Anna Bell currently writes the weekly column 'The Secret Dreamworld of An Aspiring Author' on the website Novelicious (www.novelicious.com). She is a full-time writer and loves nothing more than going for walks with her husband, son and Labrador.

You can find out more about Anna at her website:

www.annabellwrites.com

Also by Anna Bell

Don't Tell the Groom
Don't Tell the Boss

don't tell the brides-to-be

ANNA BELL

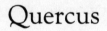

Quercus

For Ivy Scott

First published in Great Britain in 2015 by

Quercus
55 Baker Street
7th Floor, South Block
London W1U 8EW

A CIP catalogue record for this book is available
from the British Library

PB ISBN 978 1 84866 368 8
EBOOK ISBN 978 1 84866 369 5

10 9 8 7 6 5 4 3 2 1

Printed and bound in Great Britain by Clays Ltd, St Ives plc

Typeset by Jouve (UK), Milton Keynes

chapter one

Olivia Miller @livi_girl
I'm getting married in the morning . . . Just picked up my dress
& en route to the airport! See you soon @princess_shoestring
#excited

Looking up the aisle, I'm starting to tingle with anticipation. It actually looks like someone has plucked the scene out of a fairy tale. There's a perfect amount of ivy creeping over the weathered brickwork of the old hotel; the Disney-esque turrets of the medieval city wall are poking their head above the hedge line and the brilliantly bright but not too scorching-hot sun is basking the white-covered chairs in a warm light.

The string quartet is playing Adagio for Strings, and whilst I'd ordinarily miss the background beats of the

1

William Orbit version, in the ambience of the surroundings it is making me weep.

I'm gliding up the aisle, despite my heat-swollen feet feeling like they're wedged into my Louboutins. I ignore the throbbing toe sensation and instead smooth down my floaty silk dress. Finally, I feel like the princess I always dreamt of being.

'A little to the left, Penny.'

I elegantly side-step as requested, my smile not faltering.

'Actually, shuffle up to the right.'

I'm not going to let him interrupt my gliding moment. I shimmy to the music across to the path I'm having carved out for me.

'Now walk slower.'

My smile has turned into more of a pursed-lip pose. He's ruining this for me.

'Stop! Walk back and go from the top.'

I take a deep breath and try to channel the inner calm woman that I'm sure must reside in me somewhere. I brush my skirt down in an attempt to brush away my frustration.

I turn and notice that guests have started to congregate in the outdoor courtyard. I roll my wrist to check my watch and gulp as I see the time.

'Patrick, we're going to have to wrap this up. The bride

will be dressed now, and you haven't got long to get the photos of her in the ramparts before she needs to be here.'

For a fleeting moment I wish that it was me that was going to be walking down this perfect aisle towards my groom, people smiling at me like I'm the most beautiful bride in the world.

'OK, two more minutes max. Please?' he pleads.

I give an exaggerated sigh. Two minutes is fine, but I want to give him the impression that I'm doing him a huge favour. I've only been a full-time wedding planner for a few months, but I've already learnt that this is the best way to handle the artistic temperament of wedding photographers.

I walk slowly down the aisle, this time not with my princess fantasy hat on, but with my serious wedding planner hat instead. I am finally allowed to reach the spot, currently empty, where I should be meeting my groom. I wish my husband, Mark, was here. He'd have loved it. Maybe this is where we should renew our vows, when we get to that stage. Apparently a year and a half isn't long enough after our wedding to warrant another ceremony. Believe me, I've asked. He's told me that I can't ask him after I come back from every single wedding I plan. I simply can't help it; I love weddings and I love the idea of getting to be a bride again. Last time I mentioned it he said that he'd tell me when the time is right, and warned that we'll both have grey hair by then. I must be the only woman in the world that does a little leap for joy when I see a white hair sprout on my head – I see them as a sign we're getting closer.

'Perfect – hold it there for a second,' says Patrick. 'Great, all done. Thanks, Penny. You're a legend. Now, let's go and see this bride.'

I give a quick thumbs-up to the musicians, who have launched into Pachelbel's Canon as I walk past the early-bird guests. I'd even settle for being one of them right now. They're milling about, drinks in hand, sunglasses on, without a care in the world. Whereas I've entered what I call the demon hour – the hour before the nuptials start and the time where things are most likely to go pear-shaped. I've only planned five weddings since I accidentally became a wedding planner earlier in the year, and only three of those have been since I officially launched Princess-on-a-Shoestring. I've found that once the brides are dispatched up the aisle, I tend to collapse in a corner having a near ner-vous breakdown, trying to regain my poise in time for the reception.

There's always something that seems to crop up: a bride freaking out that a strand of hair is out of place; a father-of-the-bride who's gone AWOL; a bridesmaid who's got to go to the toilet because she forgot to go before she got to the church. All in all, actually making sure that the bride and groom are at the end of that aisle, almost on time, is the most important, and sometimes the most difficult, part of my job.

I hadn't intended to change career and become a wedding planner. It all happened after I started a budget wedding blog, when I was trying to fill the void left from planning my own wedding. One of my readers asked me to plan her wedding for her, and then I agreed to plan one for her friend too, which is when it changed my life. It turned out that her dad was my new boss and he almost fired me for moonlighting. It was then that I realised that my heart had been captured by wedding planning and, even though it means that Mark and I aren't going to be moving out of our two-up-two-down starter home any time soon, starting my own company is worth the wait.

Patrick and I enter the hotel and climb the stairs up to the bridal suite, where I left the bride, Olivia, in a state of peace and tranquillity thirty minutes ago. Her hair was in perfect waves flowing over one shoulder, her make-up flawless, and all she needed to do was slip into her dress. Usually I'd be worried, as I'm the one that usually gets roped into lacing the brides in if they've got a corset dress. It's a terrifying experience where you think you're going to literally squeeze the life out of the bride in their pursuit of a tiny waist and voluptuous cleavage. Luckily today I don't have to worry about that, as Olivia has a figure-hugging mermaid-style dress with a zip. Surely one of her five bridesmaids will be able to handle that.

'Penny!' Olivia screams as I open the door and make eye contact with her. 'Penny, I'm supposed to be a princess! A PRINCESS.'

Why is she still wearing the hotel-provided, fluffy dressing gown? Why isn't she in her expensive, bespoke wedding dress? I glance round at Patrick and he's not doing anything to hide the shock in his eyes, which tells me this is bad. Very bad indeed.

'A PRINCESS!'

'OK,' I say holding my hands up to try and contain the bridezilla that is threatening to rear its ugly head. I quickly scan the room first – not to try and work out what the hell's going on, but to see if there is any booze left over that I can drink to help me tackle this latest crisis. 'Whatever has happened, it's going to be fine. Now, take a deep breath and tell me what's going on.'

'A princess,' Olivia repeats, spluttering and collapsing into a chair by the ornate dressing table.

I turn and look at the others in the room, hoping one of the many bridesmaids might offer up the information.

'Her zip's stuck,' says her mother.

I eye up the champagne flute in her hand, wondering

where it came from and if there's another one, before I remember that it's my job to fix this situation. How stuck could it be?

'Let me,' I say, as if it's going to be like the sword in the stone and I'll magically be able to make it work.

The dress, which cost more than the entire budget of some of the previous weddings I've organised, is hanging on the back of the wardrobe door. It's so beautiful, with its ivory dupion silk and antique lace, that I almost can't bring myself to touch it.

'I'll give you a hand,' says Patrick.

He's got a look on his face that says this is serious business. After all, he's got to get the money shot of her in her dress looking over the castle walls before she says 'I do.'

I try the zip and it's not budging, not even a teeny tiny bit.

'Let me have a go,' says Patrick again.

I'm slightly reluctant to let him put his hands on the delicate dress, but needs must.

'Did you have problems when you had it on at your last fitting?' I ask, trying to work out what the hell has happened to it.

'It was fine, then Delia said she'd make one more adjustment to make the zip lie flatter and now it's ruined. RUINED.'

In the space of half an hour, lovely calm Olivia has turned

into a monster. Not that I can blame her, but I'm the one who's got to tame the beast and get her up the aisle to meet Jeremy – I look at my watch – in exactly fifty-two minutes' time.

'I'm sorry,' says Patrick, letting go of the dress and shaking his head in defeat.

I'd secretly been hoping that a little bit of male brute force might do the trick.

'OK,' I say, my heart racing and my head throbbing from the inevitable headache that's about to set in. 'There has to be a solution. I take it you've all had a try?' I ask hopefully in case there is anyone with magic fingers amongst us, but the look – or death stare – that Olivia has just flashed at me tells me that everyone has tried the zip, probably a billion times already.

Think, Penny, think. How am I going to fix this?

Unfortunately I don't carry the wedding planner utility belt as modelled in the film *The Wedding Planner*. Neither do I possess any sewing ability. I knew there was probably a reason I should have taken home economics or textiles as a GCSE option instead of religious education. No one ever needs you to whip up a philosophical argument about religion in the same way that you need to perform an emergency skirt repair or prepare a quick dinner after work.

'PRINCESS, PRINCESS!' screams Olivia, in a way that isn't conducive to making my brain work any quicker.

I scan the hotel room looking for anything that might help. I open a cupboard and desperately search inside: trouser press, ironing board, laundry bag. No magic zip fixing tools. What kind of a hotel is this? *The hotel.* It hits me that we're in a fancy-pants hotel. A hotel that has a concierge and might have a seamstress or at least a chambermaid who can sew. Flying to the telephone, I grovel to reception and they promise to send somebody up to help me.

If only all my budget weddings were held in elegant hotels with a problem-solving phone line. I don't usually do high-end weddings like this, but I've recently discovered that it's not only broke people that have to find cheaper solutions to get what they want. It seems that no matter how much money brides have, they always want more than their budget will stretch to. Which is how I ended up with Olivia.

I met her at Mark's best friend Phil's daughter's christening. She was moaning to me that she was going to struggle to afford to have her perfect castle wedding, and after she started telling me some details, I realised I could help. It was a short-notice wedding as Jeremy was being seconded to New York and it would make it easier, legally, if they were married. I convinced her that a destination wedding in Carcassonne, France, would work out cheaper than hiring the expensive Northumberland castle that her wedding planner was suggesting. Her guests were all going to have to fly to get there anyway, and this way they got a nice mini-break out of it. Olivia gets her wedding in a lovely hotel that happens to be hidden in the medieval *cité* of Carcassonne, which comes complete with turrets, fortified walls, horses and carts – you name it, everything to make her feel like a princess. And, luckily, it had last-minute availability.

'See, this is going to be fine,' I say calmly, nodding at Olivia in a way that I hope will reassure her.

'But what about my photos? I'm going to be late down the aisle. Jeremy will think I'm not coming.'

'Of course he won't.'

I've had nervous grooms before. In fact, at wedding number three the groom almost ran out of the church when the bride wasn't there on the dot of two o'clock. Ever since then I've tried to keep tabs on both parties right up until the start of the service.

A knock on the door interrupts us, and I let in a woman carrying a wooden box with a large handle.

'*Bonjour*,' she calls, storming into the room and heading straight for the dress. '*Je m'appelle Céline. Oh là là*,' she says as she tries the zip.

I wince as she takes out an unpicking tool and starts to unstitch. According to my watch, Olivia is due to walk down the aisle in forty-six minutes. We've already established that I know nothing about sewing, but I'm pretty sure that it's going to take longer than that to replace a whole zip.

'Are you sure . . . ?' I don't finish my sentence as Céline has thrown me a look that would rival Olivia's death stare. She certainly *is* sure. She starts rattling something off in French and I turn my attention back to my nails.

'I do hope I'm not jinxing this wedding,' remarks Patrick to one of the many adult bridesmaids. 'The last wedding I shot got called off minutes before the ceremony. Groom got cold feet.'

'Really?' says the bridesmaid. She takes a a step closer to him and tugs her dress down to reveal a little more cleavage, as if it'll help loosen his lips. 'Tell me more.'

'Well, the bride was late and—'

'Patrick,' I say watching Olivia's face, which is contorting as she struggles not to burst into tears and risk ruining her make-up. 'Why don't you go and take some photos in the courtyard of the guests arriving? If the dress gets fixed in time for bridal photos before the ceremony, then I'll come and get you.'

'Sure thing. I'll tell you that story later on,' he adds, winking at the bridesmaid.

After Patrick's departure I do my best to keep the brides-maids busy, getting them to tidy up the bridal suite and decorate it for the wedding night, in a bid to distract every-one from the alterations going on in the corner.

By the time we're T-minus ten minutes the tension in the room has reached fever pitch.

'Penny, I'm going to be late,' whispers Olivia, her eyes still riveted on Céline, who has the zip entirely in her hands now.

'All brides are late – it's the law of weddings.'

'I'm not even in my dress yet,' she hisses.

I take a deep breath and creep up to Céline. 'Sorry to inter-rupt. I was just wondering . . .'

Something tells me from her look that I'm going to keep wondering. I retreat back over to the other side of the room.

'Penny! I'm going to be more than a few minutes late. Jeremy's going to freak out, and what if he thinks I've changed my mind?'

I'm about to laugh and point out that it doesn't matter as they're technically already married, thanks to the civil cere-mony at the town hall yesterday which is a legal requirement in France. Today's more like the public show that's the equivalent of a blessing, but I know it means a lot to Olivia. 'He's not going to think that. Why don't I go and speak to him? Let him know there's a bit of a delay.'

'Yes, yes,' says Olivia nodding. 'Tell him nothing would stop me coming.'

Back out in the courtyard and, with just over ten minutes to go, it's starting to fill up with guests.

'Hi, Penny,' says Jane as she shimmies up to me. Jane is Mark's friend Phil's wife. She's the ultimate snob, dripping in designer labels, and she has a way of making me feel inadequate. I automatically look down to see what I'm wearing, but for once I don't regret my choice. I'm in my official wedding planner outfit: a lemon-coloured Karen Millen dress, and my all-important Louboutins, a present from Mark when I started the company. I desperately want to flash the soles so that Jane can see them, but I don't want to make it too obvious that I'm trying to impress her.

'Jane, how lovely to see you,' I say, air-kissing her on each cheek. Which seems less pretentious than it usually does, seeing as we are in France. I smile at her daughter Imogen, who looks immaculate sleeping in her iCandy buggy in her ruffled occasion dress, and for a second I ache, wishing that Mark and I were still trying for babies. We'd been trying for almost a year when we decided to put it on hold so I could start the business. But someone hasn't told my hormones, and every time I see a cute baby I want one.

'This is simply beautiful, Penny. I can't believe that *you* pulled it off.'

I try to raise the corners of my mouth up higher to hide the fact that I've noticed the emphasis on the 'you' in her sentence. I know what she's thinking. How could a person like me, that doesn't buy her food from M&S and in her eyes usually looks like I'm dressed for decorating, pull off a swanky wedding?

'It's lovely, isn't it?' Then I catch sight of the groom over her shoulder and remember the task in hand. 'I've got to go and speak to Jeremy – a couple of last-minute details – but I'll see you later on.'

As I approach him, Jeremy looks up at me and smiles. I pray silently that he's still smiling when I walk away.

'Pennnnnny,' he says, elongating my name for so long I wonder if he's ever going to stop.

'Jeeerremy,' I reply, trying to match him.

'This is gold standard, Penny. Simply gold standard. Couldn't have asked for anything more. I think the registrar is going to get the guests to sit down any minute.'

'Now, um, about that. I thought it best to let you know that there might be a little delay.'

'What kind of delay?' His smile has dropped, and his voice has lost its warm tone. 'Is this about that Tony man? Is he here? I'm going to kill him. I'm really going to kill him. I won't be left standing here like a fool.'

I hold my hands out to stop him from storming off

towards the hotel entrance. 'There's no Tony,' I say, wondering who Tony is. That sounds like a right piece of juicy gossip – but, alas, not what I'm here for. 'There's a slight dress malfunction, but it's being fixed. She'll be here, just a little late. I'll get the string quartet to play another few songs.'

Jeremy's narrowing his eyes at me.

'Relax, Jeremy. I thought it best to tell you what was going on. Wait another ten minutes before you get everyone to take their seats, and that way no one will even notice she's late.'

'Make sure she's here by quarter past. No later. And if I get a whiff that this was about Tony—'

'I promise,' I say patting him on the arm to calm him. 'It's all about the dress. She told me to tell you she'll definitely be here.' I back slowly away from Jeremy, smiling at the guests as I go. A few of them are staring as if sensing something is not right, but I'm not letting my face give anything away for once.

My back hits the door of the lobby and, out of sight of prying eyes, I turn and bolt up the stairs to the bridal suite to check on the state of 'Zip-Gate'. After this is over I'm never going to turn my nose up at having to lace another corset dress.

I close my eyes and pray to the god of princess weddings that I'm going to see smiles on the other side of the door. I open it slowly and I'm treated to sounds of laughter and high-pitched chatter. I open my eyes and gasp. There in front of me is a mermaid. Olivia's chestnut brown hair is in loose curls draping over one shoulder and her strapless dress is hugging her slim but curvy figure, flowing out into a fishtail that would give Ariel a run for her money. The simple shell-shaped comb holding her hair up at the back completes the mermaid look. In short, she looks amazing.

'Penny,' says Olivia. It's so nice to hear my name said at a regular level of decibels. 'Hasn't Céline done the most wonderful job?'

'She has,' I reply, beaming my most pleased smile in Céline's direction as she tidies away her tools. 'Everyone's fine downstairs. The string quartet are playing extra songs, and you've got about seven minutes to get down the stairs.'

I look down once more at the mermaid tail and figure-hugging dress and for some reason I can't get out of my mind the old photographs of Chinese women with bound feet, who had to be carried everywhere because they couldn't walk. I'm hoping that her dress has more give than meets the eye.

The make-up artist seems to have taken the hint, as she places a piece of tissue between Olivia's lips, and gets her to blot down on it. 'All done here,' she declares, smiling.

'Let's get this show on the road then,' I say.

The five bridesmaids, dressed in their pale lavender dresses with their hand-tied bouquets, hover round Olivia as I escort them down to the courtyard.

'You'd better get in there,' I whisper to the bride's father, who is waiting for us at the entrance and looking a bit nervous of the highly excitable gaggle in front of him. 'And you ladies should form the orderly queue we practised last night.'

I'm amazed as the women actually do toe the line, and after a few shakes of their heads to get their perfect hair in place and dabbing their eyes to check their make-up, they're all ready to go.

I give Olivia one last smile, and she reaches out and gives my arm a squeeze. 'Thanks, Penny, for making all this happen.'

'You're welcome,' I say, positively beaming. I'm already lost in my daydream of wondering how I got to have the most amazing job in the world, when the silence reminds me that this is my cue to go and signal to the musicians that the bride has arrived.

I look at the scene in front of me and I could cry, it looks so perfect. This is definitely going in the budget bride's wedding book I'm currently writing. It's perfect for the 'Destination Weddings' chapter as it already looks like it has been lifted out of a professional photo shoot.

The quartet breaks out into the wedding march and as I watch Olivia glide up the aisle to meet Jeremy, I experience another brief pang of jealousy. This is only my fifth professional wedding, but it's the first one to give me proper bride envy. I guess it's because it's the closest I've organised to the ultimate fantasy wedding that I lusted over for so many years. The pursuit of that dream wedding almost cost me my husband (as well as ten thousand pounds that I flushed down the metaphorical gambling toilet, but that's another story!), but watching this scene unfold in front of me is still making me pine after it again. Not that I would want to change the day I had. But if I could just convince Mark to renew our vows . . .

Speaking of Mark, that waiter in the far corner looks awfully like him. Maybe all the drama of the last hour, mixed with the heat, has made me start to see things . . .

Now I'm hallucinating that he's walking towards me, and he's looking more and more like Mark every moment . . .

'Come here often?' Mark says as he walks up and plants a kiss on my lips.

'I would do if I knew you'd be here, darling,' I reply in as lecherous a voice as I can.

We both crack up laughing. We'd be so rubbish at being those couples that pretend to be strangers on dates.

'What are you doing here?' I add, still not believing that it's actually him. How did he get here?

'Surprise.'

It's certainly that. But a lovely one. 'I can't believe you're here,' I say, grinning. 'I mean how? When?'

I hope the wind doesn't change as I'm scrunching and contorting my face, but I can't help it; I'm so confused about what he's doing here.

'I was talking to Phil on the phone last week about the wedding, and he was telling me how excited he was about going to Carcassonne and how romantic it was supposed to be. And then I thought of you, being here on your own, and I decided to fly out with Phil and Jane.'

'So you got here this morning?'

'Uh-huh, I've been camped out in their room keeping hidden.'

'Sneaky,' I say, planting another kiss on his lips.

'I know. So what time are you done with the wedding?'

'Probably not for quite a while. Eight, maybe nine? After the ceremony I've got to hang around for the speeches, the wedding breakfast, the cake cutting, the first dance . . .'

I trail off, disappointed that I'm barely going to get any time to spend with him.

'Great. I'm going to go and find a bar to watch the rugby

in and then we'll go out for a late dinner when you're finished.'

'Are you sure you're OK? You came all this way and we're only going to get a few hours here to enjoy it.'

'That's where you're wrong, Mrs Robinson. I've changed your return. We're now flying back together on Monday. I've got the day off work, so by my watch we'll have thirty-six hours together.'

'That sounds amazing.' I've been so focused since I started the company, helping others have their perfect romantic day, that I can't remember the last time we had time for a proper bit of romance of our own. Certainly not thirty-six hours' worth. I immediately get lost in a few naughty fantasies of what we can do in that time.

'Until then.' Mark kisses me again and I watch him walk away. All my jealousy of Olivia's wedding has slipped away. Mark has reminded me that I can be a princess any day of the week when he's around.

I pinch myself to check I'm actually awake. I still can't believe that this is my life. Not only do I have an incredible husband, but I get to plan these incredible weddings for a living. I look over as Jeremy bends down and kisses Olivia, and a warm, fuzzy feeling washes over me. This is what it's all about: the romance; the sparkle. It makes those chaotic and lonely days in my make-shift home office worth it.

chapter two

Olivia Gold @livi_girl

Back in Blighty – the honeymoon is officially over :(Now to sort out the move to NYC.

Penny Robinson @princess_shoestring

@livi_girl Blimey, two weeks already?! Hope you had an amazing time in Mauritius. PS have you seen the blog about your big day?

Olivia Gold @livi_girl

@princess_shoestring Just read it. Made me cry. Almost makes me want to get married again to have another big day #donttellJeremy

I've learnt a lot of things about working from home. The first is that no matter how good my intentions are to work in my office, aka the spare room, I always end up working in the kitchen. Not only is it nice and warm, but it saves me going up and down the stairs to the biscuit tin and kettle. Don't worry, I still get my exercise when I run up the stairs before Mark gets home as I don't want him to know that I don't use the office. It took him ages to dismantle the spare bed and put it in the loft, not to mention that he almost put his back out getting the new futon up there. I don't have the heart to tell him the truth.

The second thing I've learnt is how much I thrive on routine. Take today – the postman is ten minutes late. Ten minutes might seem like nothing, and I would never have noticed before, but once I'd set myself a target to hold out for another Jaffa Cake to have with my coffee when I was opening the post, ten minutes seemed like a lifetime.

My phone rings, and for a minute I forget about the Jaffa Cake crisis and answer it.

'Hello, Princess-on-a-Shoestring,' I say in my posh voice.

'Hello, Penny. It's Cathy.'

'Hi, Cathy.'

Cathy's the curator of the Surrey Military Museum that I used to volunteer at. We've been speaking a lot lately as I'm organising a wedding fair there next week.

'I was phoning to see if you had sorted out the band show-case, as I suddenly thought it might clash with the museum bells chiming.'

'Don't worry, I've already spoken to the bands about that and reshuffled the schedule accordingly. Hang on a second,' I say, opening a PDF of the document I'm working on. 'I'll send you over the new timetable now.'

I hit send and hear the swish as the email leaves my outbox.

'Thanks, Penny. It sounds like it's all under control. In that case I'll see you next week for the set-up.'

'You will indeed,' I say, thinking that it surely must finally be biscuit o'clock.

'Oh, one last thing – a wedding supplier rang about exhibiting at the fair. I said I'd get you to call her back. Let me find the name. Ah, here we go . . . Georgina Peasbody.'

I run the name over in my mind. I'm sure I've heard of her. 'Have you got her number?'

'Yes.'

Cathy reels it off and I write it down on the scrap of paper that I've been using to make notes and doodle on whilst she was talking. I've managed to draw a huge number of hearts in the short space of time we've been on the phone.

The doorbell rings. At last – the postman.

'Thanks, Cathy. I've got to run. Someone's at the door.'

'OK then, Penny, speak soon.'

I hang up and instantly jump up. I've got a smile on my face, and I realise how sad it is that I'm this excited about the post. Don't get me wrong – it's great running your own business. It's much nicer getting out of bed when all you have to do is pad downstairs. None of that freezing your fingers off whilst trying to scrape ice off your car or shivering whilst the mist clears on your windscreen. But there are days upon days where I don't see anyone and I hadn't prepared myself for that. On those days I have to try especially hard to get dressed in actual clothes and not stay in my Tigger onesie. I've found that it's quite difficult to sound professional on the phone when a prospective client calls and I'm trying to get comfy sat on a fake tail.

Up until two months ago I worked as an HR assistant for a large multinational company. I wouldn't say I missed the work, as wedding planning is so much more fun, but I do miss the people and the buzz of the office. I would even go as far as to say I miss Shelly, who'd become my work rival when we went head to head for a promotion. Don't tell her that; her ego's become as big as Simon Cowell's since she became HR supervisor, apparently.

I arrive at the front door and pull it open, smiling upon recognising Adrian the postie, who is the closest I'm going to get to a water-cooler chat these days.

'Morning, Mrs Robinson,' he says, grinning.

'Morning, Adrian. Any post?' I say – our own little joke

after he rang my doorbell one day last month and then realised he had no post for me.

'Yes, this bundle here.'

I know the letters would have easily fitted through my letter box, but luckily for me he does like a little chat. I slip off the elastic band and shuffle through the letters. It's amazing that I've only been running my business officially since August yet I already get an inordinate amount of junk mail relating to it.

'Now, you know I'm not one to gossip, but you would not *believe* what your neighbour at number seventy-four ordered.'

I fold the post under my arm, my attention rapt. Before these little chats with the postie, I had no idea what colourful lives some of my neighbours lived. *Fifty Shades of Grey* has a lot to answer for.

'Well . . .' he says, lowering his voice and looking around, signalling that whatever he has to say is especially juicy.

The phone rings behind me and I look over my shoulder with a sigh.

'I think it will have to wait until tomorrow,' I say.

'That it will,' he replies, giving me a wave as he turns round.

I rush back up the hallway dumping the post on the table, and pick up the phone. 'Hello, Princess-on-a-Shoestring.'

'Hey, Pen, it's me.'

Now, I'm usually thrilled when Mark phones, but today I can't help being slightly irritated that I missed out on the gossip for his call. Mark and I speak three or four times a day, so it's sod's law that he'd ring in the rare moment I'm having a chat with a real-life person. They're never very important calls, usually something mundane like making plans for dinner or reminders to pay the gas bill. Really it's just me needing to check my voice still works when I haven't spoken to anyone for a few hours.

'Hi, honey, everything OK?' I say trying not to let my imagination run away with me about my neighbour at number seventy-four.

'Yeah, fine. Just wondered if you fancied going out for dinner tonight?'

'I'd love to,' I say without pausing for thought. I'll do pretty much anything to get out of doing the cooking. 'What's the occasion?' I add, mentally running through my Rolodex of important dates, anniversaries of our first date, wedding anniversary, Mark's birthday . . . Nope, all clear.

'I thought we could use a date night. We said in Carcassonne that we were going to carve out time for them again.'

Before we got married we used to have weekly date nights, but for the last three months, since I started the business, they've been pretty much non-existent. I've been too busy doing research and meeting brides in the evenings.

'We did,' I say, remembering that magical night away last month. Last month? I can't believe that was over two weeks ago.

'There's that new French restaurant that's opened in Fleet. We could try there? You know, bring back some memories from our trip . . .'

I think back to that night. 'I don't think that's very appropriate behaviour for a restaurant,' I say fanning myself with the pad of paper in front of me. Is it just me or is it getting warm in here?

'Well, there's always later tonight when we get home.'

'OK, sounds great. Book it and I'll see you later.' I need to wrap up this phone call before I get too hot under the collar. Our night in Carcassonne turned out to be one steamy affair. It was as if we were trying to recreate our two-week honeymoon in thirty-six hours. I'm suddenly looking forward to what I thought was going to be a dull autumnal night in front of the telly. If only Mark and I were still trying for a baby. All this rekindling of passion seems like a bit of a waste. Well, not a total waste, I chide myself.

'Before I go,' Mark says, 'I spoke to Nanny Violet on the phone earlier and she sounded a bit weird. Can you pop round later on, if you're going out anywhere?'

I glance down my to-do list, which is getting longer rather than shorter today. I've got to make time to do the finishing touches to the sample chapters of my book at some point, but this afternoon I have to pop out to meet a florist with one of my brides, Ellie, who's getting married in December. I don't have the heart to tell Mark that I could do without going to see Violet, but his nan means the world to him and she's eighty-nine. It looks like I'll be working right up until we go out for dinner tonight.

'Sure, I'll swing by this afternoon.'

'Thanks, Pen. I'll book the table for eight.'

I hang up the phone and turn my attention back to my ever-increasing to-do list. I add Nanny Violet to the end of it, before remembering that I was supposed to call that woman Cathy mentioned. I pick the phone back up, but before I manage to dial the doorbell rings.

I glance at my watch and realise that it's half past eleven already. Not only have I not had my coffee yet, but I also haven't tidied the room before my clients turn up. I try not to have meetings at my house as a dreary terrace house in suburban Farnborough is not the most professional of settings. Added to that, I always have to spend a ridiculous amount of time cleaning, even for a short meeting.

I try and tidy my pile of papers and stack my wedding magazines as neatly as I can on the table, then hide my breakfast dishes in the dishwasher, reminding myself to stack them later.

I hurry down the hallway and open the door. 'Josh, Mel,' I say air-kissing them both as they come in.

Luckily for me, I know these prospective clients and I don't worry too much about what a state the house is in. Josh is my gambling mentor and Mel is his long-term boyfriend. When I finally admitted to myself that I had an online bingo addiction, I went to a gambler's support group and was paired with Josh. He not only helped me to stop gambling, but he helped to save my marriage too.

'Come on through,' I say, leading them into the kitchen, where I finally put the kettle on. 'Tea, coffee?' I ask, rambling slightly. I realise that I'm nervous. It's ridiculous. I know I get nervous with new clients, but I've known Josh for nearly two years and he's helped me through some pretty dark times. I would never have thought I'd get the new-client nerves with him.

'Coffee for me, please,' says Mel, smiling away.

'Not for me. I'm fine,' says Josh.

I start organising coffee bits whilst the water boils, watching Josh out of the corner of my eye. He's fidgeting in his chair as if he's trying to get comfortable. He puts his elbow awkwardly on the table and leans his head into his hand, but his elbow slips underneath him and he hits the stack of bridal magazines. He jumps back in horror as they cascade over him, as if they're poisonous.

It seems I'm not the only one that's nervous. 'So, it's exciting, you two getting married,' I say, trying to remember the type of sales patter I usually do with new clients.

'Yes,' says Mel. 'Can you believe it? We never thought this day would come.'

'You can say that again,' says Josh.

He's looking down at the floor, and I see Mel give him the kind of look I'd give Mark if he said something embarrassing in public.

'I'm excited, as not only will it be my first gay wedding to organise, but because I know you two. I hope that I'm going to be able to make it extra special,' I say.

I pour hot water into the waiting cafetière and bring it over to the table, along with mugs, milk and sugar. Luckily I bring an extra mug, as Josh seems to have forgotten he declined a drink and pours himself one before stirring it briskly, jiggling his knee at the same speed.

When I first met Josh he told me he didn't believe in marriage, and yet here he is, getting ready to do it himself.

'So, have you given any thought to what you want?' I say, looking between the two men.

'We just want it to be close friends and family,' says Mel. 'Nothing too showy.'

'Yeah, something really small and intimate,' agrees Josh.

It makes my job easier when the two parties involved agree on things. 'Great. How about when and where?'

'We haven't got that far,' says Mel. 'When they legalised gay marriage we had no reason not to get hitched any more, and when Josh finally agreed all I said was that we had to have you plan the wedding. That's as far as we got.'

'I'm a little biased, but that's a good start,' I say, smiling.

Josh is shifting uncomfortably in his chair and I'm getting the feeling that he might not be as onboard with this wedding as Mel thinks.

'I quite like the idea of having a theme though,' says Mel. He's wincing slightly and I can see why: Josh is visibly tensing all his muscles next to him. It's hard not to notice as he's got such a lot of them.

'What type of theme?' I have all sorts of awful stereotypes in my head, drag queens with tiaras and feather boas.

'I don't know,' says Mel, looking at Josh as if for answers. 'Something classy.'

'Perhaps we should stick to the basics first,' says Josh, clearing his throat.

'Of course,' I say. But now my head is in the Moulin Rouge and I'm wearing a can-can girl's outfit. 'First of all, have you set a budget?'

'Not yet,' says Mel.

ANNA BELL

'Right, well, those are your starting points. How much you've got to spend, what type of place you want to have the wedding: country hotel, quirky venue . . . and, of course, most importantly, when you want it to be.'

'We can do that, can't we, J?' says Mel.

Judging by the pale colour that Josh has gone, I'm not so sure.

'Perfect!' I say, trying to fill Josh's silence. 'When you've got a better idea of what you want, you can come and see me again.'

Mel is grinning and Josh is gurning. This has been one of the strangest initial planning meetings I've had. Not that I've had that many, but still, the ones I have had have been with enthusiastic brides and grooms.

'Thanks, Penny. I know that it's all under control with you at the helm.'

'Ah, Mel, you're too kind.'

'Right, well, we won't take up any more of your time,' says Josh, practically leaping out of his seat. 'We're off up to London to do some shopping.'

'Ooh, that sounds like much more fun than my day,' I say.

'You've clearly never been shopping with Josh,' says Mel, laughing.

'Oi, watch it, I'm not the one that spent three hours in Harvey Nicks menswear last time.' Josh is grinning at Mel in a whole different way, and suddenly it's like the Josh I know is back.

'You deserved it after your brogue hunting.'

The two of them make their way out of the kitchen, bickering over who's a worse shopper all the way to the front door.

'We'll be in touch,' says Mel as he steps outside. 'And soon. This one is so nervous, if we don't get it planned soon, he'll be changing his mind.'

I smile, but I can't help wondering if he already has.

'Great, and I'll see you at group,' I say to Josh. Thinking that I really need to go more regularly. With setting up Princess-on-a-Shoestring I've missed quite a few over the last few months, and I need to get back into the habit of going regularly. I've learnt that you're never cured of an addiction; you have to learn to manage it. And the best way to manage it is to go to the group sessions, to remind yourself what you're up against.

'You will indeed.'

I wave them goodbye and wonder if the follow-up meeting will ever happen. With the wedding planning, I'm getting a real insight into the dynamics of relationships that I usually wouldn't get to see. There are some people that meet with me that I swear aren't going to make it to the end of the honeymoon, let alone till death do us part.

I'm not saying that Josh and Mel aren't compatible – I think they are – I just think that Josh isn't into the marriage thing as much as Mel. Maybe I'm wrong. Maybe Josh will warm up to the wedding idea. I certainly hope he does. Out of all my clients, I'd love to plan him a special day to try and repay him for all he's done to help me when I got myself in a muddle with my gambling.

Speaking of odd couples, I might as well leave now for the florist for Ellie and Silent Blake's wedding. I tend to nickname all my brides to keep them straight in my head, only for this one I've nicknamed the groom as he's – how shall I put this? – *distinctive*. I've met him a grand total of three times, and on each occasion he's said no more than hello. I think it's extra remarkable as I've known Ellie for years. She's my best friend Lou's work colleague, and we've bonded over many a bottle of wine. She's one of those people who makes whoever she talks to feel like her best friend. She's warm and bubbly, but Blake by contrast is completely silent. They do say opposites attract.

I pick up my handbag, making sure I remember my new Filofax that I treated myself to when I started the company. It's a little bit nineties, but so much handier than me trying to type things into my iPhone calendar, which can be tricky with my uncoordinated thumbs.

I'm driving to the florist when I remember that I said to

Mark I'd pop in on his nan. It probably makes sense for me to go and see her en route. It is lunchtime, after all, and there's a good chance she'll be making cheese on toast. It may be the world's simplest lunch, but no one makes it as perfectly as Nanny V. She even cuts it into quarters and everything.

I drive over there, feeling a bit guilty as I realise I haven't seen her for a good month, maybe even more than that. This wedding planning isn't very good for living a Monday to Friday lifestyle. With weddings and wedding-related events mainly taking place on the weekend, and brides often only being available on Saturdays, my visits to see Mark's nan have dwindled. I must make more of an effort to take the odd afternoon off in the week, but it's just been so busy.

Whilst I haven't had many weddings yet, I've been working really hard to get lots of them booked up for next year. I've done pretty well, with fifteen bookings so far. With any luck I might start making some profit by then, and then hopefully Mark won't take such a sharp intake of breath when he opens our bank statements. We're lucky that he's got a good, stable job and most of our day-to-day outgoings are covered by him, but by starting the company I wiped out what meagre savings we had, and until the company makes money we've got no way of building them up again.

I park in front of Nanny Violet's bungalow and notice

that Ted's car is parked outside too. Ted is a former fellow volunteer at the military museum where I had my wedding. I'm always trying to do my best to get him and Nanny Violet together. They almost got it on during the war, but back then Nanny Violet was married to his best friend, who was killed in the D-Day landings. It was a tragic story of lost love that saw them both go on to marry other people. And yet here they are sixty years later – friends again.

Mark tells me that I should give up trying to get them a happy-ever-after and focus on the fact that since they became friends again his nan's much happier and doesn't keep telling us that she's about to pop her clogs. Yet, as a hopeless romantic, I won't be satisfied until I've planned them a super-duper wedding.

As I walk down the path to her bungalow the front door swings opens. Thinking it's to welcome me, I smile, but Nanny Violet walks out, followed by Ted.

'Penelope,' says Violet, stopping dead in front of me. She's looking at me like she's seen a ghost. I know I haven't been here for ages, but I hadn't expected her to look so shocked to see me.

'Hiya, bad time?' I say.

'We were on our way out,' says Ted, smiling.

I resist the urge to go and hug him, as I have to do

whenever I see him. I sort of want Ted to be my surrogate grandad.

'Anywhere nice?' I ask, thinking it might be lunch and I could tag along.

'Church,' says Nanny Violet. 'Yes . . . funeral of an old friend.'

I look at Ted in his rather-trendy-for-an-old-man chinos, and at Nanny Violet who is dressed in trousers too, very unusual attire for both of them for a funeral. Especially as Violet's a real stickler for black at such occasions and she's wearing a fuchsia jumper.

'Oh, that's too bad,' I say, wondering where they're really off to.

'Did you want anything in particular?' she asks.

'No,' I reply, thinking about the cheese on toast. 'I was on my way to a supplier and I was passing so I thought I'd pop in.'

'How thoughtful. It would have been nice to catch up as it's been a long time. Why don't you come round at the weekend? You and Mark.'

'That would be lovely,' I say, trying to look into her eyes, but she's avoiding my gaze.

'I'll see you next week too,' says Ted.

Nanny Violet gives him a look.

'At the wedding fair, I mean,' he adds, looking back at her.

'That you will,' I say, watching them climb into Ted's Micra.

They give me a wave and Ted starts the engine and they drive off.

There was something weird about that encounter. I haven't seen Nanny Violet act that odd since she thought I was having an affair and almost ruined my wedding. I get back in the car and see my Filofax sticking out of my bag. It reminds how much I've got left to do today and I should get back to my list of jobs. I'll have to interrogate Ted at the museum next week to try to get to the bottom of whatever is going on with Nanny Violet.

chapter three

'Penny, you've exceeded our expectations. You should be
very pleased with yourself,' says Cathy.

It reminds me of getting a gold star when I was at school.
Glancing down from the balcony onto the grand hall, I'm
proud of the sight before me. There's clearly no limit to my
organisational skills.

When Cathy the curator asked me if I'd organise a wedding

fair, I was more than a little bit nervous. I'd never organised an event where someone else didn't invite all the guests and get RSVPs beforehand. I had a terrifying wait this morning, when the suppliers were set up and ready to go, and all we needed were the brides-to-be. But amazingly they came, and came, and now there are bloomin' loads of them.

'Thanks, Cathy.'

'The front desk says we've already had enquiries about holding weddings here.'

'That's amazing. I've spoken to a few brides who seemed very interested in using Princess-on-a-Shoestring and another half a dozen who read my blog.'

'That's great. Looks like we'll have to make this a regular thing.'

Not only is this good for drumming up business, but it's handy for my business bank account too as I get a percentage from the takings. The problem with planning weddings so far in advance is that I won't get much money until next summer when the bulk of my scheduled events take place. To say my business is a bit cash poor at the moment is an understatement.

'Perfect. Maybe two a year?' I say, thinking off the top of my head. 'Maybe one this time of year and one just before wedding season?'

'I think that would work well.'

'The only thing I'd change is maybe restricting the food samples to wedding cakes. Can you smell that cheese? It put me right off my breakfast this morning.'

'I can't say I've noticed. But I'm a bit of a cheese fiend to be honest.'

'So am I, usually,' I say, turning my head away from the cheeses stacked up like wedding cakes, 'but it was a bit overwhelming when I came in at seven this morning.'

'Possibly,' says Cathy. 'Or . . .'

She trails off as a woman's voice rises up to us at the balcony. 'This is preposterous! There must be someone I can talk to,' squeaks the high-pitched voice.

The word 'preposterous' is never the sound of a happy customer. I look down and spot the outraged woman. She's impeccably dressed, probably in her late forties. From up here she looks like a little pixie, with boy-cropped blonde hair and angular features.

I see Ted trying to appease her, but it seems like she's having none of it.

'Did you want me to go and sort it out?' asks Cathy.

For a split second I almost take her up on the offer, but then I remember the event plan, and my name at the top as the person running it.

'No, I've got this,' I say.

'OK, well, I'll be in my office if you need me.'

41

I walk down the stairs while trying my best to guess this woman's problem. Too crowded to get to talk to the suppliers? Not enough dress designers? Or maybe it's the fact that the caterers are cooking really smelly food and like me she's finding it off-putting. Whatever it is, she seems really mad.

'I'll take it from here,' I say to Ted when I reach them. I notice his unusually frosty expression and folded arms; whoever this woman is, she hasn't brought out his good side.

'Good luck,' he whispers, patting me on the back as he leaves us. I glance over my shoulder at him as he goes, remembering that I still need to ask him about Nanny Violet's odd behaviour last week. Every time I've made a beeline to talk to him so far this morning, someone or something has got in the way – wobbly table legs; heater melting the bespoke chocolate favours; photographers warring at dawn. And now a little pixie woman with a very loud voice.

'What seems to be the problem?' I say as calmly and authoritatively as I can manage. Although I'm pretty much quaking in my boots, and before you ask, they're lovely red cowboy boots. Perfect for a showdown. Ever since I wore them at a flooded-out wedding in July this year, and had to transform the washed-out marquee into a country-chic affair, they've become my lucky boots. Surely nothing can go wrong whilst I'm wearing them.

'Are you the organiser?' she spits, before looking me up and down with a slow, deliberate pan as if she's assessing every inch of me.

'I am. My name's Penny . . . Penny Robinson,' I stutter.

'Penny Robinson,' she says slowly before shaking her head. 'What company do you work for?'

Her eyes have narrowed in concentration.

'Princess-on-a-Shoestring,' I reply, avoiding eye contact. The Tiffany bracelet on her arm and her classic Chanel houndstooth wool suit give me the impression that she'll probably never have heard of it.

'Is there anything I can do to help?' I say again, not waiting to listen to her thoughts about my company, which judging by the look on her face were not going to be complimentary. I take her by the elbow and try and steer her towards the lobby and away from the rest of the main fair.

'Yes, I want to know why you didn't let me exhibit here.'

I'm slightly dumbstruck. 'I'm sorry, and you are . . . ?'

'I am Georgina Peasbody, of Peasbody Weddings,' she says, waving her hand around as if to give herself a grander fanfare.

My brows are contorting as I try and work out where I've heard that name before, whilst I'm simultaneously staring at her hands. They are so small and delicate, it's like she's a doll.

43

'Um, I'm sorry. I didn't realise that I hadn't let anyone in.'

Georgina's flaring nostrils tell me how badly this has gone down. 'I always exhibit in Hampshire and Surrey. This is my patch!' she says, stamping her foot, which is impressive, given her towering stilettos.

'I'm awfully sorry,' I say, sounding like my mother on the phone. 'I simply assumed I'd contacted all the wedding suppliers in the area. What service do you provide?'

'"Simply assumed",' she says, laughing mirthlessly and shaking her head. 'I provide wedding planning. *Luxury* wedding planning. I happen to get a lot of clientele from this area. That's why I tried to ring you when I found out about this event last week, but you never returned my calls,' Georgina continues angrily. I swear her eyes almost glow red for a second.

'I'm sure I would have called you back . . .' Then I have a vague recollection of Cathy giving me a number last week, before the postman arrived and then Josh and Mel. Oops. 'I'm terribly sorry. I had an extremely busy week and I must have honestly misplaced your number and forgotten about it.'

I've learnt over the past year or two that I get myself into terrible situations when I try to lie and make excuses. These days I'm going with honesty as the best policy, only judging by Georgina's face and the horns that are almost sprouting from her head, I'm thinking that in this case it might not be the right approach.

I'd thought that Georgina Peasbody's name sounded familiar when I jotted down the message from Cathy. Before I established my business full-time I evaluated the local competition. Peasbody Weddings was the only other wedding planner in the phonebook, and with the look of her website and the types of high-end weddings she seemed to organise, I didn't think we'd ever be competing in the same market.

'Too *busy*? Well, I can see you have a lot to learn about this business,' she snaps, picking a bit of fluff off the lapel of my jacket. She inspects it in her tiny fingers before flicking it away, and I feel like she's using it as a metaphor for what she thinks of me, the 'competition'.

'Look, this is the first time the museum has had one of these fairs, and I'm really sorry.'

'Yes, yes, I'm sure you are. Now, what are you going to do about it? You know, to rectify the situation.' She's staring at me blankly with an eyebrow raised in expectation.

'I . . . er . . . I can add you to my supplier database and contact you in advance of our next fair?'

The nostrils are still flaring. 'But what about all these brides? They're probably crying out for a wedding planner.

They'll look down on your fair if you don't have one, you know.'

I personally very much doubt people come to wedding fairs to meet planners. People stumble across them and then think they're a good idea. I would say that, judging by the queues at the wedding-dress stands, that that's what people have come for.

'I'm a wedding planner, so people can always talk to me.'

'You? You're a wedding planner?' she says, almost choking in disbelief.

I want to revert to my teenage self and be like, *Yeah, what you going to do about it?* But I'm mindful of the brides milling about.

'That's right. Princess-on-a-Shoestring specialises in the budget bride market.'

Georgina's mouth curls up into a small smile and I see her suppressing a giggle.

I can feel the blood rushing to my head in anger.

'Good luck with that then, Penny, was it? I've seen a lot of your type over the years,' she says, pacing around me like a prowling lion. 'You come along, set up your little business, cause a few little waves in the pond, and then you get pregnant. Once you've popped out some sprogs, all of a sudden working every weekend doesn't look so attractive. Being on call for brides-to-be at all hours doesn't seem worth it, and then you disappear. I see you're already married.' She points at my rings. 'Nice diamond, by the way.'

She flutters her eyelashes at me as if challenging me to tell her she's wrong, and when I don't immediately reply she smiles and opens her overly large handbag and starts digging around.

'Have you got a business card?' she asks, opening a business-card folder.

I put my hand in my jacket pocket and pull one out to hand to her.

'Thank you. How sweet,' she says, stroking the card before putting it into her book. 'I'll pop it in this section next to all the other failed wedding planners I've met over the years.'

'I—' I stutter as the tears start to sting behind my eyes, and I feel like I've been winded. It's as if this woman has come up and licked my face, I feel that violated. How dare she make assumptions about my business. Yes, I want children, but that's not going to ruin Princess-on-a-Shoestring for me. I'm suddenly grateful that Mark and I put trying for babies on hold whilst I make the business a success.

'Now listen,' she continues, tilting her head and speaking slowly as if she's talking to a small child, 'can I perch on a table? I'll happily write a cheque for your little fee and I've got some of my materials with me. It's not like I'll be any threat to *your* business.'

I notice the small suitcase she's wheeling behind her.

'I feel it's the least you could do when you forgot to invite me or to ring me back. Such poor customer service – you wouldn't what that story doing the rounds now, would you? Not very good for the word of mouth.'

An image of Sleeping Beauty and the wicked fairy comes to mind. Not wanting this to end in a curse, I do my best to smile and weakly say, 'This way. You can set up on the table next to mine.'

I'm half tempted to put her next to the stinky cheese, but I think it's better to keep her in sight. What is it they say about keeping your enemies close? Not to mention that I'll take pride at the glee the brides will no doubt show when they find out my fees in comparison to hers.

'Thank you, Penny. I'll try not to poach too many of your clients.'

This time she's full-on cackling, as if I'm the warm-up act and she's the real thing. I try and concentrate on the exhibitor fee she'll be paying the museum and the commission I'll earn off it.

If I was childish enough to be keeping score over the brides Georgina has attracted compared to mine in the past two hours, then I'd be pleased to report I was in the lead. Her presence has only solidified my position as top wedding planner at this fair.

'I've been looking out for you specially,' says a prospective bride, laden down with goodie bags.

I'm tempted to stick my bum out, get my elbows flapping and do a victory dance to accompany the victory music in my head.

'I did want a big country hotel, but I don't know if my budget would stretch to that.'

I'm trying my best to focus on what this bride-to-be is saying, but I can see Georgina in the background taking great interest whilst fanning out her leaflets, as if she's listening in on our conversation.

'I mean, I'd really love to hire a stately home, but I thought that was laughable.'

'I like to tell my brides that nothing is out of budget per se,' I respond. 'We only have to find a modification to make it affordable.'

'My dear,' interrupts Georgina, 'I think you'll find that Penny here tends to plan small-scale events. Gazebos in the garden, pub-grub buffets. I don't think she's really into stately homes or castles. I, on the other hand . . .'

I can't believe she said that out loud, and in front of me! My mouth has dropped open and I'm worried that I'm flashing my tonsils for the whole world to see. I can't honestly remember ever meeting someone so rude. Even when I was in all-out war with my ex-colleague Shelly, we didn't stoop as low as being rude to each other's faces. This woman makes Shelly look like Snow White in comparison.

I'm not standing for this any longer. I might have taken her initial comments lying down, but I'm going to let her know that Princess-on-a-Shoestring won't go down without a fight.

'Actually, Georgina,' I manage in a tone that hopefully doesn't show that I want to gouge her eyes out with a fork, 'the last wedding I organised was in a castle. Well, almost a castle. It was in the grounds of the medieval citadel of Carcassonne. It was beautiful. The bride and groom had their photos taken on the ramparts overlooking the scenic French countryside.'

I can see from the twinkle in the bride-to-be's eye that I haven't lost her as a potential client. The word rampart is clearly working its magic.

'The bride in question had to plan her wedding really quickly as her fiancé had been offered a job in New York and it made it easier for her to go with him if they were married. She had her heart set on getting married in a castle and she'd been talking to a wedding planner who told her the only availability for somewhere like that would be some grand place in Northumberland. Yet it was stretching her budget to the extent that her groom was losing sleep over it. When I chatted to her and suggested a wedding abroad, it was like it all fell into place for her.'

'Wait a second. You're not talking about the Miller–Gold wedding, are you? Olivia and Jeremy?' says Georgina, pointing her finger at me in accusation.

Uh-oh. I suddenly realise what I must have said. I want to close my eyes and run away. Out of all the wedding planners it could have been, I'm guessing from Georgina's reaction it might have been her.

'That's right,' is all I manage to say. It comes out in a barely audible whisper.

The bride-to-be smiles politely as we both notice that Georgina appears to be trembling.

'I'll just take one of these,' says the bride-to-be, reaching forward between Georgina and me to pick up one of my leaflets. The look on Georgina's face must scare her, because she plucks a leaflet out of her pile too.

'I'll be in touch,' she says, nervously looking between us both.

With the bride-to-be out of the picture, there's nothing to break the Mexican stand-off.

Georgina is still glaring at me, pointing menacingly in my direction. 'The Miller-Golds were just about to put down a deposit with me, when I got a call to tell me they were going another way. They'd decided to have a destination wedding in Carcassonne. It had come to them at a friend's christening, they'd said. They hadn't mentioned in what form.'

I pause for a minute, wondering how I'm going to get my foot out of my mouth to answer her. I can feel that my cheeks have turned tomato-red, and they're so hot that I imagine I'd be able to cook sausages on them.

'Funny story,' I say, giggling nervously. 'I did meet them at a friend's christening, and you have to understand I had no idea that they were using your company. I accidentally overheard the two of them having a row about the cost of the wedding and I happened to suggest the wedding abroad idea.'

'You *poached* my clients.' Her voice has risen an octave and she's taken a step closer to me so that her outstretched finger, with perfectly manicured pointy nail, is only inches away.

'I didn't know it was poaching,' I say, holding my hands up and taking a small step back. 'They were truly upset, and they were friends of my very good friends. I couldn't help but suggest an option. I hadn't meant for them to dump their planner and work with me.'

'Really, you didn't want them as clients? When you took your 15 per cent . . . 15 per cent of – what was their budget? Forty or fifty thousand pounds?'

'Actually we planned it in the end on thirty, and I don't take a percentage. Instead I charge a set fee.'

'You what?'

The finger has dropped and instead of this making me feel relieved, I'm aware that she's now clenching her hands into fists. I'd be worried that one of them might come flying at my face and hurt me, if she didn't have such dainty doll-like hands.

'I charge a set amount. I've found it's really popular with budget brides – that way they know how much they are spending on my services from the start.'

'Good luck with that approach. Well, well, well. When I heard about the Carcassonne wedding planner, I naively assumed that one of the London planners had got hold of them, but *you* . . .'

I've been biting my tongue through most of this little exchange, and whilst I don't want to stoop to her level, I can't seem to stop myself. 'Yes, *me*. Olivia and Jeremy were thrilled with the wedding I planned them, and with the savings I made. I know my business model might seem controversial to you, but I'm making a go of it. And Princess-on-a-Shoestring is here to stay, no matter what you think.'

'Excuse me, are you the wedding planner?' interrupts a woman.

'That's right,' I say confidently, smoothing my hair down

and hoping it calms the hackles on my back too. I turn my gaze away from Georgina.

'Great. I wanted to talk to you about the country-chic wedding on your website, I loved it and I was thinking of having something similar.'

The bride-to-be launches into telling me about her hopes and dreams for her big day. She starts with the table decorations, before moving on to the little baskets of toiletries she's going to install in the toilets. I'm desperately trying to concentrate as she begins telling me about her ideas for the cake, but Georgina's once again distracting me as she packs up her pop-up banner and collects her leaflets.

By the time I get a word in edgeways with the prospective client, Georgina is out the door.

I pretty much just peed on my territory like a dog, but hopefully she got the message. I would do an air punch of victory, but I don't think that would woo this bride-to-be. Instead I nod encouragingly and launch into my vision of her wedding with more confidence than usual.

I feel like I've had my first test as a professional wedding planner, and that I've passed. It's made me realise that I've got to keep on top of my game, but it's worth it; I'm not going anywhere. I've told the industry I'm here, and that I'm here to stay.

chapter four

Abigail Weston @Abiwestie81

Help! I've got a bridesmaid who thinks my wedding is hers. She keeps suggesting ideas to me forcefully. What do I do . . . ?

Ruby Blair @sparklyslippers

Eep, sounds like you've got a bridesmaidzilla on your hands. How about getting @princess_shoestring to plan your wedding for you?

Laura Weston @LaLawestie81

Wish I could afford a wedding planner, but really skint ☹

Ruby Blair @sparklyslippers

She's a budget wedding planner, prob cheaper than you think. Sorted out my problem of motherinlawzilla!

I look up at the clock and wonder how it's mid-morning already. The wedding fair last week was a huge success, but it brought with it a ton of new work. Suppliers to plan meetings with, interested brides to follow up on, not to mention writing an event evaluation for the museum and giving feedback on footfall to the exhibitors. That's on top of keeping my existing brides happy, doing my daily quota of social networking and blogging and proofreading the sample chapters of my book.

After almost succumbing to doing eeny, meeny, miny, moe to work out what to start with, I plump for setting up suppliers' meetings first; after all, they have the potential to be long-term sources of income. I'm trying to build up a list of preferred suppliers to offer my clients, which would mean that I could charge commission to the suppliers for the business I bring to them. That would really help to rake in a little more cash.

The doorbell rings, and I immediately wonder if it's Adrian the postie coming to give me more gossip. I've been so busy I hadn't even realised that I skipped my mid-morning coffee.

I walk down the corridor, but it doesn't look like the postman's silhouette on the other side of the frosted glass panel. I open it, wondering who it's going to be, and am delighted to see my best friend, Lou.

'Hello, time for a quick cuppa?' she says as I open the door wider. She's already barged past me, Harry, her baby boy, balanced on her hip.

'Of course,' I say, even though this means I'm going to have to work through lunch to make up the time, meaning I'll miss *Loose Women*.

That's the one of the downsides of working from home – any time your friends or family have a day off they automatically assume that you're free to meet for lunch or pop to the shops, not realising that you're working and whatever hours they disturb need to be made up somewhere. Not that I'm complaining that much; it is nice to see another human being in the flesh.

'Great,' I mutter as I hear the kettle being flicked on. I'm about to shut the door when I see the tardy postman making an appearance. Not my regular one either.

'Good morning,' I say, beaming happily.

'Morning. Sign here, please.'

I take the parcel and batch of letters that's been thrust at me and sign in the digital box. My signature looks as good as my five-year-old niece's. He snatches it away without looking at it and shoves it back in his waist pouch.

'Cheers,' he says. And with that he turns and leaves. Usually I'd be upset that he was leaving after so little interaction, but now that Lou's here I'm pleased that I haven't got my usual chatty postie wanting to gossip about number seventy-four.

I walk back down to the kitchen and see that Lou's already pouring the coffee and Harry's sat on the floor playing with his noisy fire engine.

'You not working today?' I ask as I begin to open the parcel. I can't remember ordering anything, but I have been online shopping a lot lately. There's something about the novelty of being able to order something that doesn't involve having to queue up at the parcel office at lunchtime to collect it.

'No, I had to swap my days around as we've got a big do at work on Thursday. Then when it came to it this morning I was a bit lost, as we usually have baby sign classes on Thursdays and I didn't know what to do. So we're on our way to the library.'

'Well, I'm glad you thought to come here. And I'm even more glad you brought eclairs,' I say as I eye up the pastries that Lou's popping onto a plate from a white paper bag.

'Thought you deserved a little treat. So, what's in the parcel?'

I peel back the paper and discover that it's a framed photo of me and Mark. We look sickeningly happy. It was taken when were in Carcassonne. We bumped into Patrick, Olivia and Jeremy's photographer, on our way out for dinner and he snapped a photo of us. And it's a beauty. We look all sun-kissed and fresh, and the lights of the medieval city walls are twinkling in the background.

I rub my hand over the photo. Boy, that was some night, and some next day.

I turn the photo round and offer it to Lou.

'Ah, Pen, that's gorgeous. Wow, was that when you were in France?'

'Uh-huh,' I say as I open the little card in the package. It's from Olivia, thanking me for their day. What a lovely, thoughtful gift. In my old job in HR no one gave me thank-you cards, or presents like this. The only gifts I'd get would be if I gifted myself some Post-its when I'd been left in the stationery cupboard unsupervised.

'That bride is a hell of a lot more organised with her thank-yous than I was after my wedding. It took me months to get round to sending mine out,' says Lou.

'I know. Me too. But it was a month ago now,' I say, sighing. It felt like it was six months ago though, with all the work I've been doing since. There's a lot more work involved in getting a business off the ground and getting it into the black than I ever would have imagined.

'Was it really a month ago? This year is flying by. It'll be Christmas before we know it.'

'Don't – I've already heard Christmas music on the radio. It's only October, people!'

'I know it's a pain in the arse . . .' says Lou, bringing our drinks over to the kitchen table. I follow her over and bring the pastries. ' . . . but I do love this time of year, you know, when it gets going. The parties, the music and now with Harry . . . Ah, Pen, when you and Mark have a baby, you're going to realise how great it is.'

I smile weakly at her. Ever since she's had Harry, she's been on about my future baby. It's hard watching her with him, when I desperately want one of my own. A constantly eating, pooping, gorgeous-smelling baby to snuggle.

I'll have to suppress my broodiness for the sake of Princess-on-a-Shoestring, at least for the next couple of years. I'll still be young enough in my early thirties to start my football team of children, and that way I won't give Georgina Peasbody the satisfaction of seeing my business fail because I become a mum.

'Sorry, Pen,' says Lou as if she's just clocked the look of disappointment on my face. 'I keep forgetting you're not trying any more. But you know what they say – sometimes that's when the stork visits you anyway. It happened to my friend Denise, the one in our NCT group that had triplets.'

'Thanks, Lou,' I say biting into the eclair and talking through the mouthful of chocolate and creamy goodness, 'but we tried pretty hard before we stopped. Believe me – I don't think we're just going to magically have a random night of passion and get that lucky that we hit it at the right time to make a . . .'

I stop eating and my mouth drops open. Clearly not a great sight for Lou, who's sitting opposite. I just about remember to swallow the mouthful of cream as I start to count on my sticky fingers.

'Pen, what's up?' asks Lou. She must be concerned; she's rested her half-eaten eclair on her plate.

'I'm late,' I say, counting on my fingers again. 'I didn't have a period last month. With all that's going on, I didn't even notice. How did I not notice?'

I've never not noticed that before. I wrack my brains as if I'll suddenly remember that I actually have had it, but nothing comes to mind. I'm sure I haven't had one since early September, not since before I went to Carcassonne and spent thirty-six hours in a hotel room with Mark . . . Oh.

'That's amazing. You're pregnant, Penny!'

'I might not be,' I say, standing up from the table. 'I mean, it could be a false alarm.'

I've been down that road before. Earlier in the year I was a few days late and convinced I was in the family way, only to be crushed when I wasn't. Surely it's more likely that the stress of starting the new business has upset my body clock.

'I'd know if I was pregnant, wouldn't I? I mean, I'd feel different, and I'd be glowing. Do I look glowing?'

I'm starting to feel light-headed and the room is ever so slightly spinning around me.

'You might be though, Pen. Surely it's worth finding out. Ooh, Harry,' she says, interrupting him from playing with his fire engine, 'Auntie Penny might have a friend on the way for you.'

He gives us both a grin, and for a moment he looks like an angelic child, before he goes back to bashing his fire engine noisily around our legs.

'It's bound to be a false alarm. Mark and I did everything we could to conceive naturally when we were trying. I mean, I know in Carcassonne my legs were in the air more than usual, and we *were* rather inventive with what we were doing, but . . .' My thoughts are running away with themselves as I try and remember if I took my birth control pills with me at all. It was such a busy weekend that even if I packed them I might not have remembered to take them all as I was all out of routine. 'It's such a bad time. We said we weren't going to now, and I've got weddings booked for next year . . . I've already bought the Christmas bottle of Baileys. I'm the only one that would drink it!'

'Penny,' says Lou, as she gets up and grabs hold of me.

Until then, I hadn't even been aware that I'd been pacing around my kitchen. 'Look, first things first. You've wanted a baby for forever. There's never a good time. You'd cope. I'll do you a favour and take the Baileys off your hands. What you should be doing is going and peeing on a stick. Do you want to watch Harry while I go and get you one?'

'No need. Mark bought some a few months ago when we thought I was pregnant before. Oh, god. Mark.'

The disappointment on his face last year when we had our false alarm was enough to crush my soul. Whilst I always thought that would be the one occasion I'd be pleased for him to look at something I'd weed on, I don't think I can face upsetting him again.

'Are you going to wait until he comes home?'

'No,' I say resolutely. 'I need to know now.'

I really couldn't bear waiting for the lines on the stick to appear with his face looking at me with so much hope.

'Well, go on then,' says Lou, practically pushing me out of the kitchen. 'I'll be here when you get back.'

I'm about to refuse and tell her I'll wait until I next go to the toilet, but it's as if my bladder's conspiring with Lou and I suddenly feel the urge to go.

For a minute I'm stuck in the hallway. I feel like if I remain here everything will stay exactly the same. I can have my little hope that I do have a baby in my belly, without having to worry about the problems that it would cause for my business.

'Go on!' prompts Lou.

I sigh. She's right – hiding in the hallway isn't going to get me anywhere. I need to know now what's going on.

I go upstairs into the bathroom and hunt around in some drawers that I've been meaning to sort out for ages. There, in the middle of a lot of mess, sitting in its cardboard box, is one of the pregnancy tests Mark bought earlier in the year. I got my period before needing to use them and they've been waiting patiently there ever since. I take out the instructions and study them with more attention than I usually give those kinds of leaflets. I know desperate teenagers take and pass these tests; it can't be rocket science.

'Is it working?' I hear Lou shouting from the other side of the bathroom door.

'I've only been in here a minute.'

'Feels like forever. OK, but so you know, Harry and I are right here.'

Great. Now I'm bound to get stage fright. I was nervous enough about having to aim for the stick, without worrying that they're going to hear me weeing.

'Can't you make some noise? I'm having a little trouble going,' I say a couple of minutes later.

The sounds of Incy Wincey Spider fill the bathroom and I wish I'd kept my mouth shut. This has got to be one of the more surreal moments of my adult life.

Amazingly, despite the pressure, I manage to pee, and I think I've even done it on the stick. I quickly lay it to rest, zip up my jeans and wash my hands. I practically run out into the hallway.

'Well?' says Lou, her eyebrows arched almost to her hairline.

'I've got to wait.' I slump down on the floor next to her and start playing with Harry's fire engine, which he's discarded in favour of kicking my stair banister. Usually I'd mind the little dents that are appearing on the white-painted wood, but today I'm far too distracted to care.

I feel Lou squeeze my hand. 'It's OK, I'm here if it's not good news.'

'But what if it is? What about my business?'

I start counting the months on my fingers, nine months from my last period would take us to the end of June.

'What about it? You can take a bit of leave.'

'I can't. The baby would be due in peak wedding season. I've got five weddings in July alone. I can't be standing at the end of the aisle with a baby attached to my nipple.'

'Then you'll hire someone else. You can get an assistant or something.'

'I guess so,' I say, wondering. 'It would be different if I had a few years of weddings under my belt, but next year was going to be the year that I cemented my name in the local wedding industry. Not to mention the money that's been ploughed into it. All our savings. After everything that happened with the bingo, and now this . . . Poor Mark, we're never going to have any money.'

Next year's weddings were supposed to be the financial making of my company and allow me to pay myself and build up our depleted savings. Only all that could now be fading away.

It's like Georgina's prophecy is already coming true. If I'm pregnant, my company will fold and all that will be left of it will be a business card in her crappy plastic business-card folder.

'And what about Josh's wedding? He's only agreed to get married since they changed the law, and Mel is terrified he'll change his mind. What if me not being able to plan his wedding causes him to call it off?'

I think back to how nervous Josh was when he and Mel came to the meeting here a couple of weeks ago.

'If it would take that little for him to call it off, then you'd be doing Mel a favour. And I've met Josh – I'm sure he'd be thrilled you're having a baby.'

'And what about the book? Grace is pitching the ideas and chapter samples to publishers; the hope is it will be out next year. When am I going to get time to write it? And what if they need me to do publicity?'

'Um, do you think you're the first pregnant author? That is the least of your worries.'

'So you admit there *are* worries,' I say, aware that my voice is sounding a lot higher and shriller than usual.

'Pen, take a deep breath. It will all work itself out. You've wanted a kid for I don't know how long. Out of everyone I know, you will work it out. I mean, look at what you did the last time you were in debt. Look at the wedding you pulled off on a shoestring. Look at the new career you've built yourself. Besides, it's not good for the baby to get stressed out.'

I close my eyes. Stress the baby out? For all we know there might not be a baby. I get up off the floor and straighten my jumper.

'This is ridiculous,' I say. 'I might be getting myself all worked up for nothing.'

I scrape my hair back into a slick ponytail, take a deep breath and walk into the bathroom. I half close my eyes as I approach the stick and peer at it.

Thank goodness Mark bought the tests that told you whether you were pregnant or not pregnant in words. I wouldn't have coped right now with having to work out whether there were the right number of lines, or the right colours, appearing.

I can't help but smile as I look down at the word on the stick. For a minute I can't quite believe it, but there it is; all there in black and white. Well, black on grey.

'Lou,' I say quietly.

She comes in, Harry tucked up under one arm, and with the other hand she takes the stick from where it was resting on the corner of the bath. She looks at it and then at me and my giant smile.

'Congratulations!' she screams, throwing the hand with the stick around my neck. 'You're about to join the best club in the world.'

I'm so happy that I'm almost willing to ignore that she is holding a stick covered in my pee, and probably depositing drops of it all over the bathroom floor.

'Thanks,' I say, retreating from the hug. 'Now wash your hands.'

Lou looks at the stick and grimaces. I take Harry and as I hold him it hits me that this time next year I'll be holding a baby just like him. Although I hope my baby isn't as naughty as him, or, whilst we're at it, as heavy, as that would mean he'd have come out like a big melon (ouch).

I don't know whether it's the moment or my new

pregnancy hormones, but I experience a surge of love for the little monster in my arms. I give him a kiss and, as I smell his lavender-scented hair, I start to calm down. I, Penny Robinson, have been in bigger scrapes than this. I can handle anything. Well, almost anything . . . I have no idea how I'm going to handle waiting until Mark comes home from work to tell him.

chapter five

Lucy Cowdry @LuLuLucyC
So fellow brides with @princess_shoestring what's your biggest #weddingworry?

Ellie @Elliezgood
My H2B's mum planning to wear a white meringue dress . . . sounds like she thinks it's HER wedding! #weddingworry #princessshoestring

Nancy Best @BestieNan
Not fitting into my dress, gym anyone? #weddingworry #princessshoestring

Mel @MT125
Penny pulling out of organising our wedding. Where would we be without her?! Lol #weddingworry #princessshoestring

I really didn't give enough thought to the wisdom of doing a pregnancy test in the middle of the day, as having to wait until teatime to tell Mark has been killing me. Which is why I'm walking into the reception of his work at midday.

Lou wanted to hang out and chat babies, but I lasted all of ten minutes before I felt guilty that Mark didn't know. So I sent Lou and Harry off to the library and came here in search of Mark.

I haven't been to his work since the time when he went AWOL right before our wedding. I'm hoping that they've changed their receptionist since then as I can't have made the best impression on her. But no such luck. It's the same mousy-brown-haired woman behind the desk.

'Hello,' she says, looking up and smiling.

'Hi,' I say, praying she doesn't remember me. 'I'm here to see Mark Robinson.'

'Is he expecting you?' She squints as if she's trying to place me.

'No, he's not,' I say, looking around.

'Ah, you're his wife, aren't you?' she says in wide-eyed recognition.

'That's right!' I say far too jovially. 'I was just passing and I thought, Why not come and surprise your husband for lunch? Always a nice surprise, right?'

She gives me a look as if she remembers me as the crazy

71

wife. I've only been here twice, but both times I've behaved strangely. Last time I was acting suspiciously as I was trying to track down AWOL Mark, and the time before I recall doing jazz hands before thrusting a Tupperware tub of stinky curry leftovers at her. I'm hoping this time I can be normal enough to rectify her impression. She observes me closely for a second before picking up the phone.

'One second, I'll see if he's about.'

I watch her dial Mark's number.

'Um, hi, Mr Robinson – your wife is here in reception.'

Her tone suggests that this is not a common occurrence; manager's wives don't turn up in the middle of the day unannounced. Yet it seems to have become my signature move when coming to see Mark at work. I know I could have called him on my mobile, like a normal person, but the truth is I'm so excited about the baby that I wouldn't be able to talk to him on the phone without telling him. This really isn't news that you should give someone over the phone. I can't imagine it in the same conversation as telling him he needs to get loo roll on the way home.

'Uh-huh, that's right, in reception.'

That's right, folks, I want to add to an imaginary audience. *I am in reception!* If I didn't feel embarrassed enough, the emphasis on my location from the woman behind the desk has made me feel as if I'm walking round in public naked.

The receptionist winces, which makes me wonder what Mark has said. Surely he can't be cross I'm here, can he?

She places the receiver down.

'He'll be out in a minute.'

'Thanks.' I smile weakly and slink away into a corner in order to make myself as invisible as possible.

'Pen, did we have plans?' asks Mark as he strides out of the frosted door into reception.

'Um, no,' I say, wishing that the receptionist would at least pretend not to be watching the whole scene play out.

I'm starting to think this might have been a mistake.

Mark's tie is in an untidy knot and his hair is sticking up at the sides. I recognise that style – it's the one he has when he's stressed and has been running his hands through his hair.

'Is everything OK?'

'Yes, absolutely fine,' I say, smiling. 'Can we go somewhere?'

'Ah, Pen, today is not a good day for lunch. It's always lovely to see you,' he says, planting a kiss on my forehead and giving me a quick pat like I'm a dog, 'but it's really not a good time. One of my clients has got a tax audit and I'm having to go through his books with a fine-tooth comb.'

I'm caught between a rock and a hard place. I can't not tell him. This is far too big a secret to keep. And not only that – I made a promise before we got married that I wouldn't hide things from him ever again.

'Some other time, huh, Pen?'

I look at Mark and I catch the receptionist smirking at our conversation.

'Actually, Mark, come for lunch with me. I've got something to tell you, something that can't wait.'

'Oh no, what's going on now? Is there something wrong with the business?'

'Nope, the business is fine,' I say, gritting my teeth.

'Well, what is it? You're looking at me like you've come to tell me that someone's died. Is it Nanny Violet? Is she OK? Oh God, did Mum send you to tell me that something's happened?'

Mark's eyes are bulging and he looks like he's about to burst into tears.

'No, no one died. As far as I know Nanny Violet is fine, although her cancelling last weekend was weird, and I haven't spoken to your mum since Monday night.'

I'm lost in thought as I remember that I never did get to the bottom of Nanny V's odd behaviour when I spoke to Ted.

'Ah, thank God,' he says, sighing and running his hands through his hair again. 'So can't this wait until later?'

I'm snapped back into the conversation as I realise I'm losing him.

'But I brought a special lunch,' I say in desperation, holding up the plastic bag that I shoved it in.

Mark narrows his eyes, looking at me before taking the bag from my hands and opening it up.

'This is a special lunch?'

My cheeks flush. I know that the word *special* implies deli finest ranges and not leftover fajita wraps stuffed with lettuce and ham. I should have stopped off to get some more exciting ingredients on the way, but I was too excited to make the diversion.

'Yep, look, there's a Kit-Kat Chunky from my secret supply.'

Mark looks up from the bag. He doesn't look impressed. 'What's going on, Pen?' he hisses. 'Are you in trouble?'

'No!' I reply quickly, looking over his shoulder to make sure that the bat-ears receptionist isn't listening. 'Why would you think that?'

'Because you show up at my work at lunchtime unannounced, acting strangely.'

I'd like to deny that I'm acting especially out of character, but I know I am.

'I had something to tell you,' I say, whispering back, trying not to cry.

'Then tell me, Pen.'

I shake my head. This was not how it was supposed to

happen. Maybe this is karmic payback for not waiting for him to be there before I peed on the stick.

'I can't now. You're busy. I'll tell you when you get home.'

Mark sighs loudly. 'You came all this way. It must be important.'

'No,' I say, smiling my best fake smile. 'It can wait.'

Mark takes my hand and gives it a squeeze. 'It's a bad day, I'm sorry. I promise I'll be in a better mood when I come home. Maybe you can make me a special dinner instead of lunch and tell me then?'

'OK,' I say. I reach up and kiss him on the lips and I can't resist running my hand through his hair to tidy it up a little.

'I'll try not to be home too late.'

'See you later.' I wave as he walks back into his office. The receptionist gives me a pity smile before she picks up the ringing phone as I walk back out.

It's now 12.10, and I've got at least six hours before Mark gets home. There's no way I'm going to be able to concentrate on any work, so if he wants a special dinner, then that's what he's going to get.

By the time I hear the key go in the door at seven o'clock, I'm lying on the sofa unable to find the strength to get up. It turns out that cooking a special dinner is exhausting. Not to mention a bit of a waste of time, as the lamb I've been roasting in the oven is probably all dried out by now as Mark is nearly an hour late.

'Penny?' he says.

I just about manage to sit up and swing my legs round to the floor, but I've gone all lightheaded and feeling a little woozy. I've definitely got up too quickly.

'Are you OK?' he says, walking into the lounge and seeing me with my head in my hands. 'Dinner smells delicious. Is it lamb?'

'It is, but it's probably ruined by now,' I say holding my hand out for him to pull me up. He brings me up to standing and gives me a kiss on the cheek.

'You would not believe some people,' he complains as I follow him into the kitchen. 'My client knew two weeks ago about this audit and only thought that I might need to know about it this morning. Two whole weeks where we could have got everything into shape at a leisurely pace. I just don't understand them. I mean, talk about burying your head in the sand. But I'm home now.'

He instinctively goes over to the oven and starts to fuss around with the roasting tray, whilst I take my usual seat at the kitchen table and watch him.

He takes out the lamb, the fats sizzling in the pan, and I feel myself retch. It's obviously been cooking too long; it smells rancid.

'This looks amazing. Shall I carve?' asks Mark.

I nod and cover my mouth with my sleeve. Surely six weeks is too early to have an aversion to food smells, isn't it?

I try and distract myself as Mark cuts the meat and scoops up the vegetables.

He picks up the plates and turns as if to bring them over to the table.

'I've laid up the dining room,' I say, turning my head away from the food.

'Really? On a Tuesday? Wow! When I said a special dinner I was joking.'

I half smile and reluctantly get up to follow him in. 'You've gone to a lot of trouble,' Mark says as I see him looking around in shock. It's rare that I actually put a tablecloth on the table, but I've not only done that, I've ironed it. There really is a first time for everything. My mother would be so proud.

'I know I have,' I say, sitting down.

Mark sits down opposite me and starts scooping mint sauce out onto his plate. The smell of it hits me and I wonder if I'm going to be able to stay here.

'So, what did you want to tell me?'

I can't bring myself to look at him – the smell of the mint is too much and I've got to focus on a tiny old food stain on the tablecloth or I'm going to be sick. I push my plate away. I can't face it.

'Have you poisoned the food? Are you trying to bump me off?' Mark says, pointing at my plate.

'I don't feel like eating.'

He tilts his head and looks at me. He knows there has to be something wrong. Not a lot gets between me and my food.

'I know what it is,' he says quietly.

Momentarily distracted from the nausea, I look up. Perhaps I look different. Perhaps I look pregnant.

'You do?' I say smiling. I'm about to launch into the wonderful news.

'Yes, I mean I worried it might happen.'

'You did?'

'Yeah, with you spending all day at home, working by yourself.'

Hang on, I'm confused. I don't think there's any way that I could have got into my situation on my own. Human biology is one of the few lessons you don't forget from your school days.

'Um, I'm not following.'

'It's OK, Pen, you've been so good for so long. It's probably only a minor slip. I'm sure that we can get you through it again.'

I'm well and truly lost now.

'What do you think my problem is?'

'You're gambling again,' he says, shovelling a large chunk of lamb and roast potato into his mouth.

'What? I'm not gambling. I'm actually enjoying working from home and I, um . . . don't feel lonely.' I say, recalling my desperate need to see the postman every morning. But no matter how lonely I feel, I'd never be tempted to gamble again. The shame and upset that my online bingo addiction caused is something I'd never in a million years want to repeat. I felt I'd hit rock bottom in my life when I told my family and friends that I'd been stupid enough to throw away ten thousand hard-saved pounds in order to buy a bigger dress and spangly heels.

I am slightly hurt that Mark thinks I'd have so little resolve.

'Are you sure? I wouldn't be mad – I'm only asking as this time I'd want to support you through it.'

Despite my annoyance, sometimes I love my husband a lot. And this is one of those times. I didn't give him the chance to help me through the gambling habit the last time as I was determined to keep it a secret. I'll never gamble again if I can help it, but knowing that Mark is here for me if I did, is, well . . . it's well, oh no, I'm crying.

'Honey.'

Mark's got up and come round to my side of the table and

he's wrapped me up in a hug. 'Whatever it is, it can't be that bad. You can tell me anything. Are you ill?'

'No,' I say, shaking my head. Considering that I've been dying to tell him for the last seven hours, I can't understand why I can't get the words out of my mouth.

Instead I push his arms away and stand up.

'Come with me,' I say, taking his hand.

I lead him into the bathroom and pull the dangling light switch.

'Penny, I have to say when you dragged me upstairs I thought my luck might be in, but doing it in the bathroom doesn't really get me going. Unless we had one of those baths out of the movies, with the bubbles and candles all around,' he says, nevertheless grabbing hold of my bum cheeks and pulling me towards him.

He runs his hand up my back and for a moment I forget why we're here, especially when he starts nibbling my neck and I can feel myself pressing against him.

'Mark, stop,' I say, wriggling free. I let out my breath and focus on cooling myself down. 'Look.'

I point to the pregnancy test, which has assumed pride of place on the toilet cistern. Even though I know keeping a peed-on stick is gross, I haven't been able to throw it away – I kept having to check it every few minutes this afternoon to make sure that it was real.

'What the ... ?'

Mark picks it up and then looks up at me. I smile at him and nod. He looks back down at it and runs his free hand through his hair again.

'You're ... ? We're ... ?' he stutters.

'That's right,' I say.

His mouth falls open. I was sort of expecting him to hug me or to break into a smile, but he looks like he's been punched in the stomach. What if he's not happy? What if he is worried about the money and the business?

'I don't believe it! All that time. *All that time.*'

He sits down on the toilet seat and he's making a really weird noise. Is he crying?

'Mark, it's OK, you don't have to worry. It'll be fine. Everything will work out with the company and the money.'

He looks up at me, and I see he's not crying, he's laughing.

'We're going to be parents, Penny. Us.'

'I know,' I say, instantly relieved. This is the expression I wanted to see on Mark's face when I told him.

'We're having a baby,' he says, slowly and more to himself than me. 'That's why you came to the office and were acting so oddly.'

'Yep, Lou made me take the test this morning, and I really didn't think it'd be positive, but then it was.'

Mark stands up. 'This is the best news ever. Who are we going to tell first?'

'We shouldn't really tell anyone. It's early days. I'm only six weeks. We've got to have a scan first and then it'll be safe to tell people.'

Mark nods as if he's taking it all in.

'If you're six weeks, when was that?' He scratches his head.

'Well, actually you calculate it from the date of your last period – so the date of conception would have been a couple of weeks after that.'

More head-scratching ensues.

'Oh, Carcassonne!' he says with a laugh.

'Yep,' I say, watching his cheeks colour at the memory. 'It's due at the end of June.'

'Well, well,' he says, pulling me over to him and with his head at my tummy height he kisses my belly. 'A little French baby. Just in time for the summer.'

I sit down on Mark's knee and he wraps me up in his arms.

'Just in time for the wedding season. Perfect timing for Princess-on-a-Shoestring,' I say sarcastically.

'Don't worry about that now. I mean, you can always relaunch the company when the little one is older.'

I pull away from Mark and look him squarely in the face.

'What do you mean, relaunch? It's too late to stop the company now – I've got weddings booked all through next year!'

'But what about maternity leave? You know as well as I do that you've been planning that for years.'

A vision of me dressed in dungarees painting a nursery floods into my mind. I've been saving box sets of *Mad Men* for it and everything.

'I know,' I say, pouting. 'But that was back when I had a job that would pay me. I can't stop the business now. I've got brides that need me.'

'I think the baby in your belly is going to need you more.'

I'm about to argue that a bride on her wedding day that can't get her dress done up might be more in need, but I feel that might be missing the point.

Mark stands up from the toilet seat and washes his hands.

'So what am I going to do?' I say, placing my hands on my hips. 'I'm not shutting down the company.'

'Fine. So get someone else to do the weddings you've booked.'

'What do you mean, get someone else? They pay to have *me* organise the weddings. That's part of the service.'

I walk out of the bathroom – there's something weird about having an argument where it's all echoey.

'I know, you're the star attraction of Princess-on-a-Shoestring. All I'm saying is that there must be a way that we can work around it. There must be someone you trust to do the weddings for you.'

I think about it for a minute, but I haven't been doing the business for long enough to have any backups put in place.

'I can't think of anyone. Besides, brides are easily freaked out. It's hard to get them to choose you in the first place, let alone if you pull a switch. Oh, this is such crap timing,' I say, walking into our bedroom and sitting on the bed.

'I don't think there's such a thing as perfect timing when babies are involved. We've got another seven or eight months until the baby arrives, right? Why don't you carry on with the business and I'm sure you'll find someone to replace you,' he says.

'What, and lie to the brides to be?'

Mark's leaning against the door frame to the bedroom, undoing his tie. It's a shame I'm still feeling pretty sick, as what with the little grabby hands in the bathroom and now him looking all smouldering, I'm feeling a bit frisky.

'I'm not saying lie; just don't tell them yet that you're pregnant. I'm sure between now and your scan you can find someone to take over, and you can introduce the idea to the brides gently. You can make it a smooth transition.'

I'm not the world's best liar, even if over the last year or two I've had to keep my fair share of secrets. But I wouldn't be lying really, would I? I mean, everyone keeps pregnancies a secret for the first twelve weeks, don't they?

'It'll be like you keeping the wedding planning from your old boss.'

'And that went so well,' I say, remembering the moment when Giles found out about Princess-on-a-Shoestring and I almost lost my job. It was then I handed in my notice and started my own company. Ironically, if I had still been working at my old job, I'd now be doing a happy dance over the maternity pay I would be getting, instead of freaking out that the business will go down the pan and we won't be able to afford to buy nappies.

'It worked out well in the end.'

'Yeah, but—' I start.

'No buts. Except that it's probably sensible not to book in any more on-the-day wedding planning for the summer, until you get something sorted.'

I nod. Containment. That I can do. I wouldn't want to disappoint any more brides than I have to. I briefly wonder if I should cancel the existing appointments I've got booked with prospective clients, but maybe their weddings won't clash with the arrival of our bundle of joy.

'Keep it on the down-low for a bit and we'll figure it out.'

I laugh at Mark as he does some weird hand movement as if he's down with the cool kids.

'OK,' I say, smiling.

'We're having a baby,' he says, sitting down and putting his arm around me again.

'I know,' and, for the first time today, I let it properly sink in.

Mark's right, it's the most important thing. It's what we wanted, long before my company came along. I only need to keep it a secret for a few weeks and then I'll have it all sorted and everything will be out in the open.

chapter six

Rachel Burton @Onlyrachburton
Hoping @princess_shoestring will have better ideas than @madjimbo for our wedding . . . me entering in a zorb ball isn't going to happen.

Jimmy Jenkins @madjimbo
@Onlyrachburton That would be awesome. Almost as good as skydiving in. @princess_shoestring will have her work cut out to beat those babies.

This morning I'm meeting with my first clients since I found out the big news about the impending change to my parental status. All I've got to do is get through these two meetings without being sick on the brides or mentioning the bump-to-be.

Easy-peasy, right?

'Hi. Penny?'

I look up over my laptop at a woman with long blonde hair. I vaguely recognise her from the wedding fair, but I spoke to so many people that they all blurred into one.

'Hello, you must be Sally.'

'Yes, that's right,' she says, sitting down in the chair opposite.

'I'm sorry I'm early. I wasn't too sure about parking and I thought I'd grab a coffee. I didn't expect you to have arrived early too, and then I saw you sitting here.'

'It's fine, really,' I say, saving the document I was working on. I don't want to tell her the truth – I'm actually making a list of possible baby names. I know I've got another seven months to come up with one but you really can't start too early. Mark's already ruled out anything poncey; Chandos got banned straight off. The trouble is, one man's poncy is another one's perfect. Take Garfield, for instance. I didn't realise it could be an actual name other than a cartoon cat, yet it can. Garfield Robinson. Doesn't that sound like a prime minister or doctor in the making?

It's not like I'm idling away in work time. It's Saturday, which is when a lot of my meetings in the off-season take place so brides don't have to take any time off work.

'So, how do we do this then?' asks Sally, as she turns to face me after putting her coat over the back of her seat.

'First of all we have a bit of a chat about the wedding you want and the budget you're working to. You let me know why you want the help of a wedding planner, and from there we work out if I'm the best option for you. Now, have you got an idea of provisional dates?' I say, pulling out my notepad and pen.

'I had been hoping for 30 June.'

Of course she had. Two days after baby Robinson's due.

'Have you . . .' I cough and clear my throat as I start to choke on the words, 'set a date in stone?'

'No, not until we decide on the venue.'

'So you have got some flexibility?'

If I could pencil her in in May, I might be waddling, but at least I'd be there.

'Yes, although, I would like it to be a summer wedding. Late June at the earliest. What's your availability like for the summer?'

I'm guessing non-existent. I try to think of another strategy which would mean I could take her on as client guilt-free.

'Um, well, I've got a few weddings already booked for fully managed packages, and I don't usually take on two clients for the same day. But on those dates when I'm already booked, I'm still available for pre-planning packages. That's when I help out with the initial planning side, but I'm not involved in the week leading up to the wedding or the day itself.'

If only all my brides wanted pre-planning only, then I wouldn't have a problem. I'd be able to sort everything out for them before the baby arrived. Too bad I've already got existing brides booked in for the full package over the summer.

'I'd ideally like to have you all day. That's the appeal of a wedding planner for me. I saw my sister get all stressed out over her wedding and I definitely wouldn't want that. I've read all your blogs and I've loved all your brides' wedding stories. I imagine having you by their side on the big day was such a huge comfort.'

In the past I'd have been secretly air-punching at this point, as that would mean a bigger fee and therefore a step closer to my business turning a profit. Only now I'm slightly deflated. I agreed with Mark that I shouldn't take on any more bookings for the full package over the summer period, but with her right in front of me, it seems impossible to turn her down.

Finding someone to delegate to should be my number-one priority. After all, if I have someone to run the weddings, then it won't be a problem to agree to this one too. I scribble down a note in my Filofax to start actively finding a replacement.

'So, Sally. Have you given any thought to where you want the wedding?'

'Yes, I want it outside, in a garden or a park.'

'In the British summer?'

I shiver as memories of the wedding I organised in July come rushing back to me. The squelch of mud underfoot, the weight of sandbags as we tried to stop the flow of water flooding the marquee.

'Uh-huh. We had such a lovely summer this year, didn't we?' says Sally.

'Did we?'

That's the problem with the weather in the UK – one memory of a great barbecue in the sunshine, and your mind tricks you into thinking that that was what it was like for the whole season, rather than the dull and cloudy weather that it probably was.

'Yes.'

I'd like to point out that if we had had a nice summer this year, then we're unlikely to get two in a row, but who wants a pessimistic wedding planner? Instead I write down 'out-door' in my notes and add 'look into indoor options' as a backup.

'Tell me more about your vision for outside,' I say, taking

a sip of my decaf coffee and instantly regretting it. The bitter taste is making me feel queasy. I try and cleanse away the taste by rubbing my tongue against the top of my mouth.

'I like the idea of tropical plants, or wild flowers, or an enchanted wood.'

I start to tingle with excitement. I love this sort of design brief. I can't help but feel a bit naughty planning this when I know I shouldn't be taking this on, but this is my favourite part of my job.

'I thought I could carry it through to the details in the ceremony, hand-tied bouquets, flowers in my hair, bare feet.'

'Bare feet? In this country?'

I instantly think of the escape-and-evasion team-building day in July that I once organised for my old job, where we had to go crawling through thick mud under a deluge of rain. I don't know why people have these idyllic thoughts of English meadows in summer, as my experiences have always been far from that.

'Uh-huh. I think I'll go for a short dress, something floaty.'

Sally's eyes are going misty and I can tell she's been planning this wedding in her head for a long time. Probably since long before her fiancé popped the question.

I'm a tiny bit sad that I won't be there to see her have this wedding. It sounds so lovely.

'And then as I walk up the flower-strewn aisle I want Justin Bieber playing.'

'. . . Justin Bieber?'

I scratch my ears, thinking I must have misheard. I didn't think anyone over the age of twelve was a Belieber.

'Yep. You know the song "Baby"?'

I certainly do know the song 'Baby', unfortunately. But in case I don't, Sally has launched into an a cappella version of it, much to the amusement of the rest of the customers in the coffee shop.

It's as if the universe is taunting me with my secret.

'I know the song, I know it!' I say, flapping my arms around and trying to get her to stop. 'Why do you want that?' I ask, trying to keep my tone like I'm not judging her.

'It's mine and my fiancé's song.'

Oh wow. I guess it has to be someone's.

'OK, then. Well, I'm sure that's doable.'

To be honest, out of everything she's mentioned so far, the music will be the easiest part.

'So, Penny, what do you think? I was speaking to that other wedding planner at the fair, and she seemed to imply that outdoor wouldn't work and perhaps a marquee would be as outdoor as I get,' says Sally, draining the last dregs from her cup.

Goose pimples immediately spring up on my arms at the

mention of Georgina Peasbody. I'd tried to block that vile woman from my thoughts, but as Sally is a prospective client, I try not to blurt out my true feelings.

'I'm definitely not thinking marquee,' I say, speaking slowly and choosing my words carefully as it's not the worst idea in the world. 'I think Peasbody weddings probably have a marquee as standard as they tend to do higher-end weddings.'

'Yes, I wondered about that. You see, I couldn't find the prices of their packages. they weren't very transparent on their website.'

One of the first things I did was put my prices in black and white on my site so that brides instantly knew if they could or couldn't afford me and we didn't waste each other's time.

I begin to relax and I'm about to talk through the budget when I notice she's shifting in her chair.

'I've arranged a meeting with her too though. I hope you don't mind. It's just it's a big commitment signing with a wedding planner, and I thought it best to shop around a little.'

She's avoiding eye contact, and whilst it might actually solve some of my problems if I didn't do her wedding, a wave of professional pride washes over me and suddenly I'm desperate for her not to sign with Peasbody Weddings.

'Of course,' I say, plastering a fake smile on my face. 'It's one of the biggest days of your life, and I understand that you've got to be sure you've got the right person at the helm.'

'That's what I thought. I'm so relieved you see it that way. It's making me think that you *get* me, Penny, and that with you planning my wedding I'd be safe.'

I feel a tiny bit guilty that if I do win the business that I won't be seeing it through to the end. I try and console myself that whoever I got to cover it, I would train them, and I'd still be as involved as possible. Even if I was issuing instructions via Bluetooth while changing nappies.

By the time we finish discussing budgets and other details, I feel like I'm another step closer to having her as a client.

'Thanks so much for all your help, Penny. I've got to get to my gym class now.'

I look at my watch and gasp. We've been talking weddings for well over an hour and a half. I'm due to meet Rachel, another prospective bride-to-be, at any minute.

'I'm meeting the other planner this afternoon, so I'll be in touch early next week with my decision.'

'Great, and if you do go ahead then I'll have plenty to get on with,' I say, looking over my full page of scribbled notes and wondering if I do win the business how I'm going to do it.

'I'll speak to you soon then.'

Sally stands up, humming 'Baby' as she goes. I'm squinting at her as I wonder if she's actually guessed my secret and is making fun of me. But the sincerity with which she is humming it and the inane grin on her face are telling me not to be paranoid.

I take a moment to catch my breath before I spot a woman walking into the coffee shop whom I presume to be my next customer. She's scanning around as if she's looking for someone, and bingo! She's made eye contact and is smiling at me.

'Hello,' she says, striding across the floor with a confident spring in her step, to match her bouncing red curls.

'Hiya, you must be Rachel.'

'That's right. Nice to meet you.'

'Nice to meet you too,' I say, my smile dropping as she takes off her coat and reveals a tiny baby bump poking out of her tight wool dress.

'Oh, you've spotted it then,' she says, blushing as she fusses with putting her coat over her chair.

'Congratulations,' I stutter. I'm trying desperately to compose myself. I'm acting like I've never seen a pregnant woman before. But the truth is, I haven't seen one since I found out my news and I'm in awe that I'm going to have my own one of those in just a few months' time.

'I know exactly what you're thinking.'

'You do?' I ask, trying desperately hard to focus on her face rather than her bump.

She sits down and I let out a small sigh of relief that now it's hidden from my view.

'Yes, you're thinking what most people do, that me and my fiancé are morons for not waiting another few months, or that we're planning the wedding now because I'm up the duff.'

'Oh no,' I say honestly, 'that wasn't what I was thinking at all.'

Believe me, that was the furthest thing from my thoughts. Although now she's mentioned it . . .

'It's OK, most of our friends and our family have said it. My mum thinks we should either have the wedding earlier or postpone it for another year, and his mum thinks we've committed the crime of the century by having sex before marriage. But actually, Jimmy and I really wanted to start a family and we thought, why wait?'

'So when are you due?' I say, trying to side-step any more controversial topics.

'April.'

'And you want the wedding . . . ?'

'In July.'

'Wow. A three-month-old baby and a wedding.'

'I know, which is where you come in.'

Or not, as I think back yet again to what Mark and I agreed. If I could just get her to move her wedding.

'Have you thought about moving it to, say, September or October? I mean, six months is such a lovely age.'

And my baby would be three or four months then and it would be much easier for me to do it.

'It might be a nice age, but babies at three months pretty much sleep all the time, or at least in big chunks. Much easier than having a wriggling, awake baby.'

I wonder if I should tell Rachel now that I can't plan the wedding, yet I can't seem to bring myself to do it. I don't know whether it has something to do with Sally mentioning Georgina Peasbody, bringing back to me what she said about having babies, but I feel as if I should take on all the clients I can.

It's wrong, as I told Mark I wouldn't take on any more summer brides, yet here I am taking on two. But if you think about it, it's not like Mark would even know if they were existing bookings or not. I mean, the appointments were already booked, so technically it's like they were already clients. And I've already got to find a replacement for the other weddings I'm planning, so what's two more in the grand scheme of things. I'm clearly worrying about nothing.

The waitress comes over and takes our order. I give her my

cold decaf coffee and plump for a freshly pressed apple juice instead, whilst Rachel orders a rooibos tea.

'I'd love to have an apple juice here, but you can't have freshly squeezed juice when you're pregnant.'

'What?' I say, beginning to come out in a cold sweat. I can't not drink this one too – not only will it look odd to the waitress, but I'm getting really thirsty. How did I not know these things? What else am I doing that I shouldn't be? I'm struggling to control my breathing here.

'Yeah, it's something about fresh juices not being pasteurised. You run the risk of listeria,' she says, shrugging. 'You have to be careful with loads of things that you'd never even think of.'

The waitress comes over with our drinks on a tray and I eye my apple juice with suspicion. So much for me thinking that I was going for the healthy option.

'Did you know,' I say to the waitress as she places our drinks down on the table, 'that pregnant women can't drink freshly squeezed juices?'

I make sure I point at Rachel at this point as if I am asking for her benefit, not mine.

'That's only partly true. If you make it fresh when the customer orders it, like we do with our juicer, that's fine. There's more of a problem with ones which are squeezed and then sit there in a jug for a while.'

'Oh,' says Rachel. 'That's good to know.'

It certainly is. I tuck straight into my apple juice so that it doesn't have time to sit about cultivating bacteria.

'Thirsty?' asks Rachel, laughing.

'Something like that. So, back to your wedding,' I say calmly, thinking that I'd better do some research into what I can and can't eat.

'Right, we thought we'd hire a wedding planner as I'm going to be out of action a lot beforehand, looking after the baby.'

As am I, I want to add.

'OK, so have you thought about when and where?'

'We want to get married in our local church, and then the venue is really up for grabs. I don't care so much what the place looks like, as long as everyone has a really good time.'

'Wow, that's quite an open brief.'

'I know. Perhaps somewhere close to the church, so that our guests don't have too far to travel. And, if it's possible, I'd love something like a bouncy castle, or something that makes it a bit different. A bit crazy and a bit fun. It has to be relaxed too. I want there to be loads of laughter and noise. If there's going to be a baby screaming, we might as well blend it in.'

'OK,' I say, scribbling my notes down. I'm almost hoping it's a July wedding and my little bean is out by then, as a cheeky jump on a bouncy castle sounds awesome. And if there's already one crying baby, people aren't going to notice too much if there's another one, are they?

'Have you got an idea of budget?'

'About twelve thousand pounds, including your fee.'

'Great. That's a healthy budget.'

'Yes, the parents have been really generous. Especially Jimmy's. I think they want him to make an honest woman of me.'

'Well, it will certainly be a lovely day with that figure.'

'I know, see? All the better for wanting my little baby to be part of it. I want to carry him or her down the aisle too. You know some people have a bouquet – I want a baby,' she says, laughing.

'Aw, I think that's really sweet.'

'My mother doesn't think so. She's not much of a fan of children at weddings, but it's my baby, I want her there.'

'It's hard with mothers and weddings. I think we forget that they've been dreaming about our big day since we were born and sometimes they struggle when things aren't that traditional.'

'I guess that's true. I hadn't thought about it like that. I think the whole baby thing has come as a bit of a shock to her. I don't think she thinks I'm up to the challenge.'

'I don't think anyone is before it happens though, are they?'

'That's what I keep saying.'

Rachel's whole face lights up when she talks about the baby, and you can tell that she's going to make a really good mum.

'Have you got kids?' she asks.

'Me?' I say, almost choking on a sip of apple juice. 'No, er, not yet.' I guess it's not technically a lie. 'One day soon, I hope.'

'Not too soon – you need to do my wedding first!' says Rachel, laughing as she picks up her teacup.

My hand involuntary spasms and I send the sugar bowl flying across the table.

'Sorry about that,' I say, hoping that my face hasn't given away my secret. I hastily pick up the packets of sugar.

There's something earthy and real about Rachel. I really like her. I'd love to confide in her and tell her that I'm in the club too. She's the kind of woman I'd hope I'd meet at my antenatal classes and hang out post-birth with our little bundles of joy. But I can't. The problem is that my business is so heavily dependent on my blog and social media that if one little comment made its way online, the cat would be out of the bag. Which is a shame, as I reckon we'd get on really well at baby signing or swimming classes. Not to mention trips to Starbucks to stock up on much-needed caffeine after all those sleepless nights.

'So what do you think?'

I look at Rachel blankly, about to tell her that I think that we should sign up to baby yoga classes immediately, but then I realise that she's not talking about my fantasy where our babies become bffs. She wants to know about her wedding.

'Um, yeah, bouncy castle. I love it. Like a summer fête or something. I'll have a think, but I've got a few ideas in mind that I want to check out before I get your hopes up.'

I'm lying. I have no thoughts. Right now my thought process is stuck with my baby lying adorably on an inflatable bouncy castle, but I've learnt that in this business you can't say you've go no ideas off the top of your head as it disappoints them. Whereas by being vague and promising not to dash their hopes, they think you've taken over the cultivation of their precious dream. And it's not like I'm not going to come up with any ideas, as I will.

'I am so excited,' she says, rubbing her hands together in glee.

'So tell me about your fiancé,' I say, moving the subject away from the mystery wedding.

'Jimmy is . . . Now, how do I describe him without you thinking that he sounds like an overgrown kid?'

She laughs and I smile back and I get lost in her descriptions of him and how they met. As she speaks, my thoughts get back on track and I begin to see bright colours, balloons, ice-cream machines. Not clowns though – they freak too many people out, including me.

By the time the meeting is over I've got to try and rein in my full-blown big-top circus idea – I don't imagine they hire those out for weddings, but I'm glad that my creative juices finally seem to be flowing again.

'Thanks ever so much for meeting me,' says Rachel as she gets up. 'And who knows – the next time I see you I might be as big as a house.'

Me too! I want to scream. But in reality that's a lie. We're going to be meeting pretty soon to sort out the details.

'I doubt it, unless you've got a few of them in there. I suggest we meet in the next couple of weeks, once I've had a chance to scout out a few provisional ideas and have some suggestions. It would be nice to meet Jimmy too to get his input early on.'

'Um, do we have to?'

'You don't want him to know the details of his own wedding?'

I'm haunted slightly by the memory of my wedding, when I told Mark next to nothing about our big day.

'It's not that I don't want him to know, as I do,' she says, looking me firmly in the eye so that I can see her sincerity. 'It's just that he gets so carried away. I'll be honest with you.' She sits back down in the chair and leans across the table. 'When we first found out about the baby and decided to get married, Jimmy said he'd take over the wedding planning. I thought that sounded logical, but the next day he was on the phone to circus tents seeing if he could hire them. He wanted fire-eaters, jugglers, clowns, the works.'

Boy, am I relieved that I didn't let her into my thought process. I'd be on the scrap heap along with Jimmy. Fire-eaters and a big top would have been amazing though.

'He even wanted those trapeze people that perform whilst you're eating. I told him that seeing a woman's crotch dangling inches above my head would put me off my dinner.'

It's a good job that Rachel put such a disturbing image into my head, as up until that point that also sounded like an amazing idea. I was beginning to think that Jimmy and I could have planned the most spectacular wedding anyone had ever seen.

'Hmm, I can see how you might have wanted him to tone it down a notch,' I say diplomatically, crossing off the circus idea on my pad of paper.

'Don't get me wrong, he's great with ideas, but perhaps not so much for our wedding. I sort of thought we'd bring him in around the stage where we've narrowed it down to a venue and he has to agree on a date or something.'

'OK,' I say smiling. 'I'll be in touch, and until then we'll get together just the two of us.'

'Ha, just the three of us,' she says, rubbing her belly as she puts her coat on.

Four of us, I add silently in my head. I'm sure she's doing this deliberately.

'Until the next time,' she says, bounding out of the coffee shop.

I whimper a goodbye. Something tells me keeping a secret during our meetings is going to be hard work.

'So when's it due then?' asks the waitress as she comes over.

'I'm sorry? My friend's baby?'

'No, lovey,' she says, picking up our empties and stacking them on her tray. 'Yours. Decaf coffee, overly concerned about the apple juice. I saw the look of panic in your eyes, not to mention the wincing when you were trying to drink the coffee.'

I look up at this woman as if she's an oracle. 'June,' I say.

'Well, congratulations.' She smiles at me warmly and walks off.

I tingle with a warm glow that I've let someone into my little secret, before I sigh. I'm not going to be able to bring any more clients to the coffee shop until they know. I wouldn't want her putting her foot in it. It's a shame as I really love this place for meetings, but right now I've got to put the business first. I have to put out of my mind how warm and fuzzy her congratulations made me feel, and hope that I'll feel like that all the time when I eventually tell everyone.

chapter seven

Penny Robinson @princess_shoestring
My brides/brides-to-be can you help? RT @GeorgiePorgee
Anyone had a @princess_shoestring wedding? Would you rec-
ommend them?

Henri Eves @Harri_henri
@GeorgiePorgee Abso-bloody-lutely. Penny planned me the
best day ever. It was amazing. And she saved us a fortune too!!!

Olivia Gold @livi_girl
@GeorgiePorgee I'd never even heard of Carcassonne - can't
imagine a more perfect wedding. Book Penny now - you won't
regret it!

It's all very well keeping the baby bump secret from the
brides-to-be, but it is quite another thing to keep it from our

friends and family. I thought having Lou in the loop might help, but she's totally freaking me out with hints and tips for the birth. Talking about stitches and giving me arnica tablets, in case she forgets nearer the time, is not conducive to a relaxing early pregnancy.

When Mark first suggested breaking the news to Nanny Violet I was thrilled. I know she'll be over the moon, and she's from a generation that doesn't over-share about the realities of birth. I'm sure she'll maintain the idea that in her day the baby appeared after a few gentle pushes and no one accidentally pooped.

'Here you go, Penny, your favourite.' I look up, praying that Nanny Violet isn't holding a box of Viennese whirls and instead see lemon-curd tarts.

Ordinarily I'm very partial to lemon curd, but the thought of the sharp, bitter taste is turning my stomach. I figure this might be the perfect way to introduce the topic of her great-grandchild.

'Ooh, thanks, but actually I'm feeling a little nauseous this morning.'

I look closely at Nanny Violet's face for a hint of a reaction, but there's nothing. Not even a little sparkle. Usually with female members of my family the slightest hint of sickness or a refusal of a glass of wine gets eyebrows raising and the chins wagging. But instead of her curiosity being piqued,

Nanny Violet has looked away from me and is off offering a Viennese whirl to Mark.

'My favourite,' he says. 'Thanks, Nan.'

He lifts it up to me in triumph, making me feel even more sick. I've said many times before that the creamy jam mixture in the middle is plain wrong.

'So, Ted tells me that you're thinking of going on a last-minute cruise,' I say, as Nanny Violet pours cups of tea from the flowered china teapot. When I talked to Ted at the wedding fair, the only topic of conversation was his and Nanny Violet's plans to go on holiday.

'He did?' she says, missing the teacup and splashing her plastic floral tray with tea. 'Oh bother.'

She mops up the spillage with a tea towel.

'Clumsy this morning,' she says briskly.

Maybe I'm imagining it, but I think she's avoiding eye contact with me. I know I can get a bit oversensitive when it comes to Violet, ever since she almost broke up our wedding when she told Mark I was having an affair. It was all a big misunderstanding, but it stemmed from when she suspected I was lying to her. Ever since then, I've paid quite a lot of attention to how she acts around me. And what with her strange behaviour with Ted a couple of weeks ago, I'm starting to get an uneasy feeling.

'Anyway,' I say, watching her closely to gauge her reactions,

'Ted said that you were thinking of going to Portugal and the Canaries in December.'

I watch as Nanny Violet stirs our tea like she's beating eggs in a bowl.

'Really, Nan? In December? You won't be away for Christmas, will you?'

Nanny Violet stands up straight and wipes the creases out of the apron she's got neatly tied around her waist.

'No, of course not,' she says smiling awkwardly. 'It's only an idea at this stage. I think it's because the weather's turned so bitter so early on this winter. Our brittle old bones feel the cold so much more than you young 'uns. A little sun would be nice – all a bit of a fantasy really.'

She hands us our tea and I can't quite shake the feeling that she's lying. She's still avoiding eye contact, and whereas usually she'd be sitting in her favourite armchair listening to what we've been up to over the last few weeks, now she's picked up a duster and has turned to the ornaments on her fireplace.

'It should be a nice Christmas for us this year,' I say, changing the subject. 'A quiet one with it only being the two of us. I figure that it's best to make the most of that while we still can.'

If my hint at feeling sick was like dropping a pebble in the ocean, then surely this comment will be like throwing a boulder into a pond.

'Yes, lovely Christmas,' she says as if she's lost in a daydream. I look over at Mark and he looks back at me quizzically. I scrunch my eyebrows and twitch my head to make him realise that it's his turn to drop hints.

I'm not entirely sure he gets it, so I do an exaggerated round stomach gesture with my hands and point at Nanny Violet, who is still dusting.

'So, um, Nan. Pen and I have got something we wanted to talk to you about,' he says, coughing awkwardly and clearing his throat.

'You do?' she says, resting the duster down and turning to face him.

Her face is set and she's got an unreadable expression in her eyes. I'm about to interject to tell her it's not bad news and that she's got nothing to worry about, but just then the doorbell goes.

'Saved by the bell!' she says, laughing nervously as she leaves the lounge.

'What's going on?' I ask Mark.

'What do you mean?' His brow is furrowed, indicating he's got no idea what I'm talking about.

'I mean that your nan is acting plain weird. She didn't even blink at my baby hints.'

'What baby hints?'

I roll my eyes and tut in a way that makes me think I'm

turning into my mother. I can't believe this was the same man that thought she sounded funny on the phone a couple of weeks ago. Now she's doing it in the flesh and he doesn't bat an eyelid.

'Never mind,' I say, folding my arms and looking up at the family portraits behind me, as if to give Mark the subliminal message that he's a typical man and next to useless at reading the women in his family.

In our silence we can hear hushed whisperings from the hallway. Nanny Violet seems to be having cross words with someone at the door, and I immediately jump up, my mind on the many daytime rogue-trader and crime programmes they have on television. People are always preying on the elderly. I'll simply walk out into the hallway, pretending I'm on my way to the toilet, and that way the conman will know she's not an easy target . . .

'What are—' starts Mark, but I shush him and go into the hallway. He wouldn't get it; he's not watched the same programmes I have.

'Ted!' I exclaim in surprise as I round the corner.

'Ah, hello, Penelope,' he says. I smile as he only ever calls me Penelope in front of Violet.

'What are you doing here? Are you stopping for a cup of tea? Violet's got lemon-curd tarts and Viennese whirls.'

Suddenly I've got Operation Get-Them-Down-the-Aisle running through my mind again.

I can just see it – a wedding in the same church where Mark and I got married. Perhaps in springtime. They could have the reception at the museum where we had ours too – as Ted volunteers there. Come to think of it, he could drive the little 1940s jeep like he did at our wedding. My friend Amy could do the flowers, and Lou could help out with wedding favours. I stop my fantasy as I realise I've morphed their wedding into mine and now I'm lost, imagining myself once again on the dance floor in my lovely, lovely dress.

'Penny?' says Violet, snapping me out of my reverie. 'Are you all right, dear?'

'Yes, just a little woozy,' I say again, hoping she'll take the bait.

'That's OK then. Right then, Ted, I'll be seeing you,' she says walking over to the door.

'But I thought—' starts Ted.

He doesn't finish his sentence as Nanny Violet has already opened the front door as if he's dismissed.

'Violet, please can Ted stay? Now that I don't volunteer at weekends I only get to see him occasionally, like at the wedding fair a few weeks ago.'

I can't bear seeing that hurt look in his eyes.

Nanny Violet sighs loudly and arches her eyebrows at him. 'Very well,' she says, closing the door.

I clap my hands eagerly and rub my palms together in glee as I try and hatch a plan of how I'm going to get these two old lovebirds together. The cruise topic sounds like a good one.

Together we go back into the lounge.

'Look who I found at the front door,' I say.

'Nice to see you again, Ted,' Mark says, standing up and shaking his hand formally.

'And you, Mark, and you,' Ted replies sincerely. Mark gets up from this armchair so that Ted can sit down and comes and sits next to me on the sofa.

Nanny Violet goes into the kitchen to get Ted a cup for his tea. There's some noisy clattering of the china. This clumsiness is so unlike her.

'So, Ted, Penny was saying that you and my nan are thinking of going on another cruise?' says Mark. I can't help thinking that he's saying it a little bit over protectively, as if he's questioning Ted's intentions. The emphasis on the word *another* makes it sound as if he thinks it's excessive, as they did go on a cruise earlier in the year, but if you ask me, retirement should be all about enjoying yourself, including going on as many holidays as you can afford.

'It's just an idea,' says Violet, coming in and placing a cup into Ted's hands. Ted looks up at her and smiles sheepishly. She's not being the most welcoming of hostesses.

'I think I've almost convinced her,' he says, winking in our direction.

'I think it sounds fabulous. I'd love a bit of sun this time of year,' I say diplomatically. You could cut the tension in the room with a knife.

'Yes, especially as we're not going to be able to go away next summer,' says Mark.

I elbow him in the ribs. He looks at me and I frown and give a tiny shake of my head to telepathically tell him that we're not sharing the baby news now. I don't want to do it in front of Ted. It's one thing to let his nan know, but quite another to tell Ted, who's not family. As much as I'd love him to be an honorary grandparent, I can't tell a non-family member when I haven't even told my mum.

Mark winces and opens his mouth as if to say something, then sighs in confusion but keeps quiet. He frowns back at me and goes back to his tea drinking.

'Oh yes. I imagine you're quite busy with all the weddings you're planning next summer,' Ted says.

I'm secretly relieved that he's a typical man, not jumping to conclusions.

'I am,' I say, knots in my stomach appearing as I remember

the bookings I've got for next year. I'm trying not to think about them until I come up with a solution.

'Next week,' he says clearing his throat, 'I was wondering, or we were wondering, if you were both free. On the Saturday, like.'

I can't help but notice the look of horror on Violet's face.

'I'm sure they wouldn't be interested in coming along,' she says.

'We don't know that for a fact,' says Ted, with a look in his eyes that suggests he's attempting a Jedi mind trick.

Nanny Violet shrugs her shoulders and purses her lips. I've never seen her like this before. I'm intrigued to know what's going on.

'Um, I think we're free. I mean, I play golf in the morning,' says Mark.

'It's at eleven,' says Ted.

'I told you they'd be busy,' says Violet.

'Of course we're not. Mark can miss golf, can't you? What's it for?' I ask, ignoring the look Mark's just given me for saying he would miss golf.

'Ted and I are involved in an exhibition about the war and we'd like you to come along to the opening of it.'

'Oh,' I say, slightly deflated. The way they were talking, I thought something really exciting was happening. Mark gives me a look as if to say, 'I told you so,' and I can tell he's not best pleased that I've made him miss golf to go to an exhibition.

'Yes, a trip down memory lane,' says Ted, laughing.

'It sounds great,' I say. 'Where is it?'

'At the town hall in Aldershot.'

I nod my head. 'We'll be there, won't we, Mark?'

He reluctantly nods and mutters, 'Wouldn't miss it for the world.'

'Wonderful,' says Ted, smiling triumphantly. 'I told you they'd like to come.'

Nanny Violet looks as if she's in the same mood as Mark at the moment. Maybe this is where he gets his sulking from.

'So, Penelope, why don't you tell us about some of the weddings you've got planned for next year?' says Ted.

'I'm sure that Penny doesn't want to talk about that. I'm sure she has more than enough of weddings during the week,' says Nanny Violet.

I open and close my mouth. Something tells me that I don't want to get on the wrong side of Nanny Violet today, so I say nothing.

'Now,' she continues, 'Mark, before Ted interrupted, you said you had something to tell me.'

'Only that we're going to do Christmas Eve drinks at our house this year,' I say quickly, before Mark gets a chance to stutter and give the game away.

'Really? At your house? I'm not sure Rosemary will like that,' she says.

Neither am I. Mark's mum has been doing Christmas Eve drinks for as long as anyone can remember apparently. It's open to all of Mark's relatives and their family and friends. Last year my whole family even got an invite. It's the social highlight of a lot of people's Christmas calendar.

I instantly regret what I've said. Hosting it is a huge deal. It's not even like I could bluff it with a few mince pies and mulled wine. Mark's mum lays on a full cold meat buffet, complete with at least four different vol-au-vent fillings.

'I thought she might appreciate it – give her a rest.'

Mark is looking at me as if I've gone mad, which to be honest I probably have. I'm never going to be able to fit the forty or so adults plus five little kids in our little terraced house.

Nanny Violet surprises me by smiling warmly at me. 'It will be something nice and new to look forward to,' she says.

'Yes,' I say, wishing I was able to tell her about the other nice and new thing to look forward to.

I keep my mouth shut for the rest of the time we're in her

bungalow, afraid of what hole I might dig myself into next, and instead listen to Ted telling us about the cruise he wants them to go on.

I'm relieved when Mark and I finally leave and I feel I'm able to talk again.

'You realise now that you're actually going to have to host Christmas Eve?' he says as we climb into his Ford Focus.

'I know, I know. It was the first thing that popped into my head. I was looking at the framed photo of all of us from one of the parties on the wall behind her head when she asked you what the news was.'

I'm already starting to have mild palpitations about all the cooking involved in the Christmas Eve feast. I struggle not giving Mark food poisoning on a daily basis, and my cakes come out of the oven either chargrilled or wobbly like blancmange.

'My mum might kill you.'

'I know. We're going to have to tell her, aren't we?'

'Uh-huh. Or at least *you're* going to have to tell her. It was your idea,' he says.

I bite my lip, wondering if there's anyway we can back-track on this, but knowing Nanny Violet she'll be on the phone to Mark's mum before we've even got home.

Maybe I can tell her that it was only an idea, but now that I've thought about it I've realised it's more practical to keep things the way they are. I'm sure she'd go for that. Yes, I'm getting myself all worked up over nothing.

My mobile phone rings in my bag on my lap. I stick my hand in and after ferreting through the chocolate-bar wrappers and random pens, I manage to clutch my phone. It's Mark's mum ringing. Blimey, we've barely left his nan's cul-de-sac. I almost don't answer it, but I know how his mum works and that she'll only get more worked-up over time.

'Hello?' I answer nervously.

'Hi, Penny. Violet's just phoned me. She's says you want to host Christmas Eve this year.'

'We were thinking about it, but we totally understand if you want to do it. I mean it is your big day and I can't imagine that I would get anywhere near your hosting skills. Not to mention your house is much nicer for entertaining,' I say, embellishing as I go.

I turn my head to look at Mark, and whilst his eyes are on the road ahead, I can see the corners of his mouth turning up and he's trying to suppress a laugh. He knows I'm trowelling on the compliments thick and fast.

'Actually, Penny, I think it's a great idea. I've been hinting at Howard's Caroline to take over the reins for years. I always wanted to go to the crib service at the church and sing the carols, but I've never been able to as I've always had to get everything ready for the party. Oh, it will be glorious!

Not having to run around like a headless chicken the week before, marinating and baking. Not getting to bed at 3 a.m. on Christmas morning after doing all the tidying up so I don't have to come down to a mess on Christmas Day . . . Penny, this is the best Christmas present you could have given me.'

I'm speechless. I thought for years that it was her favourite time of year.

'Are you sure? I mean, you could still do it if—'

'No, it's wonderful. Thank you Penny.'

'Great then. That's that sorted,' I reply in defeat.

'I'll send you over the guest list of the usual suspects.'

'OK,' I say through gritted teeth. What have I got myself into? It's going to be far from the relaxing Christmas I had planned. It was already a short break, what with Ellie and Silent Blake's wedding the day after Boxing Day. I'm going to be busy enough sorting that out, let alone creating a buffet that looks like it would feed the five thousand like Mark's mum always does.

Rosemary and I say our goodbyes and I switch off my phone.

'I take it you're hosting Christmas Eve then,' says Mark, turning away from the road just long enough to give me a smug smile.

'*We're* hosting Christmas Eve,' I correct. In reality, if we want anyone other than Howard's dog Bouncer to be able to eat the food, then Mark'll have to do the cooking.

'Uh, I think this is all you, Penny Robinson. Why would you ruin such a good thing?'

'Well, I think it will actually be really nice. It could be the start of our own family traditions. Besides, we could use it as the time to tell people about the little one. I'm going to be over three months by then and everyone will be together.'

'That's not a bad idea. In fact, I think it would be a lovely way to start off Christmas.'

I smile to myself. What am I worrying about? I've given us the perfect occasion to share our wonderful news. Besides, it's seven weeks until Christmas. I'm sure between now and then I can plan the ultimate festive party. Who knows – it could be the making of my cooking skills. I'm sure between now and then my business will calm down before it ramps up again in the new year. Maybe a little bit of festive party planning will stop me getting bored.

chapter eight

Ellie @Elliezgood
@princess_shoestring Heeeeeelp!!!! Make-up trial at 11 and I've
got an upset belly. I have to pay as didn't cancel in time. Could
you go?

Penny Robinson @princess_shoestring
@Elliezgood You poor, poor girl. Rest up – I can go. Text me the
details. I've got a networking lunch, so as long as it doesn't clash.

Ellie @Elliezgood
@princess_shoestring You're an angel – and you'll be all glam
for your lunch x x x

I glance over the sea of middle-aged men with rotund bellies
and women in tweed suits and I wonder what exactly I was
thinking coming to this networking lunch.

'I think they're quite the marvel, aren't they?' asks a woman whose acquaintance I've only just made and who's got lipstick on her teeth. I'm desperately trying to focus on anything but her mouth, as I can't tell her. I'm sure she'd be mortified.

Not that I can really talk. Today is definitely not the day for me to be giving make-up advice to anyone. Before coming here I went to get a make-up trial done on behalf of Ellie of Ellie-and-Silent-Blake fame. We've both got the same chestnut hair, and whilst her skin colouring is a little more olive, we've got a similar shade of brown eyes. I showed the make-up artist a photo of Ellie from Facebook so she could see what she looked like, and from there she got to work.

The results are, how shall I put this, a little bit 'lady of the night'. It's about ten times the amount of make-up I'd usually wear during the day, but my eyes look like they are popping out of my head in a fantastic way. The things I do for my brides.

I'm only half listening to the woman as I'm thinking about all the things I could have been doing instead. I could have been researching Woodland Sally's big day now that she's paid her deposit and signed with me, or I could have followed up on phone calls to the Iron Age site for the bride I've nicknamed Viking Ruby . . .

I tune back into Fran, the woman I'm talking to; she's

been going on about the little clip-on extensions that hang on your plate to hold the stem of your wine glass for the last five minutes. I don't share her opinion that they're a marvel; to me they look like an accident waiting to happen.

'Mmm,' I say, nodding politely. I glance behind her head and see that I've been at this networking lunch for all of nine minutes and I'm counting the minutes until I can feasibly leave without seeming rude. I had a leaflet through from our local council – a networking lunch for people who run their own businesses from home. In my head I thought it would be dead exciting and like a meeting of minds. A melting pot of entrepreneurs, like *Dragons' Den* even. The reality is far less thrilling. And to think I'm missing *Millionaire Matchmaker* reruns to be here.

'So what is it you do?' I ask Fran. I've been trying to ask her that for the last seven minutes that we've been speaking. She hasn't given many clues – all she's spoken about is the buffet, the crockery and the glass holders. She looks like she's in her mid-fifties, dressed in a heavy wool skirt suit in a French mustard colour, which is a bold choice and clashes with the pink lipstick she's wearing on her lips and her teeth. Her greying hair is neatly wound into a bun. My money is on cake decorating. She seems as if she's got a lot of patience.

'I work with lace,' she says, smiling sweetly.

Images of lace trims on handkerchiefs and those funny little table covers that old people have spring to mind.

'Oh, that's nice,' I say. 'Very fiddly, I imagine.'

'It can be. Most of my designs are quite intricate. Would you like to see?'

I open my mouth to say I'd rather watch paint dry, but I calm the inner bitch that has reared its ugly head and make an 'uh-huh' noise that still sounds a little sarcastic.

'Here we are,' she says, pulling out a smart phone from her bag. She swipes a few times before handing it to me.

For a minute I'm not entirely sure what I'm looking at.

'What is it?' I ask, turning the phone sideways. It's a tiny strip of fabric tied to a string of pearls.

'Um . . .' Fran leans over to see what I'm looking at, 'those are knickers. Well, a thong to be more exact. You see that bit goes—'

'It's OK,' I say, trying to hide my embarrassment, 'I know where that goes.'

I hastily swipe the screen of the phone and the gallery is filled with similar creations. Teddies, peephole bras and a corset that is absolutely stunning. I glance from the phone to the woman. I can't really reconcile the fact that these creations are hers.

'They're amazing,' I say, handing the phone back.

'Thank you. I don't often tell people here what I do. I did

show one man last year and he practically turned purple.'
She looks round the room and points to a tall, skinny man
with wire-framed glasses. 'See him – that's the one.'

I glance over and the man instinctively looks up as if he
can sense he's being talked about. As soon as he makes eye
contact with the naughty lingerie woman, he blushes and
turns away.

'He still can't look at me,' she says, giggling. 'I was trying
to do him a favour. He told me he was a newlywed, so I
thought he might like to try a product or two.'

I laugh, and for the first time since arriving I start to
remember why I'm here.

'Well, I'm a wedding planner, and I think you're right,
your products would be great for newlyweds. Have you
exhibited at any wedding fairs?'

'Oh no, I don't think I could. It's one thing to show someone like you discreetly. It's another to lay it all out in public
for everyone to see.'

I wrinkle my nose in confusion. 'Then how do you sell
your products?'

'On the Internet.'

'Of course. Well, here's my card,' I say, pulling one out of
my pocket. 'I've started to organise wedding fairs, and if you
do change your mind, I think you would be a great addition.
We don't have any other lingerie sellers.'

I imagine she'd get quite the business with brides picking up a little something special to make their wedding night memorable.

'Thanks, um, Penny,' she says, squinting to read my card. She puts it in her wallet and hands me one of hers. 'Perhaps you want to have a little perusal yourself? I see your wedding ring. Nothing puts a little spice back into a marriage like one of my lace creations. Perhaps a little crotchless panty?'

'Oh, thank you,' I say, feeling like she could probably toast marshmallows off my cheeks as I slip the card discreetly into the back of my Filofax. There's really no need for her to worry in that department. I am well and truly off sex at the moment, and no amount of lace – or lack thereof – is likely to change that. At the moment I'm crawling into bed at nine o'clock in my flannel PJs, trying to turn my head as little as possible to stop myself from being sick.

I look round, trying to find some inspiration to change the subject, and instantly wish I hadn't when I lock eyes with someone I definitely didn't want to see. It's only Georgina Peasbody.

'Well, well, well,' she says in her pantomime-villain voice. 'It's the bride-snatcher. Jenny, wasn't it?'

I clear my throat to mask the expletive. 'Penny, actually,' I say, pasting on a fake smile to match my fake voice. 'Fancy seeing you here. I didn't think your house would have been in this council district.'

I'm sure she said she was from Guildford.

'People make exceptions for me. I adore networking. You never know when you might be talking to a future client. For me, rather than for you though, dear. Because I mean, look around – second-marriage material all over the place, and they're often the ones with the biggest budgets, you know.'

I stare at her, and in my mind I can picture her dressed in a black-and-white fur jacket, smoking a cigarette through a long cigarette holder – à la Cruella de Vil. I decide that instead of carrying on down this route, I'll introduce her to Fran.

'Fran, have you met Georgina Peasbody? She also organises weddings. Luxurious weddings,' I add sarcastically, but Georgina misses the tone and smiles with pride as if I've paid her a huge compliment.

'We have, last year,' says Fran, looking her straight in the eye with a sly smile on her face.

'We did?' says Georgina, staring at her. 'Oh, the lace woman.'

She looks between Fran and me as if trying to decide which one of us is worse.

'I see you're going for the "Essex look" today,' she eventually says to me.

131

I instantly put my hand up to my cheek and regret it, as a think layer of foundation comes off on my fingers – bright orange lumps, and miles away from being the right shade for me. If only I'd had time to rub it off and reapply my normal natural-look make-up.

A smile forms on Georgina's lips.

'I imagine you two have lots to talk about, seeing as you have similar clientele. You know – cheap. I'll see you around, ladies.' She starts to leave before turning back to Fran, 'And by the way – you've got lipstick on your teeth.'

Fran raises her hand to her mouth immediately and shoots me a look of panic.

I pick up some serviettes from a nearby table and hand one to Fran so she can sort out her teeth, using another one to wipe the foundation off my hand.

'It was only a tiny bit,' I say, trying to ease Fran's embarrassment. 'We've all been there.'

'I know, but it would have to be her that pointed it out. Of all the people.'

'I wouldn't worry. She doesn't seem to be the nicest of women.'

Fran breaks into a wide smile, exposing her teeth, now lipstick free. 'You want to hear something funny?'

'Always,' I say, wishing I hadn't judged Fran so harshly at first.

'When I met her last year, I recognised the name immediately. You see, she's ordered a lot of my products over the years. You know, for *personal use*. I'm sure there can't be too many Georgina Peasbodys in the Guildford area.'

My eyes widen in wonder as I look over at Georgina, head thrown back laughing, her tiny doll-like hand resting on the arm of the man she's now talking to.

'Well, I never,' I say, grinning.

'It's always the ones you wouldn't expect,' says Fran with a twinkle in her eye.

'I guess it is.'

That little nugget of information stays with me as I mingle my way round the room for the next hour. Every time I catch sight of Georgina I chuckle to myself rather than let her intimidate me.

By the end of the lunch I've managed to talk to half a dozen people. None with more interesting lines of work than Fran, but more interesting than I gave them credit for when I first entered the room.

I leave the main hall of the civic centre and I'm wrapping myself up in my coat and scarf when Georgina comes out to find hers.

'You're taking this business of yours seriously then,' she says, a small smile forming on her lips.

'Yes, I am,' I say.

'Well, we'll see, Jenny.'

'Penny.'

'Ah, well, I make a point of never learning my competitors' names until they've been around for a while. I learnt that lesson a long time ago. That's the problem with start-ups – most of them are predestined to fail. When you've been round as long as, say, Jan that you were talking to earlier, I might make an effort to remember your name.'

'Fran,' I say. 'Her name is Fran.'

'Are you sure?'

I nod. I try to move past her but she steps in my way.

'How did your little wedding fair go in the end? I had to leave early. I had pressing business to attend to and knew I'd already secured enough brides from it.'

And there was me thinking she'd left because I'd put her nose out of joint when she found out about Olivia and Jeremy.

'Like Sally Jessop?' I say snidely, then instantly regret it. Woodland Sally phoned me on Monday to confirm she was going ahead with Princess-on-a-Shoestring.

I realise I've managed to overwrap my scarf and it's like a snake tightening round my neck.

'I had a very fruitful meeting with her on Saturday,' Georgina says, not picking up on the sarcasm. 'I'm sure she'll be signing with me soon.'

'I don't think so. I received her contract and deposit cheque through the post this morning.'

There is a sudden intake of breath and Georgina's cheeks are sucked into her face, making her look even more doll-like than usual.

I desperately try to keep a smile from breaking out over my face.

'Don't get used to that,' she says. 'It always happens to the new ones – they get a flutter of business and are lulled into a fall sense of security. They soon realise how difficult wedding planning can be, and how a little mishap can so easily ruin the big day. If you need any advice or tips, I'd be more than happy to give them to you,' she says.

Nothing like getting a pep talk from one of my 'peers'.

'In fact, I see you try and do that yourself on your website,' she continues.

I squint momentarily in confusion. Georgina has seen my website? And if she's found the hints and tips, she's clearly had a good look around . . . odd for someone who can't remember my name. I wonder if I've rattled her more than she's letting on.

'Clearly people find my tips helpful,' I reply. 'What, with my column in *Bridal Dreams* magazine, and a literary agent pitching my book . . .' I'm not able to resist adding.

'Your book?' she asks, leaning in towards me as if she'd misheard.

'Yes, my book – my wedding planning book. My agent is sending it out to publishers as we speak.'

Her face drains of colour. I would have felt a bit guilty about gloating, but after the way she's spoken to me and Fran I think she deserves it. I'm not entirely sure who this woman thinks she is, but I'm pleased I'm able to show her that I'm not intimidated by her.

'Well, Jenny . . .'

It's Penny! I want to scream.

'Good luck with that. You let me know when it's on the shelves and I'll head to the nearest bargain bookstore and buy a copy. Help you out with the ten pence or whatever you'll get in royalties. I'd best be off, I've got to set up for tomorrow's weddings. I've got two tomorrow, even though it's November. How many have you got?'

'None,' I stutter, off guard. I can't even counter that I've got meetings with brides, as for once I'm taking Saturday off to go to Nanny Violet's exhibition opening.

Georgina smiles and turns up the collar of her coat, then walks out into the street without another glance.

I shake my head and mutter another expletive under my breath. What a strange woman. How she gets any business acting like that I have no idea.

chapter nine

Rosie Waddington @rosieredcheek
This time next year I'll be tying the knot! Hope you're prepared
@princess_shoestring to drag me down the aisle, I'm going to
be so nervous!

Penny Robinson @princess_shoestring
@rosieredcheek You'll be fine – you'll be striding down there all
by yourself.

Rosie Waddington @rosieredcheek
@princess_shoestring But just in case, that's all part of the service yeah? You'll be right by my side?

Penny Robinson @princess_shoestring
@rosieredcheek Have no fear, it's going to be the best day of
your life.

'Stop sulking,' I say to Mark, stroking my hand over his soft jumper. He looks so sexy today I can't help but touch him. Plus he's got this moody look on his face that's secretly driving me crazy.

'I'm not sulking,' he says, sighing. 'I just don't get why anyone would have an exhibition opening on a Saturday morning.'

I start to walk a little faster – it's five to eleven and we're in danger of being late. I'd hate to miss the cutting of the ribbon or whatever it is that's going to happen. Nanny Violet was insistent that we were on time, and with the way she's been over the last few weeks, I wouldn't want to get on her bad side.

'You're not the only one who had to give something up this morning,' I tell Mark. 'I would have preferred to stay in bed feeling sorry for myself.'

My morning sickness has slowly been getting worse, and the feeling of nausea has progressed to being sick within minutes of getting out of bed.

Mark takes my hand and gives it a squeeze. 'I know you're feeling rubbish, but it will be worth it in the end.'

I nod and try not to think about 'the end' as that makes me think of the birth, and I'm not even entertaining thoughts of that yet. My mind is still boggling that something so big can come out of such a small opening.

'Where in the town hall is the exhibition?' I ask, changing the subject.

'I'm not sure. Look, there's Ted now.'

Ted is looking up and down the street and when he sees us he waves. He's always dressed smartly, but today his suit looks extra special. He's really made an effort for the exhibition opening. I'm suddenly glad I went for a tea dress over leggings or else I would have felt a bit scruffy.

'Morning, Ted,' I say as we approach him.

'Good morning, Penny, Mark.'

Mark nods a hello. For whatever reason, he still treats Ted with a tiny bit of suspicion, even though he's the nicest man in the world.

'So, where's this exhibition opening?' I say, looking behind him. He's standing in front of the registry office and I wonder why he's here and not at the main entrance.

'It's this way,' says Ted, opening the door and going inside. 'And, um, you're not here for an exhibition opening – you're coming to our wedding.'

I stop and hold my hands out as if applying an emergency break.

'Your *what* now?' I say.

I turn to Mark to make sure I heard Ted right, and I know from looking at his face – the hurt in his eyes and the fact that his mouth is hanging open – that I did.

'Violet and I didn't want to tell you this way, but we thought you might all think we were rushing into it and try and talk us out of it. But this is what we want. We're in love.'

On any other day I would have laughed and said that with them being in their late eighties they're probably right to rush into things, but I'm in too much shock. I know that I don't have a monopoly on wedding planning just because of my day job, but I would have thought I'd have been the logical person to help out with this.

I'm on autopilot as we follow Ted in through the modern building to the entrance of a room where, I assume, they're going to be wed.

Ted opens the door and inside we see Mark's mum, his brother and his brother's family on one side, and another family, presumably Ted's, on the other.

'Mum, did you know about this?' Mark asks, practically storming up the aisle.

'No, I got told it was an exhibition opening.'

'Us too,' says Howard's wife.

'And what – we're going to go along with it? Even though they lied to us,' says Mark.

'Of course we are,' says his mother. 'It was their choice. Now sit down.'

I immediately do as she says, and after a slight hesitation Mark joins me. I take his hand in mine and put it on my lap.

Poor Mark. He's so protective of his nan, this is definitely the kind of news that he needed to be eased into gently.

It's not as if we don't all like Ted; we do – I want to adopt him as my grandad for heaven's sake. It's only that we've gone from thinking they're just friends to finding out they're in love and getting married. It's not only a whirl-wind romance, it's a whirlwind revelation.

I look round the room and whilst it isn't a bad room at all to get married in, I have to say I'm a little surprised that they're having a civil ceremony. Nanny Violet's a keen churchgoer and she was so insistent when Mark and I got married that we have the ceremony at her church.

The registrar walks over to Ted and whispers something to him and he stands up to take his place at the front.

'Will you all rise?' she says to the rest of us.

Ted's family look just as hesitant and shell-shocked as we do. It seems they were tricked into coming too.

Violet walks in without any music, escorted by Mark's father. She's dressed in a simple lemon suit which, if I'm not mistaken, was what she wore to my wedding last year.

Mark's father deposits her next to Ted and turns and sits down next to Mark's mum. He's not exactly beaming either.

This isn't right. This isn't how Nanny Violet and Ted should get married. There should be flowers, and music, and I should not be wearing leggings that thanks to too many times in the washing machine are slight greenish black. The inner wedding planner in me is screaming, and a million differ- ent scenarios of how they could have done this flood my mind. I'm almost on my feet, about to complain, but then I catch a sly glimpse between the two of them and I realise that this is how they've chosen to do it.

The service itself is over almost before it's begun. With no readings, no songs and a very short speech from the registrar, the vows are taken and the next thing we know we're staring at the new Mr and Mrs Hamilton. They turn and face us and it's a good thirty seconds or so before I get up and offer my congratulations. I'm quickly followed by other members of the family, but it doesn't seem to be com- ing naturally to anyone.

'Thanks for coming, everyone,' says Ted. He takes his new bride's hand and they walk out of the room, leaving the rest of us to meekly follow.

Out in the lobby we stand there like a confused mob, not knowing what to do or say. I look at Mark's mum, Rosemary, and she's dressed in a pair of grey wool trousers and a smart jumper, Mark and his brother are both wearing jeans. It doesn't seem right at all.

'Has anyone got one of those cameraphone things?' says Ted. 'It would be lovely if someone could take a snap of me and Violet.'

I start to chew on my nails to stop myself from shouting out. If only I'd known about this in advance I could have arranged to have one of the photographers I use come and take some pictures. I would have happily paid for them as our wedding present. A dodgy photo taken on an iPhone doesn't really cut the mustard in my humble opinion.

'Are you OK?' I whisper to Mark.

He only nods his head slowly in response. From the look of it, I'd say he's anything but.

I watch as his brother Howard takes a few photos on his phone, and after Ted's approved them, the couple walk back over to the rest of us.

'What's the plan now then?' I ask. 'Is there a reception?'

Rosemary looks at me. 'I never even thought of that. What have you sorted out?'

Ted and Violet look sheepishly at each other.

'We hadn't planned anything. We thought we'd go for a spot of lunch.'

'A spot of lunch?' I repeat.

'Yes, you're all welcome to come,' says Violet. 'If you want to.'

'You mean you haven't booked anywhere?' I say in frustration. Why on earth did they not ask me to plan them a wedding? A *proper* wedding. One where we could have worn appropriate clothes and given them the fuss they deserve.

'Well, no. We weren't sure if people would want to come or if you'd have other plans.'

'Other plans? This is your special day!' I say a little hysterically. 'If people had had other plans they would have cancelled them!'

'Penny,' says Rosemary, 'it's OK. We'll all go somewhere now.'

'But where? There's like twenty of us,' I say, almost not recognising my high-pitched voice.

'We could go to Wetherspoons,' says Ted. 'That's only round the corner, and it's huge.'

I look at his face to see if he's joking, but he's not. I start to have palpitations. He wants to go to Wetherspoons for his wedding breakfast. I'm about to explode again when I feel Mark's hand on my arm.

'You're not supposed to get stressed,' he whispers in my ear.

He's right. I take a deep breath and count to ten. Then I take another deep breath and continue counting to one hundred.

'That's that sorted then,' says Ted.

I hang back with Mark as everyone shuffles out of the registry office.

'Why does no one else think that going to a pub is wrong? Why is everyone going along with it?' I say, scrunching my fists up and rotating my wrists.

'Because we're all scared of Nan?' suggests Mark, his face breaking into the smallest of smiles.

'It's not right. Not right at all.'

'You can say that again. I can't believe they think that we would have tried to stop them getting married. I would have been a little surprised, but I wouldn't have stood in their way.'

'Of course you wouldn't, and likewise if I'd known I could have persuaded them to have a really lovely wedding. It wouldn't have had to be big or fancy, and I guess I get that they wanted it small and intimate, but this is crazy,' I say.

'I know,' says Mark. 'It's too understated.'

He pulls me into a hug and I feel a small tear roll down my face. I know the pregnancy hormones are making me blow this all out of proportion, but I can't help it. I feel like I was responsible for bringing these two back together. They are lost lovers reunited after seventy years; they warrant a wedding fit for that. Not a quickie service at a registry office followed by a pint and curry at a pub.

'Come on. Us staying here isn't going to do anything. We'll just have to get used to it. Besides, everyone will be wondering where we are,' Mark says, pulling out of the hug.

'I don't care,' I say. Now I'm the one sulking. 'Look at us – we're not even dressed nicely. You're not wearing a tie. Nanny Violet's wearing a recycled outfit. I know I'm always

ANNA BELL

saying that it's not about the wedding, it's about the marriage, but even I think that this is too low-key.'

Mark has taken my hand and is leading me out into the
fresh air, swinging my arm back and forth as we walk to
keep me moving.

'And your mum is wearing trousers and doesn't have a
hat on. You know your mum is a traditionalist and likes a
good hat at a wedding. Not to mention Ted's family – we've
never even met them! The least they could have done was
get us all together beforehand.'

Mark opens the door to the pub and I turn round for a
moment and wonder how we got here. I was so caught up in
my rant that I didn't even pay attention to where we were
walking.

I follow him through to the back, where Howard and
Mark's dad are busy pushing some long tables together.

'Well, this is romantic,' I whisper to Howard's wife,
Caroline.

'At least the kids are happy,' she says, laughing and pointing to my niece and nephew, who are colouring in the blank
pictures on the kid's paper menus.

I try to return her smile, but I'm far too angry. I feel hurt.
I'm taking it personally that they didn't ask me for help.
Violet knows from experience I can keep a secret; I could
have planned them a super-duper wedding.

I can feel the tears welling up again and bite down hard on my lip to stop myself from crying.

We all select seats round the table and I watch Violet and Ted as they awkwardly sit together in the middle. They smile weakly at each other before studying the menus. I can't believe this is actually what they'd want for their day.

'I'm Michelle, Ted's granddaughter,' says the woman next to me.

'Penny. I'm Violet's grandson Mark's wife.'

She looks like she's working this out before she nods again. She's probably a bit younger than Mark and me, maybe mid-twenties. She's got thick blonde hair that sits perfectly on her shoulders. I notice that she looks more like she's attending a wedding than anyone else; she's got a lovely patterned prom dress on.

'You knew!' I gasp.

'I didn't know,' she whispers, keeping a firm eye on her mother. 'I kind of put two and two together. I mean, why would grandad want us to go to an exhibition opening?'

I look at this smart cookie and I wonder why I didn't think of that before. I naively thought they'd asked us as I used to volunteer at the museum and they knew I was interested in history. It was a plausible cover story. I feel a bit foolish that these two near-ninety-year-olds duped me.

I stare down the table and watch Nanny Violet negotiating

a two-for-eight-pounds meal with Ted, and I can't help but think she'd want something more. My gut is telling me she would have, and that's when it hits me: I've got to plan them another wedding. A splendiferous one, with a ceremony befitting them and happy guests that have had time to get used to the idea.

chapter ten

Jimmy Jenkins @madjimbo

@princess_shoestring Is it on a barge?

Penny Robinson @princess_shoestring

@madjimbo No, guess again. PS It's going to be way more fun than that. From what Rachel's told me, it's going to be right up your street!

Jimmy Jenkins @madjimbo

@princess_shoestring Strip club?

Rachel Burton @Onlyrachburton

@madjimbo @princess_shoestring Um, 1) Penny would be sacked, and 2) do you think I'd actually turn up to say I do?

Today has been one of those Mondays that epitomises why it's unquestionably the worst day of the week. I've been turning the house upside down looking for my Filofax all day and I've wasted ridiculous amounts of precious time doing it. I had hoped to have started planning Ted and Nanny V's secret second wedding, after getting the green light for the idea from Mark, but I've not had a chance. Instead I've had to spend the last half-hour scouring my rough note-pads and going through my emails trying to create a backup contact list of all my brides, to keep me going in the meantime.

I'm sure that it's too early for baby brain, but I really can't remember when I last saw it.

My tablet beeps as an email pings into my inbox and I hope it's nothing to add to today's to-do list. I'm already behind and going to have work tonight after I get back from the meeting I've got scheduled at five.

I click on the email and see it's from Fran, the lace lady from the networking group. She's writing to say that she's thought about it and she'd be interested to hear more about the wedding fairs. I'm about to reply when it hits me – that's when I last had my Filofax, when I was putting away her card!

I google the number for the civic centre before dialling.

'Good afternoon, civic centre,' sighs the receptionist.

She's clearly having a case of the Mondays too.

'Um, hello. I was at the networking lunch on Friday and I seem to have lost my Filofax. I wondered if it had been handed in.'

I look down at my hands and realise that I'm crossing my fingers.

'I don't think so,' says the woman drearily. 'I was in on Friday and I think I would have remembered it. What does it look like?'

'It's about an A5-size ring binder, clipped at the front.'

'I know what a Filofax looks like. I mean, what colour?'

That told me.

'It's a Cath Kidston one, red flowers on a bluey-grey background.'

'Hang on,' she says, sighing again.

I'm not holding my breath, but if it's not there then I don't know what I'm going to do.

'Hello again. It's here.'

'Phew,' I say, relieved. 'Can I come and collect it today?'

'Yes, if you get here by five o'clock. Ask for it at the front desk.'

I thank the woman and put the phone down, relieved I'm going to get my life back. The one thing I didn't have backed up was the contact details of the suppliers I've been talking to for my exclusive partnerships, and I still need to set up

ANNA BELL

meetings to negotiate commission with the ones that have
provisionally agreed.

I look on the clock on my tablet and see it is twenty to
five.

I'll have to leave a little bit earlier and collect the Filofax
on my way to meet Big Top Rachel and her fiancé, Jimmy.
I'm going to do a venue reveal for them, and the civic centre
is on the way.

The venue is only an idea at the moment, but one that
needs to be pitched with props. I can tell that it's going to
appeal to Jimmy, who seems to be on my wavelength with
this wedding, which is why I made sure that Rachel brought
him along.

My phone rings on the way to the car and I see that it's
Lou. I can't not answer it as I haven't spoken to her yet this
week.

'Hiya,' I say slipping on my Bluetooth earpiece as I get
into my car.

'Hi, Mummy,' she says. 'How are you feeling today?'

'Worse. I've not been able to keep down anything at all.'

'What about cereal? That's what I used to eat. I went
through packets and packets of Frosties.'

I imagine the taste of Frosties and it doesn't make me
want to retch, so maybe I'll stop off at the supermarket on
the way home.

'That could work.'

'And jacket potatoes are good too. Just thinking about it is making me queasy. I'm not sure I could go through that all over again. Especially if it was another birth like Harry's. When they got the ventouse out and started suctioning his head, the blood flew everywhere.'

'Lou, stop,' I say, accidentally slamming my foot on the break in horror. I'm lucky that nothing's behind me. I double-check my mirrors and set off down the road once more.

'I was doing it again, wasn't I?' she says.

'Yep,' I sigh.

'I'm sorry. I'll try harder. Anyway, I was phoning about Ellie's wedding. She gave me the invitation at work and I was looking at the gift list, trying to work out what to go for.'

'Ooh, what are you leaning towards? I love knowing what people put on their list.'

'That's the thing. I keep trying to imagine what they'd like and I can't. I mean I know what Ellie would like, but . . . have you met Blake?'

'Uh-huh. Only a couple of times though.' I stop at a round-about and look for a gap in the stream of cars.

'What did you think of him?'

I know Lou well enough to know what she's getting at. 'He was mute when I met him, didn't say a word.'

'Well, yes, but you've not seen him when he's a bit lively.'

'Silent Blake gets lively?' I ask in disbelief as I spot my gap in the traffic and whizz out.

'Oh yes, he does.'

'I hope he's like that at the wedding then, bring out a bit of character.'

'I'd be careful what you wish for,' she mutters.

I'm reaching Farnborough town centre, and the rush-hour traffic is starting to build up.

'So what's the problem with the present?' I say, losing the thread of the conversation whilst trying to concentrate on the road.

'Well, I'm wondering whether to wait and make sure the wedding actually goes ahead,' Lou explains.

'What? I bloody hope it's going ahead – it's the only one I've got booked between now and February,' I say, thinking that my business bank balance is depending on it.

I reach the civic centre and pull into the visitors' car park.

'Why would it not go ahead?' I add. 'I mean, it's the hen do next week, and I've got a food tasting with them a couple of weeks after.'

I get out of the car, feeling like a right poser walking around with my Bluetooth on, but I need to get my organiser now or else I'm going to be late to meet Rachel and Jimmy.

'I'm sure it's nothing,' says Lou. 'I'll order the cheese grater and the wine stoppers then.'

'How romantic,' I say absent-mindedly, thinking back to my meetings with the couple to see if I remember picking up on anything not quite right, but I draw a blank. 'What gives you the impression that they'd cancel?'

'It was only a feeling. Forget I said anything,' Lou says. 'Anyway, are we still on for lunch next week?'

'Yes,' I reply, still thinking about Ellie and Silent Blake. 'Hang on a sec,' I say to Lou. 'Hello.' I smile brightly as I reach the front desk. 'I'm here to pick up my Filofax. I rang earlier – it's the Cath Kidston one.'

The woman sighs loudly and I know it's her I spoke to on the phone. She reaches into an open drawer and hands it up to me without speaking word.

'Thanks ever so much,' I say, taking it from her and clutching it to my chest like the treasured possession it is.

'Everything all right?' asks Lou.

'Yes, fine.' I turn back towards the car, flicking through the book. All the pages are still there and intact. I'm ridiculously relieved.

'So, I'll call you about lunch, and when we're there we can sort out our Christmas shopping trip,' says Lou.

I groan. It's November and I'd usually have my Christmas shopping well under way by now, or at least have created a wish list on Amazon. But I've been so busy I've not had time to even start it.

'Yes, we definitely need to do that. I'll speak to you soon.'

We hang up and I slip the earpiece off my ear as I get back in my car. I've got to get a move on to meet Big Top Rachel and Jimmy.

Luckily the rush-hour traffic hasn't got any worse and I manage to make it to the nondescript car park on an industrial estate in time. I see Rachel and Jimmy looking around nervously – I admit this isn't the most obvious of venues for a wedding. I get out of the car and Rachel grins and waves. She comes bounding over to me, her curls bouncing as she walks.

'Hello!' she bellows.

'Hi, Rachel,' I say air-kissing her on both cheeks – the standard greeting in the wedding industry.

'Penny, this is Jimmy.'

I turn my attention to him for the first time and have to strain my neck a little to get a good look. He's very tall and skinny, with poker-straight spiky hair. For a minute I'm transfixed, wondering what kind of hair their baby is going to have.

'Hi, Penny,' he says enthusiastically.

'Nice to meet you,' I say, meaning it.

I hadn't anticipated he'd be quite so tall, and I'm now panicking that he might not fit in the equipment at the venue.

'So put us out of our misery Penny,' says Jimmy. 'Where is this venue?'

'Right this way,' I say, trying to wink. I really should learn not to attempt it. I know it makes me look like I'm having some sort of fit.

I lead them through an open alleyway between an industrial carpet-fitter's and the post-sorting office. I can only imagine what they're thinking. We round the corner, and end up outside a rather nicer car park and, more importantly, our final destination.

'Here we are,' I say, holding my hands out as if I'm a hostess on an eighties game show. If only I was wearing a spangly dress rather than my skinny jeans and thick jumper.

I see a bemused look on both their faces. I can tell I've already sold the venue to Jimmy, but Rachel isn't quite so easy to read.

'Before you say anything, come and have a look inside.' I motion towards the entrance to the soft-play centre. 'All will be revealed.'

We go inside and are immediately hit by the smell of disinfectant and cheesy feet. I begin to wonder if I've made a huge mistake. The last of the children and their parents are just leaving and the lights over the soft-play have been turned off.

'Can I help?' asks a young woman with a swishy ponytail, dressed in a bright-red logoed Aertex T-shirt.

'I'm here to see Abigail.'

'Ah, are you Penny? I'll go and get her.'

As the woman leaves I see Rachel's face falling as she notices the metal ceiling with strip-lighting and the windowless walls.

'Don't worry,' I say to her, smiling reassuringly. 'It's not what you think.'

'Penny,' says an older woman with a bright red sweatshirt on.

'Abigail,' I say, holding my hand out for her to shake. 'Nice to meet you. These are my clients, Rachel and Jimmy.'

They all smile at each other and shake hands.

'Please, let's sit down,' she says, leading us over to their makeshift cafe in the corner. As we sit in the booth I can practically see tears welling up in Rachel's eyes. She undoes her coat and slips it off and I follow suit. Wow, I think I need to call her Big Bump Rachel rather than Big Top Rachel. It's amazing how much her baby has grown in the few weeks since our last appointment. If mine grows at the same rate I'm not going to be able to keep it a secret much longer.

'This place is great,' says Jimmy. 'Do we get to go on the equipment?'

His hands are practically quivering with excitement, in contrast to Rachel who's gone pale.

'All in good time,' says Abigail. 'Penny, do you want to tell them your idea first?'

I nod.

'So, I know that you wanted something fun, and soft-play seemed to tick all the boxes.'

I can see Rachel is poised to interrupt.

'But obviously this isn't going to be the venue,' I say.

Rachel visibly perks up. 'It's not?' she asks with relief.

'No, there's not the room for the reception. But what they can do is hire out the equipment so that they can recreate a soft-play area somewhere else.'

Abigail is nodding enthusiastically.

'What we thought would be best is if you went for a marquee wedding and had a main area of soft play for the kids, but with elements of it all round the marquee. Colour and fun would be the main themes of the day, with shiny helium balloons and bright, traditional village-fair bunting decorating the inside too.'

'I love it.' Jimmy's nodding.

'We can make you a big sweet-shop stand in one corner,' I say, getting into the fantasy.

Rachel still hasn't said anything and I'm getting a teeny tiny bit nervous.

'Are the adults allowed on the soft-play?' she asks finally, directing her question at Abigail.

'Of course,' Abigail replies. 'We've done this a couple of times for weddings, and what we do is set up separate sections for kids and adults, so that the adults don't injure the kids, especially after a few glasses of Pimms.'

'And it's within budget?' asks Rachel, looking at me.

'It should be. We've got to find a venue with toilets and an area big enough to accommodate a marquee.'

'What about the Water Club?' says Jimmy. 'It's where I go kayaking. They've got a big courtyard by the river, as well as a hall.'

'Actually, that's not a bad idea. It's a beautiful location in Guildford,' says Rachel, finally beginning to smile.

'Great,' I say, making a note. 'I'll chase it up. But do we think the theme is a winner?'

'Absolutely. Exactly what we had in mind,' says Rachel.

'Can we have giant lollipops, like in Willy Wonka?' asks Jimmy, his eyes lighting up. 'I can even dress like him. Do you remember that *Don't Tell the Bride* episode where the groom did that?'

'Don't get any ideas. Do you see now why I couldn't let

him plan the whole thing?' Rachel's laughing as she rolls her eyes at me.

I'm slightly gutted that I'm not going to be able to be at this wedding, as not only is the theme really playful and fun, but Rachel and Jimmy are so relaxed and easy with each other that their love simply radiates off them. I can't help but get a warm and fuzzy feeling watching them and I've only been in their company for a few minutes.

'Do you want me to show you what kinds of things you can hire?' asks Abigail, standing up. 'I think the best thing we could do is if I give you a tour round the centre and show you the freestanding equipment we rent out.'

'Do we get to go on it too?' asks Jimmy, practically leaping out of his chair.

'Of course. Lucy has probably finished cleaning the main equipment by now. If you're interested, we have an adults-only session every Thursday evening too.'

Jimmy looks like he's been told that Father Christmas is real.

'Oh no, you shouldn't have told him that!' says Rachel, laughing.

'Man, that's awesome. Wait until I tell Tom,' he says.

Rachel and I are slower getting to our feet, and by the time we reach the side of the play area Jimmy's already followed Abigail up inside the cage and hurtled himself off a giant slide into a ball pit.

'We've got to have a ball pit,' he says when he surfaces.

'Big kid,' says Rachel, turning to me. 'That's why I love him.'

I'm about to reply when Abigail pokes her head out of one of the gaps in the netting.

'Penny, do you want to come and have a try? Obviously Rachel can't as she's pregnant. Sorry, Rachel, but we don't want any accidents.'

'It's OK,' she replies. 'We're happy watching.'

For a minute I'm relieved that Rachel's got me out of it, but then I realise that she's rubbing her belly and the 'we' referred to her and her bump.

'Come on, Penny, it's awesome!' shouts Jimmy.

Rachel's looking at me expectantly. 'I need your opinion to tell me how fun it is as a normal person, not as an over-grown kid,' she says, smiling warmly.

'I can't,' I say, desperately trying to think of an excuse. Afraid of heights won't work, as there's lots of equipment at ground level. Afraid of little people's germs sounds ridiculous, but it is plausible – I mean, I bet they dribble and sneeze all over it. I know Abigail said the other woman was cleaning it, but still, how do they clean all the balls with a bit of spray? I shudder at the thought.

'Sure you can. Just take your shoes off,' says Abigail.

I look down at my jeans and wish that I'd put on a skirt or something equally impractical for traversing soft-play areas, but no such luck. I look ready for action.

'I can't,' I repeat, thinking of the little eight-week-old baby in my belly and knowing I need to come up with an excuse fast. 'I'm allergic to disinfectant.'

I hear the words as I say them and they sound even more ridiculous than they did in my head.

Rachel looks at me as if I'm joking, but I don't laugh.

'Oh, you're one of those,' says Abigail. 'We have that sometimes at children's birthday parties. I thought it was their parents making it up because they think soft-play is too rough.'

'It's real all right,' I say, trying to remember what I'd read online recently when I was trying to work out if it was safe to use my usual kitchen cleaner whilst pregnant. 'I come out in terrible hives with some cleaners. Not all of them, but I don't like to take a risk.'

'Fair enough. Jimmy will have to work extra hard then to give it a proper test,' says Abigail.

'I certainly will,' he says, climbing up a slide and jumping on to a tyre swing.

'That must be awful for you, Penny,' says Rachel.

'Oh, it's perfectly manageable. I have a few core products

that I stick to, and unless they change their ingredients then I'm usually fine.'

All the little white lies I've had to tell over the last couple of years have stood me in good stead. I've almost convinced myself of the allergy, so much so that I can feel my skin prickling.

'I'll get you ladies some photos of what we've done with weddings before,' says Abigail, climbing out of the bottom of the cage as Jimmy dives head first into another ball pit. I fear we've lost him for the rest of the meeting.

We marvel over the laminated pictures that Abigail hands us, and I know instantly that this wedding is going to be a huge success. I don't think I've had such a happy bride and groom at the concept-reveal stage before.

All I need to do is confirm their venue and this wedding will be well on the way to being organised. I rub my hands with glee. I just need to find someone to be there on the day and it will all be sorted. I discreetly rub my hand over my belly. As much as I'm excited about my baby, why couldn't he or she have come along a few months later?

chapter eleven

Penny Robinson @princess_shoestring
Planning a very special wedding today, more like a post-wedding blessing. So top secret it's Don't Tell the Bride or Groom #surprisewedding

Olivia Gold @livi_girl
@princess_shoestring Ooh, secretly hoping it's me, me, me.

Henri Eves @Harri_henri
@princess_shoestring @livi_girl Me too, love to get married all over again. Maybe a new business idea for you Pen??!!! #secondtimesacharm

Today for me is an official venue-hunting day. My week turned out to be a lot busier than I had expected, what with Grace, my literary agent, requesting more sample chapters.

I'm only now, three days after the meeting with Big Top Rachel, getting round to contacting the Water Club. Once that's done, I can finally turn my attention to last weekend's wedding shambles. I worked until ten last night, meaning that I could take most of the afternoon off today to sort out what I'm calling the 'Nanny Violet fiasco'.

'Hello, Guildford Water Club,' comes a voice on the other end of the phone. For a minute there I'd drifted off, thinking back to the nachos, which were for me the highlight of Nanny Violet's wedding.

'Ah, hello there. My name's Penny and I'm calling from a wedding planning company called Princess-on-a-Shoestring. I wanted to talk to someone about event hire.'

'For a wedding?' asks the man.

'That's right.'

'I'm afraid you'd have to go through our wedding planner for anything like that. I deal with hirings for clubs and associations.'

'OK, can I speak to the wedding planner or have their number?'

'Yes, it's Guildford 342118.'

'And do you have their name?' I ask, scribbling everything down.

'Georgina. Georgina Peasbody,' he says.

I drop my pen in surprise.

'And there's no other way to make a booking?' I ask, thinking that there's no way in hell I'm ringing her.

'Afraid not.'

'OK, well, thanks for your time.'

We say our goodbyes and I hang up the phone, knowing that I'm going to have to find an alternative location for the marquee.

I look at the clock on my phone, and it's already after 2 p.m. I don't have time to start looking for alternatives now as I need to go and see Nanny Violet.

I'm putting my phone in my bag when it beeps with a new text message from Mark.

Good Luck with Nanny V xx

It reminds me that I wasn't the only one hurt by their low-key wedding and how much it would mean to Mark and his family, and maybe even Ted's family too, if I was able to give them a proper reception. I pop the phone back in my bag and head on over to Violet's house.

I've got to get my skates on organising it as I was thinking that it would be nice to have it in a few weeks time to ease the family tension before Christmas. Mark's parents are onboard, and have kindly offered to pay for it.

'Penny,' says Nanny Violet, her eyes dropping to the ground

167

like a little child in trouble when she opens the door of her bungalow.

'Mrs Hamilton,' I say back, my arms still folded.

'Oh, that's going to take some getting used to.'

She holds the door open and I follow her into the kitchen. It's toasty and warm and I position myself comfortably by the Aga.

'Tea, love?'

'Yes, please.'

I watch her make her cup of tea and I realise that I have no idea whether Ted has moved in, or whether Violet's going to leave her bungalow and live with him. I've been so pre-occupied with stewing over the wedding that I didn't think to ask about the practicalities of their marriage.

'Are you staying here? Is Ted moving in?' I say as she hands me a cup of tea from the pot. It's as if she was expecting visitors.

'Yes, I think so. Ted's been living with his son and his wife for the last year. He's been on the waiting list for a council assisted-living apartment for a while, and they decided to sell his house so that he'd be ready to move straight in when one came up.'

Ted's even older than Nanny Violet, and for a minute I wonder if they're going to be all right living in the bunga-low together, but as I watch Violet shimmying round the cupboards trying to find the right biscuits, I know they're going to be fine.

'Come now, Penny, you've still got that look.'

She deposits some iced party rings that she usually saves for Mark's brother Howard's kids in front of me. She must be feeling bad if she's willing to give me those. I take one and the sweetness of the icing sits well on my stomach.

'What look?' I ask.

'The one that says you're still mad at me for the wedding business.'

'Can you blame me?' I say a little angrily. 'I just wished you had told me about it. I could have helped plan a lovely reception for after.'

'We didn't want to make a big fuss. You of all people know how big weddings can get these days. We didn't want anything too over the top.'

'Even still, Wetherspoons!' I say, pretending to shudder at the thought. I'm not going to admit that it has been the only complete meal I've eaten in about two weeks. Somehow their chicken nachos hit the spot. I even made Mark take me back the day after. It seems this baby only wants to eat junk food.

'I know, but we hadn't really thought that people would want to do something afterwards. I mean, it's not like it's either of our first marriages. It's my third for goodness sake.'

I shake my head. It shouldn't matter how many times you get married, it still should be special.

'At least you're going on a nice honeymoon,' I say.

'I know, I can't believe it. We'll have a tan for Christmas,' she says, laughing.

Nanny Violet and Ted are off on their two-week cruise soon. Their last-minute holiday was a disguise for their honeymoon. I'm hoping by the time they come back I'll have their perfect little wedding reception all planned out.

'I'd love a tan at this time of year,' I say wistfully.

'Well, you're going to be too busy sorting out Christmas Eve,' she says, chuckling.

I half laugh back, but to be honest I've been trying to forget about it. I've got too much to get done before I get round to thinking about that.

'Don't remind me. So, I was thinking,' I say, tucking my hair behind my ears, 'perhaps we could have a little do, before Christmas, with Ted's family and ours. A sort of "get to know you" do.'

'Didn't we do that at the pub?'

'I think we were all in too much in shock for that. Why don't you let me organise a little get-together?'

'At your house?'

'No,' I say quickly. It's going to take me long enough to do a spring-clean worthy of one party at Christmas, without adding this to the mix. 'I was thinking somewhere else. I'm not sure where yet.'

'You're not planning anything big and fancy, are you?'

'No, not at all. Just an occasion for us all to get together. I thought perhaps when you got back from your holiday.'

Nanny Violet is narrowing her eyes in suspicion. She's looking at me like she did when I was hiding my gambling secret from her. She was the only one then to suspect something bad was going on. I'm wondering if she's rumbled the fact I'm planning her secret blessing. But she soon lets up and smiles weakly at me.

'If you must then, dear.'

I do a quick fist bump under the table. It's my new signature move. Working by yourself most of the time leaves you few fist-bump options.

'Now, tell me about this cruise,' I say, picking up my tea and getting cosy once more. As Nanny Violet starts talking about their forthcoming trip around the Canaries, my brain starts racing with the details of the vintage afternoon tea I'm going to organise for them.

Having got the green light from Nanny Violet to plan something, I don't waste any time in sorting out the rest of the details.

'Ah, Penelope Robinson,' says the vicar as I approach.

Blimey, he's got a good head for names. He must have married hundreds, if not thousands, of people. I'm surprised he can remember little old me.

'Good memory,' I say, smiling my warmest smile.

'I tend to remember most couples, but your wedding was a first for me . . . what with you calling off the wedding and Mark's dramatic entrance. Then there was the fainting.' He chuckles and shakes his head. 'It was like a scene from *Fawlty Towers*.'

I bite the inside of my cheek. I instinctively want to defend our peculiar little wedding, but I stop myself as I need the vicar onside.

'Um, yes,' I say, trying to laugh along with him. 'I guess it was a little unconventional.'

He smiles, raises his eyebrows and nods. 'A little.'

'Yes, well, anyway. I've come to talk to you about Mark's nan, Violet.'

'Ah,' he says, the smile falling from his face.

'I take it you know that she got married at the weekend.'

The vicar motions for me to sit down in one of the pews, which is a relief as I find I get tired standing up at the moment. He sits down sideways in front of me so that he's still facing me.

'Yes, Violet came and told me after the service. She introduced me to Theodore.'

172

'It was so sudden. It came us a huge shock to us all,' I say. 'They tricked us into meeting them at the registry office, telling us that we were going to an exhibition opening.'

'People do that kind of thing when they get older.'

'But she was so insistent that Mark and I get married in a church, and then she goes and has a quick civil ceremony – it doesn't make sense.'

I'm pouring my heart out to Reverend Phillips as if I'm in some sort of therapy session. I hadn't meant to come here for this.

'I know, but as Violet explained to me, it was her third marriage and she didn't want any fuss. I think she was worried that if she had a church service people from the congregation would all want to come and then it would be a big affair. She wanted it to be family only.'

'Well, I guess that's why I'm here. I wondered whether we could organise a small blessing, one Saturday afternoon. Nothing fancy. I think that it would mean a lot to her.'

'I think so too, but I already suggested that and she said she didn't want people to go to any trouble.'

'I bet she did, but this is Violet, and she's special. She's worth the trouble.'

I know I had a different view of her last year when she was almost the reason I didn't marry Mark, but she really is the glue that holds his family together, and I genuinely believe that she would do anything for any one of us. If anyone deserves a bit of spoiling, it's her.

'OK, Penny. But if she's cross, I'm blaming you,' he says with a wink.

I shudder at the wink. I've seen it before, between the vicar and his wife when he was talking to our marriage class about keeping marriage alive in the bedroom. Disturbing images come into my head and I desperately try to banish them. My cheeks go purple and I stumble over my words as I struggle to slip back into wedding planning mode.

'Great, here's what I was thinking . . .'

I launch into my vision and I'm relieved by the time I leave that I've got the vicar well onboard. Now I have to sort out the venue for the reception.

I arrive exhausted at the museum where I used to volunteer. I know I'm only eight weeks pregnant, but this is ridiculous. How can anything the size of a peanut zap so much of my energy? What is it going to be like when it gets to be melon-sized?

I park my car and double-check that Ted's little Micra isn't in the car park. It appears to be all clear. I get out and walk across the gravel drive and up the main steps. It's a cool and crisp November day – and it's starting to feel as if winter is definitely on the way. I wrap my scarf even tighter round my neck and hurry inside.

'Penny,' says Cathy, the curator.

'Ah, am I late?' I ask, looking at the clock behind the main desk. I'd feel awful if she's been waiting for me.

'Not at all. I was on my way round the galleries. I need to check on an exhibit. Care to walk and talk?'

'Sure,' I say, following her as she starts briskly through the tunnel-like gallery entrance.

'As you probably know, Ted got married to my husband's nan at the weekend,' I say matter-of-factly as we pass the Napoleonic War displays.

Cathy comes to an abrupt halt, causing me to stop so suddenly I almost bump into one of the mannequins.

'He did what? Ted got married?'

Uh-oh. They didn't know. Ted's been volunteering here for the best part of ten years and I think they consider him family. I screw my face up and wish I could take back my last few words.

'He did,' I say solemnly. 'But they didn't tell anyone. They tricked us, their family, into coming and they did it in a registry office. They hadn't even booked a reception; we all ended up at the pub.'

'He got married?' she says again, as if she's really upset that she wasn't invited or even told about it.

'Yes, which is why I'm here. It was all so low-key and small and I don't think it was right. They kept saying they didn't want to make a fuss, but I thought I'd plan them something. I've told Violet I'm going to give them a small reception. I've already gone a bit beyond that – I've asked the vicar to do them a blessing and I was hoping that we could have an afternoon tea event here. I thought maybe in the billiards room?'

Cathy is looking pensive for a minute as if she's taking it all in.

'Yes, of course you can. The billiards room would be perfect.'

It really would be. It's a little room upstairs with light pouring in on three sides and it gets all the afternoon sun. It has rich red wallpaper and heavy velvet curtains, with ancient oil paintings hanging on the walls. It has classically Victorian ceilings with intricate gold-leaf work and small crystal chandeliers dangling from it. Whenever the museum dresses it for a dinner or a lunch there's a lovely intimate feel to it.

'Thank you. I was thinking vintage afternoon tea. There's a company in Fleet that hires out mismatched china crockery, so that will look lovely.'

Cathy's nodding her head but she still looks really hurt. 'I'm sure it will. Of course you can have the room for free, as Ted really deserves it.'

'We couldn't do that!' I protest. I know how much the museum struggles to bring in income.

'Nonsense. You'll have to pay for the catering, as we don't control that, but let us give you the room.'

'Thanks, Cathy. I'm sure that Ted will be really touched when he finds out.'

'No problem. So, what date were you thinking?'

'Well, I've got a couple pencilled in with the vicar. How about we go and have a look at your diary?'

Cathy nods and I follow her back towards reception, keeping my fingers crossed that everything's going to work out at such short notice.

By the time I arrive at the gambling support group a few minutes before six I'm pooped. I don't usually get all the details for a wedding sorted in one day, but with only three weeks until Nanny Violet's fuss-free celebration, I had to get my skates on.

I was tempted to send Mary, the leader of my gambling group, a text to tell her I wasn't going to make it tonight, but I couldn't not come. You see, it's not my regular Tuesday-night group; tonight I've come to a sister group's support meeting on a Thursday to tell my sordid story. It's been a while since I've admitted to anyone new what happened to me, and part of me is really nervous about reliving it.

I walk into a sea of faces that I don't know and my belly starts to tie itself in knots.

'Penny,' says Nick the businessman.

I smile with instant relief. Not only did Nick used to be in my gambling group, but I also planned his wedding earlier in the year and he's become a friend.

'Nick,' I say, kissing him on both cheeks, 'I wasn't sure you'd make it. Henri said that you're working away a lot at the moment.'

'I have been, but I've got a couple of weeks at home before I'm off to Dubai.'

'It's all right for some,' I say, about to complain that I don't get to go anywhere on work trips before I remember my raunchy weekend in Carcassonne. Perhaps I should start encouraging more destination weddings.

'I'd usually say that it's all dull, but I'm surprising Henri by taking her away with me this time. I've got enough air miles.'

'Lucky Henri,' I say wistfully. The closest Mark ever gets to air miles is visiting his clients based on the private airfield in Farnborough. I don't think we'll be going to Dubai any time soon.

'I know. She'll be pleased, but when we get back we really have to meet-up. Perhaps you could come over to ours for dinner? Or we could treat ourselves to somewhere special, like Chez Vivant. We went there a few weeks back and I couldn't believe their wine list. It was to die for.'

'Sounds great. It might have to be after Christmas now though. You know how busy it gets in the run-up – all those Christmas lunches and parties . . .'

I'm exhausted at the mere thought of them. Usually this is my favourite time of year, but when you're trying to hide a baby secret, it's a nightmare. I mean, who refuses the free wine at a work do, or turns their nose up at the fifth turkey dinner they're invited to? I'm usually a strict believer that turkeys are only for Christmas, so I have to get my fill over the festive period. Only now even the thought of cranberry sauce is making me feel queasy and I'm wondering if I'm going to be able to keep the contents of my stomach down.

I scan the biscuits on a side plate and lunge for a couple of ginger nuts. I suck slowly on one and feel instant relief.

'I'm sorry, all that talk of dinner reminded me that I didn't have time to grab any food before I came and I don't want my stomach rumbling during my talk,' I say.

'So how goes the company? Managing to get enough business?' asks Nick as he grabs a Bourbon biscuit.

It reminds me of something that Georgina Peasbody would say and I feel my hackles rising before I realise that he looks genuinely interested.

'Yes, it's been tough, but it's starting to pick up. Next year should be busy.'

179

Even busier if I don't find someone to replace me, as right now I'll be doing the weddings and nursing a baby 24/7.

'You know if you want any testimonials or any feedback for your website then don't be afraid to ask. Henri and I would be excellent advocates. You're a hot topic of conversation in our household whenever we recall our big day.'

I'm about to take him up on his offer, but Mary's calling us over to start the meeting.

I take my seat next to her, and as she welcomes everyone and introduces me I clear my throat and get ready to tell my gambling story.

It's been so long since I told it to anyone new that my stomach's churning like a washing machine. I hope that this is the last time I have to tell it, as the fear and the shame of what I did is coming flooding back.

chapter twelve

Bridal Dreams Magazine @Bridaldreamsmag
Today we're asking – what was the biggest disaster you experienced in the run-up to your wedding?

Angie Anderson @AAndersonrocks
@Bridaldreamsmag A friend made our cake (giant castle) - turrets collapsed and melted en route . It looked like it had been in a food fight.

Penny Robinson @princess_shoestring
@Bridaldreamsmag Groom thought I was having an affair (long story) and went AWOL. Eventually he turned up at the church – 20 mins late.

Becky Cartwright @PartyBCarty
@Bridaldreamsmag My fiancé got in a fight with the caterer over corkage charges and has a black eye in all our photos . . .

Becky Cartwright @PartyBCarty

@Bridaldreamsmag [2/2] . . . which was only marginally worse than the hunt to find a replacement caterer at 36 hours' notice . . .

You know when you've accidentally fallen asleep and you've got a little wet patch on the blanket you're lying on, your arm is dead from your heavy head leaning on it, your cheek feels funny as it's got an indent from the remote control and your mouth is so parched it feels like you haven't had water for days? Well, that.

'You're finally awake then,' says Mark, laughing at me from the armchair across the room.

'Have I been asleep long?' I ask, wiping my mouth to get rid of the drool.

'About an hour and a half. You were snoring.'

I smile. At least now I'm getting my own back for Mark's one-man bedroom orchestra that often keeps me awake.

'Did you want a cup of tea?' he asks.

'Yes, please. Decaf – in the green bag,' I call as he walks out of the room.

I try and haul myself into a seating position to wake myself up. Unplanned afternoon naps seem to have become a regular feature of my life lately. Not that I'm complaining. In my book that's what lazy Saturday afternoons are for.

I look over at the clock and it's already 4 p.m. This week has really taken its toll on me. What with trying to sort out details for Nanny Violet's impromptu wedding reception – sorry, family get-together – and trying to find Big Top Rachel an alternative venue. It seems that Georgina Peasbody has fingers in quite a few pies when it comes to local venues suitable for a marquee. I hadn't realised she had the market so sewn up. I also had to finish off those extra chapter samples for my book that Grace had requested.

'Feeling better?' says Mark, coming back in with a cup of tea and a packet of ginger nuts under his arm.

I don't think it's possible that I could love him any more than at this precise moment.

'Not really. I think it's going to take more than a power nap. I might have to go and have a long shower and go to bed early.'

Mark raises his eyebrows suggestively.

'I mean for sleeping,' I say, giving him an 'I'm sorry' face.

'It's fine. I can bring cheese sandwiches or beans on toast up to you if you like.'

'Thanks, honey.'

At least Mark's being understanding about my lack of sex drive. I can't even entertain the thought of being cuddled right now, let alone anything more. All I want to do is curl up in my bed and go to sleep.

I reach over and take my cup of tea from the table and watch in horror as Mark helps himself to one of my ginger nuts. I throw him a look and he takes another one. 'I stopped at Costco after golf. You have a year's supply of ginger nuts. Therefore I'm eating one.'

'OK,' I say, still not trusting him that I'm not going to run out of ginger products. Right now they're the only thing keeping my lunch down.

'I hope I feel better than this in the week. I've got three meetings with clients,' I sigh. 'It's hard enough already trying not to mention the pregnancy to the brides, let alone me having to keep my head permanently tilted and my mouth constantly supplied with sugar puffs.'

'Do you think any of your brides have guessed?'

'No,' I say, thinking through the brides-to-be I've spoken to over the last couple of weeks. 'I was dying to tell Rachel, who's also pregnant, but I didn't dare. I mean once one person knows, it would only take one little comment and then the secret could filter out. Especially as they all chat with each other on Twitter.'

'If it's so hard to hide it, why don't you tell them? I mean it's not long until the scan right? Four weeks on Wednesday. I mean, it's not like you're telling everyone. Just a few brides whose weddings might be affected by it. It might make it less stressful for you.'

I sip my tea and think about this, before shaking my head.

'It feels wrong telling people though. I don't want to jinx it. I mean, what if I tell them and then something happens?'

'There's no reason to think that anything's going to,' says Mark, taking another one of my biscuits. I'm almost tempted to get up and check how many packets he's bought.

'I know, but what if it did? Then I'd have to tell them that it had, and I'd be all upset and it would be awful.'

I can feel tears pricking at the back of my eyes as I think of the possibility that something could go wrong with the baby.

'Well, let's look at it this way,' says Mark, getting up from his armchair and sitting next to me. 'What's putting you under more pressure at the moment – keeping the secret from the brides, or the baby?'

I look up at him. He's got a point. I'm worrying about the secret and he's right – really I'd only have to tell a few of them. Only the ones who would be affected. That would only be five or six. That's like telling only your close friends, right?

'I guess it might be a bit easier if I told a few of them.'

I still feel a little uneasy about it though. We haven't told our family yet, and here I am thinking of telling my clients.

'There you go, and as we said before, it's not like they're

185

going to go anywhere. I mean I'm sure that they'll trust anyone that you get in. And once you plan them a wonderful wedding, they won't care who's there on the day. We all know that what you're best at is the ideas, and those you can do – bump or no bump.'

He's right. I know he is. I feel a little bit of tension lifting from my shoulders at the thought of being able to let them in on my secret. 'I'll not make any special announcements. Instead I'll just not lie to them. If it comes up, it comes up,' I say, deciding out loud.

That sounds like a compromise.

'There you go, much better. More tea?' he asks, pointing at my empty cup.

I look at it in disbelief. That's the first one I've drunk in ages without wanting to hurl. 'Yes, please,' I say.

I already feel happier that I'm going to let others into my special secret. I can't help feeling a bit excited at the thought. Whilst I'm waiting for Mark to bring me my drink I reach over and pick my tablet up off the table to check my emails.

I scan my inbox: nothing exciting. Even the newsletter from Boohoo does little to stir my spirits. After all, they don't have a maternity range and I'm going to be growing out of most of my clothes at some point very soon. I turn my attention to Twitter. I haven't done many @princess_shoestring tweets today, and Saturday is a great bride-to-be surfing day. I tweet a top tip idea from a friend's wedding I went to last year:

Penny_Robinson@princess_shoestring
Have games at your reception – giant Jenga, boules, swing-ball . . . Breaks the ice and may keep guests amused whilst you have your pics taken.

I make a mental note to suggest this to Big Top Rachel. It would be perfect for her fun-themed day. Then I groan – at this rate there will be nowhere to go after their ceremony unless I get something booked pretty soon.

'What the . . . ?' I exclaim involuntarily as I scan my Twitter feed. I can't quite believe what I'm reading. Any happy warm feelings from the quote have been lost instantly.

'What?' asks Mark, having flicked over to a sports channel after recovering the remote from when I was asleep.

'It's Georgina, she's . . . It says on Twitter that she . . .' I don't finish my reply as I follow the link from her most recent tweet. I can't quite believe what's she done.

'She what?' asks Mark again. I'm aware that he's waiting, but I can't answer, not until I see it for myself.

I launch the homepage of Georgina's website, and there in black, white and silver is the announcement that she's

187

offering free wedding planning. Correction, 'luxury free wedding planning', which she calls her 'Silver Service'.

'She's offering to plan people's weddings for free.'

I'm having trouble navigating my tablet as my hands are tightening into fists and my eyes are having difficulty focusing as I'm furrowing my brow so much. I could be wrong, but it certainly looks as if she's trying to go after the budget market. *My* market.

'Free? How's she doing that?' he asks.

I scan the page and eventually find my answer.

'It's free as long as you use her suppliers, and she says that she works off their commission.' I can't believe what I'm reading. 'So if you use a hundred per cent her suppliers, then she gives you a fully managed wedding package.'

I'm practically hyperventilating.

'Weren't you looking at doing something similar?'

I shake my head. 'Not quite like that, I was thinking of using exclusive suppliers to gain commission, but nothing like this. This is quite . . .' I search for the word, 'inspired.'

I hate to admit it, but this is a really good idea for the budget bride market. Everyone loves the word free, and who knows how many brides she'll get to sign up. They'd most likely be overpaying the suppliers for them to cover Georgina's commission, but they'd probably believe they were getting a cheaper deal.

'She's got a whole bloody range of packages for frugal brides.'

I click on the link and I scan through Georgina's packages. Words jump out from the page towards me: bulk-discount negotiations, high-street shopping guide, finder-only packages, planning but without the on-the-day service. It's as if she's scanned my website and found different names for everything, but it's all there. It's my market.

'So she's going into direct competition?' asks Mark, running a hand through his hair like he does when he's worried.

'Yes. Only she's got the Peasbody branding all over it. It's like she's taken Princess-on-a-Shoestring up a notch.'

'Pen, calm down,' says Mark as he switches the TV off. I look up at him in shock. The TV almost never goes off. It indicates he's taking this very seriously, which in turn makes me shake a little more.

'I can't believe she'd do this. After looking down on me for the type of clients I attracted. She kept telling me over and over again how I was going to fail. And now she's going after my market that she herself ridiculed!'

I'm expecting steam to come out of my ears at any second.

'Slow down, Pen. And sit back down,' he orders me, as I stand up and start to pace. 'You can't get stressed. Think of the baby.'

I freeze. He's right. We tried for so long for this baby, I can't risk it.

I take a deep breath and try and channel some Zen. I imagine myself on a beach: crystal clear water lapping at my feet, white powder sand underfoot. The sound of the wedding march as a bride and groom tie the knot by the sea ... and there standing next to them is Georgina flipping Peasbody! I shake my head in frustration. I can't even think my usual calming thoughts without her butting in.

How dare she! How dare she ruin everything!

I sit back down on the sofa and drop my head into my hands, pressing the heels of my hands into my eye sockets.

'Perhaps it's not all bad,' says Mark gently.

'What do you mean?' I practically scream at him as if he's a moron. Of course it's all bad.

'I mean, maybe a little competition is healthy. Besides, her contacts are all going to be in the luxury wedding market so the prices will still work out to be more expensive, won't they?'

I look up at him and instead of thinking he's from Mars, I begin to wonder whether actually he could be right.

I pick up the tablet again and look for any hint of suppliers or prices.

Scanning her website, I see a few names of suppliers listed and my heart starts to sink. Not only are not all of them high-end suppliers, but some of them are actually the very ones I approached about working with exclusively. There are also a few of the same venues listed that I enquired about for Big Top Rachel's wedding. It's suddenly falling into place why I haven't had much luck hiring somewhere for their marquee.

I read more about the planning packages and see that she's added bolt-on elements, so that you can use your own suppliers and pay for bits of wedding planning on top. There's a PDF with all the package information, and I jab at the tablet in my haste to download it. I look at the screen through scrunched eyes – I can't quite bring myself to look at it full-on.

'Can you look at the prices first?' I ask, tossing the tablet like a frisbee across to Mark.

Luckily he manages to grab hold of it before it entirely leaves my hand.

'OK, the finder's fee for finding the venue and suppliers – prices start from £300.'

That's less than my finder's fee. 'What else?'

'Um, bolt-on a wedding planner to orchestrate your day: £150.'

'One hundred and fifty?' I cry, spitting all over Mark's arm. Good job we're married – he barely blinks as he wipes his jumper on his jeans.

'Uh-huh.'

'But I charge £200 for that.' I give a low whistle, the way they do in movies when someone is doomed. The way I didn't realise I actually could whistle. If my business wasn't crumbling around me I'd be secretly impressed with myself. 'She's undercut every one of my prices. Not by a great deal, but when you're talking about budget weddings, then those sorts of sums add up.'

'But all her prices say "from" – maybe they're more expensive in reality, and what about her suppliers' charges? Who knows what the costs would end up as?'

'Then it's clever marketing,' I say. 'Even if it's a starting figure and no one actually gets it, people will still be attracted to her for the prices.'

I take my bobble out and scrape back my hair into a slick bun. If I can keep my hair under control, maybe it will somehow keep me in control.

'Why can't you alter your prices to say "from"? Beat her at her own game?'

'Because I'm not like her. I'm all about being transparent. What you see is what you get, and anyway, we don't know that's not what she's charging. Maybe she's taking a loss on the budget bride side because she doesn't want me stealing any more of her business. Big firms do that, don't they? Supermarkets don't make money on their milk so that they can make their profit on all the chocolate and pizzas and crap you didn't mean to buy when you walked in there.'

Mark turns and looks at me, a small smile breaking out over his face. 'Penny Robinson, you're starting to sound like a businesswoman.'

'That's bloody typical just as I'm about to lose my company!'

'You're not going to lose it,' says Mark, taking my hands to stop me from smoothing my hair down again.

'But what with the baby and now Georgina Peasbody . . . it's like everything is conspiring against me.'

Mark rubs his hands over mine, stroking them softly. 'Every business has its challenges. We never thought it was going to be easy to get yours off the ground.'

We didn't? I thought it would be. I knew that it would be tough on the financial side, and my lusting over designer shoes would have to be taken down quite a few notches, but I didn't expect there to be sharks like Georgina. I mean, when I looked into it I didn't think I'd have competition, and I don't want to tell Mark that I naively assumed that I never would.

'What am I going to do?'

'Exactly what you've been doing. Planning excellent weddings. Building up a reputation.'

'But what about the baby? Georgina already told me I'd have babies and my company would go down the pan.'

I take my hands out of his and instinctively rub my left hand across the place where I hope my bump will appear one day soon.

'I think you should stick with the original plan where you don't tell the brides for now.'

'Really? Didn't you say it was worse for the baby?' I screw up my face in frustration.

'No. I would go back to hiding the secret for now . . . at least until the scan, and you've found a replacement. I'm sure when you finally tell the brides they'll understand completely.'

'Really?'

'Of course. And in the meantime, you carry on working and excelling. You've got to remember that you're selling one thing that Georgina Peasbody doesn't have.'

'What's that?' I say, looking at Mark like he's mad. He's gone all serious and intense.

'You. You're the reason that your brides pick Princess-on-a-Shoestring. You've got to use that to your advantage.'

'But doesn't that go against the fact that I'm going to pull a switch with someone else when I have the baby?'

'No, the devil's in the details. As long as you plan them, then the weddings will still have that Penny sparkle. Plus, if she's been planning luxury weddings for so long, how's she going to know how to plan a budget wedding like you do? She'll have to make all new contacts; she's starting up just like you.'

I hadn't thought of it like that. I can't imagine the Four Seasons or the Hiltons of the wedding world offering prices to please Georgina's new clientele. All the top-end caterers, florists and bridal boutiques aren't going to want to be associated with that end of the market. Maybe I'm worrying about nothing.

I lean over and kiss Mark. He's right. Georgina Peasbody hasn't won yet.

'You've got that evil grin,' Mark laughs. 'You look like you're set to take over the world.'

'I have?' I respond. 'Perfect.'

I may not be taking over the actual world, but I sure as hell am going to conquer the budget wedding market in this area. I may have to keep my secret a little longer than I'd planned, and I might have to work my Penny magic a little harder, but Georgina Peasbody is going to regret slumming it on my turf.

chapter thirteen

Georgina Peasbody @PeasbodyWed

Would you like a wedding planner for free? Thought you might.
Take a look at my new 'Silver Service' free wedding planning
packages

MyWeddings Blog @Myweddingsblog

@PeasbodyWed Wow! Free wedding planning. Floats our boat.
Tell us more...

Everyone hates Mondays. It's part of the same law that says
every woman should feel like a princess on her wedding day.
Since running Princess-on-a-Shoestring I've disliked them
less, but there's still that moment when the alarm rudely
awakens me and Mark hops out of our warm little love nest
while I pine for Sunday morning lie-ins.

Today though I got out of bed when Mark did at 7 a.m. It took me three attempts to make it down the stairs, having to momentarily sit down to keep the nausea at bay. But I made it to the kitchen and managed to find the sugar puffs in time.

By the time Mark left for work I'd already written the copy for two new ads for bridal magazines and my monthly 'agony aunt' piece for *Bridal Dreams*. A bride writes in with a dream wedding idea, and I offer her a budget version of it. This month the bride wanted to arrive at her London venue in a helicopter. The budget suggestion was to arrive by tuk-tuk. Not quite as flashy, but hopefully distinctive and quirky. My mobile rings.

'Hello, Princess-on-a-Shoestring.'

'Penny, it's Grace.'

My heart starts to beat faster. Grace is my literary agent and last week she sent out my book pitch to publishers. I've been trying not to dwell on it as it sends me into a nervous wreck to think that real-life editors are reading my words. Maybe she's phoning to say I've been offered a deal. Maybe I'm going to become the Jamie Oliver of the wedding world! First a book, then a TV series, then I'll be petitioning Downing Street to get weddings back down to a sensible size. I can see it now.

'Penny, are you still there?'

I realise that I've been fantasising about my million-pound book deal and haven't actually replied to her.

'Yes, yes, I'm here,' I mutter, waiting with baited breath.

'Good. I was phoning to say there's been an offer on your book.'

I leap up from my chair and start hopping from foot to foot. Trying to dispel some nervous energy and stop myself from squealing with excitement.

'Oh really?' I say, putting on a calm and collected voice, even though I'm feeling anything but.

'Yes. Now it's not for very much money, and I don't think we should take it, but it's an encouraging start. It's with Evans who have a good nonfiction list, so they'd be a good fit.'

I'm trying to act nonchalant and not scream, 'Show me the money!'

'I'll send you an email with how the figures work out and then we'll keep our fingers crossed another publisher comes into the ring.'

'OK,' I say, a little deflated. I'd been naively thinking that when you got an offer you popped the champagne corks, but from the sounds of it I'd better keep the champagne on ice for now. 'It's a good thing, right?'

'Yes, it's a good thing. I also saw an editor at a book launch on Friday night and she sounded very interested so I emailed her the sample chapters too.'

'That's great,' I say, disappointed that I'm going to have to wait longer for my million-pound offer.

'Yes. I know this is a tense time for authors so I like to keep in close contact while I'm submitting the book. I'll be in touch at the end of the week to give you an update, if I haven't phoned you sooner with another offer.'

'OK.' I cross my fingers and sit back down in my seat. I'm suddenly exhausted, with a little post-excitement head rush. All that adrenaline from when I'd thought I'd be getting a life-changing offer has left a sick feeling. 'I'll speak to you soon.'

As Grace rings off, I'm reminded that I've got a much higher stake than Georgina has in this market at the moment. If I had a book deal that could see me crowned as the queen of budget weddings, then surely that would give me a competitive edge?

I glance at the clock, squinting to make sure I'm reading it right. How can it be only 10 a.m.? I already feel exhausted and ready for another weekend. I glance over at my to-do list and I've barely made a dent in it.

I open the folder for Woodland Sally's wedding and jot down some of the ideas I've had over the last couple of days.

I've been thinking about other possible outdoor venues and immediately vineyards and public gardens sprung to mind, yet a brief look on the tablet shows that they're well out of the price range. I google 'Garden Centres Hampshire' to see whether there are any that offer weddings. A long shot that produces no results. Back to the drawing board.

I'm researching council-run gardens when it hits me that Sally didn't say it had to be a pretty botanical garden; she just wanted an outdoor venue. I have a sudden a brainwave in the form of a local nature reserve. I know from having visited with Mark's niece and nephew last year that it has decent facilities, like the all-important toilets. I bring up their website and give them a quick ring.

After a ten-minute conversation with a volunteer named Trudi, I've found out that they do host wedding receptions and that they have a wooden pagoda on the outskirts of the woods that's licensed, so they could actually have their ceremony there too.

I can just see Sally now – her long blonde hair in loose plaits and her feet bare after all. I know I haven't known her for long, but I'm convinced that she's going to love it.

There are many great bits about wedding planning, from what I've learnt so far, and one of them is breaking the venue idea to them ... when it goes right of course. I find it either goes splendiferously well or really, really badly, with no in between. But at least when it goes badly you get a strong sense of what they don't want.

I bring up Sally's number on my phone, unable to wait to share my new idea with her. This way I can set things in motion if she warms to the idea, and if she doesn't I can go back to square one without having invested too much time in it.

'Hello, Sally speaking.'

'Oh, hi, Sally. It's Penny here.'

There's a pause on the other end of the phone.

'From Princess-on-a-Shoestring?'

Your wedding planner! I want to shout. Usually brides-to-be are dead excited when I phone them.

'Ah, Penny,' she says in a manner which sounds as if she's not pleased to hear from me at all.

'I'm sorry, Sally, am I interrupting? Is this a bad time?'

I forget sometimes now that I'm working from home, that not everyone can stop what they're doing at the drop of a hat for a phone call.

'Not at all.'

'OK,' I say, not believing her. There's something strange going on, I can feel it in my bones. 'I was phoning as I've had some ideas for your venue.'

'Oh, right. Yes, that.'

I'm wondering if she's around people that she can't talk

in front of, as she doesn't sound anything like she did when I met her. Then she was all smiles and bubbly laughter. Now she sounds cold and distant.

'I was thinking of your outdoor theme and—'

'Before you go any further, I was talking to my fiancé and we were discussing the wedding planning and I was wondering, have you cashed the deposit cheque yet?'

Have I what? My pulse quickens again, having only just recovered from Grace's call. There's only one reason that people want to know about cashed cheques and that's if they want their cheque back so they can cancel whatever it is they've agreed to.

'What's going on?' I ask as calmly and politely as I can. The cheque is still sitting in my in tray. I was going to pop it into the bank last week, but I didn't get round to it.

'Well, I got a leaflet in the post. You know that other wedding planner I met at the fair? Well, she's offering free wedding planning and my fiancé and I were talking about it and Liam was asking about the cost, and then we saw that. I wondered if I'd been a bit hasty in saying yes to you.'

My blood runs cold. I close my eyes and wonder whether this is the first of many such phone calls. If only I hadn't agreed to let Georgina take a table at that wedding fair, she wouldn't have had Sally's details to send the flyer to her.

'Oh,' I say, lost for words.

'I know that I signed a contract, but I phoned her to see what she could organise and she suggested that I have a marquee in the grounds of a hotel. You know, one of the ones with windows in so you can see the hotel gardens. That way I have my outdoor wedding, but I get the practicality of having it sheltered from the weather.'

'Right.' I bite my lip so as not to say anything nasty. There's nothing wrong with that as a wedding scenario at all, but that's the type of wedding that Sally could have organised herself; there's absolutely no need for a wedding planner's involvement. Any hotel in the area could put that together in their sleep.

'Yes, and so, I know that I signed the contract and gave you the cheque . . . but can I have it back?'

I'm wondering if Sally understands how contracts and deposits work, but I know that without my having cashed the cheque she could cancel it with her bank, and realistically I'm not going to take the case to the small claims court – to be honest, I couldn't afford the time or the money.

I also don't want the negative PR. One little comment on Twitter or an online wedding forum could spell trouble with future brides. The budget bride online community is a tight-knit little clique, and I've seen over the last year that those who comment on my site also tweet with each other and chat on wedding forums. In fact, some forums even

ANNA BELL

have an open thread about my website. I've seen how vicious some of the brides-to-be are about companies they don't like, and for a business that thrives on its online reputation, it would be a huge risk.

I begin to panic, feeling that if I lose one bride then I'm going to lose them all.

'Sally, I'll be happy to rip up your cheque if you can tell me that deep down a marquee at a hotel is the wedding of your dreams. One that will have you feeling like a princess.'

'I, well . . .'

That brief pause gives me the impression that I still have a chance. I know that, technically, one fewer bride next summer would mean one fewer problem in terms of bump management, but I still need to fight for my business.

'You see, this morning I've been trying to find you a venue and I've come up with one. How would you and Liam like to tie the knot outside, under a wooden pagoda, surrounded by woodland?'

'That sounds exactly like what I'd imagined,' answers Sally quietly.

'Look, I know that I may not be the cheapest option,' I say, not believing it. I genuinely couldn't charge any less for my services. 'But what I charge, I make up for in the ideas and the contacts I have.'

'But a free planner sounds so good.'

'I know it does. It sounds amazing. But before you jump, check how much the services are. The hotel marquee option might turn out to be a lot more expensive than the woodland one, even with paying for my services on top. Did Georgina give you any idea about the costs involved?'

'Now that you mention it, no.'

I roll my eyes, relieved that she can't see down the phone. How can she be so worried about saving money and then not even have asked about it?

'I'm really embarrassed right now. I mean, Liam was looking, and we were talking about the money . . .'

'Don't worry about it. Talk to Liam, see what he thinks about the pagoda idea and if you want to go with the other planner then I'll return your cheque to you. I only want to have you as clients if you're happy to be with me. I don't want you resenting me.'

'And now you're being so understanding. I feel awful.'

'Don't. Talk to Liam and get back to me.'

'Thanks, Penny.'

'You're welcome. Speak to you soon.'

I hang up the phone and hit my head lightly on the table in front of me. I'm quietly confident that I've managed to save her as a client, but what if she's only the first one who tries to wriggle out of her contract?

I also can't believe that Georgina has got her 'silver

service' marketing out so quickly. I shudder at the thought that she's started to send mailings out to the people she met at the wedding fair. People we both met. Sally wasn't the only potential client that came from that day.

My heart sinks. I'd been naive at the weekend when I thought she'd only attract away new business; I should have realised that there's every chance she'd try to steal away my current clients too. I pick up my client folder and leaf through the plastic wallets, mentally picturing each bride – trying to envision which of them will stick by me.

My phone rings again almost instantly, and my stomach sinks at the thought of another bride ringing to cancel my services.

'Hello, Princess-on-a-Shoestring, Penny speaking,' I say, trying to inject as much enthusiasm and happiness into my voice as I can muster.

'Hi, um, I'm Melissa Chambers. I wanted to talk to you about my wedding. I'm calling from Las Vegas.'

'Oh, hi, Melissa.'

I'm trying desperately to focus on the bride-to-be at the other end of the phone line, and not on the thought of the bright lights of the strip and Matt Goss, my pre-teenage crush from Bros, performing at Caesar's Palace.

'I'm out here working as a dancer, and my fiancé and I want to get married back in the UK, but as I'm here and not there I wanted to have someone to plan most of it for me. Once we're in the country we won't have much time to plan anything.'

'OK,' I say, wondering why anyone would want to get married in the UK and not in Las Vegas, where it's as easy to tie the knot as it is to go out for pizza. Little white chapels and Elvis pop into my mind. 'Wouldn't it be easier to get married where you are?'

'I'd love to, but it's difficult legally, with me being a British citizen and Vick being Australian. Plus my grandad has to be there to give me away, and there's no way he would set foot on foreign soil. His words not mine.'

'OK,' I say, warming to this bride-to-be. 'When's the wedding?'

Please don't say next summer; please don't say next summer, I chant in my head.

'Next year. July to be exact.'

I know I said to Mark that I wasn't going to take on any more brides, but it's even more important I don't turn down a client now, isn't it? After all, I don't know how many I'm going to lose to Ms Peasbody.

'OK, and are you wanting on-the-day help?'

'If you're free on our date, then maybe, but if not the package where you do everything up to the day would be fine.'

'Well, we can discuss that when we know your details. Have you had any thoughts on where you'd like to get married? Or what you'd like for the day?'

'Not really. We always figured that we'd get married out here – before Grandad put his foot down and we started looking into the visa practicalities.'

'How about Vegas-themed but over here then?' I say.

We might not be able to offer the same razzmatazz – or the weather – but I'm sure there must be something we could do. My thoughts instantly drift to slot machines and black tie.

'Oh, I like the sound of that.'

'Great. How about you give me your email address and I'll send you some questions to get an idea of your budget and what elements are important to you, along with my business T&Cs.'

'Perfect.'

We exchange email addresses and pleasantries before ending the call.

I haven't worked with a client overseas before. I'm sure that will bring its own challenges, but it has to be less difficult for me than my clients in this country, surely? I'm going to be able to keep my little baby bump very secret from *her*.

If only we could go to actual Vegas. I've always wanted to

go, mainly so that I could go to those amazing-sounding all-you-can-eat-for-next-to-nothing dollar buffets. Only now it wouldn't really be worth the airfare, as, despite almost reaching the twelve-week mark by which time I'd hoped the morning sickness would tail off, I'm still eating little but sugar puffs and ginger nuts.

I picture how we can turn somewhere near Farnborough into the Vegas of the UK. One of our neighbours does light up his garden in a way that looks like it could be on the Vegas strip, but unless Melissa wants an ascending Father Christmas, with reindeer that travel up the side of a house, for her summer wedding, I'll have to think more creatively.

I hear the thud of post on my doormat, and I'm a little sad that the postie had no need to knock today. I hadn't real-ised it had got so late. I glance at the clock on my way past and see it is indeed past eleven, almost time for my ginger nut. Flicking through the normal mix of bills and junk mail on my way back to the kitchen, I spot an expensive-looking envelope with flicky italic handwriting on the front. It's the type of handwriting you'd hope to have if you were writing your own place settings for a wedding.

I freeze. I know instantly from the way my spine has started to tingle that it's from Georgina. The silver envelope matches her branding. My hand shakes with anger as I pull out a card advertising her 'new business angle'. Then I see that there's a comp slip attached to it. It's on really thick textured cream paper, with her logo embossed in black ink.

Dear Jenny,

You seemed so adamant that there was a market here, that it seemed like too good an opportunity not to.

See you soon.

Georgina x

I stare at the note in disbelief. If I thought I was being para-noid about all this being personal before, then here is my proof. I knew I was going to have to up my game, but this has made me more determined than ever to put Princess-on-a-Shoestring firmly on the wedding planning map. I'm going to have to go above and beyond the call of duty for my brides – I'm not going down without a fight.

chapter fourteen

Ellie @Elliezgood
I haven't eaten since yesterday lunchtime in preparation for our food tasting today. Can't wait.

Ruby Blair @sparklyslippers
@Elliezgood Yum. I went to seven tastings before I picked the final caterer. Now I'm off to WeightWatchers – lol.

It turns out what I thought was morning sickness was only the tip of the iceberg. I'd been pretty much able to cope with the mild nauseous feeling, and the loss of appetite. I spent a week or two fancying only sugar puffs, cheese rolls and plain jacket potatoes, but at least I was eating and not becoming acquainted with the toilet pan. Whereas now I've got full-on morning sickness, only it's not confined to the mornings.

The odd time I can get out of bed and make it through a shower without the urge to throw up, but other mornings I've had to hop out with conditioner in my hair. I've been sick in some odd places: the toilets at Asda during my weekly shop and very discreetly when visiting my mum.

How anyone hides morning sickness when they're working in a busy office I'll never know. Right now I've never been more thankful for the fact that I work for myself and that, now we're not in wedding season, I'm usually alone. That means I can sit with my just-in-case bucket next to me, and no one notices that I'm eating a single sugar puff every couple of minutes to keep the sickness at bay. Mark has started to call the baby 'the honey monster'.

Whilst it's been relatively easy to go on as I usually do, today is going to prove to be a challenge. I'm going food tasting with one of the brides-to-be. These are usually the best types of meetings to have with the clients – who doesn't love free food? Eleven-week-pregnant me, that's who.

Even walking into the hall of the former Victorian school that now acts as a conference and wedding centre, I'm hit with the smell of garlic and my stomach is instantly in knots. I look at my watch and mentally try to calculate how long I can stay without it seeming rude.

'Penny!' screeches Ellie, today's bride-to-be. She's sitting with Silent Blake alone at a table in the centre of the room.

I sit down at the third place setting, and wish for a moment that I'd suggested bringing Mark, to even things up a little.

There are a few other people sat at other tables, ready for the tasting as well. It looks like a mixture of brides-maids and parents have been dragged along too, and for each table I try and play guess the bride. They're usually easy to spot – they're the ones that have a look of expect-ation and excitement etched on their faces.

I wave back, a little less enthusiastically, and join them at their table.

'I'm so happy you could make it,' she says.

'Wouldn't have missed it for the world,' I lie, thinking I'd rather be anywhere but.

'When you said you hadn't heard of the caterers, I knew I had to have you in on the tasting session. I wouldn't have trusted myself to make a decision on my own.'

'I'm sure your taste buds would have been fine without me,' I answer, thinking my palate isn't really going to be any help at all. But I didn't want let her down. Not only because she's a good friend of Lou's, but also because I'm trying to impress the socks off my brides so that they wax lyrical about me and don't defect to the opposition.

'John said he's going to bring out the canapés to start with. A whole plate of different ones. Yum, huh?' says Ellie.

Blake as usual doesn't say anything.

'Yum indeed!' I try to match her enthusiasm.

True to her word, a tray of canapés is shortly delivered to our table by a very confident teenage boy:

'Now, here we have mini sausage rolls with wholegrain mustard, beef in Yorkshire puddings with horseradish, duck liver pâté on plum brioche, smoked salmon roll with lemon-infused crème fraîche, and steamed langoustine in garlic and chilli. Over here we have beetroot and goats cheese on a crusty ciabatta and asparagus in hollandaise. Enjoy!'

He lost me somewhere around 'liver pâté'. I'd had high hopes that there might be a posh cheese on toast that I could feast on, but everything sounds very rich and far from anything I could safely ingest this early.

Luckily for me, there aren't three of everything, so I'm going to go for the tactic of eating one item very slowly in the hope that they gobble down the rest. I grab the mini sausage roll quickly and place it on the plate in front of me, trying to subtly scrape off as much of the mustard as I can.

'Oh, wow, this is delicious,' says Ellie through a mouthful of langoustine. Usually I'd have fought her for that one, but today I'll be grateful if I don't have a rerun of the apple juice incident. I made sure I did my research of the banned food lists before I came.

'Mmmm,' I say, fighting my gag reflex. 'Tasty.'

I swallow the sausage roll and, actually, when it hits my

stomach something magical happens: I don't want to throw up. With a little too much gusto I make a swipe at the mini Yorkshire pudding and shove it in my mouth, hopeful that I've somehow been cured of my morning sickness.

'Ah,' I moan, trying not to spit it back out.

'What's wrong?' asks Ellie, fear and panic written all over her face.

'Nothing,' I reply, grabbing for a glass of water. I've only been able to drink water in small sips lately, but now I'm practically downing a pint of it. Man alive. 'That horseradish was a little on the hot side. Nice though. I'd simply forgotten that he'd said they had it in.'

'Right,' says Ellie, nodding in Blake's direction. 'Perhaps we won't pick those then.'

I watch her scribble a note and instantly feel guilty. I'm going to have do a better job of hiding my displeasure.

'So, Ellie, have you got all of your RSVPs back?'

Her wedding is on 27 December, only six weeks away. I was initially a bit peeved about having to work between Christmas and New Year, but now that I'm into the planning I'm really excited. It's meant that everything has been given a festive feel, from crimson candle-lined tables with holly decorations to mistletoe hanging from the ceiling. I get to wear the really cute faux-fur Jasper Conran wrap I bought for a 1940s fancy dress party, which goes perfectly with my baby-blue Reiss shift dress. Not that my outfit is the first thing I planned about this wedding or anything.

The only little fly in the ointment is the family party I'm now hosting on Christmas Eve, which means I won't get quite the relaxing break I was hoping for. But that's what January is for, right? I can plead post-Christmas poverty and stay in and have a good rest.

'More or less,' replies Ellie. 'Only one or two outstanding people now. Mainly on Blake's side of things, but he's going to chase them up this week, aren't you?'

Blake nods and goes back to chewing his asparagus. I'm thinking back to what Lou said about him being lively at times, and I wonder if he's just incredibly shy – is he even going to be able to say 'I do' when the time comes? And what it is about him that has Lou doubting their suitability as a couple? Surely being shy doesn't rule him out of being a good husband.

'Only one or two? That's pretty good going then.'

'Yes, so now we know the food allergies and the numbers of veggies, we can choose the food, and apart from the little crafty bits, we're all set.'

I love the way she says little crafty bits, as if they'll be whipped out in an afternoon, but muggins here is doing those – creating the seating plans and the table centres. I was planning to make them out of leftover holly on Christmas Eve to get me in a festive mood, but I think I'll have to leave it until after the big day now as I'll be busy hosting Mark's mum's party. I guess Boxing Day won't be spent queuing outside Next for the sale or lying on the sofa in a chocolate coma; instead I'll be channelling my green fingers. Luckily for me, the table centres are quite simple and don't require much skill. I tried and failed at flower arranging when I was planning my own wedding, despite doing a course and everything.

I'm slightly dreading the coming six weeks as, from experience, I know that this time is the worst in terms of crazy bride behaviour. They trick you with this easy breezy calm exterior, but a broken nail or mis-cut fringe can suddenly tip a delicate bride over the edge.

While the guests continue tasting, I pull out the rough table plan I've done for the venue, and look around the hall to make sure that there aren't any structural bits I've missed, so that I don't sit great-aunt Martha or whoever in a space that's actually a chimney. But this hall is pretty much as I remember it. It's perfectly rectangular, with a large circular lead-latticed window at the far end above the stage. It's like it was designed with weddings in mind. There's a lovely old wooden chandelier that hangs down in the centre of the room, and I've been given the go-ahead to get the florists to trail ivy over it, with a huge sprig of mistletoe hanging down in the centre.

'Is that the layout?' Ellie asks, peering over my shoulder.

'It is,' I say, making one final note of the location of the plugs on the stage to tell the band. I hand it over to her and she pores over it.

'Oh, I can't wait.' She claps her hands together.

'Where's the top table?'

I look round, wondering where the male voice is coming from before I realize it's Blake.

'We're having a round top table – that way we can all chat and people don't get stuck on the ends,' says Ellie.

'My mother won't like it,' says Blake.

'Well, tough. Your mother doesn't get a say.'

'Oh, this is another one of the "my parents are paying for the wedding, so your parents get no say"? I see.'

I'm slightly taken aback by Blake's tone. There was me thinking he was the strong silent type.

'Blake, we've been through this before. You know that's not true. When Penny and I were talking through the options, I thought it sounded nice to have a round table. It's more laid-back, and I actually thought that your parents would prefer it as they could sit next to each other.'

'Oh, so you're bringing the wedding planner into this

decision now? Why won't you admit that *you* want the round tables and be done with it?'

'Fine,' hisses Ellie. 'I want it that way, but on the day you'll see it's for the best.'

If I didn't want to be here before, I certainly don't want to now. Talk about awkward. I look around the room, trying to pretend I can't hear what is turning into quite a heated argument. I can see a few of the other people looking this way and whispering.

I'm relieved when the starters are delivered. Blake has reverted to incommunicado and Ellie is red-cheeked, I'm worried she's about to burst into tears.

I have to say that this is a first for me. I know I've not been wedding planning that long, but even from this brief exchange I'm getting the feeling that Ellie and Blake might not celebrate that many wedding anniversaries together. I've been known in the past to get a sixth sense when a couple are on their last legs and to predict a break-up within a two-month window of accuracy. Unfortunately for this couple, they're sending out all those signals to me – I can now see what Lou might have been getting at.

'So, guys!' interrupts the waiter theatrically. 'We have three starters for consideration. Goat-cheese-stuffed mushrooms, smoked salmon with a balsamic dressing, and seared scallops with quail egg. Enjoy.'

He winks at me and walks off as if he knows what I'm in for.

'Um, these are interesting starter choices,' I say to start the conversation for the table. Interesting in the sense that I am not supposed to eat any of these foods, let alone the fact that the sight of the oozing white cheese is making me want to head to the nearest toilet.

'Who wants what?' asks Ellie in a less than chipper voice.

'Why don't you tell me what I want? You seem to be good at that,' replies Blake snidely.

'How about we cut up the three we've got and each have a little bit,' I say, pulling the plate towards me. That way I can cut myself the smallest servings possible and then pick at the bits I can eat.

'OK,' says Ellie, watching me hungrily as I cut.

I manage to sneakily take the parts of the food I can eat – a bit of mushroom here, a bit of rocket there. The two of them don't seem to notice. They're too busy using their forks as proxy swords, batting each away from the food.

'Here are some wines for you to sample,' says the teenager, arriving with a tray of bottles. 'The sauvignon blanc goes especially well with the seafood, whereas the pinot noir compliments the meat dishes.'

Blake lunges for the first bottle in reach and generously fills his glass.

'Penny, which would you like?' asks Ellie, staring at Blake as if he's been rude not offering it to me first.

'It's not even half ten,' I say, double-checking the time. I have been known to declare wine o'clock at some dubious hours, but not even I would indulge this early . . . Well, not unless I'm on holiday.

'Yes, I know, but we've got to taste it, haven't we?' says Ellie, pouring a glass as large as Blake's.

She hovers the bottle over mine and I put my hand over to cover the glass.

'I'm fine, thanks. It's a bit early for me, and I'm driving.'

'That's a point,' says Ellie to Blake. 'Who's driving home?'

'I drove here,' he replies.

'And? What, do you want a medal? I drove to your parents' house last week so that you could drink.'

'Yes, because I needed to drink to drown out my mother whinging about the lack of input in our wedding.'

'If it was up to your mother we'd be getting married in St bloody Paul's to impress her old crony friends.'

'Oh, great. We're back to this again, are we? Well, that's perfect.' He turns to face Ellie, holding her gaze for a moment before picking up his wine glass and downing it in one.

Ellie gasps at him in shock and looks longingly at her own glass.

'Why don't I drop you both home, after the tasting?' I say, worried that this fight is going to escalate even further. 'You can come and get your car tomorrow. I'm sure if we asked the venue they won't mind.'

There seems to be a temporary ceasefire. Ellie picks up her glass and has a large gulp.

'Thank you, Penny, that's really kind of you.'

'No problem.' I take a deep breath. We've still got two more courses to go.

The main course passes in a bit of a blur for me. I spend most of the time pushing the steak round the plate, my stomach lurching as little bits of blood escape the rare slab of meat. The vegetables are honey-glazed and look cooked to perfection, but even they can't tempt me. The only good thing about the focus I put into playing with my food is that it passes the time and I can pretend I'm not noticing the silence that has descended on the table. Every so often Ellie and Blake turn and stare at each other, deep into each other's eyes. I'd usually find this quite worrying, but today it serves as a distraction while I subtly transfer bits of my unwanted food onto their plates. By the time we finish, they've managed to eat a portion and a half each and not notice.

'Wow, that was a fantastic course,' says Ellie, wiping her mouth with a serviette, before draining her glass. 'I was a bit worried when I saw the size of it as I thought that it wouldn't fill me up, but it seemed like loads.'

I nod my head and smile politely, trying not to laugh. At least on the day of the wedding she'll probably barely eat, so hopefully won't realise when she only gets a regular-size portion.

Blake doesn't say anything and Ellie seems to have stopped looking in his direction. She picks up the chalkboard menu and reads out the desserts before placing it between her and Blake. It's like the Berlin Wall has gone up between them.

Our plates are cleared away and I begin a polite conversation about the table decorations, trying not to wince at Ellie and Blake who seem to be having a race with the wine to see who can finish their bottle first.

Finally dessert is served and I sigh with relief. Not only is it something I can eat, but it also signals that the tasting is nearly over. I stare at the mixture of puddings and lust over the chocolate brownie, rubbing my belly in anticipation. All this non-eating has made me really hungry. This poor little baby – it's living on a diet of rubbish and prenatal vitamins.

'What's the verdict on the catering?' I ask, taking my first bite of brownie, then instantly wishing I hadn't. I go to retch and I wonder if I'm going to be able to keep the mouthful down. I curse the little bean again for turning me off chocolate. He or she obviously takes after Mark's family, as no member of the Holmes clan would ever turn their nose up at chocolate.

'Excellent,' says Ellie. 'I've loved it all, especially the wine. The wine is good.' She taps her wine glass and nearly knocks it over. I'm fairly surprised that she knows what she's tasted given the amount she's had to drink. She's absolutely hammered, hardly surprising seeing as it's mid-morning and she's consumed a whole bottle of 14.5% Californian Pinot Noir.

I push my plate further away as the gooey brown mess is making my stomach do somersaults.

'Are you OK, Penny?' asks Ellie. Her mood seems to have lightened, maybe because Blake has just placed the chalkboard back in the centre of the table. It feels as if the Cold War between them might be thawing.

'Yes, I'm fine.' I wince as the contents of my stomach threaten to come up. 'Will you excuse me?'

I hotfoot it out of the reception room towards the nearest toilet. I don't have time to care that there are other people in there who might hear me being sick. Right now, the baby is making its feelings quite clear.

Emerging from the toilet, I feel light-headed but so much better. The really weird thing about morning sickness is that you can feel so utterly rubbish one minute and then fine the next. In fact, that leftover apple tart at the table is starting to call to me. I hope they haven't taken away the desserts whilst I've been in here.

'It wasn't any of the food, love, that made you sick, was it?' says a woman who has all the tell-tale signs of a mother of the bride.

'No, no.'

'Oh, pregnant are you?' She winks.

See, Nanny Violet? That's the normal female reaction to another woman's stomach sickness.

'No, absolutely not.' I cross my fingers behind my back. 'Shouldn't have had so much wine this early in the day.'

She looks at me disapprovingly and I dry my hands, wishing for the billionth time that I could tell people. How anyone keeps it a secret for the full twelve weeks is beyond me.

I brace myself before walking back to the table. I wasn't sure what I was going to come back to, but I definitely wasn't prepared for what's in front of me.

Ellie and Blake are kissing . . . no, not kissing, making out. Like they do in American teenage dramas, all tongue and hands everywhere. As if they haven't already had enough attention from the other people in the room, all eyes are now on them.

I sit back down at the table, a little embarrassed at the gross PDA. I feel as if I'm at the warm-up to their wedding night, and I'm sure I'm not the only person here that thinks they should get a room.

I tap my empty wine glass with a knife. It makes a jingling clang and it's just enough to prise them apart.

'Ah, Penny, there you are,' says Ellie, wiping her mouth and giggling as if they're teenagers caught by their parents.

I'm about to reply, when John, the manager of the catering company, comes over and introduces himself.

'First things first, did you like the food?' he asks.

I can see now where the teenager got his repertoire from; he's like a mini John and their mannerisms are uncannily similar. He has to be his dad.

'We did. It was absolutely divine,' gushes Ellie, waving her arms around. 'I know exactly what courses I want for my wedding, although I think we're going to discuss it more when we get home to make sure we're *both* happy.'

I see Ellie look over at Blake, and he looks pleased, although I notice that now that they're not arguing he's gone back into mute mode.

'Great. I'm thrilled to hear it. Just give me a call a few weeks before your wedding.' He glances down at his clipboard. 'So, let's see, the wedding is on 28 December, which means . . . let me know in about two or three weeks' time.'

'It's the twenty-seventh actually,' says Ellie, grinning away. You can tell the wine has gone to her head. If most brides had heard the wrong date they would be breaking out into a cold sweat like I am.

John looks down at his paper. 'It looks from my notes like it *was* the twenty-seventh, but it has been amended to the twenty-eighth by my wife. It's her writing.'

'It's definitely still on the twenty-seventh. It's obviously just a mistake,' I say, thinking back to the nightmare I had, trying to find a florist, caterers and a venue that would be open between Christmas and New Year. I wouldn't want to go through that again.

'I'll change it back.' John makes a note. 'It's no problem with us – we've got no other bookings until New Year's Eve and I haven't organised that week's rota for the casual staff who do the silver service yet.'

He shrugs as if it's no big deal. Ellie and Blake don't seem overly concerned, but it's enough to ruffle my feathers.

'Perfect!' says Ellie.

I smile anyway, as a happy bride is a happy client after all.

John turns to me. 'And you must be the wedding planner. I'd love to catch up with you at some point. I could give you another tasting – for you and perhaps a partner, free of charge of course. It would be great to work with you further.'

The thought of going through another tasting session fills me with dread.

'That would be lovely. After Christmas would be best for

me.' *Hopefully my morning sickness should be over by then*, I add in my head. I reach in my handbag and pull him out a card. 'Drop me an email and we'll pop something in the diary.'

'OK, great. I'll give you a shout. Now then, Ellie, Blake, have you got any questions for me?'

As usual, Blake remains quiet.

'Can't think of any,' says Ellie. 'That's the beauty of having a wedding planner – you don't have to think of the difficult stuff yourself.'

'You are lucky indeed. Your big day will be a breeze with someone like Penny by your side, I'm sure,' says John.

'I know,' Ellie sighs. 'I could not imagine the day without Penny. It's almost as important to me she's there as Blake is.'

I bite my lip involuntarily. Thank goodness she's not having a summer wedding.

'Cheers,' says Blake.

Uh-oh. Speaking Blake is back.

'You know I didn't mean it like that.' She waves her hand as if she's dismissing him.

'Did you roll your eyes at me?' Blake demands angrily. 'I hate it when you roll your eyes at me. How many times do I have to tell you that?'

'I'll leave you to it,' says John, standing up and giving me a wink in solidarity. 'I'll be in touch about the tasting, Penny.'

'Thanks, John.' I smile apologetically. I hope he doesn't think all my clients are like this.

Ellie and Blake don't seem to have noticed that John has gone, and I sink back into my chair trying to make myself invisible. I hope that these two make it to at least their wedding day, or else I will have put myself through a personal hell for this tasting all for nothing. I just hope that tomorrow's attempts to keep my brides happy goes better.

chapter fifteen

Penny Robinson @princess_shoestring
Off to a venue with a bride this morning and a wedding fair this afternoon. #notmyusualsunday

Sally Jessop @Jessoplady
@princess_shoestring Ridiculously excited, been up since 5 a.m. – is it nearly time yet?

Penny Robinson @princess_shoestring
@Jessoplady I hope you like it! #underpressure

Usually the thought of having a day 'out of the office' with one of my brides would be a lovely treat. Past highlights have been cake tasting (pre-morning sickness), dress shopping and my absolute favourite – shoe shopping, yet today I can't muster much enthusiasm. I'm meeting Woodland

Sally and we're off to see the venue I'm suggesting . . . on a Sunday. This whole going above and beyond for brides is exhausting. Especially after Ellie and Blake's food tasting yesterday. I feel like I need at least a week to recover from that.

Don't get me wrong, it's not that I don't like the nature reserve we're going to. It's a wonderful place run by spirited volunteers, they serve an excellent flapjack in their shop and it's a great place for a nice country walk where you know you're not going to get lost. This is a bonus for me, with my very poor map-reading skills/lack of knowledge of how to use the GPS on my phone. It's just that it's mid-November, it's starting to get brass monkeys cold and it's even begun to sleet. I'd much rather spend my Sunday lazing round in my PJs and a fleece, but with Sally already having a wobble, I can't risk cancelling on her in case she changes her mind again and heads off in Georgina's direction.

Instead I've manned up and dug out my walking boots. I haven't worn them since the summer, when I went on a work team-building escape-and-evasion trip across the South Downs. I'm surprised that the boots had finally dried out; they were so wet I honestly never thought they'd ever be dry again. Mark had obviously treated them, as there were old bits of *The Times* newspaper stuffed inside, and they're no longer caked in mud.

'Sally!' I say, putting on my fake smile when I see her getting out of her car.

'Wow, I almost didn't recognise you,' she laughs.

I have got a whole lotta layers on, including my extremely warm alpaca bobbled hat and my purple snood from a few seasons ago pulled up to my nose.

'I'm not great with the cold,' I reply.

'Me neither. Let's hope it's not like this in July.'

I try not to think about the horrific weather at the wedding I organised last July.

'Fingers crossed,' I say. Now with every wedding I organise I try to make sure there's a freak-weather contingency plan – as, like our nation's football team, the weather disappoints often.

'So. First impressions . . .' says Sally, looking round the car park.

I grimace slightly. It doesn't look the best. The car park is made of dirt and stones, which after the weeks of rain we've had recently have become mostly mud. It doesn't help that there's a giant skip at one end and piles of branches strewn nearby.

The brick visitor centre sits at the end of the car park, and next to that there's a small field that has barbecues round, with what's usually a dense wood surrounding it, but it's now bare trees that have recently lost their leaves.

'I'm sure by the summer it will—'

'Don't panic, Penny.' She smiles at me. 'I can see all the mess is superficial. I'm sure by the summer it will be lovely here.'

I wish I shared her optimism.

'Now we have to go through the visitor centre to reach the education pagoda, which is where they are licensed for weddings. We're going to meet one of the volunteers along the way.'

I pull my snood further up round my mouth, but soon pull it down again when I discover it's all wet and cold. Out of all weather conditions I think I hate sleet the most. It's as if it's taunting you that it's almost cold enough for snow, but it has none of the fun that goes along with it – no making snow angels or building snowmen.

We walk into the visitor centre and gravitate to the shop area. Warmth is pumping out from a small convection heater on the desk. I'm not entirely sure that's very health and safety, but since I left that world behind with my HR career I calmly smile and introduce myself to the man behind the counter. As he radios for the volunteer we're due to meet, we busy ourselves in the little tubs of pocket money items in the shop.

'Just getting some ideas for wedding favours,' says Sally, picking up pencils and rubbers.

I'm not entirely sure that a pencil is the right way to go for a favour, but I remind myself of the golden rule of wedding planning: I'm not the bride.

'Uh-huh,' I say, casting my eye around the shop to see what I would pick if it was me. My gaze falls on packets of seeds in the corner. 'What about these?'

The bags of seeds are printed with the conservation centre's logo, and according to the sign they're all wildflowers that grow within the grounds.

'They're perfect, so in keeping with the theme,' I say.

Sally nods in approval and I realise then and there that she's already decided this is the venue for her. I don't think she even needs to go and see the pagoda if she's skipped ahead to the wedding favours.

I do a quick cross of fingers behind my back and secretly hope she's going to say that we don't need to go out in the cold, but all of a sudden she's shaking hands with a middle-aged man in full waterproofs, the only part of him exposed to the elements the little round hole for his face. This must be Malcolm.

'This is Penny, the wedding planner,' says Sally, gesturing towards me.

I put down the seeds and give him a big grin. 'Nice to meet you.'

'Likewise. Now, are you ladies ready for a little bit of mud?'

I gulp, worrying how long it's going to take to dry out my walking boots this time.

'At least you've both got decent footwear on,' he chuckles.

We follow Malcolm out into the cold again and I immediately regret not dressing like him. The woodland might have been pleasant when I walked with Mark's niece and nephew, in the spring or autumn, but now, in what feels like the depths of winter, it's pretty bleak. Big drops of sleet are dripping from the overhanging branches on to my alpaca hat, and I can feel the rain seeping through to my scalp. The ground is a thick wet clay, which makes every step feel like I'm wading through treacle. It doesn't appear to bother Malcolm, but Sally and I are lagging a bit behind.

'Thanks for coming with me. I know it's not the nicest of days,' says Sally. 'I'm sure I could have come on my own.'

'All part of the service,' I say through gritted teeth. *Above and beyond*, I repeat over and over in my head.

The 'little bit of mud' could rival Glastonbury on a wet year. I'm glad I didn't put wellies on – they would probably still be lodged right outside the visitor centre.

I go to take a step and the next thing I know my foot has slipped, and I'm about to fall over. Fear spreads over me as I desperately try and keep upright.

'Woah there!' says Malcolm.

I look up at him in relief as he stretches out his hand to

catch me and I double over, catching up on the breath I missed when I thought I was going to fall. All I could think of was the baby and how I'm supposed to be doing my best not to be Miss Clumsy-Pants.

'Thank you, Malcolm.' I stand up straight again.

Both Malcolm and Sally look at me with suspicion. That probably seemed like a huge overreaction.

'I did not want to ruin these trousers.' I laugh unconvincingly.

Sally gives me a look and I can see she is taking in my combat trousers, which are still stained from a muddy dog walk I did in the summer with my brother-in-law's dog. Bouncer's indelible paw prints are all up the side.

They both give me a faint smile, as if they thought I was trying to be funny, and I want to crawl under one of the many slimy rocks that litter the path.

Taking slow and steady deep breaths, I tread carefully the rest of the way. I'm analysing every footstep, trying to step on the firmest pieces of ground.

'Oh, it's perfect,' says Sally beside me.

I look up and realise we've reached the pagoda.

It really is. It's even better than I remember. It's a long dark wooden structure, open at the sides, with a rustic, natural feel to it.

'You can put flowers up over the eaves there. Then

hanging some over the banister along there looks pretty,' says Malcolm.

Sally is walking round, spinning in circles.

'Better than a marquee in a hotel?' I ask, mentally giving Georgina Peasbody the finger.

'Definitely. The only thing is, where would we have the wedding breakfast if it rained?'

'I've thought all about that,' I reply triumphantly. 'I spoke to Malcolm here about the possibility of you hiring a yurt. I think it's in keeping with your theme, and they've got a firm that they often use who will give us a discount.'

Sally's looking at me as if I've told her that the Easter bunny does exist and that there aren't any calories in the chocolate he would bring.

The next thing I know she has enveloped me in a hug.

'I can't wait! I wish the wedding was now.' She lets go of me and starts doing a jig on the spot.

I gaze out at the muddy scene that resembles a hippo enclosure at the zoo, and at the bare trees. For the first time I'm actually glad her wedding isn't until July.

'What happens now? Can we talk through some more details?' asks Sally. She's now singing from a very different hymn sheet than when she was asking for her deposit cheque back.

'Um.' I glance at the time, then wince. 'I can't, I'm sorry.

I've got to go to a wedding fair this afternoon, for another bride.'

'Oh, OK.' Her smile fades.

I do some mental maths to try and work out what's the latest time I could leave here to still make the wedding fair. I've got to do everything I can to keep my brides happy.

'I've probably got time for a quick chat over a cup of cof-fee,' I say finally.

Her smile reappears. 'Great, I want to hear more about these yurts.'

I feel a warm fuzzy glow that I've managed to retain her as a client. Now all I've got to do is keep the rest in smiles and I'll hopefully save my business.

Up next on Operation Keeping the Brides Happy is this wed-ding fair. It's the first one I've been to since starting the company that I'm attending like a normal punter. I'm scop-ing out some ideas for a couple of my brides and hopefully going to make some new contacts. It's really hard to do that when you're exhibiting. Before the brides-to-be arrive everyone's frantically setting up, then everyone's way too busy chatting up potential clients, and afterwards every-one's knackered and wants to pack up and leave as soon as it finishes.

I've travelled to Winchester for this wedding fair, a little bit out of my usual patch, but they've got a casino hire company here that I want to see in action for Vegas Melissa's wedding.

What's also great is that Mark's coming to keep me company in the car, as he suggested going for an early dinner at a country pub on the way home. I'm not dragging him round the fair though – he's not the biggest fan of weddings. We called ahead and the bar of the hotel has Sky Sports, so he's going to watch the football.

The trouble with wedding planning is that so many of my appointments are on Saturdays so I don't get to spend a lot of time with Mark. Then when I told him that I had to meet Woodland Sally on a Sunday and then come here this afternoon, he suggested coming along. It's probably only like what we'd be doing at home anyway, him watching the game and me surfing for wedding ideas.

If I hadn't stopped for coffee with Sally at the conservation centre then I might have been tempted to pop to the Christmas Market in Winchester en route. I still haven't bought a single present, and I don't know when I'm going to find the time to do any shopping.

'I had no idea this was going to be so big,' says Mark, as we drive into hotel grounds.

'Neither did I.' I take in the people in high-vis jackets directing us into the overflow car park on a field.

We reach the next available space, and a boy who looks no older than twelve starts to direct me into a space he's standing in.

'I can't go any closer to you,' I say, enunciating my words as clearly as possible to let him lip-read. Honestly, it's like he wants his toes run over. I think that they should only employ people to park cars who actually drive and understand how much room cars need.

He's still frantically waving at me to come forward. Brave man, what with my clutch control today. I take a deep breath and shift forward. I'm wearing some very lovely boots with spindly heels. I'd been obsessing over them in Schuh for ages, stroking them and visiting them whenever I went to the store. Then Mark bought them for me for my birthday. Or at least I bought them and he wrapped them up. I haven't driven in them before though, and you know how the soles of different shoes can be weird to drive in? Well, that's what's happening to me today.

'Just go forward,' says Mark.

I turn and look at him, slightly exasperated. I feel like I'm being ganged up on. The trouble is, he's always berating me for wearing impractical footwear and I can't give him the satisfaction of letting him know my predicament.

I narrow my eyes, cringing as I shunt forward slowly, expecting to feel a thud at any minute. Through my narrow field of vision I see the young boy making the stop sign with his hand and I pull up the handbrake. Who knew this was going to be so stressful?

'How long do you think you're going to be?' asks Mark.

'I've got one supplier to see for sure, and then I thought I might speak to a couple more.'

'You might as well make the most of it whilst you're here. Speak to as many of the suppliers as you can. You know, for research purposes.'

I turn off the engine and look at my husband quizzically.

'What?' he says. 'I'm trying to be supportive.'

I slide my seat belt off and open the door. 'Who's playing?' I ask suspiciously.

'It's Arsenal versus Man U.,' he admits.

'Uh-huh? I'll see what I can do.'

I smile to myself at how easily pleased Mark is. I'm secretly glad he's so eager to stick around, as I can't wait to get lost in the wedding fair. They're the perfect place for inspiration.

I get out of the car and immediately sink down a few inches. I look down at the muddy field and even though it feels quite firm underfoot, it's clearly not made for people dressed in spindly-heeled boots. The sleet has started to come down again and I know I'm going to look like a drowned rat by the time I make it inside.

Mark and I make our way towards the entrance. The main hotel car park can only be about a hundred metres away, but the effort required to pull each foot out of the mud only for it to sink down on the next step is immense.

'Bloody boots,' I mutter.

'What's that?' asks Mark.

'Nothing.' For the second time in as many minutes I can't tell him that my footwear choice is less than practical. After a few strides I look up at the hotel, but it seems to be getting further away with each step. Mark has gone on ahead. When he realises I'm not next to him, he turns round and looks for me.

'What are you doing? We're going to get soaked.'

'My heels are getting stuck,' I say with a pout, hoping he'll throw me over his shoulder in a fireman's lift. A quick flash of Mark dressed like a fireman flits through my mind and I feel my pulse start to race. Now there's an idea . . .

'Will you give me a piggyback?' I ask, as he walks back towards me.

'What? No, come on.'

I try and take a couple more steps and I pout again. 'Please, Mark.'

'Pen, I can't. You know my back's sore at the moment. Plus there's two of you now so you're bound to be heavier.'

I hit him with my handbag and he laughs at me.

'Seriously! I don't want to have to go to the chiropractor again this month. Change into your walking boots – they're in the back of your car.'

I'd forgotten that I have my perfectly functional, perfectly muddy walking boots in the car from my trip to the nature reserve. I look down at my carefully chosen skinny jeans and pristine, belted white-wool coat. I hardly think they're going to go with walking boots. I look back up at the venue and realise that it's going to be mid-afternoon before I make it there if the last few steps were anything to go by. Seeing as Mark won't help me, I've clearly got no other option but to do as he says. I do a quick change, hovering under the boot of my car to keep dry. Noticing my raincoat in the back too, I slip it on over my coat, hoping there will be somewhere to hang it when I get inside.

In my more appropriate gear for the weather conditions, I make the journey without effort. And when I finally go through the hotel entrance, I'm so relieved to be in the warm that I almost forget I'm wearing the world's weirdest outfit.

'Don't rush,' says Mark over his shoulder as he heads for the bar.

I don't even have time to reply before he's inside the heavy doors.

Deciding not to dwell on my rapidly departed husband,

I follow the shrill sound of excited women through to the main ballroom. I head straight for the casino hire company, figuring I'll get that out of the way before I get distracted.

This fair certainly is busy and I'm soon joining in elbowing people to get them out of the way. I'd forgotten what it was like to be this side of the tables and how ruthless brides-to-be can be. It's then that I realise that walking boots were a wise choice after all. I've already had my feet trodden on by pairs of heels and had I been wearing my beautiful, but delicate, leather boots, I'm sure my toes would be badly bruised by now.

I make it to the casino company table and the staff are busy chatting away to brides-to-be. I take in the roulette wheel and the blackjack table. They're actually set up with croupiers, and people are playing them. A small ripple of excitement passes through me and I realise this is the closest I've been to anything gambling-related since I went cold turkey from playing Internet bingo.

A woman gets up, leaving an empty seat at the blackjack table and the croupier looks over at me.

'Do you want to play?'

I look at him as if he's speaking another language. I'm pretty sure it isn't real gambling, there's no money involved and it's only for fun. I can't quite bring myself to say yes, so

I nod my head and gravitate towards the empty stool, wondering if I'm doing a bad thing.

As I sit down, I smile weakly at the woman next to me.

'Good luck,' she says.

'Ha, it's all for fun, right?' I ask, checking that I won't actually be gambling for real.

'No, look.' She points at a board. 'The one with the most chips at the end of the day from a twenty-minute session gets a free casino night.'

'Huh.'

I begin to think how cool it would be if I could win Vegas Melissa a free casino . . . that would certainly be going above and beyond for a bride. But then I look back at my neighbour and I recognise that look of true desperation on her face. I know then that I'll just play for fun, as there are brides-to-be here whose need is greater than mine.

The dealer deals the first card and I instantly curse. Nine. Who wants a nine? I wait patiently for my second card and it's a seven. Sixteen. I feel my heart starting to race as I wonder whether to risk it and then I remember that I have nothing to lose.

'Hit me,' I say.

The dealer turns over a five. Twenty-one. I do a little air-punch in victory, and then I instantly feel guilty about the woman next to me. She gets eighteen and the dealer busts at twenty-five, meaning I win.

I feel a buzz that I haven't felt since my bingo days. The dealer gives me the extra chips and I look down at them like they're poisonous. It's as if something has awoken inside me that wants to keep the pile growing and growing, despite them being worthless, and I don't like it one little bit.

What an earth am I doing? I shouldn't be anywhere near this. I feel a cold sweat break out over me and my breathing becomes laboured. How could I have thought that I could even do pretend gambling and it not bring back feelings from my bingo days?

'Can you all act natural?' says a voice behind us. I turn round to see a big camera lens and the body of man lost behind it. 'Promotional pictures for the wedding fair,' he explains.

The dealer deals the next round and I pretend to be playing for the photograph. As soon as I lose the round (I bust at twenty-six) I relinquish my seat and join the queue to speak to the staff who manage the casino hire. I need to get away from those tables and quick.

After a good long chat with the LuckyCasino staff, I've potentially negotiated a deal for Vegas Melissa's wedding. Not longer after, I managed to find a brilliant chocolatier. Not that many of my brides can afford bespoke chocolates, but you never know when one might want to have some in the shape of her and her partner, cameo-brooch style. I glance at the large clock at the end of the hall and I do a double take; I've been here for two hours already. Being married to Mark, I feel I should know how long a football match is, but I'm guessing I'm almost out of time.

It's a shame. In these walking boots I'd be up for treading these floorboards all afternoon. Sure, I would have blended in with my neat little heels, but this way even after two hours on my feet I don't have sore toes or aching feet. If it wasn't for the ever-present pregnancy tiredness, I'd be begging Mark to watch more sport so I could stay longer.

Knowing him, even if his match has finished he'll be watching Sky Sports News. He likes to know how random teams like Accrington Stanley or Crewe Alexandra have got on, for reasons I can never fathom.

I walk over to the coat rail in the corner and slip into my white wool coat, before putting my raincoat over the top. I'm about to leave the room when I catch a glimpse of some home-made bunting that looks amazing. I'm sure I could leave him one minute more while I have a quick look at this stand, and besides, it would go perfectly with the afternoon tea idea for Nanny Violet's surprise wedding reception.

I'm not paying attention to where I'm going and I manage to tread on someone's toes.

'I'm so sorry,' I say, turning round.

I swallow a lump in my throat as I realise that it's Georgina Peasbody. Of course it is.

'Georgina!' I apply my fake smile.

'Penny.' She grimaces, then reaches down and rubs her baby pink Mary Janes.

At least she's called me by the right name. 'I'm so sorry about that. I wasn't looking where I was going.'

'No,' she says. 'I see you're sporting your "tramp" look.'

I look at her, confused.

'It's what the Kiwis call hiking, and seeing as you're dressed like one . . .'

I stutter as I try to process what she's saying. Yes, I'm wearing walking boots, and I've got my raincoat on, but I hardly think I look down and out. I feel my bottom lip start to tingle in anger and I realise I've got to change the subject before I say something I'll regret. Well, perhaps not regret, but I'll get in trouble for.

'Are you exhibiting here?' I ask.

'Yes, I work with this wedding fair company all the time. I don't really have time to chat to you today. Far too busy. I'm on my way to the powder room whilst the fashion show takes place. It usually goes crazy after that, just FYI – in case you ever do a big show like this. But I'm guessing that's pretty unlikely.'

She gives me a sly smile, then eyes me up and down again and gives a small giggle.

'I'll see you around.'

'Not if I see you first,' I mutter to myself as she walks out of earshot, which is not very far at all; the noise volume in this place is unreal.

There's something about bumping into Georgina that deflates my good mood. No matter how happy I'd felt about the good work I'm doing for my brides today, she still makes me feel inadequate.

I walk into the lobby and see Mark standing there tapping away at his phone. He looks up at me and his smile turns to an expression of concern.

'Pen!' he says in surprise. 'I was texting you to see if you were finished. I had a quick look, but it was bedlam in there.'

I reach my arms around his waist and nuzzle my head into his shoulder.

'Georgina's here and she was mean,' I say, reminding myself of being at infant school and running out to my mum at home time after fights with my friends.

'Don't worry about her, Pen. She's probably a lonely old bag. Come on. Let's get you to the pub and you can tell me all about it. And more importantly, we can talk more about baby names.'

I look up and smile. He knows how to cheer me up. I think about our baby and our upcoming scan this week.

As we go to leave I see Georgina heading back into the wedding fair and the fog descends again. I don't know what it is about that woman, but whenever I see her it's like a chill has passed over my body and I can't quite shake it off.

chapter sixteen

Jimmy Jenkins @madjimbo

I like big bumps and I cannot lie . . .

Rachel Burton @Onlyrachburton

@madjimbo Very funny. You're not going to next year when I can't fit into my wedding dress.

I sit bolt upright in bed and gasp for breath. I feel clammy and sweaty all over and it takes me a good moment or two to realise it was only a dream. I was at the hospital and the sonographer was trying and failing to find my baby. The ultrasound machine was beeping loudly to signify there was a problem and it wouldn't stop. My ears strain and I realise that the beeping noise from the dream didn't end when I woke up, and I glance at my table and realise the noise is coming from our house phone.

Mark rolls over and puts a pillow over his ears and I reach over and grab it.

There's always something scary about a phone ringing in the middle of the night. My blood runs cold and my immediate fear is that something's happened to one of our relatives.

'Hello?' I croak before trying to clear my throat as quietly as I can.

'Hello, Penny?'

I'm still half asleep and I'm trying to place the voice.

'It's Melissa Chambers here.'

'Melissa?' I say. 'What time is it?'

I rub my eyes and squint at my alarm clock. It's 6.45 a.m., but it feels like it's the middle of the night.

'Oh no, did I wake you? I assumed you'd be up by now. I'm on a break at work.'

'It's quite early here – quarter to seven.'

'I'm sorry, I'm terrible with working out the time difference. I always phone my grandad at this time and I forget not everyone gets up at the crack of dawn. I'll call you back later.'

I slide out of bed and slip my feet into my slippers, grabbing my dressing gown as I walk past on my way out of the bedroom.

'No, it's fine. I'm up now. My alarm was due to go off in a bit anyway. What can I do for you?'

'It was about that information for the casino hire that you sent over. I loved it.'

'That's good to know,' I say, thinking that could have been said in an email.

'Yeah, it was great, and it got me thinking . . . What do you think about Elvis?'

I groan. I'm not a fan. I'm especially not a fan since they did all those re-releases a few years ago and I had to do body-pump to 'A Little Less Conversation'. Every time I hear it now my biceps spasm in fear.

'It doesn't matter what I think. What do you think?' I say diplomatically.

'I think he's cheesy, but he screams Vegas. I was wondering if you could see if you could get an Elvis impersonator?'

'You want Elvis for the whole evening?' I ask.

'Not the whole evening, but part of it. And maybe we could get him to marry us.'

Again I curse the fact that they can't get married where they are. I'm sure I could organise this wedding in a few hours out there, and still have time to catch the evening performance of Matt Goss. It's making me think about suggesting to Mark that perhaps we go to Vegas for our wedding anniversary when I remember the bump. I think it'll be a long time before Mark and I will get to do a weekend city break like that again.

'I'll see what I can do.' I wander into the kitchen and fill up the kettle.

'Brilliant. Thanks, Penny. And sorry for the early-morning call – next time I'll try and ring at a more appropriate time.'

'That's OK, I'll speak to you soon.'

'What was all that about?' asks Mark as I hang up the phone. He makes me jump. I hadn't even heard him come down the stairs.

'My Las Vegas bride. She got her times muddled up.'

Mark sighs loudly and passes me the coffee.

'Decaf for me,' I say.

He reaches back into the cupboard and hands me out my jar.

'Sorry she woke you,' I say as I make the coffee.

'It's OK. It's probably done me a favour. I could do with popping into the office before we go to the hospital anyway. Not long now.' He rubs my belly.

We've got our first appointment at the antenatal clinic this morning, and we're having an ultrasound of our baby. I'm feeling ridiculously nervous about it.

I stir the coffee and think back to my dream. Closing my eyes, I try and clear it from my mind. *It wasn't real. Our baby is happy and healthy in my belly*, I repeat over and over in my head. Ever since the wedding fair on Saturday I've been feeling uneasy.

I would usually chalk it up to the post-weekend blues, but this feels different. Seeing Georgina again rattled my confidence. It seems like I can't do anything at the moment without her being there, taunting me and my company.

It's as if the negative thoughts she makes me have seep into all areas of my life and have made me start to worry about the baby.

'It's going to be fine,' says Mark suddenly, as if he's reading my mind. He takes his coffee and goes back upstairs.

I decide that the best thing to do is distract myself with work until it's time to go to the hospital later on this morning, and seeing as Vegas Melissa is fresh in my mind I might as well look into this Elvis idea.

When Mark gets back from work at ten, I'm giggling so hard at the computer screen that I don't hear him come into the kitchen.

'Are you ready to go?' He pokes his head round the door. 'What's going on?'

I wipe away the tears of laughter and point to the You-Tube video.

'What the hell is that? You call that work?'

'Do you know you can actually get Elvis to marry you in this country?'

'So he *is* alive, and there was me thinking he lived in Argentina.'

I shut down my laptop, still grinning.

'It's nice to see you smiling,' says Mark. 'Today's going to be amazing.'

I take a deep breath. 'I hope so.' The smile slowly fades as the nerves take over once more. I'm so nervous about seeing our baby for the first time. I know that I won't see much more than a blob, and it's not like we'd be able to find out the sex, but until I hear that heart beating I'm going to worry.

'Get your coat on then. We don't want to be late.'

'OK,' I stand up and gather up my coat and bag as slowly as I can.

'Pen, you're not still worried after that film, are you?' says Mark.

After the wedding fair on Sunday, already in melancholy mood, thanks to Georgina, I watched *Marley and Me* on TV, and I wept at the scene where she miscarries her baby. I may have taken it as an omen.

I look at him, narrowing my eyes and wondering when he learnt how to read my mind, whilst I'm still very behind at my married couple telepathy.

'But it could happen. I mean, they had a positive pregnancy

test, and then it wasn't there,' I say, a lump catching in my throat.

'You've been as sick as a dog for weeks now. Doesn't everyone say that means the baby is healthy? Look, it's not going to put your mind at rest if we miss the appointment, is it?'

'I guess there's no point in delaying the inevitable,' I say glumly.

I pop back into the kitchen and collect my large bottle of water. The NHS website says to have a full bladder for an ultrasound.

The car journey passes quickly, with Mark for once dominating the conversation. He's been talking about his plans to get our little one to play sport professionally so that he or she can support us in our old age. I'd usually be interjecting – trying to break it to him gently that our little one might not be into sports – but today I let him run away with his fantasies of his offspring playing for England while I sip my water.

'Have you drunk that whole thing already?' says Mark as we pull up in the car park.

I look at the empty bottle. 'I guess I have. I wanted to be prepared. They say that if you have a full bladder it's easier to see the baby and I wanted to make sure they can.'

Mark reaches over and squeezes my hand. 'Of course they're going to see it, Pen.'

We get out of the car and start to walk into the main hospital. I do an involuntary shudder, which happens whenever I visit anywhere like this. The smell of disinfectant makes me feel queasy at the best of times, let alone with my morning sickness. A smile flickers over my face as I remember my ridiculous lie to Big Top Rachel and Jimmy about the disinfectant allergy. I'd have given anything to go in that giant ball pit; it looked like amazing fun.

'That's the spirit, Pen!' says Mark. 'You should be excited. We're going to see our little one for the first time.'

He takes my hand in his and pulls me in for a quick hug.

'Ooh,' I say. 'Not so tight. You'll make me wet myself.'

I pull away laughing. Perhaps a whole two-litre bottle of water wasn't the smartest idea.

'Did you want to stop at the loo?'

'No, I can't. I've got to have a full bladder.'

We walk through the soulless corridors to the antenatal and gynaecology unit. I honestly feel like if I stop moving then I'm going to wee.

Mark opens the door into the unit and I step through to reception.

'I've got an appointment,' I say to the receptionist as I shift from foot to foot. 'Penny Robinson.'

'OK, take a seat. They're running about twenty minutes behind schedule.'

Perfect, I think. Twenty more minutes of jiggling on the spot.

'Why don't you go to the toilet?' says Mark. 'Get another bottle of water on your way back, a smaller one this time.'

'I can't! What if it doesn't go through me in time? It said in my pregnancy book that you're bound to be uncomfortable, oh, and that when I go to the loo after I'll probably feel faint as my bladder has been holding so much water.'

Mark rolls his eyes at me.

'I'm sure you'd be fine without it, but it's *your* bladder,' he says. 'All this talk is making me need a wee. I'll be back in a minute.'

He heads off in the direction of the disabled toilet at the other end of the waiting room and I stare at the back of his head incredulously. I know it's ridiculous of me to be mad at him for going to the toilet, but I sort of feel that if I can't go, he shouldn't go. Almost like he should have to cross his legs in sympathy.

I keep jiggling about, walking in circles. In a bid to distract my bladder, I eye up the other people in the waiting room and try and guess by the size of their bumps how far along the other mums-to-be are. The woman next to me is huge and I'm worried that she's going to pop at any minute. She's wincing as she moves and looks as if she's in pain. I don't know why I'm so worried – there are worse places for her to go into labour; we are in the antenatal department of a hospital after all.

A door opens to one of the consultation rooms and I hope that the woman behind the desk got it wrong and I'm going to be called in.

A couple shuffle out, thanking the medical professional they've been dealing with. It isn't until they turn to face the waiting room that I lock eyes with the woman.

'Penny!' says Big Top Rachel, her face lighting up.

I close my eyes for a second in the hope it magically makes me invisible.

'Rachel, Jimmy,' I say, my mind whirring as I try to come up with a cover story.

'What are you doing here?' she asks.

I open my mouth and close it in rapid succession. My mind is blank. I look over Rachel's shoulder for inspiration and my eyes fall on a poster for cervical screening.

'Nothing serious, just a smear,' I say, noticing I've made Jimmy look away in embarrassment.

'At the hospital?'

Damn my bad lying.

'Yes, I had some abnormal results and I'm getting everything checked out.'

Now I'm wishing I'd kept up to date with my smear tests as I feel like I'm jinxing it by lying about it.

'I hope everything will be OK,' says Rachel, concern written all over her face.

'It'll be fine,' I say. 'Everything's going to be normal.'

Mark walks up behind me and rubs the small of my back. 'Of course it is.'

I instantly flinch, Mark has no idea that Rachel and Jimmy are clients of mine and that I've just told a very big porky pie.

'Are you Penny's husband?' asks Rachel. 'I'm so glad that you're here with her. I was going to offer to wait around in case she needed anything.'

'I am, and I wouldn't miss this for the world,' he says, kissing me on the cheek.

I clutch at his shoulder and laugh nervously, whilst trying to send him a telepathic message.

'That's so lovely,' says Rachel. I swear she's got tears in her eyes. 'I'm sorry. I get so emotional.'

I can see Mark looking confused.

'Mark, this is Rachel and Jimmy, two of my clients, getting married next year. I was telling them about my abnormal test results.'

'Your wh—'

I raise an eyebrow at him and wish for once he'd pick up a hint.

'Yes, of course,' he says, giving me a look which I know means we're going to have words later.

'Penny's putting such a brave face on it,' says Rachel.

'She certainly is.'

Mark's got a scolding look on his face.

'So what are you here for?' I say, changing the subject. 'Everything OK with the baby?'

'Oh, yes, look!' Rachel hands us a printout of an ultrasound and I'm amazed that you can see a whole little baby. I always imagined it would be like looking at a Magic Eye print from the late nineties – you know, when you had to squint and then pretend you saw the flying shark or, in this case, the baby's head.

'That's so clear. Look, Mark!'

He takes the picture and congratulates Jimmy as he hands it back to him.

'Penny, good news. When I was at kayaking last night I spoke to the manager of the Water Club, and he said as I'm an existing club member, that we didn't need to go through their wedding planner. If you phone him up again, he'll book us in.'

I'm so happy with the news that I have to fight the urge to wrap my arms around him and give him a big squeeze. Not only would it be inappropriate with a client, but I'd also burst my bladder.

'Thank you so much, that's brilliant news. I'll phone them right after this.'

'No hurry,' says Jimmy. 'You might have more important things on your mind.'

I curse the fact that I can't let them in on our secret.

'We should be going,' says Rachel. 'We're meeting my mum for lunch to show her the photos. Fingers crossed for you, Penny.'

'Thanks, Rachel.'

'Nice to meet you both,' says Mark as he shakes hands with Jimmy again.

'They're a really nice couple,' I say to Mark.

'They seem it.'

I turn away and hope that's the end of the conversation. I pick what must be the most uncomfortable plastic chair in the waiting room and grab an out-of-date magazine from the stack in front of me.

'So,' says Mark, sitting down next to me.

I squirm on the seat, guessing what's coming.

'So,' I repeat.

'Penny Robinson!' calls a voice.

Phew! I sigh with relief and almost wet myself as I momentarily forget my desperate need to wee.

We follow the smiling woman into the clinically white room and stand nervously just inside the doorway while the sonographer confirms my name and date of birth.

'Right, then, Penny,' she says after she's satisfied herself that I am who I say I am. 'Let's see what we've got.'

She pats the chair with the shallow back and stirrups for me to sit on. No sooner have I sat down, than she pulls down the top of my tracksuit bottoms and lifts up my T-shirt.

'This is going to be a bit cold,' she says as she squirts on the gel.

She's not wrong. I wince as she rubs it around with the edge of the ultrasound stick.

Mark and I are transfixed by the empty screen. I feel him squeezing my hand, but I can't look at him. Not until I see the baby.

The woman pushes my belly this way and that, and all I can think of is how I wish I'd taken more than one pregnancy test. When I phoned my GP surgery they laughed at me when I asked when I should come in for a test. Apparently they take your word for it. But what if the test was faulty?

I'm terrified that she's not going to find anything in there at all. I've been so ungrateful about the timing, what if Mother Nature doesn't realise how much I want this baby?

The screen continues to turn light and dark as she moves the stick around, and it's quiet. Aren't we supposed to hear a heartbeat?

'Ah,' says the woman, 'here we are.'

And suddenly everything stops whirring around my brain. There's my baby.

'Why can't I hear it? The heart, is it beating?'

The woman presses a button and a tinny mechanical noise starts booming.

'That's its heartbeat?' I say in disbelief.

'Sure is.'

'Oh, Mark.' I turn and exhale the breath I didn't realise I'd been holding.

His eyes are shining and he's wearing the biggest grin I've ever seen. 'That's it, it's official, we're going to be parents,' he says.

We really are. Suddenly thoughts of the business and worries about getting everything done in time for Christmas fade away and I realise that our baby really is happening.

I've been so preoccupied with Princess-on-a-Shoestring and how the baby is going to impact on the company that I haven't really stopped to think about the baby itself. But there it is on the screen, all alien-like and wriggly.

Mark squeezes my hand tighter. 'Told you everything was going to be OK.'

He smooths my hair down and pulls my head into him, giving me a hug.

'I'll print your pictures,' says the sonographer, 'and that's it.'

She removes the little prodding machine and wipes the gel off my belly; not very well actually, as when I pull my tracksuit up again it feels all slimy and wet.

I'm sad when she turns off the monitor; I could look at the blurry grey screen all day.

I still don't know how I'm going to juggle the company and the baby, but there's something about seeing that screen, and the future ahead of me, that makes me so excited.

chapter seventeen

Ellie @Elliezgood

It's 9 a.m. and I've already seen two men's penises. Got to be a great start to a hen do #lifedrawing

Penny Robinson @princess_shoestring

@Elliezgood Oh dear. London watch out — girls on tour. Looking forward to seeing you later.

Ellie @Elliezgood

@princess_shoestring I would say the same but I doubt I'm going to be able to see anything by the time you arrive — already on my 4th G&T.

I absolutely love a good hen do. I'm usually first in line to throw on a T-shirt with a dodgy one-liner and wear anything bright pink and tacky. Hen dos are amazing, especially when

267

they're not your own. Yet when I said I'd go on Ellie's, I hadn't counted on the little bean in the belly.

'Are you sure you still want to come?' asks Lou as I get in the back of the taxi next to her.

'Yeah, I'm trying not to spook any more of my brides.'

'Ellie's not like any bride though, is she? I mean, she's a friend.'

'I know, but she's more your friend than mine, and I can't tell her my secret. All it would take would be one little tweet, and what with Georgina—' I say at a rate of knots.

'And breathe. Blimey, I know it's stressful not telling people, but it's only a baby.'

'Lou, you made up a fake hangover to get out of wine tasting at my house because you didn't want to tell me you were pregnant, and I'm your best friend!'

I see her shudder at the memory.

'I've got to be careful about my online image at the moment. I can't afford to have any little slip-ups.'

'OK, but how are you going to get through a cocktail-making lesson followed by a night out?'

I look out of the window, hoping that inspiration will strike before we meet the others.

'I'm not sure yet. I'm amazed she didn't guess after the food tasting.'

'I forgot to ask you – how was that?'

'Interesting. Blake actually spoke.'

'Spoke, or fought with Ellie?'

'Fought. I take it that's a common occurrence?'

'It's only happened every time I've seen them.'

'They seemed to make it up and were pretty hot and heavy after.'

'Sounds about right. Now do you see what I was getting at the other day?'

'I'm sure they're fine. You never know what goes on behind closed doors, right?'

I don't want to confirm Lou's suspicions too much, I feel wrong speculating on the future of Ellie's marriage when we're off to her hen do.

'Guess not.'

Lou knows me well enough to know when I'm changing the subject. 'So what are you going to do about the alcohol then?' she asks.

'Well, all I know is that I have to make them think I'm drinking.'

Lou rolls her eyes and grins at me. 'And what are you going to do with your drinks?'

'Well, I'm thinking that's where you come in.'

'Oh no. Don't you rope me into your little plan. You know I'm a lousy drunk.'

'Please,' I say, making a big lip.

'Nuh-uh.' She turns and looks out the window.

'I'll make you godmother.'

She snaps her head back round, as quick as a flash. 'Um, excuse me, you'll be making me godmother no matter what, Penelope Robinson.'

'So think of this as you doing your first nice godmotherly deed. It's practically your duty, protecting him or her from alcohol.'

Lou raises her left eyebrow at me; I've always been jealous that she's able to do that. 'OK then, but you've got to babysit Harry for me next week. I'm in desperate need of a haircut and I can't face taking him with me again. Last time he jabbed a toy car into my foot while they were cutting and I now have one section of hair three inches shorter than the rest. I've had to wear my hair up ever since. Look.'

I stare at Lou's hair. She's hidden it really well by strategically pinning the sides up at the back. She's lucky she's got wavy hair or else she wouldn't have got away with it so easily.

'Deal,' I say. How long can a haircut take? An hour max? Harry's not the best-behaved toddler, but I think even I can handle an hour. It will be great practice.

Lou smiles at me with a twinkle I haven't seen for a while.

The twinkle is still there when we arrive in Covent Garden, where we are meeting the other hens.

'Lou! Penny!' shouts Ellie as we walk into the bar.

I can tell by the way she's wiggling her hips as she totters across the floor in her heels that she's been on the sauce for a while. She and most of the other hens caught the train up earlier to do a life-drawing class, followed by a pole-dancing lesson. Having tried pole-dancing once at the gym and almost breaking an ankle, I'd luckily opted out of that months ago, blaming my clumsiness.

'We're going to get started in a minute,' Ellie says, giving us hugs and almost knocking me out with the fumes from her boozy breath.

Maybe I won't have to worry about having the staying power to make it through to the nightclub – I'm sure if Ellie bows out (aka gets dumped in her hotel room) then I can make a speedy exit back to Waterloo and be tucked up in bed in time to watch *X-Factor*.

'Can't wait,' I say, peering into the corners of the dark and dingy bar. It's all mahogany tables, leather couches and dim spotlights. The place is deserted apart from a barman dressed all in black and the rest of the rabble there for Ellie's hen do. It looks to me like Ellie isn't the only one who might be headed for an early night. One of the hens is already trying to climb on the bar, having to be physically removed by the man in black.

'Oooh, Sheryl's pulled!' shouts one of the girls.

'Down, tiger – leave some men for the rest of us!' calls another.

Up until now I haven't missed alcohol. Yes, I know I've only known for six weeks that I'm pregnant, and it's not like I drank a lot before. A glass of wine, cough, or two, after work a couple of times a week . . . and then a few at the weekend, so it's hardly been a big sacrifice. But today is one of those occasions where you need to have consumed at least three shots to feel at ease with the situation.

'Right, ladies, welcome to The Lounge, I'm Bill. If you can control yourselves, let's get shaking,' says the barman in a strong Australian accent.

'I'd shake anything for you,' says Sheryl, demonstrating.

Considering they've been pole-dancing beforehand I might have expected her to be wearing a bra with a little more support. Not that it seems to bother the barman; he doesn't bat an eyelid. This is clearly not his first hen do. He's got a knowing look on his face, and what with his chiselled jaw, and a smile that looks like it's going to do a Colgate ping, I'm thinking he probably thrives on this type of thing.

'Now, we're going to get started with some margaritas.'

My stomach lurches at the thought of tequila. Pregnant or not, I don't believe in tequila-based drinks before 11 p.m. I seem to be in the minority though, as whoops and cheers go up around the room.

'We're going to start with a tasting.'

I look at Lou and she puts a finger in her mouth, making a vomiting signal.

I feel a tiny bit guilty about making Lou drink my drinks, but I'm sure I'll end up with the worse side of the bargain when I babysit Harry.

The barman hands us two shots each, one a golden colour and the other clear.

I hold them up to the light as if I'm studying them studiously, but really I'm wondering how the hell I'm going to be able to pull the switch with Lou.

Luckily there's no countdown or any forced down-in-ones (yet). It seems the other hens are listening to Bill describe the different production techniques that affect the colour. There are a looks of concentration . . . albeit very drunk concentration. There's a lot of swaying going on and people sipping the shots like they're fine wine.

'Hand it over,' whispers Lou.

I look round at her and she's holding one of her glasses in her hands, obscuring the contents. We look around to make sure no one is watching, before we swap glasses. She downs the drink and shakes her head in disgust.

Poor Lou. She hasn't got the benefit of having consumed her body weight in drinks like the girls that started drinking this morning.

She looks at me and makes a face as if she can't possibly drink the next one and I lean over to the hen next to me and accidentally bump into her, knocking my drink over in the process.

'Oh, sorry,' I say to her.

'No bother,' she says. 'You spilt your drink though! Don't worry – I'll attract Bill's attention to get another.'

She's looking in his direction and about to raise her hand when I grab hold of it.

'No, don't worry. I'm sure there's plenty more coming up,' I sigh, wondering how I'll get out of drinking the rest.

'So, if you want to gather round, I'm going to give you a margarita masterclass.'

We squeeze in close to get a better view of Bill. He begins to open bottles and throw them up in the air like Tom Cruise in *Cocktail*. Each time he catches something he flashes the Colgate smile and I swear he winks at Ellie. He's clearly got hen dos down to a tee.

I don't think it's perhaps the best idea to give the girls the idea of throwing bottles around their heads. I hope Bill's going to be handing out crash helmets to go with our ingredients.

When his container is full he shakes it around his ears then turns round and shakes his bum, much to everyone's delight. Even I can't help feeling a little flushed. Of course, as a happily married woman I wouldn't say his bum is as nice as Mark's, but it's pretty perky. Especially in the tight trousers he's wearing.

'And that's all there is to it.' He laughs and pours out a little bit of his drink from the silver mixer into each the glasses in front of us. I do a sniff test and instantly wish I hadn't. I take the glass up to my lips and do my best not to inhale the fumes coming up. I don't taste it, but instead place my drink back down among the throng of glasses and hope no one notices the difference.

'Now, along the bar are the ingredients you're going to need. Don't worry – or be offended that the bottles are all plastic – we've had a few butterfingers moments in the past.'

Phew. No crash helmets required after all.

'You can customise the margaritas to whatever flavour you fancy. There's cranberry, strawberry, vanilla, pineapple, banana – the world is your oyster. Maybe you can mix it up a little.'

'I'm one for mixing it up,' says Sheryl to raucous laughter.

'When you're finished, I'll judge them to see whose is the best. I've got a special prize for the winner.'

I happen to make an excellent cocktail, or at least I think I do. I might not be able to shake the bottles over my head, but I'm pretty good at making a tasty concoction potent enough to get you pissed. I'd usually be first up to the bar, scouring the ingredients to make an award-winning drink. Yet my usual strategy of including the most alcohol I possibly can whilst still making it drinkable isn't going to work this time. I've never made a mocktail . . . I guess there's a first time for everything.

I go up and find the strawberry and banana flavourings, taking care to remember to pick up the tequila for appearances' sake.

I get to work shaking, stirring and pretending to add alcohol into my fruit drink. I get a little bit carried away, measuring the fruits out so that they balance. I throw in some mint leaves to give it a twist and shake it like a Polaroid picture. Despite everything, I start to relax and, dare I say it, enjoy myself.

'Nice shaking,' says Bill, winking at me.

I giggle like a schoolgirl. He's such a charmer.

'Time's up, ladies!' calls Bill a few minutes later.

I see Ellie add an extra splash of tequila to her glass, clearly for luck. I think Bill saw it too, but he seems to be turning a blind eye. I go to protest, but I hesitate . . . she *is* the bride, and I did swear I was going to go above and beyond to please them. Accusing her of cheating on her own hen do would probably go against that.

'Right, line them up, ladies, and stand proudly alongside your own little beauty.'

I see Sheryl pulling her top down to reveal her little beauties a bit more. I love the way she's subtly trying to influence the voting. If I were drunker, younger and unmarried, I imagine I'd probably be hitching my skirt up a little higher in the same way. What is it about these things that brings out the slutty worst in people?

'How did you get on with yours?' whispers Lou, whilst Bill walks along sipping each of our drinks. He's a very clever man, keeping half a metre of bar between himself and us. Yet with that look in Sheryl's eyes, I'm not sure even the wooden bar is going to keep her away from his bum.

'It's pretty spectacular-tasting,' I tell Lou. 'Just the way I like my margaritas . . . without tequila.'

'Ha, I couldn't face much either, so mine's only got a splash in.'

Bill picks up my drink and I watch him nervously. He looks up, licks his lips and gives me a smile. If he's guessed my cocktail is lacking, he's kind enough not to say.

He reaches the end of the row, and there's an excitement brewing. It seems I'm not the only one who wants to win.

'It's between two,' says Bill. 'I think I'm going to award Ellie best classic margarita, and this one – what's your name?'

My jaw drops open. He's pointing at me. 'P-P-Penny,' I stutter in confusion. Surely he can tell that mine's got no booze in it. He must do this week in and week out. How could I have fooled an expert?

'Penny, yours wins best original flavour. It was a hard choice though, ladies. You all did really well.'

I look around, a little embarrassed that I've won. A few of the women give me an arm rub and offer up their congratulations.

'I want you all to taste the winning drinks, so I'm going to pour them round.'

I look in horror as Bill takes mine and Ellie's drinks and starts pouring them into shot glasses for everyone else to try.

The girls dive in to grab them as I watch on, grimacing. Ignoring the fact that that was supposed to be *my* nice virgin drink that I could have enjoyed, now they're going to guess my little secret.

I start to feel a little flustered. I wish I hadn't been so competitive. If only I was as bad at making cocktails as I am at baking cakes.

'Wow, Penny, this is delicious,' says Ellie, shooting hers back in one.

'It's gorgeous,' says another.

'All that flavour really masks the bitterness of the tequila,' says a third.

I realise the ladies haven't even twigged that there's no alcohol in there.

I look at Lou and do a mock wipe of my brow and she gives me a little wink. I see she's swapped my shot of Ellie's with her shot of mine. I smile in relief and shoot both non-alcoholic margaritas back. It really does taste delicious. I'm gutted I'm not able to enjoy a whole glass of it.

'I said that there would be a prize for the winner.'

I clap my hands in delight. I'm always up for winning a prize. Got to be a free T-shirt, or a pint glass. I do love a good freebie.

'You get to have one of my extra-special cocktails.'

At this point I would have settled for a branded coaster. Anything but another drink to try and get rid of.

'What's your poison, Penny?'

If I was stuttering getting my name out, I'm positively falling over my words now.

'Um, um . . .' I'm trying to work out what the least-alcoholic cocktail is. That's the one I'd usually avoid, as I always believe in ordering ones with the most types of alcohol in to get the best value for money. Think, Penny, think.

'She'll have a banana daiquiri, just like me,' says Ellie, looping arms with me. 'Well done you,' she beams.

'Thanks,' I reply, trying not to breathe in her exhaled breath. I could get drunk off that alone.

'I'm so glad you came.'

'I'm happy to be here,' I say, feeling guilty that I've dreading coming all week.

'You're the world's best wedding planner, and I'm so lucky to have you.'

'Ahh, thanks. That means a lot.'

I want to try and free my arm, but I get the feeling that I'm the only thing holding her up.

'You really do anything your brides ask, don't you? I mean, coming to my tasting, stepping in for my make-up trial. And I see on Twitter that you're going to venues on behalf of a bride from the US.'

I nod. I would usually take the professional pat on the back, but it acts as a stark reminder that my brides-to-be all are active on social media, and any hint from one of them that I'm pregnant might cause a mass exodus over to Georgina's camp.

Bill comes round the bar to present us with our drinks and I wonder how I'm going to get out of this. There's no way I'm going to be able to pass this off as Lou's. Not only is it in a tall glass and canary yellow in colour, but it's also got a bright pink umbrella in the top.

My heart is starting to race and I'm beginning to wish that I hadn't read that recent report on foetal alcohol consumption. Before that I'd probably have been inclined to think that one wouldn't hurt. I wonder if I can give my drink to Ellie as a special hen-do treat, or if I should 'accidentally' knock it over.

Bill gives Ellie a kiss on the cheek as he presents her with the first drink, and I think I hear him wishing her a happy hen do. He then leans over to me and whispers, 'Don't worry, it's a virgin.'

I look at him in surprise. He gives me another wink and a flash of his perfect smile. I return the smile and my shoulders practically drop to the floor with relief. I take the smallest sip first just in case, but there's not the tiniest hint of alcohol taste. I'm expecting to feel sick drinking it, yet there's something about this drink that reminds me of the banana antibiotics I used to get as a child. It slips down surprisingly well.

I see Lou's mouth fall open in shock, presumably at me drinking.

'Don't worry – it's alcohol-free,' I say, using my hand to shield my mouth so that the others don't hear.

The music that was playing subtly in the background kicks up a notch, and before I've had a chance to finish my drink, the hens are up on the dance floor, throwing some shapes to 'It's Raining Men'. And what shapes they are. It's only four in the afternoon. There's head-flicking, foot-stamping and girl-on-girl grinding. If these are the dance moves they're pulling now, I dread to think what it's going to be like by the time we get to the main event.

'Do we dare?' asks Lou, squinting.

'Considering you've had all those drinks and *you're* hesitating, can you imagine I want to?'

Lou squeezes my hand. 'It gets easier. Only another few weeks and you'll be able to tell everyone. Your secret will be out in the open.'

'That's what I'm worried about.' I slump down on a bar stool and lean on my elbow, propping my heavy head on my hand.

'Why wouldn't you want to tell? It's not like your best friend is getting married and is going to freak out because your baby bump would ruin her hen do or her wedding pictures,' Lou says, pulling a comical face.

Can you believe that Lou was afraid to tell me she was pregnant because she thought I'd go all crazy? Well, you probably can't believe it now because I'm generally so relaxed about weddings, but there was a time when I might have been described as a bridezilla-in-waiting.

I pull a sarcastic smile and sip some more of my banana drink, which I'm beginning to think is probably all sugar.

'Lou, did I tell you about that snooty wedding planner I met recently?'

'The one who had been planning your French wedding before you?'

I nod. Bill comes over to us, and without speaking places two more drinks down in front of us. Perhaps this hen do isn't that bad after all.

'That's the one. Last week I found out that she's started to do budget weddings too.'

'Ah,' says Lou.

'Ah, indeed. One of my brides tried to defect to her.'

'What? Really?'

'Yep, and all this before my summer brides know I'm pregnant.'

'Oh,' says Lou, pulling a sympathetic face. 'But you'll get someone to run your weddings next year, won't you? It's not like you're going to leave them in the lurch.'

'I know. It's just that the business is so new and I'm going to find it really difficult to get someone that I trust to run it. I mean, it's part of me.'

She gives my arm a quick squeeze. 'I'm sure you'll find someone. The sooner you start looking, the easier it will be.'

I sigh heavily. I've been putting it off as I don't really want to think about it.

'Penny, things always work out for you, so why would this be any different?' continues Lou.

I let out a loud laugh. 'That's *so* not true. I spent all my wedding savings on Internet bingo, remember?'

'And then you had a spectacular wedding.'

'OK, but then I practically got fired from my job.'

'And then you became an entrepreneur and set up your own business.'

The word entrepreneur conjures up all sorts of images and makes me think that I should be preparing to go on *Dragons' Den*. I can see myself now: trembling in a skirt suit, sweat beads forming on my forehead as I try to get my gross profit straight from my projected forecast. Of course all the Dragons would fight over me, and I'd take a deal with Peter and Duncan, my two favourites. Although quite what I'd want them to invest in, I don't know, but I'm sure I could think of something.

'Yes, but that could fail now. Then I'll be a mum with no job.'

Lou's laughing at me. 'Pen, your business is not going to fail, and if it did—'

I breathe in sharply at the thought that she thinks it possibly *could* fail.

'If . . .' she says, placing extra emphasis on the word to reassure me. '*If* it does, then you'll enjoy your maternity leave and find something else to do after.'

I know she's right, and had I been in my job I would have

been taking a year off anyway, but now I desperately want Princess-on-a-Shoestring to survive.

'Anyway, there's no saying that your brides are going to leave you. It was only one bride, and you say she *tried* to defect. What happened with her in the end? Are you still planning her big day?'

'Yes. I managed to convince her that I had a better idea of what she wanted than Georgina. She's now booked to get married in a pagoda at the nature reserve, with her reception in a yurt. Can you believe Georgina had suggested she forego her woodland theme and have a marquee at a hotel?'

I roll my eyes and shake my head. Saying it out loud makes this whole thing seem ridiculous. I *get* my brides. I get their dreams.

'See, that's why your brides are going to stick with you. Bump or no bump, you're still going to have those ideas.'

'Am I? Aren't I going to get baby brain and put my phone in the washing machine and my deodorant in the freezer?'

'According to Russell, baby brain is a myth.'

'What would he know?' I laugh at the thought of Lou's husband telling her that. Mark would say exactly the same. He'd also probably point out that I do that kind of thing as a matter of course; once last summer he found the remote control in the dishwasher. Luckily it was finished and I'd opened it up to get a spoon for my cereal – I'd just put the remote in its place.

'I told Russell that he should give birth to something the size of a rugby ball that is constantly attached to your boob for the first month and never lets you have a minute to yourself. Then he'd understand baby brain.'

I've clearly pulled a face because Lou's expression suddenly changes.

'But those newborn snuggles and that smell – ah, Penny, you're going to love it.'

I try to ignore her comments about the rugby ball, even though it all seems a lot more real now that I've seen him or her on the ultrasound.

'You're going to be great. It's all going to work out, you'll see,' says Lou.

I smile weakly at her. I wish I shared her confidence.

Whatever happens with the baby and the brides, one thing's for sure: this time next year my life will be completely different.

chapter eighteen

Nerinda Designer Dresses @nerindadress

New collection launches today! If you were a wedding dress what would you be called? One lucky bride will win her dress! #nerindadresses

Rachel Burton @Onlyrachburton

@nerindadress Lola – I'm a showgirl at heart – despite my big baby bump :) #nerindadresses

Sally Jessop @Jessoplady

@nerindadress Elowen – it's cornish (like me) for elm tree, as I'm getting married in a wood! #nerindadresses

'It's so lovely of you to come,' says Nerinda, giving me air kisses on both cheeks.

'I wouldn't have missed it for the world,' I say honestly.

An afternoon with a designer at a gorgeous little bridal boutique, with chocolate and cava (or sparkling apple juice in my case), what's not to love? And as if the treats weren't enough, Nerinda is showcasing spring and summer wedding dresses to press and industry contacts. There are dresses delicately exhibited on mannequins scattered around the room, and others being modelled by gorgeous women.

'Have a good look. There's a real range of prices, depending on the fabric and cut. There's a lot more sheer lace around next season, and I've got quite a few short dresses this time round too, perfect for brides zipping off to hotter climes.'

I nod and make some notes. This kind of stuff is great for my blog, and it's always useful for me to spot an on-trend bargain on the high street.

It's times like these that I go a bit gooey and melty and I remember why I wanted the big Vera Wang princess dress in the first place. I balance my juice in one hand with my notebook and run my other over the full skirts of one of Nerinda's more extravagant creations. My heart flutters slightly.

'I've got a special one for you to see,' she says, whisking me to the other side of the shop. She takes me to one that's cream in colour with almost a hint of yellow – it's short and looks like it would float in the breeze, perfect for a destination wedding.

'It's beautiful,' I say, admiring it on the mannequin.

'It's called "Penny",' she says.

'It is?'

'Yes, I was in the process of designing it when you and your bride came into the shop, and I thought that your personality suited the nature of the dress, so "Penny" it became.'

I blush slightly, I've never had anything named after me before.

She smiles at me. 'I've got to go and greet some other people. If you've got any questions after you've looked around, come and find me.'

'Thanks, Nerinda,' I say, still touched about the dress.

I take a photo of the 'Penny' and continue looking round. I'm tempted to take a few dresses into the changing room, to see what they look like on, before I bring myself back to reality. When would I ever need another wedding dress?

Instead I go around taking notes on the shapes and fabrics, and snapping photos on my phone of the models wearing the dresses beautifully.

'Jenny!'

I hear Georgina calling whilst I'm taking a photo of a dazzling dress that's practically dripping diamantés. Her voice is so distinctive that I couldn't miss it. I'm about to turn round, when I tell myself that she could be talking to anyone. There might actually be a Jenny here for all I know.

'Jenny Robinson!'

I turn round, chiding myself for responding to the wrong name. I smile at her through gritted teeth whilst holding my hand out to finish taking the snap. Perfect photo obtained, I thank the model and turn properly to Georgina.

'Hello,' I say.

'I wouldn't have expected to see you here.'

That old chestnut? I wonder if she's going to say this every time we meet.

'My brides wear dresses too.'

'I know, but these are the types of dresses that my high-end girls have.'

'Actually I looked here for dresses with Olivia Miller.'

It's an effort not to add 'So ner!' to her. There's something about speaking to her that brings out my inner child, and throwing in her face the fact that I came here with the bride that I accidentally stole off her is a new low for me.

Thinking of Olivia and her dress makes me shudder at the memory of the zip disaster that could have ruined the whole wedding. If only she'd fallen in love with a Nerinda dress back then. From the look of how they're made, I can't see one of them falling foul to a dodgy zipper.

'Is that so?' asks Georgina.

'Yes, and you know that I write for *Bridal Dreams*, so I'm sending my report to them.'

Liar, liar, pants on fire! I was thinking about sending Jane the editor a few of the photos, as they do have a feature on local boutiques and I think Nerinda's designs would be perfect for it, but I was only going to send it as a suggestion for a story, not a story itself, but Georgina's really bringing out the worst in me.

'*Bridal Dreams*? I think they've gone downhill lately – all those tacky new features. I still prefer my *Weddings of Style* magazine.'

'I guess your weddings are a bit more traditional than mine.'

'Yes, but maybe I'll have to start doing more research. Did you get my flyer? Did you see I'm expanding the business?'

'I did. I thought there wasn't a market for budget brides?'

'Who said anything about budget? They're simply my type of weddings on a smaller scale.'

'Of course they are.' I nod. I sip my apple juice, wishing it was something stronger.

'I've already had a lot of interest. I might have to take on another full-time planner to cope.'

'That's great. Well, if you'll excuse me. I've got to get a couple more photos before I leave.'

'Somewhere to go, have you?'

I'm not just making excuses to get away from her; I do have to go. I've got my gambling group meeting to get to.

But I can't very well tell her that and I definitely have to be there today as we're deciding on the Christmas do. I would have offered to plan something special, but with all the work I'm doing for the brides at the moment, and my own Christmas Eve family party to organise, I don't feel I've got the time.

'I've got a wedding venue to scope out for one of my guests.'

'Oh really? Anywhere I might know? I have a lot of contacts in the area and I might be able to pull a few strings for you.'

'I'm good, thank you.'

My poor cheek. I'm having to bite it to stop myself from saying something mean and nasty. Georgina's still staring at me as if she's going to say something more.

'It's not one of your quirky venues, is it? I heard that you convinced that Sally woman to get married in a forest.'

'That's right,' I say, the corners of my mouth twitching into an involuntary smile. 'Yes, I am off to another of my "quirky venues". One that isn't your run-of-the-mill hotel . . . I'm sure your brides wouldn't be interested.'

'I'm sure you're probably right.' She laughs and I laugh along with her – a fake tinkle that makes me hate myself for not standing up to her.

'See you around,' I say, wishing that the wedding industry in North Hampshire wasn't *quite* so small.

'Maybe not for very much longer, Jenny.'

She's got that 'your business is doomed' look on her face, but I ignore her and walk away.

I still feel her eyes on me as I take the last of my photograph. I'm starting to feel a little paranoid. Surely she's got better things to do than stalk me.

'Nerinda, the dresses are fabulous, as always,' I say to the designer when she turns away from the people she was speaking to.

'Thanks, Penny.' She grabs my hands and gives them a squeeze. 'I'm always terrified before these events, but it's nice to get good feedback.'

How could anyone be nervous when they've created dresses that look like they've been woven by fairies?

'I'm sure you'll get more than good feedback in the reviews. I've got to run now, but thank you so much for inviting me.'

'You're welcome, and thanks for coming.' She smiles at me warmly and I hope I have another bride that I can bring back here soon. There's something special about this shop.

I wave goodbye and walk out with a smile on my face. I'm trying to think whether any of my brides-to-be are looking for a dress like one of Nerinda's when I see that Georgina is behind me.

'I've got a bride to meet,' she explains as she hurries past me to her car. 'So many to fit in, so little time!'

My smile disappears. Georgina makes me so mad. I spend the entire journey to my gambling group fuming and thinking of wittier comebacks that I wish I'd thought of at the time.

As I walk through the doors of the community centre my shoulders relax when I see one half of a couple that surely won't desert me. Well, not unless Josh gets cold feet and they don't get married at all.

'Hi, Josh.' I say, going over to my mentor. He's strategically placed himself next to the biscuit table and I'm in luck this week – there are ginger-nut creams.

'Hey, Penny. Haven't see you for a couple of weeks. How have you been?'

He's looking at me with such intensity from his gorgeous blue eyes that I feel he's searching my soul, as if he can sense I've been gambling again.

I don't have much colour in my cheeks at the moment anyway, and any that was there drains and I immediately feel guilty about my little blackjack moment at the wedding fair. I know that money didn't exchange hands, but the rush

I felt when I won brought back really horrible memories. For the last eighteen months I've been brilliantly behaved and not really been tempted to gamble, but in that split second I felt exhilarated and it made me remember how I used to feel back in the good days of my gambling habit. And by 'good days' I mean the ones when I was oblivious to how much I'd been losing.

I know it's the kind of thing that I should tell Josh about, with him being my mentor, but I can't bring myself to talk about it. I know that it would lead to him wanting to talk about my feelings and what's going on in my life, and right now I'm trying to hide my baby bump from him and Mel. I can't risk him taking any more interest in me than he needs to, and it's not like the fake casino blackjack has led to me falling off the wagon. It was like an amber warning light, alerting me to be careful.

'OK, busy, not a lot to report,' I say, plastering a fake smile on my face. Good job I've had practice from my conversations with Georgina. 'It's been the best week. The bestest!'

Josh gives me one of those looks where I think he's trying to work out whether I'm actually a sane human being.

'That's always good to hear. Any reason?'

'No,' I say bluntly. There's no reason at all why I've had the bestest week in the world other than that I'm a crap liar. 'Just love my job.'

Awesome recovery, Penny, I think to myself. My cheeks are hurting from trying to keep that smile in place.

'Ah, well, speaking of your job . . . I'm glad you're here tonight. I've been talking to Mel and I think we're ready for one of the "proper meetings".'

'Yay! I'm so thrilled to be planning your wedding.' I rub my hands together in genuine glee. I notice the look on his face, which seems to suggest I tone it down, so I pick up a ginger-nut cream and start sucking on the biscuit-y goodness instead. 'I mean, yeah, let's get together and sort out some details.'

Josh is a man who didn't believe in marriage and has been recently converted by his partner. Therefore I'm aware I should tread carefully. He's a bit like a wild horse – I wouldn't want to spook him as I think Mel might kill me.

'So, what have you decided on so far?'

'We've picked a month. We're going to have it in August. You know – easier for Mel with him being a teacher, not because it's a traditional month for a wedding or anything.'

Josh is looking down at his toes and I can tell he's as uncomfortable talking weddings with me as I was talking about my gambling habit to him.

'That's a start,' I say. I'm grimacing slightly at the thought. There's a good chance my replacement will be handling that one, as I'm probably going to be nocturnal by that point.

I'm wondering if I can confide in Josh as he's sworn to secrecy under our mentor/mentee relationship. Also, I hardly think that he would be the type to tweet with my other brides like his boyfriend Mel, aka @MT125, does, and I already know from experience he's an excellent keeper of secrets.

I'm about to take him away from the rest of the group to tell him in the corner, when a look of panic breaks out over his face.

'What? Is August a bad month? It's a cliché, right? Getting married in August. The venues will all be fully booked, and it will be too hot for everyone, and—'

'Breathe, Josh,' I say, rubbing his arm. OK, now is definitely not the time to be telling him about the baby. If he's that freaked out about the choice of month, then he's not going to react well to the baby bump.

'August is fine. It's a great choice. Perfect. In fact it's the bestest.'

Uh-oh, there's the look again. The one that reminds me an awful lot of the look Mark used to give me when I was lying to him about my gambling. Are men better at spotting my lies?

'Is there anything else you want to tell me about your week, Penny?' Josh continues, suddenly dropping the nervous groom act and reverting back to his role of mentor. As he looks at me I again feel like he's trying to stare into my soul.

'No,' I reply quietly, shrugging innocently. 'It is the bestest.'

I take an extra ginger-nut cream to stop my stomach churning which, this time, I think has nothing to do with the baby and everything to do with me feeling guilty about the blackjack. I take my seat in the group horseshoe, ready for Mary, the group leader, to call the group to action. If ever there was a time that I needed to listen to the horrors of gambling, it's today. I need to remember how dark gambling can be so that those feelings replace that little memory of the buzz from the blackjack. I've got enough problems in my life with Georgina, and the baby secret, I mustn't add resurrecting my gambling addiction to that.

chapter nineteen

Ellie @Elliezgood

Wish I'd taken out wedding insurance :(

Rachel Burton @Onlyrachburton

@Elliezgood OMG – What's up????

Ellie @Elliezgood

@Onlyrachburton Groom's being an A**hole. Wanna cancel the whole thing. Plucking up the courage to phone Penny . . .

Rachel Burton @Onlyrachburton

@Elliezgood :(xxx

'Are you sure you're OK with this? If not, I can cancel,' says Lou, unpacking a huge duffel bag on to my kitchen table.

I'm only babysitting for the time it will take Lou to get a

haircut, yet she's brought more stuff for baby Harry than I'd take away on a week's holiday. I feel a light sweat run over me; I might have bitten off more than I can chew. But then I remember this will be me in a year's time. I'll be the one carrying round the duffel bag. If I can't cope with an hour, then how am I going to cope as a mum full-time?

I can feel my breath catching in my throat and my airways are starting to close up.

'I'll be fine,' I squeak. I saw the desperation in Lou's eyes when she was unpacking the bag. I can tell she needs me not to change my mind.

She takes out the loveliest little set of dungarees, which I'm sure I saw Prince George wearing in *Hello!* magazine. I'm slightly mesmerised by how cute they are, and I hadn't really considered that I'm going to get to dress my little one in outfits, day in and day out.

'. . . and this one's for if he's got a temperature.'

I blink and realise that I've not been paying attention to Lou. She's arranged a load of medicines along the mantelpiece.

'Temperature? He's all right now though, isn't he?'

I look over at Harry and he's already found the weak spot in my lounge – he's pulling the scent sticks out of my diffuser. My very expensive DayNa Decker diffuser, which was a thank-you gift from a satisfied bride.

I bend down and scoop them up and back into the pot, placing them out of his reach. Harry's bottom lip quivers and he pauses for a second before he lets out a huge wail. Before I know it, Lou's swooped in and presented him with a plastic digger from her voluminous Mary Poppins bag.

She clearly knows all the tricks of the trade. Harry's frown has gone and he's smiling away once more.

'Here's a list of phone numbers: my doctor's, my mum's mobile number, NHS Direct.'

I look at the list and then back up at Lou.

'You're only going to the hairdressers', right?' I scratch my head, trying to remember whether she actually got me to agree to a longer stint of babysitting.

She tips her head back and laughs. It's the nervous laughter she does when she's uncomfortable. For an awful minute I have one of those blind moments of panic that she's going to do a runner and leave me literally holding the baby, but then I watch her cuddling him and I know that she'd never be able to leave him longer than necessary.

In fact, that could be a problem. She seems very reluctant to go.

'Aren't you going to be late?' I ask, eyeing up the clock on the wall.

'Probably. I'm sorry, I'm rubbish at this. It's bad enough leaving him with my mum or Russell. I practically chuck him at the childminder and run, as it nearly breaks my heart. Not that he cares. As long as he's got his toys, he's more than happy.'

'He'll be fine,' I say, trying to pick Lou up off the ground and release her grip on her son. 'If there are any problems, I'll give you a call. And you're only going to be an hour, aren't you?'

Lou stands up and throws her handbag over her shoulder.

'Yes, that's right, an hour. Or maybe a bit longer as I'm having a colour put on. But I won't be more than two hours tops. Mummy loves you!' She blows Harry a kiss.

He's oblivious and carries on playing.

Lou raises her eyebrows at me, and then before I know it she's legged it out the door. For someone who seemed to be unable to leave a minute ago, she sure scampered quickly.

I look over at him playing away, banging his plastic digger into the foot of the coffee table. I wince slightly as it's teak, and easily scratched. I'm about to move him when I realise that if that's the abuse it's going to get in five minutes, then our little one is going to do a whole lot worse.

Instead I breathe out and let it go. *It's only a table*, I say to myself.

'Right then, little man.' I sit down on the floor next to him. 'What are we going to do for an hour?'

He looks up at me, then around the room, and before I

know it the big lip is back. Uh-oh. What was it Lou did? . . . She picked up a toy.

I pick up his digger and thrust it under his nose, but it's too late. The tears have started to fall and wailing has taken over his body.

Poor boy, he's realised that he's been left alone with me. I look between him and the mountain of paraphernalia and lists left by Lou and I wonder what it is I'm supposed to do. It's the first time I've been left alone with a baby. I'm about to start crying myself, thinking if you can't beat them join them, when a little voice inside my head tells me to pull myself together.

'Harry, Harry, look!' I pull a silly face and shake my head from side to side. He unwrinkles his eyes for a second, enough to see what's going on, and the wailing stops. He continues to whimper as he watches me, yet the more I distract him, the more the lip goes back down. Maybe I'm a baby whisperer after all. Maybe I'll be the most natural mum in the world! He's back to playing with a truck now and I start to relax. This hour is going to fly by.

I walk over to the pile of toys and wonder if Lou's emptied his whole toy chest into her bag. Surely one little boy can't play with all these toys in an hour, can he?

As if reading my mind, Harry gets up, walks in his wobbly way to the pile and pulls out two monster trucks. They're the noisy kind that screech and flash – you would think they'd instantly give you a headache.

'Why don't you play with these instead?' I pick up some nice board books. I flick through them and see the different textures om each page. These seem much quieter.

'Tuck,' says Harry in response, pulling the noisy trucks backwards and letting go so that they shoot forward at an alarming rate.

I manage to move my feet out of the way just before one of the trucks nearly takes my toes off. I try not to take it personally – I'm sure he didn't mean to send it flying in my direction.

I've barely recovered from my near death experience when the other truck starts heading towards a tall vase that's currently got lilies in it. I race over and swoop up the vase just in time. I'm beginning to realise that my house isn't as child-friendly as I thought when I offered to have Harry at mine rather than go to Lou's.

I've literally turned my back for a second, and now he's in the fireplace, taking out the fake coal.

'No, Harry!' I shout, grabbing his hands away. I recognise the bottom lip rising up and his eyes starting to clench shut.

'Digger.' I pull out his favourite toy.

He seems happy with the bright orange toy, and for a

pure blissful moment he sits in one place. In fact, he seems *so* content that I chance a quick business phone call.

'Hello, In Bloom?' says the voice of someone who sounds very busy.

'Oh, hi, can I speak to Antonia, please?'

'Speaking,' she replies quickly.

'Oh, hi, it's Penny Robinson here, from Princess-on-a-Shoestring? You're doing the flowers for one of my brides, Ellie French.'

'Oh yes,' she says with a small sigh. I've clearly caught her at a bad time. 'You're not phoning to change the colour again, are you? It's hard enough ordering flowers around Christmas as it is.'

I'm speechless for a second, trying to process what she's talking about, but before I can ask her I notice that Harry's about to bite into the wooden giraffe ornament that stands in the corner of the room.

'Change of colour?' I move the giraffe. 'I think you must have the wrong bride.'

I hold the phone with my chin as I scoop Harry up into my arms and place him back over on the other side of the room. He seems able to move from one side to the other in a blink of an eye.

Antonia sighs loudly. 'No, definitely your company. I think I spoke to your assistant.'

'My assistant?'

'Yes,' she says tersely. 'She phoned to say that Ellie had changed her mind about red and now wanted hot pink.'

I gasp in shock at the thought of hot-pink flowers; they'd clash with everything – the bridesmaid dresses and *all* the decorations are going to be blood red.

'No, no, no!' I say, shaking my head.

Harry looks up at me and drops his toys in response. He's got that shocked look on his face and I know the tears are about to start falling.

'Not you,' I say, covering the mouthpiece of the phone, but it's too late, the damage has already been done.

I remember how often I've seen Lou appease him by offering him a treat. I run over to the bag of snacks and pick out some fruit and yogurt drops, which look more like hamster food than something you'd give a child. It's amazing how quickly his tears disappear as soon as the treats are in his hands.

'I don't have an assistant, and there's been no colour change – the flowers should definitely be red.'

'Then who did I speak to?'

'I don't know.' I scratch my head. I'm sure that Ellie wouldn't have done it. The only person that would have any motive to sabotage that wedding would be Blake's mother, but surely she wouldn't be that mean, would she? 'Can it be changed back again?'

'I suppose so. I don't put the order through until the week before anyway.'

'That's great,' I say, trying to grab some dried cranberries away from Harry before he grinds them even more into my cream rug. 'If you get any more requests like that, can you let me know?'

'Sure.'

'Thanks. Now I was phoning about another wedding I've got in March,' I say, trying to focus on the job in hand rather than wondering who would have changed Ellie's flowers. I rattle off the date to check she's got availability and arrange an appointment for the bride and me to talk it through with her. It seems weird organising appointments for the new year, but with only four weeks left of this one, everyone seems busy with Christmas events and shopping.

I hastily say goodbye to Antonia as the yogurt drops begin to be pushed up Harry's nose. I don't fancy spending the afternoon in A & E.

'How about we play with this puzzle?' I sit down next to him. Finally a jigsaw puzzle that even I could complete . . . but then again, it's only got four pieces and giant ones at that. I think even Harry could manage that.

Or maybe not.

I try not to cringe as he puts the pieces in the wrong place. After all, the longer it takes him, the longer he's not busy destroying my lounge.

I pick up the phone, content that he's quiet and sitting still.

'Hello!' snaps Ellie.

'Oh, um, bad time?' I wince.

'Oh, Penny. Sorry, I thought you were Blake.' Her voice warms with a laugh.

That's reassuring. She said it like it was OK that she practically bit his head off . . . hardly a good sign before their impending nuptials in a few weeks' time.

'And yes, it's a pretty bad time. The wedding is off.'

'Off?' My throat closes up slightly.

'Yes, off. He's done it this time. You'll never guess what his mother did.'

'It doesn't have anything to do with flowers, does it?'

'No, what's wrong with the flowers?'

'Nothing,' I say quickly. Well, there's nothing wrong now. 'A slight mix-up, but it's all fixed now. Don't worry, I always double-check with my suppliers a few weeks before to make sure the details are all correct.'

Or at least I will now.

I'm thinking about these flowers before it hits me that it

doesn't matter who changed them if there's no wedding. And if there's no wedding, then my company is never going to get out of the red.

I've got to get this wedding back on track.

'What's the problem with you and Blake?' I ask.

'His mother has gone and invited a whole other table of her cronies. Without asking. Apparently Blake had told her it would be OK. He's got no backbone when it comes to his mother, and if he won't stand up to her now, he never will.'

I sigh. This is not really within my remit as wedding planner. I rub my eyes, thinking that Lou's hour at the hairdresser seems to be dragging.

Harry seems to realise I've been distracted and wriggles off the sofa in search of his toys. He settles on the floor and I turn my attention back to Ellie.

'Is that all? Mark, my husband, has this weird relationship with his nan, and I realised a while ago that it's easier to accept it and ignore it.'

'I can't though. This woman is so infuriating! She's practically tried to stop the wedding. I'm sure Mark's nan didn't do that.'

'Actually –' I giggle at the thought – 'she did. Look, when you get married and your Blake's wife, things will change gradually over time. And I'm sure if you have kids it will speed up the process.'

Speaking of kids, I glance at the empty spot where Harry was just moments ago. I continue talking while I start looking for him. Behind the sofa, behind the curtain drapes, but there's no sign of him. I'm starting to panic and I'm barely concentrating on what Ellie's saying.

I finally find him under the dining-room table and I exhale with relief.

'And that's why I can't marry him,' she says.

I look at Harry's cheeky grin and I wonder what I missed whilst I was distracted. I can't ask her to repeat it. Instead I decide to channel her inner bride.

'Oh, that's a shame, as I was on the phone to the florist and the details of your bouquet sounded amazing. And then those delicious canapés,' I say, practically retching at the thought. 'It's going to be such a shame to cancel it all, as I think it was going to be one of the prettiest weddings I've ever planned.'

I'm convinced there's a bride in most women. I'm sure most girls put tea towels on their heads and wore their mum's old wedding dress when they were kids, and I'm hoping this will pull on those bride strings.

'You really think it's going to be that pretty?' she asks, changing her tone.

I pull Harry out from his hiding place underneath the

table, walking him back into the lounge, and close the dividing doors between the two rooms.

'*So* pretty. Such a shame you're cancelling it.'

'I guess that I could work on Blake and his mother's relationship,' Ellie says pensively.

'Really?'

'Yeah, I mean you're right. It would be wrong to cancel the wedding now; we're so close to it after all.'

'That's true.' I sigh with relief. I give Harry a hug, but instead of hugging me back he pulls my hair. Delightful.

'What were you ringing about? Are the flowers OK then?' she asks. The wedding's clearly back on.

'Oh, they're fine. Listen, I've got to run, but I'll call you next week to discuss final arrangements,' I say quickly. I notice that Harry has set off around the coffee table and I'm wondering what he's going to grab next.

I hang up the phone and want to scream. If I thought I was going to be able to run my business whilst looking after my baby, then I've got to think again. I never imagined that it was going to be this tough.

My phone rings and I pick it up off the table to see who it is, thinking I'll call them back later as I'm exhausted from the last few phone calls, but when I see it's my literary agent, I can't help but answer it straight away.

'Hi, Grace,' I say brightly.

'Penny, hi. Great news. I've had a call back from an editor at Talbots and they love the book.'

'That's fabulous!' I say, trying to stop Harry tugging at the curtains in the bay window.

'Yes, they're going to make you an offer.'

'They are?' I drop Harry's hand. I'm too astounded by the news to react to the fact that he's now yanking the curtains even harder.

'Yes. Not too sure on figures, but they should have something over to us by next week. So that's two in the running. It's excellent, really excellent.'

'I don't know what to say,' I reply honestly.

'It's definitely heading in the right direction. I think I should set up meetings with the two editors. How's your diary looking for a week on Wednesday?'

I mentally run my schedule through my mind. It's the week of Nanny Violet's surprise wedding, but that shouldn't get in the way. That reminds me – I must phone her to make the arrangements for our shopping trip to get her an outfit.

'It's pretty clear,' I say, turning my attention back to Grace.

'Great, I'll let you know when I've confirmed.'

'OK. Sounds good.' I sit down and try to take a deep breath.

'I'll be in touch in a few days, Penny.'

I say my goodbyes as best I can and collapse onto the couch. It really looks like my book is going to happen.

I blow out a whistle, but before I can smile I see that Harry's climbing up on the armchair and is starting to lean out towards the bookshelf.

'Harry, no!' I scream, jumping up, as I remember that any celebrations will have to come later.

The doorbell rings and jolts me awake. My mouth feels dry and my mind's foggy and I wonder how long I've been asleep. Ah, a little afternoon nap. Then my eyes fly open and I nearly jump up in panic when I realise I'm supposed to be looking after Harry. I vaguely remember him crawling onto my lap and closing his eyes . . . and there he is, still in my lap, sleeping soundly. He looks like butter wouldn't melt in his mouth.

I lever myself out from under him and position him on the couch with cushions buffering him from the edge, before going to get the door. I look at my watch on the way and see that it's past three o'clock. Lou's been gone nearly three hours? This better be her standing on the other side of the door or she really has done a runner.

'Hey,' she says, barging straight in. 'I'm so sorry, the appointment ran over.'

She marches down the hallway and stops in the doorway of the lounge, her hand over her mouth.

'Bless him. I take it it went well? I was worrying for nothing.'

I hesitate, wondering whether to tell her about it. Between rearranging most of my front room, the dirty nappy (with a smell worse than the bathroom after Mark's used it) and lunch, which has probably stained our table permanently green, there were tears – both his and mine. I know that looking after a kid was supposed to be full-on, but I really had no idea.

'Of course you were. We were fine,' I lie. 'Do you have time for a cuppa?'

'Always,' says Lou. 'I'll just go and pop Harry on the floor.'

I go into the kitchen and put the kettle on. I feel like I've gone ten rounds in a boxing ring.

'Did you enjoy it then?' she asks, taking a seat at the kitchen table.

'It was bloody hard work,' I admit. 'I know you said it was, but flipping heck!'

Lou tilts her head and gives me a look of pity. 'It's worst at first.'

'What, worse than that?' I can't contemplate it.

'Yeah, but don't worry, you get used to it.'

'I hope so.'

I bring the cups of tea over to the table and sit down opposite her.

'Don't worry, Pen, you're going to be a great mum.'

'Thanks, but it's not the mum thing. I don't think it hit me until today how little time I'm going to have. There was me thinking I was still going to be involved in my summer weddings,' I say, letting out the mother of all sighs.

'I've been thinking about that,' says Lou. 'I've had an idea.'

'You have?'

'Yeah, you know how you were saying that you were finding the idea of trusting someone difficult?'

I nod my head. I know I keep putting it off and I'm only making it harder for myself.

'Well, how about me?'

'How about you what?' I'm not following.

'How about I do the summer weddings?'

I look at Lou properly for the first time since she came in. Firstly I notice that her new haircut is lovely, then I notice that she looks nervous. Not as nervous as when she was leaving me with her son, but nervous nonetheless.

'I mean, I know I've not done event planning before per se, but I was thinking I could shadow you at some of the weddings beforehand.'

'But what about your job at the MoD?'

'I'm going to cut down my hours after Christmas. Russell

and I have been looking at our finances and to be honest my wages just about cover our childcare bill each month. So we figured that I'd cut back on my hours, save on the childminding. Then, when you said about the weddings, it sort of hit me that perhaps I could fill in. I mean, I wouldn't be able to work full-time during the week, but I talked it through with Russell and he said he'd be happy to have Harry for the weekend days when I'm doing the weddings.' Lou's waving her arms around as she talks. 'You don't have to say yes. I'd understand if you wanted to get someone with more experience . . .'

I shake my head. 'Lou, you'd be perfect. There's no one I'd trust more.'

She visibly relaxes.

'There's one teeny-tiny thing though. What about your lateness?'

Lou's cheeks flush. She can't deny that she's always late to meet me whenever we have plans.

'I knew that might come up, but I'm never late for work and I don't think I'd be late for the weddings. I mean, I wasn't even late for my own.'

I'm about to point out that that was because I was bridesmaid and ran the clock with military precision, as I always do, but I hesitate. At least with Lou, I'd know what I'm getting into.

'Let's give it a go. My next wedding is Ellie's, and obviously you're a guest at that, but how about you give me a hand with the one after that, in February. We can see if you like it and how you get on.'

'Fantastic,' says Lou.

She's grinning from ear to ear, and for the first time in weeks I begin to feel like a weight has been lifted off my shoulders. Even without the trial, I sense that Lou's going to be perfect.

'To Princess-on-a-Shoestring's newest recruit!' I raise my mug of tea.

Lou chinks her mug against mine and we laugh as we sip our tea. Perhaps I've been worrying about nothing when it comes to my business. I start to believe that everything might just work out after all.

chapter twenty

Ellie @Elliezgood

Shopping trip later on for clothes for my honeymoon. Not long now #4weeksandcounting

Penny Robinson @princess_shoestring

Why not take a look at a @LaceyFran creation? I'm sure you'll find something there to knock more than Blake's socks off.

Ellie @Elliezgood

Oo-er, missus, they're special. Won't tell you what I've gone for — but Blake's in for the treat of his life #whathappensonhoneymoon . . .

For the first time in a long while I wake up excited and happy, rather than feeling like I've had a serious altercation with a bottle of tequila the night before. Of course that feeling returns as soon as I get in the shower, but at least it's a sign of improvement.

But not even the morning sickness can keep me down today. I'm on top of the world. The more I think about it, the more it makes sense for Lou to take over from me with Princess-on-a-Shoestring. I can continue to help out as much as I can, and it won't matter if I'm briefing Lou on details whilst I've got my boobs out feeding the baby, with hair that hasn't been washed in days. Over the years I'm sure Lou's seen me in worse states. I think back to some dodgy holidays to Tenerife in our late teens and early twenties and a couple of music festivals I can't quite remember.

'Are you feeling better?' asks Mark as I practically bounce into the kitchen and over to the kettle.

'No,' I say, grinning from ear to ear. 'I feel pretty rubbish still, but I'm taking Nanny Violet dress shopping today.'

'Oh, I should have known.'

Mark pulls me into him and gives me a slow kiss on the lips. Usually I'd be pulling him in for a longer, deeper kiss, but not today. Not with that coffee breath.

I push him gently away and subtly reach for the packet of Cheerios on the side, hoping they'll calm my stomach.

'I hope she had a nice time on her cruise,' I say between mouthfuls.

'I'm sure she did.'

Mark seems to be concentrating quite hard on arranging the bread in the toaster so that they're perfectly spaced. I can see the look of sadness in his eyes. I know he's still upset that she went behind his back with her marriage to Ted. I'm hoping that the get-together/secret wedding will help to ease the tensions in the family before Christmas.

Also, now that Nanny Violet is back from her holiday, we'll be able to tell the family about the baby. Mark and I have decided that we're going to share the news at Ted and Violet's reception next week. Everyone will be together, and after the day I've got planned, they'll be in a great mood.

'I wonder if she might have got a little bit of a tan, as I was thinking that perhaps an ivory suit – almost a pale cappuccino in colour – might be a nice option for her. Bring out the brown in her eyes. Or do you think I should go with something with a colour to brighten things up, like a lavender to match her blue rinse? She always strikes me as someone who should wear more colour.'

'Mmm.' Mark's intently watching the toast and I know he's not paying attention to me.

'Of course, we'll have to go to Ann Summers and pick out her underwear. I was thinking a basque too, maybe something see-through, with tassels. You know, give Ted a thrill in his old age? Or I could order a pearl and lace thong from the woman I met at the networking lunch.'

'Mmm, sounds lovely,' says Mark, still distracted. 'Hang on – what?'

'I knew you weren't listening,' I say, as he turns away from his toast. 'She didn't mean to upset anyone, you know. I don't think they realised how much it would bother everyone.'

Mark shakes his head. 'I've been thinking about it all this time, and I still can't understand how they didn't realise it would upset people.'

I butter his toast for him, spreading a thin layer of Marmite on the top, just the way he likes it.

'I know,' I reply, handing him the plate of toast, 'but she's happy. This past year since Ted's been in her life again, she's been smiling more than I've seen in as long as I've known her.'

'She has, and I know he makes her happy, but I'm still upset about how they went about it. Anyway – have a fun day, and no Ann Summers shopping.'

Mark picks up his last bit of toast and kisses me on the top of my head. 'I'll see you tonight.'

'Have a good day, honey.'

He turns and walks down the hallway and I sigh. Poor Mark. It makes me appreciate how important today's outing is.

Speaking of which, I said I'd be at Violet's at nine and it's already eight o'clock. If I'm going to be showered and ready in time, then I'd better get my skates on.

I pull up outside Nanny Violet's bungalow and her curtains are still drawn. That's odd. Her curtains are always open at the crack of dawn, which is when she gets up. How else is she supposed to monitor what's going on in the cul-de-sac? Perhaps she's just tired from her cruise, or jet-lagged . . . although jet-lag and Tenerife don't usually go hand in hand.

I turn the engine off and hesitate before getting out of the car. What if the curtains are drawn because Ted and Violet are still in bed? They are newlyweds after all. I shudder at the thought. It's one thing to joke about peephole bras, but it would be another to discover I wasn't far off the mark.

It *is* unlike Violet though, as we did say nine o'clock and it's five to now. I get out of the car and decide to be brave. It's not like I'm going to let myself in; buzzing at the door should disturb anything that's happening.

I ring the doorbell and hear it echo on the other side. I wait, expecting to hear footsteps and the noise of the scrambling of the chain letting me in, but there's silence.

I bend down and peer through the letter box. The house

is quiet. There's no TV or radio blasting away, and with Violet's hearing they're usually at a volume so loud that most of the street can hear whatever she's listening to.

I can't stop my pulse from racing. There's a nasty taste that's developed in my mouth and I'm starting to feel uneasy. As I pull out my phone to ring her number my hand starts to shake.

I can hear the phone through the letter box, but no one's picking it up.

I look up at the house again and wonder what to do. I don't want to call Mark – I can't worry him – when I'm sure there is some perfectly innocent explanation, like she's slept in and doesn't have her hearing aid in.

I call Mark's mum. She's always calm in a crisis. I'm sure she'll know what to do.

'Hello?' she answers.

'Hi, Rosemary, it's Penny. I'm at Violet's house. We had plans to go shopping this morning, only she's not answering the door.'

Mark's mum is the queen of multitasking and it sounds as if she's busy putting away pots and pans in her kitchen.

'She's probably nipped out to get a paper – you know how she can't resist reading the *Daily Mail* first thing in the morning.'

'Um, I don't think so. Her curtains are still shut.'

There's a pause at the end of the line. It's gone eerily silent.

'All of them?'

'Yes.'

'I'm coming over. In the meantime, the neighbour on the left, the one with the red door – Mrs Oakes – has got a spare key. See if you can get in. If not, I've got keys and I'll be five minutes at the most.'

'But what about Ted?' I ask. 'Surely he's there too?'

'No, he was still at his son's house this week packing up his things. We're going to help him move at the weekend. I'm setting off now, so I'll see you soon.' She hangs up.

If I had a sense that all was not well beforehand, then Rosemary has just confirmed it for me. I jump over the small wall that runs between Nanny V's and Mrs Oakes's garden, which feels like trespassing, but I'm sure under the circumstances I'll be forgiven.

I ring the doorbell and almost immediately the door is answered. I can't help but wonder if I've been watched all this time.

'Hello,' I say to the woman. 'I'm Penny, I'm married to your neighbour Violet's grandson and I've been over there and she's not answering the door. We had plans this morning and all her curtains are still shut, which isn't like her.

I've phoned Mark's mum, Rosemary, and she said you had a spare key?'

The seriousness of the situation is written all over Mrs Oakes's face. 'I'll get it now.'

I'm left on the doorstep. I take a few paces back and stare desperately over at Violet's bungalow, willing the curtains to spring open.

'Here we are, love.'

Mrs Oakes is back and she's dangling a key on a blue ribbon. She slips on a coat and some Crocs and shuts her own door behind her.

'Thank you. I'm sure she's just asleep. She was recently on her holiday and maybe she's tired.'

Mrs Oakes gives me a look that lets me know exactly what she thinks of that theory. We arrive at the front door and she takes charge. She's got that no-nonsense kind of attitude that you need in this situation.

The key turns in the door, and to my surprise it opens easily.

'Violet always puts the chain across at night,' I say, my voice faltering.

Mrs Oakes pushes the door open and we both go in.

'Violet?' she calls.

'Nanny Violet?' I echo behind her.

Mrs Oakes heads to the kitchen and I march into the

lounge, looking all round the room in case she's fallen over somewhere. But she's nowhere to be seen. A teacup sits half empty on the coffee table.

'She's here!' calls Mrs Oakes. 'In the bedroom.'

I rush to find them. Nanny Violet's lying across the bed, her eyes closed and her face as pale as a sheet.

I stare at her closely and I can see her lip quivering as she breathes heavily. I almost fall to the floor with relief; for a moment I feared the worst. Mrs Oakes has one hand on Violet's neck and other clutching the landline phone to her ear.

'Ambulance. 11 St Paul's Close, Farnborough. I'm with a woman in her eighties, a neighbour, it looks like she's had a stroke.'

I gasp. I only spoke to her yesterday. I rack my brain to try to remember if she sounded different on the phone but she didn't. She sounded normal.

'I don't know. The curtains were shut, so sometime after it got dark yesterday . . . uh-huh, OK. Thanks.'

Mrs Oakes puts down the phone and props Violet's head up on more pillows. 'Can you give me a hand? We need to roll her onto her side.'

I position myself at her feet and on the count of three we roll her over.

'How do you know she's had a stroke?' I ask, realising that

I would have been completely clueless if I'd come in by myself.

'I used to work in a care home,' she says, stroking away a few of Violet's loose strands of hair. 'I think you probably need to sit down.'

She's right, I do. I don't know how I haven't fallen down already. My head's spinning and I feel like I'm going to faint.

All I can think is, *How am I going to tell Mark?* I know that I've got to. He'll want to meet us at the hospital. I sit down on the chair in the corner of the room and hold my head in my hands.

'Do you want me to call any of her family?'

I look up at Mrs Oakes and think that she must be a mind-reader.

'Her husband. Ted. She got married last month, did you know? He should be told first. I don't have his number. I don't know how to get hold of him. He's with his son and I don't know where his son lives, I don't—'

'It's OK, love. Calm down. Let's start with her son. Have you got his number?'

I nod and stare at the phone in my hand as if I've forgotten how to use it. Before I can figure it out I hear Mark's mum calling.

'Violet? Penny?'

'We're in here,' replies Mrs Oakes. She gets up from the bed and goes to meet Rosemary in the hallway.

I instinctively go over and take Nanny Violet's hand. It's strange – I've never held her hand before. It's wrinkled and weathered but still warm.

She looks like a different woman to the one I saw a few weeks ago at her marriage ceremony. She seems smaller than she was then.

'Penny?' says Rosemary as she walks in.

She noticeably gasps and then comes and puts her arms around my shoulders, before reaching down and patting Violet's hand, which is still resting in mine.

I hear a noise in the hallway and I realise it's the paramedics.

Rosemary gently pulls me back off the bed and we go into the kitchen, leaving the professionals to do their job.

'What are we going to say to Mark?' I look up at his mum.

'I'll do it if you want. I've got to phone his dad, and I guess I should call Ted.'

'Poor Ted,' I say.

'Poor all of them. There are going to be three distraught men in a few minutes.'

We look at each other as if we both know what a mammoth task we've got ahead of us.

But before I can reply one of the paramedics pops his head in.

'We're taking her to Frimley Park. If you head to A & E, they'll point you in the right direction.'

We watch them as they wheel her out and Rosemary thanks them. I'm too stunned to say anything.

'Penny, do you want to come in the car with me?'

There's no way I can drive. I can barely stand, let alone think straight enough to navigate the roads of Farnborough.

I nod.

'We'll phone the men before we set off though.' She squeezes my hand.

I look down at my phone and take a deep breath. It's only going to get worse the longer I leave it.

'Hey, Pen, what's up?' says Mark cheerily when he answers his phone.

'Mark, I'm really sorry, but it's your nan . . .' I say, a lump catching in my throat.

I walk on autopilot to Rosemary's car and fill Mark in the best I can, and I pray we all make it to the hospital before it's too late.

I'm standing outside a curtained-off cubicle in A & E when I see Mark come rushing through the doors. 'Are you OK?' He takes hold of my hands and pulls me into a hug.

I've managed to keep the tears at bay so far, but now I start to sob.

'I'm fine. The doctors are with your nan at the moment. We don't know anything yet.'

Mark pulls out of the hug and wipes away my tears.

He seems to notice his mum's next to me for the first time and goes to her.

'Mum,' he says, before hugging her.

'I'm OK. Your Dad and Howard are on their way.'

'And Ted,' Mark almost whispers.

'His son's bringing him.'

He nods and turns back to me. 'Do you want to sit down? Shouldn't you be sitting down?' He looks round as if he's trying to spot a chair.

'I'm fine, Mark, really,' I say.

'No, you've had a nasty shock and you can't, I mean I don't want you fainting or anything.'

'It's fine,' I repeat, taking hold of his hands again. 'We've had sugary tea from the vending machine, and I've had some chocolate.'

I notice that Mark's mum is looking at us as if she's trying to figure out what's going on, but before she can say anything the doctor appears from behind the curtain.

'It looks like Mrs Hamilton has had a stroke. We don't know yet how severe it was. With strokes it's all about how quickly it was caught. I believe it was several hours before she was found.'

The doctor pauses to look up from his chart for a moment before his eyes go back down and he flicks through his papers.

'I'm afraid now it's a waiting game. We're all waiting to see when, or even if, she regains consciousness and from there we can assess the impact. Now, are any of you her next-of-kin?'

'That's my husband, her son,' says Rosemary. 'He'll be here in a few minutes.'

'No, he's not,' I say, shaking my head. 'It's Ted, *her* husband. Her *new* husband.'

'Right,' says the doctor, looking at each of us in turn as he speaks. 'He'll have some difficult decisions to make. He'll have to decide whether he thinks she'd want to be resuscitated as we don't have that information in her notes.'

I take hold of Mark's hand and squeeze it, and I feel him squeezing back hard.

'I'll let you know if there are any further developments.'

'Are we allowed to go in?' asks Mark.

'Of course. Go in and talk to her normally – the sound of familiar voices can sometimes help to bring patients round. Right now it's a case of wait and see what happens.'

We thank the doctor and go round the other side of the

curtain. If I thought that Violet looked small and shrunken before, it's nothing compared to how she looks now that she's hooked up to drips and monitors.

Mark goes over and scoops up her hand, and for the first time in a long time I see him cry. I stand alongside Rosemary and let him have his moment with his nan. I can't hear what he's whispering to her.

'My Violet!' says Ted as he rushes into the cubicle, followed by his son.

I gently go over and take Mark's hand as he backs away. Mark surprises me by turning to Ted and giving him a hug.

After a couple of moments Ted pulls away and pats Mark firmly on the back before going over to Nanny Violet.

'I should have been there,' he says, taking the hand Mark had been holding.

'You weren't to know,' I say quietly.

'Still, she shouldn't have gone through this alone. Thank goodness you went round when you did. I'd called her this morning and thought she must be in the bath when she didn't answer.' He shakes his head and I see a small tear roll down his face.

'Don't beat yourself up,' I say. 'All you need to do is be there for her now.'

Ted sits down on the chair. 'Has the doctor been round?' he asks.

Rosemary sits down in the chair opposite him and explains what the doctor told us.

'We'll give you some space,' says Mark, before taking my hand again and leading me away.

Outside the cubicle I lean into his shoulder and he pulls me in close.

'I've barely spoken to her since the wedding,' he says. 'I've been mad at her and now she might never wake up.'

I almost don't recognise his voice it's all faint and shaky.

'You weren't to know.'

'But she doesn't know how much she means to me.'

'Believe me, she knows. She'd know that you weren't going to be mad at her for long and that you wouldn't have been mad at her if you didn't care so much. And you'll be able to tell her. She's going to wake up. She's Nanny Violet. She hasn't waited this long for a great-grandchild from you not to be around to see it be born.'

'Great-grandchild?' asks Rosemary, startling us.

Mark and I pull apart. I hadn't realised she was there.

'Does that mean what I think?' she asks. Her eyes contain a mixture of joy and sadness and for a moment none of us knows how to react or what to say.

I nod my head and give a weak smile.

'Ah, Penny!' she says, giving me a hug. 'You've given me a little ray of sunshine on an awful, awful day.'

'We've only just had the scan. We were waiting until next week – Violet's reception – to tell everyone,' I say by way of explanation.

'Of course. I won't say anything, but please tell Violet when you can.'

'I will,' I say. 'I will.'

I just hope she'll hear me.

I step back, and for the first time since arriving at Nanny Violet's doorstep I take a moment to reflect on what's happened. I can't believe how quickly the day descended from being one of hope and expectation to being the worst day I can remember in a long time.

Any petty worries I had about keeping the baby a secret from the brides-to-be, or about Princess-on-a-Shoestring's future, fade away, and all I can think about is Mark and his nan.

chapter twenty-one

Ruby Blair @sparklyslippers

@princess_shoestring Penny, are you not getting my emails?

Rachel Burton @Onlyrachburton

@sparklyslippers She might have a bit on her plate at the moment, I'm sure she'll get back to you when she can.

Ruby Blair @sparklyslippers

@Onlyrachburton Sounds cryptic . . . #whatsgoingon?

Rachel Burton @Onlyrachburton

@sparklyslippers Not my place to say – but I'm sure she'll answer you when she can.

Rachel Burton @Onlyrachburton

@princess_shoestring Hi Penny, hope all went well last week with you-know-what. Let me know if you need anything xxx

It's been three days since I found Nanny Violet after her stroke, and I feel as if I've been treading water. Every day has been the same: Mark and I get up and drift around the house like zombies until visiting hours begin. Mark's supposed to be working from home, but I keep catching him staring into space. I've been making him endless cups of tea, and I've even been baking cakes. They've been coming out a bit burnt and they're only borderline edible, but the process of making them is the only thing that seems to take my mind off everything.

Ellie's wedding is rapidly approaching, as is the Christmas party I'm supposed to host, and I can't face thinking about either. It seems callous to be doing such trivial things when Nanny Violet is so desperately ill.

The morning sickness seems to be waning, and whilst I thought I would be stuffing my face to make up for all those lost calories, I've got no interest in food.

I've been trying to keep up the pretence of working, but I've had no inclination to do any real work. I would have thought that planning a happy event would cheer me up a little, but it really hasn't. I've barely opened my emails or looked at Twitter. All that work to keep the brides-to-be happy with all their little whims, and now I can't even face returning answerphone messages. I can't seem to find any enthusiasm or be bothered to fake a happy voice these days. Instead I've been taking cowardly ways out and texting them to say I'll be in contact soon, too worried that my voice would wobble and I'd erupt into tears.

'My mum just phoned,' says Mark, coming into the spare room. Since he's been working from home it's forced me to use the office upstairs. It's pretty cosy up here, with the little radiator and the futon that I've packed with extra cushions. I've got a packet of biscuits and my big commuter cup of tea. It makes me feel a bit more like I'm at work rather than at home. Ironic, as I now don't feel like working at all.

'Any change?'

'No. Still the same.'

He sits down on the futon and I swivel my chair round to face him. 'She'll wake up, Mark. She's a strong as an ox, your nan.'

Nanny Violet hasn't opened her eyes since the stroke. She's mumbled a few words and answered a few of the doctor's basic questions about who she is, but we're not too sure if she's aware of us or not as her eyes remain shut.

I rub his knees and he shakes his head in frustration.

'What if she doesn't? What if she dies and she never knows how sorry I am? It all seems so stupid now. If marrying Ted made her happy, why was I so resentful?'

Mark's been giving himself a tough time. He's even finding it difficult to sit by her bedside and he's camped out instead in the visitors' room at the end of the hallway of her ward. His entire family have taken it over and they seem to gather there at most visiting hours.

'You weren't to know; no one was.'

'I know, but it seems so stupid now. And seeing Ted at her bedside, well, you can see how much she meant to him.'

If there was anyone to feel sorry for more than Mark, it's Ted. He looks awful. He's been there every visiting hour too, but he's withdrawn and quiet, a shadow of his usual self.

I can't even begin to imagine how he must be feeling. I know that he went through a lot when his first wife died a few years ago, and now here he is again with a wife who's critically ill.

'Anyway, I was thinking I might give visiting a miss this afternoon. Mum was saying that the doctor reckons that if she hadn't come round right away it might be a while, if at all.' His throat catches on the words. 'I was thinking that it might be better if I go into work and then go to the hospital this evening instead.'

'I think that's a good idea,' I say, meaning it. It's probably doing neither of us any good moping around the house together. We'd do better to try and focus on other things.

'Do you? You don't think it's too soon? You don't think I should be there – just in case?'

'No.' I continue to pat his knee in what I'm hoping is a reassuring way. 'I think that your nan would hate you taking time off work to hang around that waiting room. You know her – she'd probably wonder what all the fuss was about.'

Mark laughs a little. It's nice to see his smile. They've been as rare as rainbows in our house this week.

'You're probably right, but it doesn't make me feel any less guilty.'

'I know. We'll go tonight though, and your mum will let us know straight away if there's any change.'

'Yeah. Right, I'd better go and get changed into my suit then.'

I watch him go out of the room, and despite neither of us being particularly good company, I'm going to miss him being around the house today.

I look at my neglected to-do list and I wonder what I can face doing. I squeeze 'Phone Ted' in near the top of the list. I've wanted to be at the hospital to check he's OK too and give him some moral support. Underneath that, I've written 'Cancel Violet and Ted's surprise wedding'. I've been in denial about the whole thing, expecting her to wake up any day and miraculously be all right for Saturday week. But the longer she keeps her eyes closed, the more it starts to register how much care she will need if she does come round. Even after the best prognosis, a reception next week is out of the question.

Reverend Phillips at the church already knows about her medical condition and told me not to worry about cancelling until I was ready. Which leaves Cathy. I sigh and take a deep breath. After her I'll have to phone the caterers and Violet's flower-arranging friend from church who had agreed to do the table centres.

'I'll see you later on then,' says Mark despondently as he pokes his head round the door frame on his way out.

'OK, honey. Have a good day, and phone me if you need to.'

'Will do.'

His footsteps sound heavy down the stairs and the house shakes when he slams the door. The sound of silence fills the room and I suddenly feel lonely as a wave of sadness passes over me. I can't face ringing Cathy just yet. Instead I pick up the tablet and go downstairs to check my emails whilst I make a cup of tea.

I'm halfway through checking my personal Facebook account, seeing what everyone's had for breakfast and which babies have been keeping their mummies up all night, when I hear the notification pings of tweets and emails.

The tablet's ringing out with beeps and squeaks and I

wonder what's gone on. It hasn't gone this mental since I ran a competition when I first launched the business for one lucky bride-to-be to win a free wedding planning package.

I start with the emails, and see that three of my brides have messaged me, as well as other people.

From: Sally <SallyWally@rocketmail.co.uk>
To: Penny <Pen@shoestring_princess.com>
Subject: Is it True????

Is it true?????? Please tell me that it's not. And to think I had the chance to go with Peasbody weddings. I'm sure that it wouldn't have happened with them! CALL ME ASAP.

I read the email twice and wonder what on earth Woodland Sally is on about. I quickly close her email and open the next one.

From: Ellie <Ellie.elliezgood@hotmail.com>
To: Penny <Pen@shoestring_princess.com>
Subject: none

You all right hun? I take it my wedding's OK?

Call if you need

E xx

I can't read the emails quickly enough.

From: Shelly <<u>RobertandShelly@orange.co.uk</u>>
To: Penny <<u>Pen@shoestring_princess.com</u>>
Subject: wow

Blimey Pen, you work with someone for years and never realise. No wonder you wanted to start your own business, huh?! We'd always take you back. Now that I'm HR supervisor I could hire you back no problem. Robert had a problem with the bookies a while back, but he's all sorted now. If you want us to help with anything let us know.

Shelly xx

What the hell is going on? Why is my old work rival Shelly talking about her boyfriend's gambling habit?

My blood runs cold as I try to connect the dots between the emails.

I flip open my twitter app to see if my twitter stream makes any more sense.

Hayley Fowler @HayFow1982
@princess_shoestring OMG! Is it true? Those poor brides.

Weddings R Me @weddings_r_me
@princess_shoestring I'm disgusted. One wedding professional to another, it's like you've broken a code.

Knot Tying Blogger @Knottyeblog
@princess_shoestring I can't believe it. You were one of my blogging idols #letdown

There are loads of disappointed people tweeting me. What am I supposed to have done? My eyes scan down the list until I see a RT with a link.

The Wedding Guru @Wed_Guru
Scandal alert: RT @weddingwoohoo: Wedding planner gambles away brides' deposits @princess_shoestring wp.me/GTY5HI

My index finger starts to shake as I hover over the link and I press it, closing my eyes momentarily, not knowing what to expect.

What appears is a wedding blog, one that I've never read before, and staring back at me is a picture of myself sat at the blackjack table. It's taken side on, so you can see me throwing a chip down and smiling at the same time.

I walk slowly backwards and find a kitchen chair. I need to sit down before I faint. I can't believe it. I almost can't bear to read it.

Wedding Planner Gambles Away Brides' Deposits
Wedding blogger turned planner Penny Robinson, from Princess-on-a-Shoestring, has a secret. She's a gambler. Pitching herself as a budget wedding planner, she preys on her unsuspecting victims and takes their hard-earned money to use it for her gambling fixes.

I can't believe anyone would write this. I mean, it's such lies. The only proof they've supposedly got is a photo of me playing a game of blackjack at a wedding fair, and no money even changed hands. Why on earth would people believe that?

Poor Penny has been seeking help, attending Gamblers Anonymous meetings – yet from the recent snap of her at a casino, we can see it's a lost cause.
Her brides have been reporting all week that she's been impossible to get hold of. Has she gone on one big gambling binge? Has she spent all their money?
We love a good gossip in the wedding world, but shame on you, Penny, for ruining people's dreams.

I stare open-mouthed at the picture of me standing in one of my gambling support group meetings. I'm standing up in the horseshoe, talking. The faces of the other members have been pixelated, like they do on the telly, but you can see me there as clear as day. And in case people assumed this was any old meeting or event, there's a pile of books on the table behind where we're sat, and every single one is on a gambling theme: *Get Over Your Gambling*, *Roll Away Your Addiction*, *Gamble No More*.

I feel myself starting to shake. How could anyone possibly have found out? I scour the blog to see if I can find any personal information about who wrote it, but there's nothing. In fact, the blog is pretty new with only a few entries on it, including this awful exposé.

It reminds me of Ellie's flowers that mysteriously changed colour. With everything that's been happening with Nanny Violet I hadn't given it another thought, only now I can't help thinking that it's all connected.

I stare at the photo, willing it not to be true, and rub my eyes to try to stop the tears from falling, but I can't. I've been trying so hard to stay strong for Mark, but now, in the face of this, I can't hold it together any longer.

The doorbell rings and my first thought is to ignore it. What if it's going to be one of those scenes like in the movies where the unsuspecting victim finds herself in the centre of a media storm? It happens all the time, doesn't it? Small story on a blog gets picked up by a local media outlet, and then it snowballs from there.

I'm going to stay firmly here, hidden away from the paps, whilst I'm in my PJs.

'Pen?' I hear, through the letter box. 'Pen, are you in there? Open up.'

I sigh with relief. It's just Lou.

I practically run to the front door and open it, collapsing onto her in a hug.

'There, there,' she says patting me on the back. 'I came as quick as I could when I saw.'

She pulls back from me, leads Harry through to the kitchen and deposits a mountain of toys on the floor for him to plough through.

'When you didn't answer your phone I was so worried.'

'My phone?' I say slowly. 'Oh, I've left it upstairs. I'll go and get it.'

'No, you sit down. After the shock you've had, you need to rest. I'll pop the kettle on and go and get it. Is it in your office or the bedroom?'

'Office,' I reply feebly. I take Lou's advice and plonk myself down on a chair.

Whilst she goes upstairs I help myself to some kitchen roll, blow my nose noisily and wipe away the tears.

'You've had quite a lot of missed calls,' says Lou, walking in and handing over my iPhone. I look down and see I've had seventeen missed calls in the last fifteen minutes. Mostly from brides, but some from Lou and Josh. Oh no. How does everyone know already?

'I can't believe this. I mean, who would do it?'

'I don't know. Where was the photo from?'

'It was from that wedding fair I went to a couple of weeks ago. I'd gone to talk to the casino hire people and they were busy, so I thought I'd give it a test run. It wasn't for money,' I say hurriedly. 'The person with the most chips was going to get a free hire at their wedding and I'd thought, if by some miracle I won, that I'd give it to Vegas Melissa.'

'You didn't know your photo was being taken?'

'I did, that's why I'm smiling and posing. They said it was for the promotional material for the wedding fair. This makes no sense.'

'OK,' says Lou authoritatively. She walks over to the freshly boiled kettle and makes us both tea. 'Let's think about this logically. When was the other photo taken?'

I think back to the day I spoke to our group. 'I was talking about my ideas for the Christmas do. The photo makes me look like I'm confessing my shameful sins, but I was standing there trying to work out whether more people thought we should do traditional Christmas or go for a curry.'

'OK. When was that?'

I close my eyes and try and remember. I barely know what day it is at the moment, let alone what week it is.

'It must have been last week. I didn't go this Tuesday because of Nanny Violet and –' I pick up the tablet and squint – 'that's Josh next to me. We talked about his wedding. So definitely last week, as he wasn't there the week before.'

'Does it narrow down who it could be? Someone at the wedding fair and also at your gambling group?'

I shake my head. 'No, it can't be anyone from there.'

I try and think back to what I did that day and who I met. It had been a busy Tuesday. I'd been running around like a headless chicken, trying to get my work done on time to make it to Nerinda's dress launch.

'Oh,' I say quietly.

'What?'

'Georgina Peasbody.'

'That other wedding planner?' says Lou, placing the tea down and sitting opposite me at the kitchen table.

'Yes, that's right, the one who's launched her own budget weddings and has been trying to steal my brides.'

'No!' Lou screeches, causing Harry to drop his toy in alarm, hunch his shoulders and wail. 'Oh, Harry sweetie, I wasn't talking to you.'

She sweeps him up over her shoulder and starts kissing him on the cheeks as she pats his back.

'Mummy was talking to Auntie Penny.' She rocks him from side to side. 'I can't believe she'd do this though, would she?'

'It has to be her. She was at the wedding fair and then she was at the wedding dress preview. I told her I was off to scope out a new venue and she must have followed me. That's why she was rushing to her car. Cheeky cow.'

'She thought that you were onto some new hot lead and what she found was your group.'

'Uh-huh, and then she used it against me. Now I'll be lucky to keep any of my brides. From the state of my twitter account, my reputation is in ruins.'

'It might not be that bad,' says Lou.

That line might have worked if she'd said it on the phone, but I can see the face she's pulling.

'It's worse than bad. All that hard work . . . These last few weeks have nearly killed me, running around after all the brides, and now they're all going to go over to Peasbody's.'

'You don't know that.'

'I do.'

Across the table my phone starts to vibrate and I reach over to look at it, expecting it to be a bride-to-be, but it's my literary agent. I'm hoping she hasn't seen the blog. I pick up the phone, wincing.

'Hi, Penny,' she says calmly.

'Hi, Grace. How are you?' I stammer nervously.

'I've been better. Listen, I've just had a phone call from Joanne, the editor at Evans, and it looks like they've seen the blog this morning and they've cancelled the meeting.'

'They've seen it?' How has it gone viral this quickly? 'But it's not true! You've got to tell them it's not true. I would never do anything like that.'

'True or not, it's all over social media and it's put a lot of people's noses out of joint in the wedding community. Joanne feels that this type of thing could hang around for a while. It might be best to cease trying to sell the book at the moment, and give it a go next year when the dust has settled.'

'Right,' I say. I feel like I've been punched in the gut. I don't have the energy to try to argue or plead with her to change her mind. 'Thanks for letting me know.'

'I'll be in touch soon, Penny. Chin up.'

She hangs up and I wonder if that's the closest I'll ever get to a book deal. I put the phone back down on the table and lay my head next to it, closing my eyes. This really is turning into the worst week ever.

chapter twenty-two

Suzie K @floozie_sooz

Please call me back @princess_shoestring. I don't want to believe it's true, but with this radio silence I can't help but think it is.

Ellie @Elliezgood

@floozie_sooz I've known Penny for years and I can't imagine that she would do this. She cares too much. There must be another explanation.

Suzie K @floozie_sooz

@Elliezgood I hope you're right, I really do. I'm waiting for the lake house to get back to me to confirm my booking #fingerscrossed

'Right, that's it. I'm not going to sit here all day and read emails and tweets full of hate,' I say, finally lifting my head off the table.

'What are you going to do?' asks Lou, folding her arms and giving me one of the sensible looks she's adopted since becoming a mother.

'I'm going to go and confront Georgina, give her a piece of my mind. She can't go around writing things like that. It's slanderous, or libellous, or whatever it is, she can't do it.'

I've started pacing the kitchen, which is a lot trickier to do when it is littered with toddler toys. I almost break my neck on a flashing fire engine and decide that perhaps I'd better be furious on the spot.

'Calm down, Penny,' says Lou, getting up from her chair and directing me back to mine.

'I can't! She's destroying my livelihood. I've worked so hard to get this business off the ground, and she's destroying it.'

'She may have put a fly in the ointment, but it will come down to how you handle it as to whether you can salvage it or not.'

I don't think Lou understands the severity of the situation.

'How an earth can I salvage it?'

'For starters, you can phone your brides back and tell them that it isn't true.'

I glance back down at the tablet as it pings at the arrival of yet another email. I don't want to even look at it.

'What am I going to say to them? That a person made it up, and that there's an innocent explanation but by the way I *am* a former gambler?'

'Well, yes,' says Lou, draining her tea.

She lifts her cup to ask if I want another. I nod my head. There's something so comforting about tea in these types of situations. Thank heavens I'm well enough to drink it now.

'I can't tell them about the gambling; they'll never trust me again.'

'What choice do you have?'

'I could ignore everyone's calls, eat ginger nuts, then take extended maternity leave.'

'No, you can't. I'm counting on you for a job, remember?'

I'd forgotten about that. In the past I've let myself and Mark down, and now I'm adding Lou and my brides to the list. All because of my gambling. It's like a shadow that never goes away. It's going to haunt me forever.

'I'm sorry, Lou.'

The rage that had temporarily subsided starts to bubble up again. If it wasn't for Georgina Peasbody, then I wouldn't be in any of this mess. I also wouldn't have had to keep the baby bump secret, and therefore I wouldn't have been acting suspiciously around my brides. I wouldn't have had to go out of my way to keep their bookings, and I might have been enjoying my early pregnancy.

'I need to have it out with Georgina.' I stand back up.

'You will do no such thing,' says Lou, giving me a glare.

I slump back down in the chair. Since she's become a mum she sure has turned into one tough cookie.

'But she can't get away with it!'

'No, she can't, but you can't fly off the handle. That's probably what she wants to happen. Plus, you haven't got any proof it was her.'

A sarcastic laugh comes out of my mouth. 'Who else would it be?' I roll my eyes.

'I know it's *probably* her, but getting mad is not going to help your business. Right now you need to sort yourself out and devise a strategy. Have you told Mark?'

'No,' I say. 'He's got so much on his plate with Nanny Violet, I can't tell him about this.'

'You can't tell him about this when he's at work, you mean? You are going to tell him when he comes home, aren't you?'

I look sheepishly around the room, focusing on Harry, who seems to have found a loose bit of skirting board underneath my kitchen cupboards.

'Penny, you will tell Mark, won't you?'

'Lou, I can't. He's barely speaking and he's so upset – this would send him over the edge.'

'But you promised him no more secrets.'

'I know, but it's not like I'm deliberately hiding this from him out of malice. I'm trying to protect him.'

'But Mark always knows what to do.' Lou deposits the freshly made tea in front of me. She's made it extra milky and sugary, and even though it's piping hot, if I take teeny tiny sips I can just about drink it.

'Usually he does, but he's not thinking straight at all at the moment – although I'm sure he'd support me in my need to go round to Georgina's and give her a good telling-off and maybe a cheeky slap.'

Lou raises her eyebrow at me. 'You know as well as I do that that's not true.'

I sulk for a minute. She's right; Mark would side with Lou on that one.

'Look, we've got to make a plan of action. Why don't you write a list of all the brides that have contacted you and start by phoning them, followed by the ones that haven't got in touch.'

'Really, Lou, I can't face it.'

'I don't want to hear it,' she says, thrusting pen and paper at me.

There's not much more I can do to protest. I hastily write my list and Lou pushes my phone closer to me.

I look at the first name and take a deep breath as I dial the number of a client that I've dubbed Maze Katerina. I planned the majority of the details of her wedding back when I took her on as a client a couple of months ago and now we email occasionally just to keep in touch before her wedding next April. Out of all my brides, she's one of the less demanding ones, yet I've had four missed calls from her this morning.

'Penny!' she practically screams as she answers the phone.

'Hi, Katerina. I take it you've seen the blog post?' I say, screwing up my face and hoping the missed calls were merely a coincidence.

'Oh yes, I've seen it,' she says snidely.

'I want you to know it's not true, and that your venue and deposit are more than safe.'

'Are they really?' she splutters down the phone. 'Then how come I've phoned the venue and they said that you'd cancelled the booking? Where am I going to get married now? And where's my money?'

'There must be some mistake. I haven't cancelled any venues – yours or anyone else's.'

'Oh really? And I suppose you're not a gambler either.'

I pause. I want to scream and tell her that I'm not, but I can't lie.

'I did have a gambling problem once. But I would never have used anyone else's money and I certainly wouldn't have ruined anyone's wedding,' I gasp.

What on earth is going on? How could the weddings have been cancelled?

'You've got a week to send me the money you owe me,' she says icily.

'But it wasn't me,' I say feebly.

'Whatever, Penny. All I can say is, thank God the wedding's not until April and I've found out now. At least I've got time to organise something else. It's a good job that person wrote the blog post.'

I'm too shocked to reply.

'Next week, Penny. Or else I'll take you to court.'

The phone line goes dead and I stare at my handset. What is happening?

'Did it go badly?' asks Lou. She's nervously nibbling on a HobNob.

'You could say that. It's making no sense. I've got to phone another one,' I say, practically on autopilot.

'Hello.'

'Hello, Kirsty?' I say, keeping my fingers crossed that this phone call goes better. 'It's Penny from Princess-on-a-Shoestring.'

'Oh, it's *you*,' she says in an accusatory tone. 'I wondered if I'd be hearing from you today. I've just got off the phone with the marquee hire company, and they said that they've never received my deposit.'

'But that's impossible!' I distinctly remember addressing the envelope with the cheque inside. It was a few weeks ago, I think. I slipped it into my Filofax and into my bag. My Filofax is on the table and I do a quick flick through to make sure that it isn't still in there. But a quick shake confirms that it's empty.

'Oh, is it? Because from where I'm sitting, it seems like that blog post was telling the truth.'

I'm lost for words again. I thought it would be a case of phoning and telling people that it was lies and that everyone would be pissed off but essentially relieved and that they'd forgive me. I never imagined they'd find any truth in it.

'I don't know what to say.'

'I don't think there's much you can say. I want my money back, Penny.'

'Of course,' I say. 'I'll get to the bottom of this and return it to you.'

We say our tense goodbyes and I put the phone down and start to cry.

'I don't understand, Lou. The brides are saying it's true and they've phoned the venues.'

Lou's face confirms how serious the situation is. 'You're going to have to phone more to see how many are affected.'

'Do I have to?' I screw up my face.

'Afraid so. I'll make more tea.'

I take a deep breath and decide on a change of approach. This time I do a quick phone call first to the venue to check. Relieved that they've still got the booking, I dial the bride.

'Hi, Sally, it's Penny here.'

I hold the phone a few inches away from my head as Woodland Sally starts screeching.

'Penny, I've been trying to reach you all morning! Not to mention all week. Where have you been? Is it true?'

'No, the majority of that article is lies.'

'The majority. So some of it's true. I *knew* it. That's why you wouldn't give me my cheque back because you'd already spent it.'

'No, that's not—'

'And to think I almost didn't go with you. Is my wedding safe? Am I still going to be able to have it at the nature reserve?'

'Of course you are.' My cheeks are burning. I'd expected these phone calls to be difficult, but I at least hoped that

I'd be appeasing people. This is so much worse. They actually think that I'd ruin their weddings. 'Sally, I would never spend your money. Your wedding is safe. The article is by a bitter woman trying to ruin my business, nothing more.'

'But you said that there was some truth in it.'

'Well, technically there is, but—'

'No buts, Penny, I gave you a second chance before. I'm not going to give you another one. You're always vague when I talk about what you'll be doing on the day, and now I know the reason. I understand that usually I wouldn't get my deposit back, but is there anyway we could come to some arrangement? I'd obviously like to keep my wedding the way you'd planned it . . .'

'Just not using my services,' I say with a hint of sarcasm.

'Right.'

'So the work I've put in already, finding the venue and suppliers so far, you wouldn't want me to be paid for any of that.'

There's silence on the end of the phone.

'Sally, your wedding is going to happen exactly like we planned it. Please let me explain the whole story. I think your wedding will be amazing and I'd love to see it through.'

'I don't know, it's all been such a shock. You wake up thinking that you're going to have your dream wedding, then a couple of hours later your whole world falls in and you realise that it was built on lies.'

I bite my cheek in frustration. Believe it or not, this was how I used to view weddings. That they were the be-all and end-all. I nearly ruined my relationship with Mark on a quest to have my own magical fairy-tale wedding.

Unlike Woodland Sally, I woke up this morning worried that Nanny Violet wasn't going to recover from her stroke and that that would make the world a sadder place. Not to mention how it would hit my husband terribly hard. It's as if Woodland Sally has made me remember what's important again.

'Your whole world, Sally? As I see it, nothing has changed. Your wedding is intact. You've still got a wonderful fiancé to marry, and a venue where the deposit is safe. If you want to know why I've been avoiding you this week, it's because my husband's nan had a stroke and is in hospital. If I've ever been vague or distant about your wedding, it's because I'm pregnant and my baby is due in the summer. I'm training up my best friend Lou to do the weddings whilst I have my baby and whilst it's a newborn. I've been waiting until my three-month scan and until Lou was confirmed to work for me, so that I could break the news with her present, and so that my brides can get to know her.'

There's a moment of silence on the other end of the

phone and I wonder if I've gone too far. At this moment in time though, as much as it pains me to let one of my brides go, it's not worth the hassle. If she doesn't want to believe me, then fine. I've realised that in the grand scheme of things, it's not important. The whole company is likely going to fail anyway. If it's this hard to convince Sally, how am I going to convince new brides once they see that article plastered all over the Internet?

'I see,' she says eventually. 'I'm going to have to talk to Liam and call you back. I'm not entirely happy with the situation, but if you say that you still have our money . . .'

'I do.' I sigh as silently as I can.

'I'll talk to Liam.'

She hangs up without so much as a goodbye and I stare at my phone in disbelief. Three down, fifteen to go.

'I take it that didn't go so well either,' says Lou as she comes back in from the lounge, where she's put Harry down to sleep in a travel cot.

The old Lou I used to know would come round to get ready for a night out and often forget to bring her heels or her make-up, yet this new mummy Lou seems to travel with every piece of equipment sold in Mothercare. It's a shame that Princess-on-a-Shoestring is about to go under, as she'd have been perfect to handle the on-the-day wedding emergencies that crop up.

'You could say that.' I drain the last of my tea and wish that it wasn't so frowned upon (or so damaging) to have a large glass of wine during pregnancy. I can't face any more tea – unlike wine, there's a limit to how much tea I can drink. 'But at least her venue's intact.'

'Well, that's good, right?'

I'm beginning to wish that Lou had taken Harry home for his nap. Her usually welcome positivity is starting to grate.

'Right, Penny, phone the next one on the list.'

'Do I have to? I feel like I'm going to be sick.' I pull my best sad face and droopy eyes.

'Pen, you've got more colour in your cheeks than I've seen for weeks. You're forgetting that I've held your hair back more times than I care to remember, I'm well versed on what you look like just before you vomit, and now isn't one of those times.'

I stick my tongue out at her, only half joking.

'Pick an easy one. Someone you know either won't have seen it or won't mind.'

'Really, can't I take a break?'

The look in Lou's eyes says that I can't. Instead I see Ellie's name on the list. Her wedding is nowhere near the summer, which means the baby reveal won't play a part in it, and as I've known her for a long time, I'm hoping she'll believe my version of events.

As the phone rings, Lou gives me a thumbs-up of encouragement and I stand up from my chair and walk over to the corner of the kitchen to give myself a bit of space.

'Hello?'

'Hi, Ellie.' I take a deep breath before exhaling as I launch into the explanation.

Managing to convince Ellie to stay with me doesn't feel like much of a victory as she's almost a friend; if anyone was going to stand by it would be her.

'It could be worse,' says Lou as she packs up Harry's toys.

'How? I've lost two brides and I've only spoken to four, not to mention that Woodland Sally is on the brink of defecting. I'm scared to phone any more. At least this way I can pretend that the rest of them are all going to use my services.'

'Of course they are. Those two brides had rubbish weddings anyway. Who wants to go to a wedding on a property that has a maze?'

'Me,' I say sadly. 'It looked really fun.'

'Yeah, but I bet there would be drunk people doing it in the middle by the end of the reception.'

'Lou!' I wrinkle my nose up.

'I've got to make you smile somehow.'

'No chance of that.' I run my fingers through my hair. I'm sure I washed it this morning, but it feels all knotty and greasy now – I've been taking out the frustration of my phone calls fiddling with it. 'I can't face speaking to another one of the brides.'

'Perhaps we need a different plan of attack.'

I look up at Lou in horror. I expected the same panto-mime sketch that we'd had before the other four phone calls. *I don't want to call, but you have to. Oh no, I don't. Oh yes, you do.* Only now she seems to think it's a bad idea, and that's got me even more worried.

'What do you mean?' I ask as calmly as I can.

'I mean that perhaps you need to break your Twitter silence. Tweet to tell people it's not true.'

'As if anyone will believe me. It's my word against Geor-gina's, and then there are the photos.'

'So explain them. Maybe you should come clean. Tell people the real story.'

I take a sharp intake of breath at the thought. How could I admit to people that I used to gamble? It's shameful enough that *I* know that I used to do it, let alone if everyone in the wedding industry knew it too.

'I can't do it,' I say, shaking my head. 'There's got to be some other way.'

We both look at each other as if we're trying think of a magical solution, but from the look on Lou's face I know that she's got the same as me: absolutely nothing.

'Don't forget, there's always Mark,' she says.

The cry from the lounge lets us know that Harry's awake and Lou goes to him. She's right about Mark – he would know what to do – but I can't burden him with this.

In the end I decide on a new plan of action: to do absolutely nothing. I reach over to my tablet and turn it off. I do the same to my mobile, before feeling guilty and turning it back on in case there's a call about Nanny Violet.

I like my new plan. This mess isn't going to go anywhere; it will still be there when I want to stop hiding from it, which, if I can help it, isn't going to be anytime soon.

chapter twenty-three

Georgina Peasbody @PeasbodyWed
For any brides recently let down by @princess_shoestring, check out my free wedding planning service wp.me/344hrkr

Sally Jessop @Jessoplady
@PeasbodyWed Starting to wish I'd gone with you after all #hindsightisawonderfulthing

I've been in the shower for almost fifty minutes and realise I can't stay in here any longer. Getting out, I notice my hands are wrinkled like prunes and when I wipe away a patch of steam from the mirror I see that my eyes are just as puffy as they were before. They were so swollen from all the crying that it looked like I'd had an allergic reaction. I had been hoping the shower would improve things, but no such luck.

I've been trying to wash off the day, but the utter misery of the situation is pretty indelible.

As I can't hide in the bathroom forever, I decide instead to get ready before Mark comes home. We're supposed to be off to see Nanny Violet tonight, but I might get him to go alone. I don't know if I've got the energy. Seeing Ted sitting by her side, looking like a broken man, and me trying to be strong for both of them.

'Pen?' I hear from outside the bathroom door.

I must have been in the bathroom longer than I thought if Mark's home already.

'I'll be out in a sec,' I say, slipping into my dressing gown and wrapping a towel round my hair.

I open the door and walk into the bedroom. Mark's sat on the edge of the bed, loosening his tie. The shadows under his eyes have grown darker as the day's gone on.

'How was it?' I try to avoid eye contact so that he can't see that I'm looking guilty.

'It was OK. There was lots to do, so the day went by pretty quickly. Quicker than if I'd been here. Mum was pretty good too – she kept texting me every couple of hours to tell me that there was no news.'

'That's good of her.' I go over to my chest of drawers and dig out my pyjamas.

'Are you not coming to the hospital?' he asks, pointing at my legs. I've got one leg in my checked flannel PJs.

'No,' I say as I continue to get dressed. 'I've got a bit of a headache.'

My heart sinks as I lie, but it's actually not untrue. The stress of the day's events has left my head pounding.

'It's been a tough week, and especially with you in your condition. You should take it easy. Put your feet up and watch a movie. I can bring up the DVD player and hook it up to the TV in here if you want.'

'It's fine,' I reply limply. He's being so lovely, it's making me feel terrible. 'I'm sure there's something on TV I can watch. To be honest, anything will do right now.'

He nods and starts to take off his work clothes. 'I'll cook us some dinner before I go to the hospital.'

'You don't have to. I'm not really hungry.'

'Nonsense. You have to eat something. What about cheese on toast? You still OK with that?'

'Yes. Thanks.'

The doorbell rings and the two of us look at each other, trying to work out who it could possibly be. We're not expecting anyone.

'I'll go,' I say, as he's in his boxers and socks. Not a winning look in any situation.

ANNA BELL

The closer I get to the front door, the more a feeling of uneasiness comes over me. I worry it's going to be press, and like that scene out of *Notting Hill*, that I'm going to get papped.

I open the door and squint through scrunched-up eyes, then sigh with relief when I see that it's Josh.

'Josh!' I burst into a smile, my shoulders dropping. For a minute I thought it was an angry client on the doorstep. The smile fades from my face when it dawns on me that he *is* a client. 'Don't tell me you've heard.'

'I have,' he says. 'I thought you might need someone to talk to.'

I hear the stairs creaking and I briefly consider slamming the door on Josh before Mark makes it halfway down and sees who our visitor is. But I'm guessing that Josh would ring on the doorbell again and I wouldn't want to confuse both men any further. The best I can hope for is to encourage Mark out to visit Nanny Violet, and for me to talk to Josh alone.

'Hello, Josh,' says Mark, reaching the bottom of the stairs. 'Come in out of the cold. It's freezing out there.' He gives me a look as if I've forgotten my manners.

'Of course, yes, come in.'

Josh does what he's told and I shut the door behind him. For a minute we all stand there and no one says anything.

'What brings you here?' asks Mark, looking between us. 'Or is it secret squirrel stuff that you can't tell me about?'

Mark's laughing, but he's hit the nail on the head.

'I came round to see how you were. I heard the news this morning.'

Mark nods and I break out into a cold sweat. How does Mark know, and why didn't he say anything to me?

'That's really kind of you,' says Mark. 'It was a bit of a shock for Pen, finding her like that.'

I can see the confusion on Josh's face. He goes to open his mouth, probably to protest, but I seize the opportunity to talk before he gets a chance.

'That's right, it was a huge shock finding Nanny Violet unconscious but it's not led me to think about doing anything silly gambling-wise,' I ramble, my eyes scarily wide. I hope that Josh can take a hint.

'Right,' he says, thankfully playing along. 'How is she now?'

'No better. We're hoping she'll wake up, but we really don't know.'

Mark's eyes glaze over, and I rub his back in support.

'Why don't you head off to the hospital now?' I say. 'We can have our tea when you get back.'

'Are you sure?' he asks, looking at me, concerned.

'Yes, I'll eat a couple of biscuits.'

He gives me a small smile. 'I'll bet you will. Josh, you and Mel will have to come for dinner at some point soon, when things settle down.'

'Absolutely,' says Josh.

Mark picks up his winter coat and puts it on. 'I'll see you in a bit.' He gives me a quick peck on the cheek and picks up his keys from the hall table.

'See you then,' I say.

I shut the door behind Mark and I lead Josh into the kitchen.

'Penny, what are you doing keeping secrets from Mark again?'

I sink down into the chair that I spent most of the afternoon in. Josh perches alongside the sink. He's got that James Dean poster-boy look going on, and he almost looks like he's posing for a photo shoot.

'I didn't want to, but he's so cut up about his nan that I couldn't put this on his shoulders too. How did you find out?'

'Mel follows you on Twitter.'

'I'd forgotten that,' I say.

'After he decided that we were going to use you as a wedding planner, he started reading me out your tweets on a daily basis until I agreed to ask you. He told me about your blog this morning, and I've been trying to contact you ever since. When you weren't answering your phone, I was worried.'

'I'm sorry about that. I saw you'd called and meant to return it. It's been manic. As you can imagine, it's freaked out a few of my brides. You know it's not true, don't you?'

I can see Josh hesitating before he answers. 'Is there no truth in it at all? You were acting really strangely last Tuesday, and when I saw the photo of you at the blackjack table, it suddenly made sense.'

I'd forgotten that I'd washed my hair, and my hands get stuck in the wet tangles as I try to run my fingers through it.

'It wasn't what it looked like. There was no money involved. It wasn't even at a casino – it was at a wedding fair. Other than that, I haven't done any gambling at all. Everyone's money is safe. Mine included.'

Josh smiles and comes and sits down opposite me at the table. 'How did the blackjack make you feel?'

I narrow my eyes at him in surprise. Out of all the elements of the story, he's focused on that. 'It made me feel pretty guilty.'

'Is that why you were acting funny at the group?'

'Yes, and no,' I say, taking a deep breath. 'I should have told you about the blackjack, but I was embarrassed about the buzz I felt when playing. I thought that it would be harmless and it wouldn't mean anything. I mean . . . it wasn't like I was going to win anything other than a chip that had no monetary value. But I felt great when I won, and then I felt terrible, like I'd let myself down.'

'So what did you do when you started to feel bad?'

'I stopped playing,' I say, looking up at Josh, who's nodding at me. 'What?'

'Don't you see? You've come so far. You stopped when you realised you were doing wrong.'

'But shouldn't I have not done it in the first place?' I rub my eyes in tiredness. The day has really caught up with me.

'You probably shouldn't have, but you stopped as soon as you realised. You put yourself in control again.'

'I guess.' I shrug.

I hadn't thought of it in that way. I'd been so focused on berating myself for putting myself in that position that I hadn't stopped to put it in perspective. If everything else wasn't so awful around me, then I might even have been the tiniest bit pleased with myself.

'So what was the other reason you were acting funny?'

I hesitate. I don't really want to tell Josh about the pregnancy. I lost my cool and told Woodland Sally and I've felt guilty ever since. I feel bad that I'm telling people out of order. Mark's mum knows, but mine still doesn't. It doesn't seem right that I should tell Josh before her.

'I can't tell you. Or at least I don't want to tell you yet.'

'OK,' says Josh slowly. 'Does it have something to do with my wedding?'

'Yes and no,' I say again, knowing that I sound ridiculously cryptic.

'Well, we haven't parted with any money yet, so I know that at least we're safe on that score.' He winks at me.

Gosh, Josh is beautiful. If he wasn't gay and I wasn't married, I'd have seriously melted at that wink.

I gurn in his direction to show my displeasure at his joke and he smiles even more.

'Being serious though, what are you going to do? How are you going to tell everyone the truth?'

What is it with everyone and their insistence on the truth all the time? What's wrong with living in denial and burying your head in the sand? They're two underrated coping mechanisms in my book.

I've started fidgeting involuntarily and I'm fiddling with my fingers, hoping that Josh will take that as a sign to back off.

'Penny, you are going to tell everyone that it's not true, aren't you?'

I squirm a bit more.

'Penny, you have to clear your company name!'

'Do I? Do I really?' I ask, knowing full well what his answer will be.

'Yes, you do.'

I sigh like a teenager.

'You remember what it was like coming clean to Mark when you had your gambling secret, and do you remember how much worse you made it when you tried to hide it?'

'Yeah, but he had to forgive me as he was in love with me.'

I think back to how even that forgiveness was touch-and-go, and how after the misunderstanding in the summer, when he thought I was gambling again, I realised that our trust is still pretty fragile.

'That might be true, but you've got to tell people.'

'What do you recommend? Doing another cheesy video?'

I think back to my pleading video, where I explained to Mark about my addiction and what I was doing to try to cure it.

'There are worse ideas. You could put it on YouTube.'

'YouTube?' I screech, practically hyperventilating. It's bad enough having had most of my family and Mark's watch the original video and know about my gambling habit, let alone the whole world.

'Yeah, it would set your story straight.'

I shake my head. 'I can't do it. I'd rather see the business fold around me. I can't have everyone knowing what I did.'

Josh looks at me and I can tell he's disappointed.

'OK, but I'm here if you need me,' he says.

'Thanks, Josh, I appreciate it, but as usual I've made my own mess, so I'll have to lie in it.'

Only with the mood I'm in I want to lie in it for a long time. I'm going to go back to being an ostrich and hope that when I take my head out of the sand this will all have been forgotten.

I jolt awake, not remembering when I fell sleep. The lights are on and the TV is blaring away. That seems to be a common theme of my pregnancy at the moment – one minute I'm awake and the next I'm waking up having dribbled all down myself.

'What time is it?' I ask, rubbing my eyes to focus them on Mark, who's leaning up against the door.

'Sorry if I woke you. It's just gone half past nine. I'm a bit late as I dropped my mum off home.'

I sit up in bed and prop myself up. I came up after Josh went, mainly because it's the warmest room in the house and my bed is so snugly and cosy. I had been planning on watching TV, but I don't remember seeing anything.

'Did you eat?' I ask, my stomach lurching at the thought of food.

'Sort of. I grabbed a pasty at the hospital. I was going to make something now though. Do you want anything?'

I shake my head and reach over to my pack of crackers by the side of the bed. 'I'll have a couple of these.'

'Are you OK?' Mark sits down on the bed and puts his hand on my forehead.

'I'm fine.' I smile, ignoring the little voice in my head that desperately wants to tell him the truth.

'Are you sure?'

'Uh-huh.' I grin as best I can. 'How was your nan?'

Mark's sigh says it all. 'No better. In fact she seemed worse. I was toying with the idea of taking tomorrow morning off. I know that mum kept me up to date today, but she can't get there till later tomorrow and I keep thinking what if something happened and no one was there?'

'Ted's going to be there, isn't he?'

'Yes, he is, but then I don't think I'd want Ted to be on his own, if . . .' He tails off, unable to put into words what we're all dreading.

'I know.' I squeeze Mark's hand. 'How about I go? I feel bad not going today, and then it would save you from having to take more time off.'

'But what about you? You look shattered. And what about your work?'

I would do pretty much anything to distract myself from my work at the moment.

'There's nothing that can't wait until tomorrow afternoon.'

Mark leans over and gives me a hug. 'Thanks then, that would mean a lot. It would be comforting knowing you're there.'

I feel ridiculously guilty for not being honest with him, but I'm shielding him for his own good, aren't I?

'I'm going to make my dinner.' He gets up. 'Are you sure you don't want anything?'

'No, thanks, honey.'

'OK then. I'll let you get back to sleep.'

He walks out of the room and I feel my heart ache a little more. When we got married I promised him I wouldn't keep any more secrets and here I am lying again. It doesn't matter that I've got his best interests at heart; it still feels like I'm doing the dirty behind his back. It seemed like such a perfect plan this afternoon, but I'd forgotten how awful lying to Mark makes me feel.

chapter twenty-four

Louise Marsden @justharrysmum

Uck, feel so useless. My best friend is going through a really rubbish time and there's not a lot I can do to help.

Ellie @Elliezgood

@justharrysmum Is she OK? Thank god my MIL isn't on Twitter. If she got a whiff of this she'd be trying even harder to stage a wedding coup.

Louise Marsden @justharrysmum

@Elliezgood She's going through the mill all right. Can't wait to meet your mother in law at the wedding . . . !

Ellie @Elliezgood

@justharrysmum Ha – you're the only person! The less of her I see on the day, the better. Give Pen my love xx

It's strange, you'd think walking into the hospital to visit Mark's sick nan would plunge me into sadness, but for a split second when I walk in the door I feel a sense of relief. It's like visiting Violet has legitimised my morning off work, and my avoidance of the fallout from the blog post.

I find the ward where Nanny Violet is, remembering to take a dollop of hand gel as I go in. I'm rubbing it in when I spot Ted sitting by Violet's bedside. He's clutching her hand and he looks a million miles away. I feel a pain in my chest as I imagine what it would be like if that was Mark and me in many years' time.

I realise that I'm standing still in the middle of a busy ward, but I don't want to interrupt what looks like an intimate moment.

Ted looks up, as if he's sensed my arrival, and waves me over.

'Hi, there,' I say, sitting on the spare plastic chair by the bed.

'Hello, Penelope. Nice to see you, love.'

'Any change?' I ask hopefully, but Violet is looking paler and thinner than she was two days ago. Her face is beginning to look gaunt, and despite the drip in her arm feeding her, she looks like she's wasting away.

'None. The doctor's rounds were much the same as the last couple of days.'

I look back at Nanny Violet. Maybe Mark's right to be thinking the worst.

'What I can't get over is how quickly it all happened. I mean, one minute she's on that cruise with you, and the next she's here like this.' I wave my hand across her body.

I look up at Ted and he's staring at his hands. I get the feeling he's avoiding eye contact.

'Ted, it was unexpected . . . wasn't it?'

I see him fidgeting in his chair before he meets my gaze. 'It wasn't a total shock, not to me,' he says quietly. 'Look, don't tell Mark or any of them as Violet made me promise not to, but she had a mini-stroke in the summer.'

My jaw drops slightly as I take in what he's saying. 'A mini-stroke? How did we not notice it?'

'There weren't any lasting repercussions, so it was easy to hide. We might have missed it too if Violet hadn't been going to the doctor's for her flu jab. She happened to mention that she'd had some difficulty writing a cheque that morning and the doctor sent her to the hospital for tests.'

'But why didn't she tell anyone?'

'You know Violet – she didn't want to make a fuss or for anyone to worry.'

'So she knew this was going to happen?'

Ted's head seems to shrink down further into his shoulders.

'The doctor at the hospital warned her that an event like that is often the precursor to a bigger stroke. He told her to be prepared and gave her some advice of things she could do to lower the risks. Of course, Violet said she didn't want to change how she was living at her age and that she was happy that she'd had her time.'

'Is that why you got married so quickly?'

The pieces are falling into place for me now. 'Yes, but we didn't imagine this would happen when it did. The doctor said it could be months or years. If I'd have thought there was any chance, then I would never have left her on her own.' He shakes his head.

'You can't blame yourself for that. It could have happened at any time.'

'I should have been with her.'

I'm reminded of the conversations I've been having with Mark. If only he and Ted knew each other better – they have a lot more in common than they think.

I look back at Violet with fresh eyes. If she'd just told everyone about the mini-stroke. There's no way that Mark would have been so mad at her, and there's no way he would have been sulking with her when she fell ill.

'You know Mark's never going to forgive himself for being so cross with her about your wedding,' I say.

Ted nods. 'She knows how much he loves her – she told

me on the cruise that Mark would come round. She understands he was just in shock.'

'I don't think that will be any consolation to him.'

I wish that we could go back a few weeks and all this could have been done differently. I think back to the time in the registry office and if we'd known about this ticking time bomb then I'm sure that all of us would have looked on the situation differently. I'm sure there wouldn't have been so many down faces at Wetherspoons, and we'd all have been a lot more understanding.

'I'm sorry, Penny. In hindsight it would have been better to tell everyone.'

'Honesty's always the best policy,' I mutter hypocritically.

Ted's gone back to stroking Violet's hands. 'I really love her, you know. I can't bear the thought of her getting ill when she was there all on her own. It took a lot of convincing to get her to marry me.'

I smile warmly at Ted, wishing I didn't feel too awkward to go and give him a big bear hug.

'Do you know she made me sign a prenup?' He chuckles.

'She did? Wow, I never knew that Nanny Violet was so up on modern matters.'

'Oh yes, she didn't want anyone to doubt our intentions. After the mini-stroke she got all her affairs in order.' He shrugs. 'I didn't mind. It's not like I needed anything she had – it was only her I wanted.'

My heart starts to break as I hear the pain in Ted's voice. 'I think, whilst you're here, I'm going to go and get a spot of lunch.'

I look at my watch. It's just after eleven. Talk about an early-bird special.

'OK, I'll keep her company,' I say, taking her hand in mine.

'Thanks, Penny. I'm glad you're here.'

He pats me on the shoulder before walking off down the ward. I turn back to Nanny Violet and stare at her.

Alone with my thoughts, I start to think about the blog and I feel the anger rising up in me until I realise that I'm probably squeezing Violet's hand a little too strongly.

'I'm sorry Nanny V,' I say. 'I'm not having a good week.'

I look round the ward self-consciously to see if anyone is looking at me as if I'm crazy to be talking to an unconscious person. But no one is paying me any attention.

'It's Princess-on-a-Shoestring,' I say with a sigh. 'Some woman's written this blog, and argh –' I shake my head – 'let's just say it's probably ruined everything and my business is going to fail. I haven't told Mark yet. He's so worried about you, I don't think he'd be able to handle it. I've tried to take your advice and be honest with him since we've been married, but I've never seen him this upset before. And then there's the baby.'

I look up Nanny Violet's face and gently rub her arm. 'Of course you don't know about that, but Mark and I are expecting our first baby at the end of June.'

I shut my eyes and try to stop myself from crying. I can't imagine Nanny Violet not being around to see our little baby.

I hear a mumble and open my eyes to see Violet stirring. Her eyes are still shut.

'Pen . . . Pen . . .'

'Violet!' I lunge forward. I can't believe she's spoken.

'Baby . . .' she murmurs.

'Don't try and talk. I'm going to get a doctor.' I look at the buttons by her bed and am trying to work out which one I'm supposed to press to call a nurse. I've been watching too many episodes of *Grey's Anatomy* lately and I don't want to accidentally summon all the doctors to rush here with crash carts. In the end I push the big red button and cross my fingers, hoping for the best.

'Baby . . . Mark baby,' she mumbles.

I grip her hand tighter. 'That's right. Mark and I are having a baby.'

I look around frantically, hoping that a nurse will come quickly.

'Ted's here. Well, not now this minute, he's gone to get some food, but he hasn't left your side.'

'Ted,' she repeats. It sounds muffled, like she's talking underwater.

I flounder for my phone and scroll hastily through my numbers. I find Ted's, having put it in my phone when Violet came into hospital, and I press call.

'I'm ringing him now,' I say, still holding her hand and trying to keep her with me. 'He'll be here in a minute.'

'Hello?' answers the voice down the phone.

'Ted, come back, Violet's awake!' I say, as if using any more words would send her back into her sleep.

'I'm coming,' he replies.

It's like we're on the same wavelength as he hangs up immediately.

'We've all been here – Mark especially. He feels terrible that he was so cross about the wedding.'

'He shouldn't worry.'

Her speech is slower than normal, and it's all gravely and hoarse, which is understandable seeing as it's been days since she's last spoken, but at least she's speaking. I vaguely remember the doctor saying something about that, but I don't think I took it in.

'You know he loves you very much,' I say, wishing he was here to tell her himself.

'I know.'

I sigh with relief. Nanny Violet's awake – that's the main thing. I hope that Ted gets here quickly as I'm desperate to phone everyone else to tell them.

'Tell Mark about your problem.'

'Oh God. Did you hear me wittering on before you woke up? Don't worry about that – you've got much more important things to think about than my silly problems.'

'Tell him.' She sounds firmer.

An uneasy feeling starts to sweep over me as I realise that she hasn't opened her eyes. She's talking but her eyes are still firmly shut.

'What's going on?' says a voice behind me.

I turn and see the short, stout nurse who was here on Violet's first day. She has one of those warm smiles that you don't forget.

'She's woken up. Her eyes are still shut, but she's talking.'

The nurse comes closer and leans over the bed. 'Violet? Violet, I'm Janet the nurse – can you hear me?'

'Yes,' replies Nanny V.

Janet looks up at me and I'm trying to gauge what her look means when Ted turns up.

'Violet, it's me, darling.' He swoops past me and scoops up her hand.

'Theodore,' she says slowly with a large exhalation as if she was waiting for him.

I walk slowly away. It's bad enough that they've got to speak to each other with the nurse there. They don't need me earwigging too.

I practically run into the relatives room and dial Mark's number.

'You'll never guess what!' I say as soon as he picks up and before he's even said hello.

'What – she hasn't?'

'She has, she's woken up! Well, not completely, her eyes are still shut, but she's talking, making sense. She knew who I was!'

'I can't believe it. I'm coming straight over.'

'OK, see you soon.'

I hang up the phone and clutch it to my chest. I've now got to phone the rest of Mark's family.

I take a second to process what Nanny Violet said to me: tell Mark the truth. She's right, and with her awake it will make it easier to tell him.

It feels amazing to phone Mark's family and give them the good news. I'm hanging up the phone from my final call when I see Ted coming towards me.

'How is she?' I ask.

I'm sure by now that she's wide awake and asking to

see everyone else. I can let her know that they're all on their way.

'She's gone again,' he says, his eyes dropping to the floor, but not quickly enough to hide the sadness in them.

'But she'll wake up again soon, won't she? I mean, it's a good thing that she woke up at all.'

Ted comes all the way into the relatives room and sits down on one of the padded chairs, his head in his hands.

'The doctor said that she might wake up again, or . . .'

He brings his head up to look at me and he fiddles with his hands, which are trembling. A lump catches in my throat.

'Or what?'

'Or she was just having a surge before . . .'

He doesn't need to finish the sentence.

'No, that can't be it,' I say, firmly shaking her head. 'She's got to talk to Mark and Howard and . . .'

I stop as the reality sinks in.

'Pen? Is it ok to go and see her? Is the doctor with her?'

I look up and see Mark hovering in the doorway, hope etched on his face. When his eyes meet mine I can see him register that something is up.

'What's wrong?' he asks, looking over his shoulder, ready to bolt in her direction.

'She's gone back to sleep,' I say slowly. 'The doctors aren't sure if she'll wake again.'

'No,' Mark mutters. He turns and walks off in the direction of the ward.

I let him have a few minutes' head start before I go after him.

'I should have been here,' he says as I wrap my arms around his shoulders.

'You weren't to know she was going to wake up; she could have done it at any time.'

'I know, but I could have told her.'

I pull back and retrieve the other chair from the far side of the bed. Putting it next to Mark's, I take one of his hands. 'She told me that she knows how much you love her.'

'She did?' He breaks his gaze, which has been focused on Nanny Violet.

'Uh-huh. I also told her that we're going to have a baby.'

Mark smiles and a tear rolls down his cheek. 'I bet she was pleased.'

'I think she was.' I smile at him and start to gently rub his hands.

'She's not going to wake up again, is she?' asks Mark, turning back to look at her.

Looking at her now. the tiny amount of colour she'd had has drained away.

I squeeze Mark's hand tighter as if to give him an answer and he begins to sob silently, his shoulders moving up and down. I let go of his hand and pull him into a hug. My poor, poor husband.

As I hold him as he rocks and shakes, I think of Nanny Violet's last words to me and I know that I've got to tell him about Princess-on-a-Shoestring. But not just Mark. I realise I've got more people to tell than him. Lou and Josh were right – it's time to be honest with everyone.

chapter twenty-five

Katerina @KrazyKat

Of all the wedding planners to pick, why did I pick @princess_shoestring? #epicfail

Ruby Blair @sparklyslippers

@KrazyKat I doubt the blog is true. There's something else going on. There's got to be #princessshoestring

Katerina @KrazyKat

@sparklyslippers I don't think so, I've had my venue cancelled

Ruby Blair @sparklyslippers

@KrazyKat You have?? Yikes, poor you. I'm hoping there has to be more to it . . . @princess_shoestring please tell me there is.

'There's something else that Nanny Violet said to me earlier,' I tell Mark as we arrive back home to our terrace. The doctor had told us initially that it could be days before the inevitable happened, but she's gone so rapidly downhill in the last couple of hours that Mark's dad suggested we all say goodbye to her one by one, leaving Ted and him to be alone with her when the time comes.

Rosemary invited us all to their house so we can be together, so we're just popping back home to freshen up before we go over there.

'What?' asks Mark, sitting down on the couch.

'She told me to tell you the truth. Now, before you say anything,' I say quickly, as I can see the look he's starting to give me. 'I'm not hiding a big secret like last time. Something happened with Princess-on-a-Shoestring and I haven't wanted to tell you because of your nan. Now, this is no better timing, but your nan told me to tell you, so here goes. Someone, I'm presuming Georgina Peasbody, has been sabotaging Princess-on-a-Shoestring.'

'What? How?'

'The colours of the flowers were changed for one of my weddings and then there's this blog post,' I say with embarrassment. 'They wrote a blog about me, claiming that I've gambled away my brides' deposits.'

Mark isn't saying anything, but he's looking at me in disbelief.

'I know it's terrible timing.'

'It's just not the timing. I'm trying to keep up. Why would she write that in a blog and what did it say?'

The easiest thing for me to do is to pick up the tablet that's lying on the coffee table. I load the blog and hand it to him to read.

I pace around the living room as he takes it all in, and when he whistles through his teeth, I go and sit back down next to him.

'The photo is from when I went to that wedding fair with you, remember? I played a hand of blackjack – just pretend, not for money – before I spoke to the hire company.'

Mark nods at me before reaching out a hand and finding mine.

'I can't believe you've known about this for twenty-four hours and you haven't told me. Are you OK?'

I let out an enormous breath which I hadn't even realised I'd been holding. I don't know how I expected Mark to react, but this wasn't it.

'I've been better, but mostly I've been ignoring it. I've lost two brides already, one's on the fence and I've still got loads to call.'

'They don't believe her, do they? I mean, one simple phone call to their venues will tell them that this is all a pack of lies.'

'That's the really strange thing. The two that cancelled their weddings checked with the venues and both *had* had their bookings cancelled. From the texts and answerphone messages, I think they're the only two, but it doesn't help when I'm trying to convince people it's not true.

'It also hasn't helped that I've been acting weird, what with the hiding the baby bump, and then this week I've been hard to contact because of Nanny V. I think the brides have put two and two together and got five.'

'Have you spoken to Georgina?'

I shake my head. 'I don't have any proof that it's her. The blog is anonymous and only has a few other entries on it. When I spoke to the venues where the weddings had been cancelled, they told me that someone from my company had phoned. That got me thinking about the colour of the flowers being changed at Ellie's wedding.'

'How do you know that wasn't a mix-up at the florist's?'

'She told me that someone from my company phoned and changed them from blood red to hot pink.'

I can see a hint of a smile on Mark's face. 'Sounds like a disaster.'

'It would have been for Ellie – the flowers would have clashed with everything.'

'And you think it's Georgina that's done that and written the blog?'

'Who else could it be? I saw her at the wedding-dress launch, which was right before I went to my gambling group.'

I try to come up with a different explanation, but I can't.

'And what about the flowers? How would she have known about them?'

'That's the bit I can't figure out. Unless she went to the florist's and saw the information in her book.'

I rub my eyes as if trying to make my brain work harder.

'The only places I've got that information are in my wedding files, which live upstairs, and in note form in my Filofax, which is here,' I say, holding it up.

'What about that time you lost it?' asks Mark, looking at it suspiciously.

'I got it back, and it was right where I lost it,' I answer, before I feel the colour draining from my face as it hits me.

'What?' asks Mark.

'The woman on the phone said that it hadn't been handed in – she'd have remembered as she was working on that Friday. What if Georgina took it and then returned it later?'

'I'd usually tell you you were thinking crazy, but after reading that blog post I don't think you're jumping to false conclusions.'

I think about the other information in the Filofax and I gasp.

'I bet it was her that changed the date with the caterers on Ellie's wedding too. That's why the chef had the day after written in his notes. He'd said that it had been changed by his wife, and he thought it must have been in error, but what if it wasn't?'

My blood's running cold – what if those aren't the only things that she's changed?

'What are you going to do about it?'

'I don't know. All I know is that I've got to tell the truth and let everyone know that this isn't me.'

Mark puts his arm around me. 'We'll figure something out, Pen.'

I lean into him and hope that he's right.

'If you're going to tell the truth, including about the baby, there's a few people we need to tell first,' he says.

I nod my head. I'd been thinking that too.

When we pull up outside Mark's parents house, we sit in the car for a minute.

'Are you sure you're ready to do this?' he whispers in my ear.

'Absolutely,' I say. 'Are you sure it's the right time?'

'Yes, it's only family, and you're right – it's best if they find out before everyone else.'

We walk into Mark's mum's house, where everyone has

gathered. I'm apprehensive to be there at first – it feels like we're all in limbo whilst we wait for something bad to happen. I soon join in with Howard's family, who are sitting on the floor looking at old photo albums.

After a few minutes I realise that there's something comforting about us all being together at a time like this. It's turned into a sort of celebration of Violet's life as we laugh over the pictures. Amongst the funny photos of Mark with his curtains in his teenage years, and him and Howard in matching dungaree sets as little kids, there are wonderful pictures of them all happy with Violet.

I look down at the photo in my hands of Violet holding either Mark or Howard as a baby and I'm struck by how happy she looks. If only she'd got to hold our baby.

'Didn't you have something to say, Penny?' asks Mark mum, looking at me with a twinkle in her eye.

I look around the room, at Mark's family, most with red, puffy eyes from fresh tears. I really hope we're doing the right thing. We asked Mark's mum earlier what she thought, and she agreed that now was a good time to break our news as it would give people something happy to focus on.

'Actually, I do. Everyone – Mark and I have some news.'

Howard and his wife Caroline look up from the photo album they're leafing through, and their two boys stop playing in the corner.

'We're having a baby,' I say slowly, as if testing the water with each syllable.

'Ah, Penny, that's great news!' says Caroline, jumping up.

'It is,' says Howard. 'Congratulations, bro.' He slaps Mark on the back.

The two little ones come over and fuss around my belly and start giggling about their new cousin and for a minute or two it's like everyone's forgotten why we're all here.

The front door slams, and we all look at each other, knowing that the only person who would be walking through the door right now would be Mark's dad.

He walks into the room and his face says it all.

I reach out to Mark and he's staring open-mouthed. His dad shakes his head, and a single tear rolls down his face.

'It was so peaceful,' he says. 'She just slipped away.'

Rosemary hugs her husband and I watch as Caroline brings her two children to sit on her lap and whispers to them before hugging and kissing them as they begin to cry.

Howard and Mark remain frozen, as if they're processing what's happened.

I stroke Mark's hand and he looks over at me.

'At least she knew about the baby.' He tries to smile, yet the pain's evident in his expression.

'Yes, and she seemed pleased,' I reply.

He reaches over and pats my belly as if he needs to feel the new life as Nanny Violet passes on.

Ted slinks into the room quietly, and after rubbing Mark's arm I walk over to him. He looks dazed and confused. I steer him over and sit him down on the sofa next to Mark and I pat him on the back.

'I hope I'm not imposing,' he says to me. 'Alan offered, and I didn't want to be on my own.'

'Of course. I'm glad you're here. I would have been worried about you if not,' I say.

'I didn't know if I'd be imposing on your family,' he repeats, the words catching in his throat.

'You're part of this family,' says Mark. 'Nan would have wanted that.'

I'd been keeping the tears at bay, but at that moment, watching Mark reach out his hand to take Ted's, my heart seems to ache and the tears fall.

'You missed out on the news,' says Mark's mum to his dad.

'What's that, love?'

'It looks like you're going to be a grandad again,' she says with a small smile.

Mark's dad looks over at Caroline.

'Oh, not me this time,' she says, pointing to me and Mark.

'Is that right? Another baby Robinson?' He looks hopefully over at us, and I smile and nod.

'Mark, Penny, I'm so happy for you,' he says, walking over. Mark and I stand up and I give him a hug.

'I couldn't have thought of a better time to have news like this. It really is circle-of-life stuff.'

I try not to let *The Lion King* drift into my mind at such a serious and poignant time, but I can't help it. The tears that had started to trickle earlier are now coming out in waves as the whole plot of *The Lion King* plays out in my mind and I see that moment where the father dies and it's like a delayed reaction to Nanny Violet passing.

'Pen,' says Mark, giving me a squeeze.

'It's OK,' I wail. 'I'm OK.'

But I'm not. Ever since I've been part of Mark's family, Nanny Violet has been such a key part of it. We've had our differences and she may have tried to stop my wedding, but I think that only brought us closer together. The thought that she's not going to be around any more is almost too much to comprehend.

It makes me even more determined that I've got to keep my promise. I've got to save my business and tell the truth.

chapter twenty-six

I wake up with my eyes and head heavy from the emotion of the day before. We spent a good few hours at Mark's parents house. Everyone, except me, cracked open the Bailey's, in honour of Violet's faux-pas when she drank half a bottle, not realising it was alcoholic, and it led to a lot of laughter and funny stories about her. I'm sure it was what she would have wanted, rather than us moping around feeling sad.

On the way back to our house, we stopped by and told my parents about the baby. My mum practically had kittens, and then made us Skype my big sister Becky, who was also delighted. The miracle of new life is truly a lovely thing to have happening at such a horrid time.

'Are you sure you want to go through with this?' asks Mark as he sits up beside me in bed. It's almost becoming his catchphrase.

After Nanny Violet dying yesterday, all I want to do is stay in bed, snuggle with Mark and watch movies, but I know I've got to sort out Princess-on-a-Shoestring.

'Yes, it needs to be done,' I answer resolutely. I don't know how I keep getting myself in such stupid situations. As far as I can tell, this one isn't even my fault. 'I'll go and get in the shower,' I add, but I'm only delaying the inevitable.

An hour later, Mark drops me outside the civic centre. Thanks to the modern technology of Twitter, I know that Georgina is definitely going to be at the networking meeting today.

I see her trademark Mini in the car park with the small gold writing on the side that discreetly says 'Peasbody Weddings'.

Mark pulls up the handbrake in that screechy way that

sets my teeth on edge, and that's my signal to get out. Only my legs have turned to jelly and I'm beginning to think this is a bad idea. I've been so angry with Georgina, yet now that I'm here it's nerves rather than anger that fills my belly. I'm not good at confrontations. I always fear that I'm going to trip over my words or get tongue-tied. But Mark's right, I need to speak to her first, to know why she did it before I put my version of events out there.

'Did you want me to come in with you?'

'No, thanks,' I reply, gritting my teeth. 'I've got to do this myself.'

I take a deep breath and then launch myself out of the car, knowing that if I sit in it any longer I won't want to go anywhere.

As I approach the door to the civic centre, I hear Georgina's cackle emanating from the lobby. It sounds like she's finishing up a phone call on her mobile. It's perfect, as it means that I can talk to her without anyone in the network meeting earwigging.

She ends her call and, as she puts her phone back in her handbag, she looks up and catches sight of me. She looks shocked at first, yet quickly composes herself.

'I wasn't expecting to see you here today. I would have thought you would have been a bit busy.' She brushes imaginary dust off her shoulder.

'I thought I better come and speak to you, face to face.'

She tilts her head to the side and I see a flicker of a smile. 'What are you talking about?'

'The blog post.'

'Oh yes, I saw that. Quite the scandal, eh?' She lowers her voice. 'I imagine something like that would be quite damaging to your business.'

'Isn't that what you hoped when you planned it?'

'What do you mean, "when I planned it"? Penny Robinson, I don't like what you're insinuating.'

I'm momentarily distracted by the fact that she's called me the right name for once, but any pleasure from that is instantly lost as I realise she's distracting me.

I can feel my legs shaking – they don't like confrontation any more than the rest of me.

'I'm not *insinuating* anything,' I say. 'I *know* it was you who wrote that blog.'

'Oh, do you now? I'm sure I have better things to do with my time than write things like that,' she says, a sly smile pasted firmly on her lips.

'I know it was you, because my husband's friend works in IT and he traced the IP address of the blog post to you.'

Georgina's smile is wiped off her face and she starts opening and shutting her mouth like a guppy fish. I can almost see her neat hair start to come out of her bun and her cheeks are flushing through her perfect make-up.

'I, um . . . but that's preposterous! I wouldn't. How can they run those kind of searches? Surely that's an infringement of data protection?'

'Everything on the Internet has to be traceable for public safety and for the prosecution of crimes,' I say virtuously.

If Georgina can hear the fear in my voice that's causing it to wobble then she isn't showing it.

'Prosecution?' she repeats in a high-pitched voice.

I try not to smile. I seem to have Georgina on the back foot for once.

'Yes, prosecution. You know, for crimes: fraud, paedophilia, there have also been people done for libel – do you remember those people that named that peer on Twitter as a paedophile and it wasn't true? He went after them in court. It seems that you can't hide behind a computer screen any more.'

I try to remember what else Mark briefed me on on the way over. He doesn't have a friend who works in IT, or at least not one that would be able to hack into people's IP addresses, but he was right that Georgina wouldn't know any better.

'Mark's friend has compiled the information and we've got it ready to take to the police.'

'The police?' Georgina says with a sharp intake of breath.

'That's right. I think they take this kind of thing very seriously these days.'

Georgina's winding her little hands around her pearl necklace and tugging it so hard I'm worried that she's going to snap it.

'Of course, if you were to tell me the truth, then perhaps I wouldn't *need* to get the police involved.'

I look at her with as firm an expression as I can muster. I'm worried that she's going to see right through my act.

'Tell the police then,' she says, folding her arms and looking squarely into my eyes.

She's calling my bluff and I feel like I'm going to wet myself.

'OK, but don't say I didn't warn you.' I look into her eyes, trying not to blink. She arches an eyebrow in return.

'Right then.' I turn. 'Next stop: the police station.' I walk towards the revolving exit door of the civic centre.

'Wait!' she says.

I turn round slowly and see desperation written all over her face. I'm the one now who's folding her arms.

'Why?' I say.

'I admit it. I did it,' she says slowly.

Even though I suspected her, her confirming it feels like she's punched me in the stomach.

'But why?' I gasp. 'It doesn't make any sense.'

'Because look at you, Penny. I've been doing this business for years, slogging away, bending over backwards to please the most demanding of brides, growing a reputation the old-fashioned way – good old word-of-mouth and satisfied customers. Then *you* come along.'

She says the word 'you' with such venom it's almost like she's spat on me.

'You've got your business all built up, you write for *Bridal Dreams* and you've got a book deal in the offing. Twelve years I've been doing this. *Twelve.* I was doing it before people even knew what a wedding planner was. Before that god-awful film, before the reality wedding programmes. You've popped up overnight and I couldn't take it. When I found out that Olivia and Jeremy had used you, it was the last straw.'

For once she doesn't look like the perfectly put-together woman I could only ever aspire to be. She seems normal and insecure, and almost human.

'Georgina, I worked really hard to get over my gambling addiction. I can't believe you would use it to ruin my business.'

'I didn't mean to do that,' she says with a hollow laugh. 'You just had it all too easy. I wanted to throw a curve ball.'

'What about the bookings that were cancelled, the dates

that were changed and the flowers? You stole my Filofax, didn't you?'

'Oh, Penny, you're such a rookie. That Filofax is your most important business asset. You should never have let it out of your sight.'

She's talking as if her behaviour was entirely justified.

'Well, you should be happy,' I say. 'The publishers who were interested in my book have cancelled our meetings, and two of my brides have pulled out already. So it looks like I'm not having such an easy ride after all.'

'I admit, it might have got a little out of hand,' she says. 'I mean, it was meant to be a bit of healthy competition.'

'We weren't in competition until you launched your free bridal packages! Before that, I would have been happy with the budget-bride market, and left you to your fancy-pants weddings. There are enough brides to go around, you know.'

'Oh well, I'm sure that I've done you a favour in the long run. It's not like you would have lasted long anyway. You would have been like all the others: a flash in the pan.'

I didn't think that I could get any angrier than I was. When she confessed I thought I glimpsed a more compassionate side to her, but I realise now that she doesn't seem to have one.

I'm at a loss as to what to do. It's not like I can go to the police – I have no evidence –and even if I did, they'd hardly care.

I'm about to turn and walk away when a man comes over to us. He's tall and skinny with a goatee beard that makes me think that he's trying to look older than he is.

'Adrian Richards, *Farnborough Herald*,' he says, flashing his badge and squinting at Georgina's name badge. 'Can I get a quote from you, Ms Peasbody?'

Her eyes start to bulge.

'From what I've overheard of your conversation, this is quite a juicy story,' he adds, scribbling in a notebook he's pulled out of his pocket.

'I don't know what you think you heard . . .' She smoothes her hair back.

'I think my iPhone does. It was handy that I was recording a voice memo when you two started arguing.'

I'm staring between Georgina and Adrian in amazement. Instead of leaving defeated with my tail between my legs, I'm beginning to think that there may be some justice in the world after all.

'You can't use that. Surely it's illegal.'

'I think that . . .' He looks straight at my chest. I'm hoping he's looking for a name badge rather than ogling my bigger-than-usual boobs.

'Penny,' I offer, thinking that he wouldn't be that obvious at taking a sneaky peak.

'Thank you. I think that Penny here will give me enough of the facts of the story, won't you? "Local businesswoman sabotages a competitor's business" – especially as it's got viral roots.'

He's rubbing his hands together in glee and the smile on his face implies that he's sniffed out the story of the century. In comparison to some of the local news stories he probably usually has to cover, he probably has.

'Penny, you wouldn't really speak to him, would you? I mean, think how low-class that would be, airing your dirty laundry in public like that. What would it do to your reputation?'

'I hardly think my reputation would be of much concern to you after what you did,' I laugh. This woman is incredible.

I can see her visibly biting her lip.

'Adrian, what kind of quote do you need from me?' I continue.

'Penny, don't do this,' says Georgina, her voice high and tense. 'What if I rescind the blog and write that it was made up?'

'The photos are out there – what makes you think people would believe you?' I say.

Her face is a picture. If she hadn't tried to single-handedly ruin my business, I would feel bad about how much she's squirming.

'It's a start,' she says. 'I'll do anything, Penny. Name it.'

'Adrian, do you have a card? I'm going to think about that quote.'

'Of course.' He digs into his pocket. 'Don't wait too long. It sounds like you need your side of the story put out there.'

'Penny –' repeats Georgina feebly, but I ignore her. I haven't decided yet whether I'm going to take Adrian up on his offer, but I'm quite enjoying leaving her hanging.

I walk out of the civic centre as confidently as I can and over to the car. My legs might not be wobbling quite so much as before, but I'm still shaking.

I get in and tell Mark to drive.

'So?' he says as we pull out of the car park.

'It was her, and she confessed to everything.'

'That's great. Is she going to write a retraction?'

'She wasn't going to, but then a reporter bowled up. He'd heard the whole thing and he wants to write a story about what she did.'

My heart is still beating really fast and I can feel the blood pumping in my head. Clearly adrenaline was keeping me going in there.

'Really?'

'Yeah, he wants me to give them a quote and tell my side of the story.'

'That's great, isn't it? You won't have to tell your brides about your secret now.'

'I know, but I feel like I'm stooping to her level and that it's mudslinging. I think I'm going to stick to the original plan.'

'You are?' He looks at me quickly before turning back to the road.

'Yes, I want to end this thing once and for all. The journalist can write whatever story he wants, but I'm going to clear my name, my way. I don't want it hanging over my head any more.'

'OK, then. It's your decision.'

I tip my head back against the headrest. I hope I'm doing the right thing.

'The only thing I'm worried about is that it's still not going to change the fact that I'm pregnant and that some of my brides are going to get Lou.'

'I've been thinking about that,' says Mark.

His eyes are staring at the road ahead, and from his pause I think he needs some encouragement.

'You have?'

'Yep, I want to help.'

A picture flies into my mind of Mark standing in a church with a wedding planner utility belt like in the J-Lo film, calming a bride down before she goes down the aisle. As much as I love Mark and think he's capable of most things, I get the impression that he wouldn't have the patience for weddings.

'You do?' I wonder how I can tell him diplomatically that I don't think he's quite got what it takes.

'Uh-huh.'

'I'm really happy that you want to be involved –' I pause, not wanting to offend him or sound ungrateful – 'but I don't know if it's quite your thing.'

'But you're always telling me that I'm great with kids.'

I glance at Mark and wrinkle my nose in confusion. 'What have kids got to do with it? I thought you were talking about the weddings.'

Mark turns and raises an eyebrow. 'Me, help with the weddings? I don't think so!'

Thank goodness for that. At least we're both on the same page with that one.

'Then what *do* you mean?'

'I was thinking of taking extended paternity leave. Instead of taking two weeks, I thought I could take six to eight. Then it would mean I could give you help with the baby and around the house and you could then help Lou. I mean, I know you won't be able to do the actual weddings, but at least you could be involved.'

My mind's slow to process it. I hadn't realised that Mark had pulled over until he noisily pulls up the handbrake again and turns to me.

'What do you think?' he says.

'I think you're wonderful.' I lean in to give him a kiss. 'Are you able to take that much time off?'

'You know as well as I do we go pretty quiet in the summer, and besides, why should you get all the fun of staying home to look after our baby?'

I'm about to laugh and tell him some of the stories Lou's told me about what it's like in the early days, but I bite my tongue. I don't want to scare him off. This baby is going to be a massive shock to the system and I rather like the idea that we'll be going through it together.

'Thanks, honey,' I say.

He kisses me again, before checking his blind spot and pulling back out into the road.

Suddenly my shoulders feel lighter – if only the day continues like this. I may have got the confrontation out of the way, but I've still got the rest of the brides-to-be to speak to, and I've just got to hope that that goes as well as my chat with Georgina did.

chapter twenty-seven

Ellie @Elliezgood

Off to @princess_shoestring HQ to hear what's going on.

Sally Jessop @Jessoplady

@Elliezgood Me too. She'd better tell us the truth.

Penny Robinson @princess_shoestring

That I will. Stay tuned, folks — I'm going to break radio silence
on #gamblinggate . . . Be prepared for a full explanation.

'I, Penny Robinson, founder of Princess-on-a-Shoestring, am
a gambling addict. However, I've not gambled for over eighteen months. I would never gamble away anyone else's
money and I would certainly never jeopardise the dreams of
any of my brides.'

I take a deep breath. Here comes the hard bit. I try not to

wince, as I don't think I look at all attractive when I screw my face up.

'My husband and I had enough money in our wedding fund for me to have a dream wedding. OK, so it might not have been able to take place in the castle of my dreams, but really, getting married in the same castle as Madonna was always going to be a pipe dream.

'I could have afforded my Jimmy Choos though, and a Vera Wang wedding dress, which I thought, at the time, were key ingredients for a successful marriage. Thinking I needed even more money, I gambled to try to win it. What I did instead was lose ten thousand pounds. Ten thousand hard-earned, hard-saved, pounds. My husband and I aren't rich, we live in a two-up two-down terrace in a London commuter town, and it was certainly more money than we could afford to throw away.

'More shocking than my losing our money was the deceit that followed. Unwilling to tell Mark (my then fiancé) the truth, I decided to plan my wedding *Don't Tell the Bride* style, where I didn't tell the groom anything about it. I did everything I could to plan a budget wedding that looked fit for a princess so I could con my fiancé into thinking that I'd used all the wedding savings. In the end, it almost cost me my marriage.

'It was then that I realised that my husband-to-be was the

DON'T TELL THE BRIDES-TO-BE

most important part of the wedding, not the shoes, or the dress, or the castle. I was lucky that Mark forgave me for my gambling, but it's always going to follow me round like a shadow haunting me.

'This time the haunting is in the guise of photos published on a blog. One is of me playing blackjack, which I did, although it's not what you think. I was actually at a wedding fair, and there was no money involved. One of my brides-to-be wants a Vegas-themed wedding, and what I was doing was researching and booking LuckyCasino Hire.

'The second photo is me in my gamblers' group meeting. I go every week without fail to remind myself of that horrible time in my life and to help others to stop so that they don't make the same mistakes. It reminds me how far I've come, how much I've changed and how I'm stronger than that girl who played bingo to buy a pair of Jimmy Choos. Whilst I still lust after shoes that are neither practical to wear nor obtainable on my salary, I will no longer stop at nothing to get them.

'I understand that there are some brides-to-be out there that will never be able to trust me because of my former addiction and I respect that. However, as a person who came so close to losing her wedding, and who gets what it's like to not be able to afford to have your dreams come true, I'm probably more passionate than most people about being able to understand your big day and being dedicated to making happen in a way that's as close to your dreams as you can afford.

'For those brides that are willing, I'm always here to help you become a princess on a shoestring!'

'That was great, Penny,' says Josh, smiling.

'It was?' I reply, wondering if it was a bit waffly or whether I mumbled in places.

'Yep, it was perfect. I'll upload it straight away.' He takes the camcorder off the tripod and plugs it into his waiting laptop.

'What? Don't you need to edit it?'

'Why would I? It was a clean take. It was heartfelt and full of emotion. I don't think you'd be able to do it again as perfectly.'

I would usually smile with pride that it went so well, but now that I've put it on tape, I'm nervous about it going online for everyone to see.

Josh is going to post it on YouTube and on Princess-on-a-Shoestrings' Facebook page and blog. All I'll need to do is share it on Twitter, and I think even I'll be able to do that.

There's no time to dwell on whether I'm doing the right thing, as I can already hear the doorbell ringing. I've invited my brides-to-be round, in the hope that I'll be able to convince them face to face what happened.

I can hear Mark ushering them into the living room, and I realise that I can't hide up here forever. Even though I want to watch what Josh is up to.

Lou pokes her head around the door of the spare room.

'Hey.' She smiles. 'I think it's time.'

'OK.' I take a deep breath. We all agreed earlier that I'd wait upstairs so I could tell my story to everyone at once without getting embroiled in individual conversations.

'Thanks, Josh,' I say as I walk out the room. He smiles at me, and I wonder what I'd do without him and his technical skills. He'd said he wasn't originally serious about putting the confession video on YouTube, but we realised it's the easiest way to get my message out there.

I follow Lou downstairs and I can feel my palms starting to sweat. I walk into my living room and the noisy chatter falls silent.

Talk about making an entrance.

'Hi.' I smile nervously. It's been a bit of a squeeze to get everyone in, and there are people sat on the arms of the sofa and even a few on the floor. I look around and spot the faces that usually I'd beam at. There's Big Top Rachel, Woodland Sally, Ellie of Ellie and Silent Blake, amongst others, and I desperately hope they stay with me as clients as there isn't a bride in this room whom I don't want to help tie the knot.

'Thanks for coming at such short notice. I'm sorry that I've been really bad at returning your calls this week.'

I see Woodland Sally look away.

'It's been a difficult time for a number of reasons,' I say vaguely, not wishing to go into the Nanny Violet story. I don't want to use it as an excuse. 'And I should have spoken to you before now, as that blog was written a couple of days ago.'

'What we want to know is, is it true?' asks Viking Ruby. 'One of your brides said on Twitter that her wedding had been cancelled.'

I shake my head. 'It's not, but I owe you the whole truth,' I say.

I take a deep breath before launching into my 'Don't Tell the Groom' story.

If it wasn't my business dangling by a thread I'd probably laugh at the expressions on the faces of the women in front of me. I've been telling my story for the last half an hour and I've never before had such rapt attention during a presentation.

'. . . and then, I fainted,' I finish with a small laugh, relieved that the story is almost over. 'Luckily, Mark still wanted to marry me, and we had the best day ever.'

I look up at the brides and they're all staring from Mark to me and back again.

'It's all true,' he says with a shrug.

'I can't believe you almost didn't show up!' says Big Top Rachel. Her bump has really grown since the last time I saw her.

'Well, I thought she'd cheated on me,' Mark explains. 'I'm sure some of you would have done the same.'

There are a few murmurs in the room and I realise we've gone off-topic.

'OK, ladies. So that's my gambling addiction. I've not gambled for over eighteen months now, and there's no way I'd have touched your money in that way. Any payments that came in my direction have gone to the venue or supplier that they were intended for.'

'Then why have you been acting so strangely?' asks Lakehouse Suzie. 'You get really shifty whenever I talk about you coming to my mum's house the night before the wedding to help make the centrepieces.'

A few other brides start to nod.

'That's a slightly more simple explanation and one of the reasons why I have my friend Lou here. You see, Mark and I are expecting a baby, which is due in July.'

I hear a few sharp intakes of breath.

'I know – terrible, terrible timing in terms of the wedding season. I've desperately wanted to tell you all, but I've been holding off till after my three-month scan, which was last week.' I catch Big Top Rachel's eye and she opens her mouth to speak but stops herself. 'But don't worry – Princess-on-a-Shoestring will be operating as normal. I'm going to do as much of the planning as I possibly can in advance, and Lou here is going to take over the main wedding coordinating duties from June. Mark will be taking extended paternity leave, which means that on a day-to-day basis I should also be able to continue working in a minor way. Lou will be keeping me up to date, and I'll be able to advise her.'

I finish my spiel and realise that I haven't spoken so quickly since I was a teenager delivering class presentations. I needed to get it all out before anyone interrupted me. But now that I've finished, no one is saying anything. The silence is deafening, and I feel so sweaty that I'm doubting whether I put deodorant on this morning.

'I take it that was what you were really doing when we met at the hospital,' pipes up Big Top Rachel from her corner of the room. 'I've been really worried about you.'

'I know, and I'm sorry I lied. I just couldn't risk it slipping it out on social media before I'd put anything in place.'

'Well, congratulations.' She smiles. 'We're going to be bump buddies!'

I smile back in relief that she isn't throwing one of the cake slices at me. I tried to pick the softest cake option, forgoing the chocolate cornflake cakes in fear that they'd hurt if used as projectiles.

'Congratulations,' says another voice, and I can make out whispers of '*She should have told us*', and '*That's completely understandable*', and I could cry with happiness.

'I thought by having you here today, you could all meet Lou. I'll also understand if any of you still want to cancel your wedding package with me.' I pin my gaze on Woodland Sally, who's looking at the floor. 'I'm here to answer any of your questions.'

'I've got one,' says Ellie, holding her hand up.

All eyes in the room fall on her. I raise an eyebrow to suggest I'm all ears.

'Who wrote the blog post and why did they do it?'

'Ooh, that's a good one,' says Marquee Marie, topping up her teacup from one of the teapots.

I bite my lip. For a moment I'm about to tell the Georgina story, but I hesitate. That would only reduce me to her level.

'A disgruntled competitor,' I say, deciding to downplay it. 'So does that mean that everyone's still happy to go ahead with the new Lou and Penny combo?'

'I am!' says Lakehouse Suzie.

'Me too,' pipes in Big Top Rachel.

I look over at Woodland Sally and she nods her head too.

'I don't think anyone else would get my wedding as well as you do,' she says sheepishly.

I sigh with relief. I may have lost two brides this week, but it seems as if the rest will be staying with me.

I pick up a teacup and hold it up. 'I want to raise a toast, to the new chapter in Princess-on-a-Shoestring. To me and Lou.'

Everyone picks up their teacups and raises them in our direction before drinking.

Lou beams across the room and I finally feel like things are looking up. Mark comes over and rubs my belly and I start to believe that we might have saved the company.

An hour later, when the last bride-to-be has departed, Josh comes downstairs from where he's been hiding.

'You're never going to believe what's happened,' he says.

'What?' I ask nervously, the good feeling evaporating almost immediately as fear takes over.

'You've had over two hundred views already.'

'In two hours?' I say in disbelief.

'Yep. A few of the big wedding sites picked it up from your Facebook page.'

I start to feel uneasy, knowing that two hundred more people now know my deep, dark secret.

Mark reaches over and rubs my knee. 'You did good, Pen. You did Nanny Violet proud.'

I put my hand over the top of his. 'Thanks, honey.'

He's been holding it together well today. I think my drama has kept his mind off his nan passing.

'You've also had loads of comments on your Facebook page,' says Josh, waving his computer in front of me.

'Good ones?' I ask, crossing my fingers.

'*Really* good ones,' says Lou, reading over my shoulder. She scrolls down. ' "Good on you for being so honest",' she reads. ' "My dad was a gambler, you've done well to quit." There's tons more like that.'

'There's the odd one or two that call you an idiot for what you did, but they're in the minority,' says Josh, grinning. 'Oh, there's another share. Huh! *Bridal Dreams* magazine just shared it!'

'It's going viral, Penny! This could be great for the company profile,' says Lou.

I pick up the tablet and stare at my inbox. I've got loads of emails already. I skim through, and then freeze.

'You're not going to believe this one.' I'm laughing in disbelief.

Lou, Mark and Josh look up from Josh's laptop.

'It's only the *Sun* newspaper. They want to pay me to tell my "Don't Tell the Groom" story.'

The others look as stunned as I am.

'Bit of a step up from the *Farnborough Herald*,' says Mark, laughing.

'Are you going to do it?' asks Josh.

I look over at Mark, and he smiles and nods in encouragement.

'I guess so. If it stops someone else making the same mistake, then why not? It might not be bad for business either.'

We go back to reading our respective screens and I feel a warm glow run over me. Maybe Georgina did me a favour. For once in my life everything's out in the open and the dark shadow that's been following me round since I started playing bingo finally seems to be shrinking away.

epilogue

Penny Robinson @princess_shoestring
Signing off for Christmas. Hope you all have a good one! Not much of a break for us as we've got the wedding of @Elliezgood on Thursday! x

Ellie @Elliezgood
@princess_shoestring Ha, that's if I don't call the wedding off after spending Christmas Day at my mother-in-law's!

Penny Robinson @princess_shoestring
@Elliezgood Don't even joke about it. What would I do with all the table centres I've made!?!

⸻

I place the final dish down in the dining room and sigh. I might not have slept much over the last few days, but I'm feeling confident that I've managed to lay on what Nanny Violet would have called a good spread.

'This all looks delicious,' says Rosemary, coming up behind me. 'And do you know what? It's going to taste all the better because I haven't had to prepare it.'

I smile weakly. All those years I'd gone to her Christmas Eve shindigs and never once given a thought as to how much effort she'd gone to. I've been baking for the past week, and over the last twenty-four hours I've stuffed one hundred and twenty-two vol-au-vents, and eaten a fair few. I thought I was never going to get it all done in time. Especially given the month I've had.

After the *Sun* ran my 'Don't Tell the Groom' gambling story, I received so much interest in Princess-on-a-Shoestring that I've got enough weddings booked to keep my baby in nappies for a long time. One of the publishers that had been interested in my non-fiction book came back and made an offer – quite a generous one too – so I've been trying to squeeze in time to write that in advance of a March deadline.

For once, what I'm looking forward to on Christmas Day isn't stuffing my face or the presents, it's the fact that I'm going to spend the whole day in my PJs on the sofa.

Not that the rest will last long – my usual Boxing Day trip to the Next sale will have to be forgone in preparation for Ellie's wedding the following day. That's if she and Blake actually make it down the aisle. I've still got my doubts about those two. I don't think I'll properly relax until they say, 'I do.'

I look over the buffet again. I've tried really hard to make it extra special, as everyone's been a bit down since Nanny Violet's passing. I even baked and decorated cupcakes – only burning the first two trial batches. The edible ones look fabulous, they're reindeer faces with pretzel ears. I almost thought I'd struck onto a new business venture, a perfect compliment to Princess-on-a-Shoestring . . . only then I realised that it had taken the best part of two whole days to make and ice eighty cupcakes. Not a very good business model.

'You've done so well, and given your condition . . .' says Rosemary.

I pat my belly, which now has the tiniest hint of a bump. To be honest, it looks like I've been bloating myself on bread, but I know it's a baby.

Now that everything's out in the open and everyone knows, I seem to be sticking my belly out more and more.

I follow Rosemary into the living room, and I have to admit it's nice to see all our nearest and dearest squeezed into our little terrace. Christmas is quite literally in the air, thanks to my cinnamon-and-winter-berry candle, with Mariah Carey screeching away from the stereo.

'Here she is!' says Mark, grabbing me and pulling me down onto his lap.

I think the eggnog I made may have had a little too much rum in it. I couldn't taste it as I went along like I usually would, so I erred on the side of 'you can't have enough booze'.

'My baby mama,' he slurs at me.

I can't help but smile as he dangles some mistletoe above our heads. I give him a quick kiss.

'I still think she looks like you,' says my mum, handing back the printout from our baby scan, which has taken pride of place on the mantelpiece.

I take hold of it and squint at the grey blob that looks more like an alien than a person.

Mark wraps his arms tighter around me. 'This time next year we'll be getting ready for baby's first Christmas,' he says.

I stare harder at the photo. I can't imagine how that little thing is going to grow into an actual baby. And that it's going to come out of me. I start taking deep breaths like I'm probably going to be doing in labour. The thought that the thing with the giant head will be coming out of me is already making me sweat at night. The less I think about that part of it, the better.

'It's crazy to think how much can happen in twelve

months. This time last year I was still working in HR. I hadn't even planned my first wedding.'

'I know. I wonder what the next year will bring?' Mark says.

There's almost too much to look forward to. Aside from the baby, we've got Josh and Mel's wedding and my book being published in the autumn. And those are only the things I already know about.

'I know one thing for sure – there aren't going to be any more secrets,' I say quietly.

'I love your shoes, Penny,' says my sister Becky, coming to sit down next to me. 'Aren't they Alexander McQueen?'

I feel my cheeks begin to burn. I'm wishing I wasn't sat on Mark's lap and that he hadn't heard that. They were a legitimate business purchase – I needed them for the *Sun* photo shoot . . . yet I still hid them from the shoe police, aka Mark.

'These old things?' I say, choking on the words. I stand up, about to head to the kitchen to hide, but Mark pulls me back down and wraps his arms around me tighter.

'You're a terrible liar when it comes to shoes, Mrs Robinson. What were you just saying about no more secrets . . . ?'

I try to wriggle free, but Mark's not letting me go, and instead he's planting tickly kisses on my neck.

'I'm not going to keep any important ones,' I say, giggling. 'Shoes are the exception.'

Looking around this room at all our friends and family, I realise I'm ridiculously lucky with my life. I've got the most wonderful husband, a business that's about to go into the black and a baby (or mini-alien) on the way. Maybe it's because I'm becoming a mum and I'm finally beginning to feel like an adult, or maybe it's because I've realised there's too much at stake, but I've had my fill of keeping secrets.

From now on I'm going to live my life like an open book. Surely I can't get myself in any bigger a muddle telling the truth than I've got myself into over the last few years keeping my secrets . . .

. . . can I?

acknowledgements

Because of the arrival of Baby Bell, this book was one of the toughest I've had to write, as I found myself squeezing writing into the tiniest of windows. I'd like to thank my husband Steve for taking him out for walks so I could write and being an all round fab cheerleader. Baby Bell himself deserves a mention as he not only gave me a great insight into Penny's morning sickness but he also gave me lovely newborn snuggles to keep me calm near the deadlines. Thanks to my Mum Wendy and Mother-in-law Heather for babysitting duties too.

A huge thank you, as always, to my lovely agent Hannah Ferguson at Hardman and Swainson. As well as to everyone at Quercus, especially my eagle-eyed editor Kathryn for all your help and guidance!

A big thank you to former real-life wedding planner, and friend, Zeenat Turner, for your suggestions on what naughty things Georgina could get up to – who knew those in the industry could be so devious (or paranoid!). Any mistakes on this front are all mine and I plead artistic license.

This time round, I don't think too many of my friends weddings made it in here this time – I think only Kaf's (it was an awesome wedding Mrs Johnn). Also reviewer Chick Litter Eve deserves a mention for inspiring the bits around Nerinda – after asking me what wedding dress I'd be called. Who knew wedding dresses had names – although I still think *Daydreams with Words* would be an awesome name for one . . .

Lastly, the biggest thanks of all has to go to my lovely readers. Thanks for reading the series and for all the tweets, emails and Facebook messages. It's an amazing feeling to know that people have not only read my books but enjoyed them too.

My Nan Ivy hugely inspired the character Nanny Violet – and I only wish she'd been around to read the series as I know she would have loved Penny's adventures, and I'm sure she would have been super proud of me, showing all her friends what I'd done. So Nan, this book is for you.

436

penny picks – top 5
unusual venues

If you're going to splurge on anything for your wedding, it should be your venue. Having a show-stopping venue will distract your guests from some of the less expensive (or missing) elements of your big day. Look locally for museum and heritage sites and other tourist attractions.

If I could get Mark to agree to another wedding, here would be my top five unusual picks . . .

1 – Alnwick Castle, Northumberland

Everyone knows that I always wanted a castle wedding – and what better castle than one that featured in not only the first two Harry Potter movies but also Robin Hood Prince of Thieves? It would be as close to getting married in Hogwarts as I could get.

2 – The Treehouse, Alnwick Gardens, Northumberland

Adjacent to the castle are the Alnwick Gardens that offer you a more rustic and enchanted affair – so how about an actual treehouse? It's a bit Swiss Family Robinson – with actual wooden bridges – and it would provide the most magical backdrop for photographs.

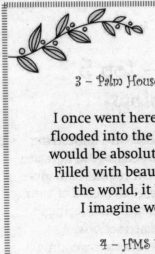

3 – Palm House, Sefton Park, Liverpool

I once went here and loved the light that
flooded into the Victorian glass house – it
would be absolutely perfect for a wedding.
Filled with beautiful plants from around
the world, it has a lovely ambience
I imagine would be hard to beat.

4 – HMS Warrior, Portsmouth

If getting married on a warship floats your
boat then the Warrior might just be for you.
Docked in the historic dockyard, you'll treat
your guests to a location steeped in history with
beautiful harbour views.

5 – Titanic Belfast

It's all about *that* staircase for this venue.
You know the one where Jack waited for Rose
in the movie. Imagine descending down it, your
dress swishing down the stairs . . .

penny picks – top 5 wedding blogs

I'd be lying if I said that Princess-on-a-Shoestring is the only wedding blog worth reading, so here are a few of my favourites that I visit regularly to give me ideas for my brides-to-be.

Rock My Wedding

www.rockmywedding.co.uk
Before you even get to the content of this blog the design blows you away oozing elegance and style. I especially love the DIY Projects section – giving you heaps of fab ideas of how you can make your own elements of your wedding.

Courting Whale

www.courtingwhale.com/blog
Now this site is pure wedding porn. Their wedding trailers transform a wedding to make it look like a Hollywood movie.

Boho Weddings

www.boho-weddings.com
The tag line says it all: 'create the wedding you want, not the wedding you're told to have!' I couldn't have said it better myself! Full of tips, trends and inspiration.

Before the Big Day

www.beforethebigday.co.uk
An excellent blog jam-packed with inspirational posts and they also keep up-to-date with sample sale information too – so maybe you can afford to get yourself a glam dress.

Style Me Pretty

www.stylemepretty.com/destination-weddings
Beautiful real-life weddings from provincial France to far-flung exotic locations. A must see for anyone planning a destination wedding.

penny picks – top 5
high street

If you're looking to keep costs down, then a great place to start is buying from the high street.

Dress and Accessory Shopping

Debenhams have a fantastic array of dresses, and bigger stores often stock Coast dresses too. Monsoon is a must visit for any bride-to-be looking for a high street wedding dress. BHS bridal departments in the larger stores are great for bridesmaid dresses, especially when trying to match colours of adult and junior bridesmaids. They're also fabulous for all the little accessories – garters, tiaras, wraps, shrugs, headbands for little bridesmaids (I could go on all day).

Shoes

The best advice I can give you about shoes on your wedding day is: think comfy. I love Next occasion shoes. They're usually super comfortable and excellent if you have big/wide feet! Accessorize also do spangly flip flops that are perfect for a change for an evening boogie.

Cake

We might all want a Choccywoccydoodah cake, but if you can't afford a bespoke cake then there are some great high street alternatives. Major supermarkets stock plain occasion cakes, that you can jazz up after you buy them. My pick would be M&S as they often have offers on their cakes, and you can order them up to a couple of months in advance. They also have cutting cakes so you can mix and match your flavours.

Get Crafty

Embrace your inner crafty self and make your own favours, table centres, table plans and place cards. Stock up on supplies from places like Wilkinson's and Hobbycraft. M&S now do favour packs and Lakeland do great moulds if you're going to make your own edible favours!

Designer Bargains

If you desperately want to go designer, but want to bag a bargain then look at TK Maxx's for wedding and bridesmaid dresses. Also check out designer outlet villages – Bicester Village near Oxford has a Jimmy Choo outlet – if only I'd known that before I might never have started playing bingo . . .

hello again, penny here!

For more information about upcoming books, events and other fun stuff, you can go online:

www.annabellwrites.com

www.quercusbooks.co.uk

@AnnaBell_writes

@quercusbooks

lots of love,
penny x